MW00650552

# Angel Found

## Virgil Varvel

ISBN 978-1-0980-8800-2 (paperback)
ISBN 978-1-0980-8801-9 (digital)

Copyright © 2021 by Virgil Varvel

All rights reserved. No part of this publication may be reproduced, distributed, or transmitted in any form or by any means, including photocopying, recording, or other electronic or mechanical methods without the prior written permission of the publisher. For permission requests, solicit the publisher via the address below.

Christian Faith Publishing, Inc.
832 Park Avenue
Meadville, PA 16335
www.christianfaithpublishing.com

Printed in the United States of America

When Aaron Todd awoke to blue skies and the smell of flowers in the spring air, he didn't expect to end the day hiding in the trunk of a car on scorched asphalt, surrounded by flames of every color and the odor of death. But then again, that would probably be true of anyone no matter what the day. He should have listened to Malone. Dreams are significant, even if they are nightmares. Although he felt like his life was over, an adventure leading him back to himself was about to begin.

*Several weeks earlier*

Aaron was restless, his sleep interrupted, not by the tangible but by the subconscious. His dreams were once again failing in their purpose. They were not providing rest but rather restlessness. Fear, confusion, and strife had overtaken his sleeping hours. Dreams, the window to his soul, were open to a soul he did not know. Perhaps, rather than a window, his dreams were acting more like a door, but this particular door was struggling to bar entry from something most unwelcome.

As the door to his mind opened, his dream began to manifest. As with all visions, the dreamer was not acutely aware of its illusory nature, adding to the tension that Aaron was feeling. A voice could be heard, first as a whisper, and then slowly building over time as if seeking out his ear in the dark unformed void in which he found himself. The voice followed him, chased him, unrelenting, presenting a warning, "We're looking for you."

"We will find you," the voice continued its threatening tone, approaching closer through the darkness. Sounding deep and raspy, like a movie voice-over with a hint of echo, the modulated voice emanated from every direction as the sound engulfed him. It was not a voice he knew, but its repeated presence in his dreams was lending it a familiarity. Having delivered its warning, the voice laughed maniacally. Building in a crescendo, it suddenly ceased as the darkness equally as suddenly became blinding light.

Breathing heavily, Aaron blinked as his eyes adjusted to the newfound light that slowly filled the room. Sweat from the heat beaded on his forehead and covered his shirt. Without thinking, he ducked behind the nearest large object he could find: a desk. Confused, he tried to orient to the surroundings. It was clear at the surface that he was in an abandoned office building, based on the large room lined with cubicles filled with metal desks, but this precise office would be the hell reserved for evil receptionists.

Dull gray paint peeled from the walls covered in demonic graffiti that appeared to be written in blood. No windows existed to let in light or to let out the odor. What light did exist came from randomly flickering and buzzing overhead fluorescents. Scorch marks, tarlike residue, and garbage covered every surface. Any remnants of the previous workspaces were broken and in disarray. If the internal disgust felt by the average office worker were to manifest itself, this space would be the result.

The random desk Aaron initially found himself under emanated the putrid stench of burning hair. It was more than Aaron could stomach. Before he added to the stench with his own bile, he decided to run quickly to the nearest door with the intent of escaping this depressing chamber. As Aaron ran, he could see that in addition to burned-out fire detectors and wireless Internet nodes, security cameras lined the ceiling. Unlike everything else in the environment, these appeared in perfect working order. Was he being watched? It seemed prudent to remain low in an attempt to remain hidden from whomever or whatever was watching him.

The floors were layered with carbon residue, leaving puffs of black as Aaron scuttled across them. Dodging the assorted trash littering the floor, he passed through the broken door as silently as he could, despite the one remaining rusted out hinge holding it in place. He continued in this manner through several doors, not stopping to think. However, by the fifth room, he paused, standing in the doorway. He had come to the realization that each room appeared identical to the one before it, or perhaps he was simply exiting the room from one end to immediately reenter the same room on the other in a simple two-sided tesseract. No matter what the explanation, continuing to sneak through this endless enigma was pointless. He slowed down and leaned against a halfway decent desk to catch his breath and think. At least he was getting used to the smell.

"Are you getting tired?" the voice asked. "Look at the delicious sweat."

Aaron wasn't sure what to think. His efforts to remain hidden had clearly been wasted. Someone was watching him, but he knew not who, why, nor to what purpose. With his best voice of confidence, he proclaimed under his breath, "Tired of you, yes." Not able to think of anything clever, he added softly, "I can do without the commentary."

The last statements were more for himself. Whatever twisted thought process was playing out in his mind, there was no reason to argue with a voice. For all he knew, it was his own subconscious revealing some bizarre struggle within. Was he sleeping? He was not sure. Aaron was tired, but not just of the voice. Speaking those words made him think of how truly weary he was. Moving from the desk to slump in the nearest doorway, he knew that he had not slept well in weeks. More depressing was not knowing what to do about it. But he was resilient. He would not surrender to some voice.

At that moment, he had a semblance of a plan. He spent the next few moments memorizing everything he could about the room—where the red-handled scissors were on the first desk, the way the floor was burnt a deep reddish tint toward the middle of the room, the number of tiles missing in the ceiling—as many details as he could fit in his short-term memory. Then he left the support of the doorway, walked through the opening slowly, and proceeded to the next room, whispering to himself, "Step one."

Quickly it was evident that each room was, as well as he could tell, identical. He had accomplished his first task but only succeeded in frustrating himself further. By now, he had come to the clear subconscious realization that he was dreaming, and for some reason, he was placed within an endlessly repeating scene from some clerical hellscape. At least knowing he was dreaming was empowering. Within dreams, he had the power to perform any miracle his mind could imagine. His fear began to subside.

Aaron grabbed the desk with the red scissors on it and flipped it over. "Step two," he told himself. "If nothing ever changes by itself, then you do the changing." Once again, he crossed the room, but this time disrupting everything in his wake. Each desk he passed was flipped, each chair knocked down, and every reachable item thrown across the room. Lastly, he stabbed a pair of scissors into the wall. It would be incorrect to say that he was destroying the room as it was clearly already in a state of destruction. There was no way that he could make it more disgusting in its filth, but he could at least reorganize that filth. Furthermore, this act was quite therapeutic, providing an outlet to some pent-up hostilities toward the dream.

Being satisfied, he kicked in the door on the opposite side, intent on its destruction with a furor that matched his frustrations. He peered into the next room. Nothing was changed. The room behind him was even more of a mess than when he entered, but the room in front was reset. *Ugh!* he thought. *So whatever force constructed this maze has repeated the same state, resetting every time I go through the door.*

"Okay, then step three." He ran, almost like a wild man, busting through each door with no regard for his surroundings, only counting. *One. Two… Twenty… Thirty.* He kept running with the wild abandon of a frenzied animal, not caring for anything other than to just keep moving. The rooms continued. He slowed as his breath began to lapse. There was no escape that way. "My subconscious is limited in its creativity it would seem, serving up shortcuts as one's mind tends to do. Why generate entire worlds when a smaller one can simply be repeated?" Aaron had taken to speaking out loud to provide his inner voice as a companion.

Seeing no imminent danger other than the risk of doubling over from the terrible odor and disgusting visuals, he relaxed a bit and spent another moment in thought. "What to do next?" he whispered. He hadn't formulated a step four yet. He often read about escape rooms where people were presented with challenges in order to get out of a room serving as a puzzle. As interesting as he found the concept and having wanted on several occasions to complete one himself, he was not finding this experience pleasing. Then he remembered a previous thought he had on the subject.

The one logical flaw in these puzzles, despite all their trappings, was that they always followed rules. But real life, and dream life even more so, followed no set rules. Telling a lion not to eat a man just because it is in a circus does not mean the lion was necessarily bound to follow. Aaron was about to be an unruly wild lion.

Having a small rest behind him, Aaron stood and stated a confident, "Step four." Stopping in the middle of the room, he turned right. *Let's give this a try*, he thought. Walking perpendicular to his previous path, Aaron continued to the decrepit wall. "It can't be that stable in its current state," he said out loud as he ran his hand across the surface. The wall was coated in greasy residue and soot, leaving his appendage sticky to the touch. Wiping off his hand on his clothes, he knocked on the wall several times, attempting to locate a stud underneath. He was right about its lack of stability. His knocks alone felt as if they would crumble the disintegrating barrier.

With a swift motion, his fist smashed into the wall. Repeating, a smile formed on his lips. "It's working!" he thought out loud. In a feverish pitch, his punches extended to kicks as the wall gave way to his force. Shards of gypsum fell around him as dust filled the air. Frantically, he pulled the remnants away, revealing the gap he had created. His endless room, previously having two doors, was now presented with a third. He coughed from the disgusting debris filling his surrounding, temporarily covering his mouth with his shirt to prevent inhaling any more of the germ and grime-infested air.

Still breathing and perspiring heavily, Aaron passed through his opening, then sat silently, slightly forlorn. It had not worked. The room was the same. "One cannot fool one's own subconscious, it would seem," mumbled Aaron. He wondered how long he would be trapped in this prison. For that matter, he wondered how long he had already been there, having lost track of time.

Struggling to configure a step five, Aaron noticed an actual change. A new odor, metallic, difficult to place, began to fill his nostrils. As he sniffed, he noticed that the walls too were changing. Red drops beaded up everywhere, bubbling as they formed. The dream was reacting to his latest strategy. Aaron did not need to inspect the red substance to conclude that the walls were bleeding, and the popping appearance and sound suggested that this blood was boiling. He felt a little disappointed in how cliché his dream was being. The beads, however, gave way to drops which gave way to streams of liquid splashing to the floor. "That's just plain disturbing," he said to himself.

Standing, unsure what to do, Aaron watched as the flow continued until his bare feet were standing in a puddle of warm viscous fluid. He became aware of his clothes for the first time, despite having wiped himself clean on them several times and having covered his mouth repeatedly with his shirt. Consisting of only a once white pair of shorts and matching white long-sleeved shirt, long since covered in grime as the dream had progressed, they stained deep red as he leaned an instant against a cubicle wall. Quickly, Aaron regained his composure. The bleeding was not stopping. He had to do something or he would surely drown a most horrible way. Once again, he traversed from room to room, always running or moving quickly, always unable to rest. Each room reset as before with new blood soon to enter.

At last, he entered a room that reset to the beginning with no blood. His mind was apparently presenting him with a moment of rest. But then the voice returned. "You've been running for so long," the voice spoke. "Soon there will be no more running. When we find you, there will be nowhere to run."

The taunts were beginning to anger Aaron. As he thought to himself, he came to the realization that he was, in fact, completely oblivious to what or from whom he was running. It seemed that the unknown was his true terror. Furthermore, the voice said, "When *we* find you." The voice was in a group, meaning someone else could be in control or he needed to see a doctor about some repressed schizophrenia. Also, even though the voice was clearly watching him, it didn't know where he was. They were trying to find him. So he was, in fact, hiding without intent and apparently doing a good job at it. With every room the same, even the voice didn't know which one he was in.

With new resolve, Aaron responded, "I'm not running anymore." Standing straight, Aaron continued, "I'm not hiding either. I'm right here out in the open, albeit a disgusting, actually sort of hellish room. I have no fear. Look for me all you want. When you find me, you can even try to kill me if you want. But I'm tired of being the prey. I will hunt you down through the depths of this hell if I must. The angel of death itself will shudder at the extent of my wrath. How does that sound?"

Aaron was being somewhat glib. He had, in fact, been running and hiding, but he committed to cease moving away and instead attempted to face whatever was wrecking his rest. "You know what else?" Aaron added. "The Lord is my shield and my strength. Maybe you're the one who should be running. Come on, go ahead, find me. What are you waiting for?" His voice rose as he continued.

The voice returned, clearly angered by what Aaron had spoken. "Listen, you impudent fool. You've been hiding since the day your flesh was born, and we will make that flesh ours. Our patience knows no end. It has taken us years just to find your dreams, and soon, we'll find your reality. When we do, we will end it."

Aaron was tired, both physically and metaphysically. He struggled to concentrate, to discuss even partially logically with the voice. "I'm too tired, so just shut up. I'm going to ignore you now that I've gained some small sense of my surrounding. Maybe I'll just curl up under this desk." Looking under the desk and witnessing the pile of feces underneath, Aaron quickly recanted, "Or I'll just curl up on top of the desk." Sitting on the desk, he continued, "Let's see if a nap within a dream counts as restful sleep, shall we?" With that, Aaron laid down on his back, closed his eyes, and attempted to rest.

"Ridiculous fool! Everything makes sense when you know the truth. When you know why we're looking for you. When you know why we have to find you."

The voice tried to continue, but Aaron interrupted, "Yeah? And what truth is that? Nope. See, that was a rhetorical question. Well, not even that really. I don't care about your little 't' truth, at least not right now. I just care about sleep. Go sell your truth to TV, and maybe I'll catch an episode. Better yet, give me the trailer. I'm good at figuring out a story from a ninety-second sneak peek."

"Well, aren't you the amusing one? Poor little man can't sleep and isn't afraid," taunted the voice. "Your death will be so exquisite. Then you can sleep only to awaken to the truth. Then we will have you."

"I'd settle for just one good night's sleep, thank you very much. Someday, I will sleep like you are trying so artfully to pun. But I'm a religious man, and that sleep will end with heaven. Your threats of death don't scare me."

Angrily, the voice began to respond, "Dare speak of heaven again, and—"

"And what? You'll kill me?" Aaron snickered ever so slightly. "You really need to learn how to temper your threats. If you start with death, you have nowhere to go. You've already spent your number one card. Next time, start smaller, like with hours of torture involving sleep deprivation. Then build up to a painful death leading straight to hell. Then threaten to keep chasing me through hell. I'll fight back and escape, though, winning the day and saving the girl. That's how I would end this story."

"Thanks for the guidance, impetuous fool," the voice sarcastically replied. "You will surely die, but you will not be reborn as you think. We want you. We will have you, and if we cannot have you, then your torture will be our delight."

"Quiet, you. I don't care. I don't care…I really don't care!" Aaron paused to compose himself. His head slumped, and he smiled slightly at a sudden moment of clarity. He sat up, hopped off the desk, and picked up a toppled chair near him. Taking a seat backward in the chair and turning as if to face the person he was talking to, Aaron said, "This is a quandary. You see, I don't even know if you are real or just some subconscious trouble stewing in my mind. For all I know, I could be doing all of this to myself."

"That must be it," Aaron scoffed at himself. "What is wrong with me? If a voice is speaking to me in my dreams, then it must be my own inner voice, which begs the question, why am I tormenting myself so?"

The voice laughed. Aaron's bewilderment was clear on his face. "Great, I figure it out, and now my subconscious is laughing at me," stated Aaron as the laughter subsided. "Tell me, wizard behind the curtain, what's so funny?"

"You. Isn't it obvious?" replied the voice.

"Nothing is ever as obvious as it should be. Life and dreams are like any story, full of twists and turns. Just when you think you know the ending, something comes to light that changes everything," replied Aaron. "You know, for the past few nights, my sleep has been restless as I run from and argue with you—or is it myself?—without being able to figure out why. I'm apparently trying to find myself. Maybe some kind of midlife crisis. If I could afford it, I'd go see a psychiatrist." Aaron's frustration could be heard in his voice.

The voice continued, "You think you have it all figured out, do you?"

"No," answered Aaron, "quite the contrary. I feel like I have nothing figured out. I'm borderline questioning my sanity right now."

"How delicious your insanity would be. Almost as delicious as your loyalty…or your pain," remarked the voice.

"Wow, I'm beginning to worry about how seriously twisted my subconscious appears to be," considered Aaron.

With those last words, Aaron started to experience unexpected pain. Up to this point, the dream was about running, hiding, taunting, and in some previous dreams, full out *Kung-Fu Theater* style demon battles, but something new was happening. Suddenly, as if transported to some child fantasy world, the floor melted away, turning slowly to lava directly underneath him. Searing his right foot, Aaron jumped back onto the nearest desk. The legs and body of the desk quickly burned and melted away; however, the top was inexplicably immune to the heat.

Aaron's heart began to race as this new predicament presented itself. New sweat formed on his brow both from heat as the entire room engulfed in flames and from worry. *Well, this is new*, he thought as he covered his mouth to help him breathe in the desiccating heat.

Stabilizing himself on all fours atop the desk, he looked around the room. The walls and ceiling cracked and opened to reveal a flowing pit of lava for kilometers in every direction against an orange-red backdrop and a cave ceiling riddled in stalactites. Steam and smoke rose from the lava, singeing the inside of his mouth as he tried to breath. He could not fly away as the cave ceiling was only feet above his head. "Now how in the world am I supposed to get out of this situation?" he asked sardonically. "There's always been a door before."

It wasn't so much death that Aaron feared as he was rather certain he was dreaming, and in his dreams, he could pretty much survive anything. However, he didn't want pain. That thought was unpleasant.

The lava began to flow more vigorously. While the bottom of the desktop seemed immune, as spurts of magma hit its top, small holes were melted into it. Within several seconds, the support was reduced to swiss cheese. The remnants of the desk began to slowly sink into the molten earth.

Aaron was afraid. He knew he was dreaming, but he foresaw pain and wondered if he would die in real life if he died this way in his dream. It appeared he would soon find the definitive answer. Aaron was also confused. Why would his subconscious want him dead? Was he wrong about doing this to himself? And if so, then who was entering his dreams?

Before he could process that question, he let out a scream. The heat was unbearable. His legs had reached the lava. As his legs spontaneously combusted, his screams began to echo over and over in his head, "Ahhh! Ahhh! Ahhh!" Just as he felt life begin to slip away...

*Beep, beep, beep!* Aaron's alarm shouted next to him in perfect sequence with the screams of his dream. He abruptly sat up in his bed, continuing one last scream before realizing his new surroundings.

Aaron, now awake but still tired, was wet with sweat. Slightly confused, his heart racing, he rolled over and turned off the alarm with a moan. "Holy you know what, I can't take those dreams anymore. I don't want to get up. I don't want to dream. I just need my sleep."

He looked at his cat that came into view at the foot of his bed as he was roused. "Why is my subconscious trying to kill me, McStuffins? These dreams are lucid and freaky, and I want them to stop buddy."

McStuffins rolled over. As usual, he didn't care what anyone else did or said as long as they left him alone or fed him.

"Well, I can see you are as caring as usual," Aaron quipped, giving the cat a quick rub. The cat responded temporarily, then jumped off the bed and left the room. "You can be replaced, you know!" Aaron called out after the cat.

Aaron continued to try to make sense of his dreams, speaking to himself, "Maybe I do need a psychiatrist? Then again, if it's not my subconscious, then what is it? And more importantly, what does it want? Are you listening to yourself, Aaron? Get your head on straight. You'll figure it out."

2

Aaron stayed in bed for as long as he could, trying to settle down and relax—what he should have been doing in his sleep. For many days, he had been having nightmares, each one linked or in sequence to the one before, recurring enough so that he could remember important portions. There was always a voice with a warning, always a lot of running, and he was always restless.

He couldn't stay in bed forever, though. Aaron slowly rose and moved toward the bathroom in his more mundane morning ritual. Walking through the door, he paused and leaned his head back out to the hallway. Ever so slightly off his routine, he almost forgot one very important thing. He shouted across the hallway, "Za, sweetie, time to wake up!" He couldn't forget his initial attempt to wake his seventeen-year-old daughter.

"Mmm," was all Aaron heard in reply, but that would do for now.

Aaron loved Za with all his heart, but in the mornings, she was a bit of a chore, never wanting to get up for school. It had been worse since she started senior year of high school, but in his mind, she was still his little girl.

As he continued, Aaron enjoyed a welcome bit of adrenaline, perhaps provided by the ending moment of his dream. He refused to let the dream or anything, for that matter, get him down, and besides, a little extra energy wouldn't hurt. "Look on the bright side" was always his motto.

The man who entered the bathroom and undressed was a standard male specimen, albeit slightly taller at six feet. Stepping into the shower, his slender, muscular build, a testament to his busy lifestyle and near nightly workouts, was quickly cleansed as he sped through his routine. Washing his head, the graying hair made him appear deceptively older or perhaps a little more distinguished than thirty-nine.

As he showered, he could not inhibit remembering his dream from the previous night or the many times he had similar recurring dreams. This one was particularly memorable. He had not conversed so extensively with the voice before, nor had the dream ended in a pit of lava waiting to painfully engulf him. Remembering the dream gave him chills, but as all dreams do, it slowly faded from memory by the end of the shower until the next time it would be recalled as the dream resurfaced.

Quickly brushing his teeth and shaving, Aaron continued through his morning. As he threw on the jeans and shirt that he had grabbed from his bedroom floor, he could hear Esperanza stirring but still in bed. "Wake up, Za!" he yelled. One more yell when he'd dressed should finally wake her fully. Aaron then ran a brush through his hair that was short enough to make a brush unnecessary. One last look in the mirror, he stepped out into the apartment, ready for the day.

The home in which he meandered was nothing special, bordering on the bland mundane. It included three small bedrooms, one large bathroom with a bath/shower, an eat-in kitchen, and a living space in a small house, albeit average for the area south of Chicago. The windows were shut as the night temperatures were still a little too cold for Aaron that early in the spring, and he worried sometimes for his daughter's security. Their home had no especially nice furnishings or points of interest.

The bedrooms were lightly furnished. The spare room included only a bunk bed, serving the sole purpose of providing a point of rest for those in need. The kitchen was at least large enough for a rounded four-person table. The four chairs around the table were mismatched but comfortable. The counters were uncommonly bare as Aaron preferred to keep everything neatly in its place. The couch and recliner, offset by a small table with lamp, dominated the living room. An average television, on which the two occupants regularly watched movies and British television or played video games, hung from the wall opposite the seating.

An apartment would have worked just fine, but Aaron had wanted Za to have a yard to play in, even if the yard was small, and they usually played at the park. He also wanted the extra bedroom. Having been homeless once as a child, he always kept a spare room just in case someone needed it, and unlike today, it was often occupied. They were not what one would call poor, but Aaron had instilled a charitable attitude on the family, causing most of their wealth to be spent on others.

Heading to the kitchen, Aaron let out one last loud call to Za, "You up?" Always by the third or fourth "Wake up," she was out of bed. Sometimes she would join him as he read a little before breakfast; but other times, she was ready with just enough time to dress, eat, and maybe brush her hair before it was time to leave. "Forty-five minutes!" Sometimes she would suddenly appear right about then. She knew that Aaron liked her to read the Bible with him in the morning, but he had left it up to her. If she didn't show, he would read it himself while waiting and eating breakfast.

In the pinkish room down the small hallway, a young girl blinked and then tried to return to her rest. The petite redheaded girl slept with a smile on her face, always positive no matter what her true emotion. She turned over but only to grab the covers and place them over her head to shut out the light from her window. She knew that she needed to wake but eventually fell back into a light sleep. Her father would serve as her snooze button.

Za's room included a white canopy bed with a similarly styled chest of drawers and nightstand. The nightstand had various small pieces of trinket jewelry, a box of tissues, and a clock that rarely had its alarm set. Instead, the clock was mostly used as a nightlight with a glowing LED feature at its top. It was also used to charge her phone through a port in the back. The walls were covered almost completely in posters common to many teenage girls' rooms with a slight video game tendency. The modesty of the surroundings was slightly offset by her expensive computer and other electronic gadgets sitting on a small desk as well as her large book collection that crowded the small room.

The small individual occupying the room was known as Za, as already stated, but she chose her name to shorten Esperanza. She liked her full name and knew why her father had given it to her, but Za just sounded right to her. She acquired her name, according to her father, from the feelings she gave him. Having a child had given him new hope for the future. Not that he didn't always have hope. It was probably his defining attribute. No matter how terrible the world around him appeared, he always found the silver lining. But when her mom died in childbirth, he needed some extra reassurance that all would get better. Za gave that feeling to him. Even with the sorrow one would expect at the death of a loving wife, her father also felt happiness that Mom was in heaven and in how he would forge a closer bond between himself and Za to compensate. That was seventeen years ago. He was right; they were inseparable.

Interestingly, her name was somewhat prophetic. If hope was a spiritual gift, it would be hers. She had the odd ability to brighten up a room and say what needed to be said when it needed to be said. This gift didn't work in reverse, though. There were times when she needed someone to say the right thing to her.

Those thoughts led Za to begin to think of her mother. Za was becoming a woman herself, and sometimes (or oftentimes, depending on the day) missed having a mom in the house. Her father was great and easily her best friend, but there was no complete substitute for a mother. Her friends tried to give her motherly advice, but that fell short as well. No need to think too hard on having a mother, though. She had tried to match her father with dates many times, but he always just said that he was devoted to her. That was nice, but sometimes a mother would be nice too.

She wanted to return to the dream of her mother that was in progress when Aaron's yell woke her. She had no true memory of her mother. That would be impossible since she had never met her. She also had no video, and there were only about fifty photos of her mother too, most of them displayed somewhere in the home. But she had created her own picture of her mother based upon her dad's stories and what pictures there were. This idealized substrate created a myriad of possibilities for the mother of her mind.

But the sleep would not return. She was awake and knew that her father wanted her reading with him.

"I'm up, Dad! I'll be ready in a minute!" Za shouted back. At the last call from her father, she jumped out of bed and quickly dressed in the clothes she had whimsically pulled out the previous evening. No time to shower, she tied her hair back and was ready in a much less regimented manner than her father. She proceeded into the kitchen to join him.

Aaron was already reading his Bible. Za grabbed hers and joined him. Aaron had raised her to be connected to God, and their morning Bible reading was part of that connection. Aaron always read at least ten minutes, and if he awoke early enough, he would read anywhere up to an hour.

Lately, Aaron had been interested in verses referring to angels. He pondered the conversion biblically from angels often bringing death in the Old Testament to angels bringing good news at the birth of Christ. Although the Bible did not specifically talk about an angel of death, the number of references to such a character in other writings and religion added to Aaron's confusion. With Za in attendance, he brought her into his thought process. "So, Za, what do you think? Is there a specific angel of death? Or is it just any angel needed at that moment will do?" he asked.

"Really, Dad? You're starting the day out pretty heavy," she replied, barely awake enough to fully process the question. "I mean, isn't there an angel of death? What about the angel that took the first sons of Egypt?"

"Right, but was that a specific angel of death? Or just an angel or angels tasked with that specifically horrid task at that time?" he continued his questions.

"Dad, I'm seventeen. I was born in the new millennium. If the movies tell me there is an angel of death, then I tend to think that there is one. Besides, it seems like there are so many paintings depicting it that there must be something biblical about it. Doesn't he even have a name?" she asked back.

"Not specifically that I know, other than being referred to as the destroyer, and that's the thing. There is no named angel of death in the Bible. Sure, there are other sources to go from, but not in the Bible. There are angels that bring death, primarily in the Old Testament, but is it a single angel specifically tasked with bringing death? What a terrible life for an angel that would be," said Aaron.

"I suppose so. I mean, I don't know about whether there is an angel of death in the Bible. I always thought that there was, but you would know more than me. But, yeah, that would be a terrible job. It seems so contrary to the love of God," Za replied. "Now I'm going to feel sad for the angel of death, all day thinking about what a terrible job he was given."

"Well, there's a lot of death in the Bible, so I sometimes think maybe there was an angel created for just that task to spare all of the others," continued Aaron. "At least by sparing the others, they don't have to be sad about it. That might help put a happy spin on it."

"Makes sense," Za agreed.

"Or—and I'm just thinking out loud now—was it an angel that brought death or, wait for it, was it an angel that led those from death to God?" Aaron felt like he had said something very profound, but this feeling was quickly dismissed by his daughter.

"What?" responded Za, not understanding what her dad was saying. She could see a slight level of disappointment in his face as if he was expecting a different response.

"Think of it this way. Is death always a bad thing? Yes, I was in tears, distraught, and lost when your mother passed, but, and I've said this before, she went to heaven. She was at peace. Any angel that took her away from us also took her to God or at least enabled her to go to God. That can't be all bad," Aaron tried to explain.

Za was slightly unhappy that he brought up her mom, but she didn't let it show. Instead, she was slightly engulfed by the topic. Thinking quickly, she responded astutely, "I can't wait to be with Mom, and that is a good thing, but is it one angel to deliver people to hell with another angel or no angel needed to take them to heaven? For every happiness, it seems that there is a sadness, and I'm the one that usually looks for the happiness."

"Wow, you are the clever one," Aaron said, admiring her thoughtfulness. "We can't have good without the bad, I suppose. Maybe angels or an angel takes care of the souls that go to heaven while a fallen angel handles the others. Or maybe no such angel is even necessary, which brings me back to my initial question really. Is there such an angel?"

"Is such an angel even necessary?" Za added.

"Now you're getting it," said Aaron. "I'm definitely going to spend some time reading up on angels this week," he added. Then Aaron began to think just about angels in general. "You know, I believe in angels. I don't really see how you can believe in God and not believe in angels."

"Yes," responded Za, indicating that she was still in the conversation.

Aaron continued, "I also believe that there is at least one angel for every human, but are they alive in the physical sense only or in a mental sense too?"

"Well, you've lost me now," admitted Za.

"Clearly, angels can think for themselves or there would be no fallen angels, but how independent are they?" He constructed a questioning metaphor in his head that he decided to run by Za. "Think about this idea. Is man to a faithful dog as God is to an angel?"

Za's face cringed. "Are you trying to make me remember the ACT?"

"Sorry," Aaron said through a slight smile.

"Okay, though, so an angel is like God's faithful dog," said Za.

Aaron continued, "If a man or woman brought home a dog and gave that dog a cage (let's call the cage Earth) but allowed the dog to do anything it wanted to do in that cage, even destroying it, then that dog would be alive in both the physical and the mental sense. How does that compare to an angel that is not allowed to do what it wants but is instead always doing the bidding of God. Would that angel be happy? A dog that is forced to only do the bidding of its master can't be truly happy, I feel."

"Well, Dad, I think that is where your metaphor breaks down," responded Za.

"How so?" Aaron asked. "Would the dog be happy? What if the dog were chained up with no freedom, forced to do only what its master ordered? Would it be happy to serve? Would it be beaten down? Or would it want to rebel?" It was a metaphor in progress but nevertheless one that made Aaron think.

"The metaphor breaks down because a dog is not an angel, and God does not beat down those he loves. An angel knows God and knows that God knows best. A dog just knows you as its master, not as a benevolent all-knowing being, although perhaps some dogs do think that way," explained Za.

"You've got something there, sweetie." Aaron would continue that thought later. As he took the first bite out of his toast that had been sitting in front of him, his mind was ready to move on. "I don't think it really gets to what I'm wanting anyway. Now that I think more, it makes me wonder what people are to an angel."

Za started on the yogurt she had taken out of the refrigerator during their discussion. "That brings it back around. I'm guessing we are something different to different angels." Za smiled. "You see, now you have me invested in your angel talk."

Aaron smiled.

Za continued, "If there are billions of angels, perhaps even one that does death, maybe nothing more than death, then angels probably look at us in a lot of different ways."

Aaron's Bible had been opened beside him during the discussion, but he closed it now that his concentration was fully on the conversation at hand. "So, then, if there is an angel of death, then its demeanor could be one of disgust toward humans, just so that it could easily complete its task. Then again, maybe it is one of sadness. It could also be happy that it gets to bring souls to heaven."

"Now you've done it," said Za.

"Done what?" Aaron asked.

"You've completed the circle. You still have no idea if there is an angel of death or how such an angel, if it exists, would feel." Za raised her hands as she spoke and completed a hand gesture as if she was dropping a microphone, ending the conversation on her reflective statement.

Aaron laughed gently and granted Za the last word. They both smiled and continued with their breakfast. They ate quickly around the kitchen table and still had time for the usual morning banter afterward.

It was clear that the two deeply cared for one another. Aaron saw the young woman that Za was becoming and the traits of his loving wife passed down to his daughter. Za saw the man who always showed her love and affection while teaching her how to be a good person.

Aaron smiled. Looking at Za, he recognized her appearance for the first time. "You definitely got your mom's way of throwing herself together in the morning. Really dear, you must get up and actually prepare for the day. You're a mess, as usual. Make sure to bring a brush to fix your hair in the truck. Are those clothes even clean?"

"Yes," Za answered.

"By clean, I mean, have they been cleaned since you wore them last?"

"Yes…maybe…no…I'm not actually sure," Za smiled.

With a smile himself, Aaron ran his hand through Za's hair. "You realize that you gave every possible answer to that question? Yep, you really are turning into your mother."

"I love you too, Dad." Za did love her father, but she wished he would move on from comments about her mother this morning. Thankfully, he appeased.

"And I love you. How can anyone help but love you? You're such a great girl, always helping out at work and at home. Where would I be without you?" Aaron said truthfully.

"You'd be lost, just like your head sometimes if it wasn't attached."

Both laughed.

"Someday, maybe I'll come to work for you for real rather than just helping out. Do you think that you can afford me?" said Za as she rubbed her fingers together to signify making money.

"Afford you?" laughed Aaron. "I think you're getting ahead of yourself. Let's finish high school first."

"Ah. Do I have to?"

"Uh, yeah."

"Okay, but only because you said so," said Za, but in reality, she enjoyed school for the most part. She just didn't like people to know that.

"Why do you say that? Is everything going all right? Grades? Friends? I don't really see that many friends around here, you know," queried Aaron.

"Everything is fine," reassured Za. "And I've got friends," she said defensively.

"You say that, Za, yet you still spend all of your time with me here or at church. You're always telling me to date. Maybe it's time for you to get out there too. A pretty girl like you must have all kinds of boys interested."

"Oh, really?" Za smiled wryly.

"Wait. Scratch that. I'm not saying get out there and start dating. You can do that when you're thirty. I mean spend more time with friends."

"Did I see a little bit of red in your cheeks there, Dad?" Za understood what her dad was trying to say, but it was fun to see him uncomfortable. It didn't happen that often. She decided to continue to reassure him. "It's fine. I've got a few friends, but I guess I could spend more time with them. I like hanging out at work with you, though, at church. To be honest, Malone is probably my best friend more than the girls at my school anyway." Seeing her dad's eyes look up, she added, "And don't worry, we're just friends."

Aaron was not blind. He could tell that Malone and Za were having a bit of puppy love if not more. Who knew if anything would come of it? As much as he wanted to keep Za safe, he knew Malone and sort of looked to him like a friend, almost a son. Za was seventeen, and he couldn't keep her away from boys forever. But he wasn't sure he was ready for her to date just yet. What she really needed were more female friends. Having no ideas on how to solve that problem presently, he moved the conversation forward.

"Malone's a good kid, but that's enough about boys. What about your grades?" Aaron asked, shifting the subject.

"I'm passing. Don't worry. I mean, I don't think I have any As, maybe one, but I don't think I have any Cs or Ds either."

"School comes first, sweetie." Aaron paused. "Listen, I love that you would want to work with me, but let's get good grades, and then you can make up your mind when you finish school and can be anything you put your mind to. Get good grades so you can have a choice."

"Okay, I'll do my best, and we'll wait and see." Za would wait and see, but in her heart, she really enjoyed working with her father. At the very least, she would probably go to a Christian school and pursue something in mission work.

Both sat there for a while. Both had more to say, but they couldn't find the words. Perhaps it was best to simply finish their breakfast.

As they quickly finished their breakfast, the early morning had passed. Getting ready to leave, Aaron made sure that he had his laptop and that Za was prepared for school. He checked the calendar on the refrigerator to verify that she had a hot lunch today. Then he grabbed his wallet and keys as they exited through the front door.

The two exited the house into an unusually warm spring day. The flowers were blooming in the neighbor's garden, adding just enough needed color and scents to the drab mist of the morning. The red truck they entered with all of its rust likewise contributed some color, but probably not in the same way.

Driving down the street, Aaron allowed the silence to continue. He thought to bring up his dream, which he had shared with Za in the past, but decided that silence was golden. The atmosphere continued comfortably quiet as they drove.

M eanwhile, in the dark recesses of hell, a meeting started. High-
level demons from the cardinal sins were in attendance. The
identification and definition of the chief sins had been fluid throughout human history, and due to human conventions, in accordance
with the belief that as above, so below, the sins were also in flux in
limbo and hell. However, since the last major reworking completed
almost fourteen hundred years ago, they had been mostly stable. At
that time, seven sins had held precedence over all others, even if all
sin was equal in the eyes of God.

To a demon, it was a high honor to represent a deadly sin. It
was also an honor to attend a secret meeting, which is why they
seemed to happen so often. This meeting, however, was especially
secretive with only certain trusted demons invited. Demons loved
secrecy. Some feared it as well. That fear swelled from the fact that
if Lucifer knew of this meeting, several of them would probably lose
their heads. Their heads could usually grow back, but while demons
in hell were nearly indestructible, they could still die. Unlike the
humans they hated so voraciously, if a demon died in certain specific
and secretive ways, they ceased to exist. For that reason, any politi-
cal movement in hell was always of potentially deadly consequence.
Only Lucifer, for reasons unknown to all of the other demons, could
not be killed in any manner in hell, and some higher demons had
tried. Who those demons were, no one could remember as even their
memories ceased.

There was no light in the meeting hall. They were too far under
hell for any light to reach. Besides, demons didn't need light to see.
They could see the energy patterns given off by their surroundings.

Light, being only a very small part of the energy spectrum, was unnecessary for their vision.

There were no windows or doors to the room either. The only entrance was through mental movement. In this realm, one could travel by thinking where one wanted to be; that is, if one was a demon. The same would also be true of any representative of heaven, but the probability of any such individual knowing of this space or wanting to reach it was zero.

With no light, there was no need for color either. Everything was a shade from brown to gray to black. A large five meters across round black stone table filled the center of the room. Nine gigantic gothic chairs with high backs and sturdy legs circled the table. Twenty such chairs could easily have fit, but they would not need that many. With only six demons expected in attendance, nine chairs were placed. Nine were needed to allow for decisions of who to sit next to and, more importantly, who not to sit next to. Not everyone, as would be expected in a demonic circle, appreciated everyone else. The table could have been smaller, but many meetings were held in this room beyond the current secretive assembly.

Nearly ten feet separated the table from the wall, but even that was insufficient for some of the beasts in attendance. The same was true of the twelve-foot ceiling. For that reason, demons agreed to take humanoid form, although they would have called it base form. Choosing a base form reminded them of what once was from a time when they were angels. It also simplified preparations as their varied demonic forms would require specialized accommodations.

Ten demons had been invited to the meeting. The leader believed that only ten demons knew of the meeting as well. Six of them were attending. These six served as representatives for six of the seven principle sins and three of the four great kings of hell. The fourth great king had no knowledge of this meeting. If he had known, then Lucifer would know, and that would not serve their purpose.

Representing *Avaritia*, or greed, was Duke Buné. His great form was of a dragon with three heads: a dog, serpent, and man. His demand for riches from his followers led him to relish in the sin of greed. Commanding thirty legions of demons and being highly ranked, he was welcome at the table.

Representing *Luxuria,* or lust, was King Gaap. One of the four cardinal kings of hell, it was no small feat to garner his attendance, even if he only commanded thirty legions of demons. His great form was of a large angelic figure turned red with bat-like wings but lacking the horns so often depicted of demons. He had the ability to make women better lovers; but in so doing, they were rendered infertile. He saw that as an improvement.

Representing *Invidia,* or envy, was Alabasandria, the only female demon invited, not that demons or angels had true genders like humans. Almost any demon could represent any of the sins, but not all were willing to admit their envious nature. Further, not all demons would be willing to take part in this plan. Alabasandria was willing to do both. Her infertility made her envious of other women, leading to her desires to punish others with the same sin. Not being one of the seventy-two ranked demons, she did not command demonic legions, but she commanded a hundred legions of sinful men enraptured by her lust.

Representing *Gula,* or gluttony, was Prince Seere. Although lower in rank, he still commanded twenty-six legions of demons. He was mostly indifferent to the evil most demons embodied, but he grew weary of hell and would just as soon see his existence end than to continue as a fallen angel. Therefore, he felt he had nothing to lose by taking part in the plan about to be discussed.

Representing *Ira,* or wrath, was the mighty King Beleth, another of the cardinal kings of hell. He commanded eighty-five legions of demons through ferocity. His base form was similar to Gaap but with a large rhinoceros-shaped head. He was also the highest-ranking demon in attendance, knowledge of which made several others in attendance secretly desire that he was leading.

No one represented *Acedia,* or sloth. Several were invited, but they were either too lazy to care or too prideful to admit their own sloth.

Leading the meeting and representing *Superbia,* or pride, was King Asmodai. His normal form was a strong and powerful bull torso with three heads: one bull, one ram, and one a man that could spit flames from its mouth. When formed with a humanoid torso, he would ride a dragon into battle, carrying a lance and commanding seventy-two legions of demons. He was the third of the four cardinal kings of hell in attendance and also the mastermind behind the plan currently underway. Although this form was unknown to Aaron Todd, he would most likely recognize the voice as the one from his dream.

There was no speaking as the demons arrived. One after another, they teleported into the room and took a seat, sometimes shifting to gain a more favorable arrangement. As they sat, they placed their hands on the table. A hum resonated from below before a deep voice emanated from the table. "Approved," was heard for each. As all of the higher-ranking demons could take many forms, it was necessary to verify the identity of those present. No one could afford to talk until they were sure Lucifer or other demons had not infiltrated their plans.

Once everyone had been approved, the first to speak, in part to proclaim his importance, was Beleth. "We waited seven hundred years for this opportunity, Asmodai, tell me your plan is working. It's been a year since our last assembly. Azriel hasn't been seen for over forty years now. Some, myself included, believe that he was erased this time. Tell us what you've been doing for the last year."

At least half of those present agreed. No one had felt the presence of the angel of death in over thirty years. He had never been absent for such a protracted time frame before. Surely, his disobedience had been punished by God, a name that would not be mentioned in current company. Their plan was dependent on finding the angel of death, Azriel, and without him, the plan was done.

Asmodai was not pleased by this request, but it was exactly as expected. Azriel had been missing before, and a similar group of demons led by Asmodai had attempted this same plan. In those instances, they had been able to find Azriel in twenty years. This time, it had been forty. As expected, each year, more demons left the cause, believing that it was futile to search for an angel that no longer existed. Twenty years ago, all twenty chairs were needed around the table. If Asmodai could not show results today, this council of demons would disband. But that would not be the case.

Asmodai considered drawing out the discussion as he loved deceiving other demons, but he also didn't want to risk unrest. "Well, my dear compatriots, I can tell you with absolute certainty that Azriel has not been erased."

"You said that same thing last year, Asmodai. I will not sit and be lied to again," said Gaap. Asmodai was correct to get straight to the point. Gaap was preparing to leave as he spoke. He had no interest in farfetched plans. He was more interested in returning to the pit to exploit its growing numbers. While he was for the plan in the beginning, he was beginning to enjoy the current state of things.

To put it simply, the current state of the afterlife was limbo. Without the angel of death, no other angel had been placed in charge of leading the dead from the purgatory known as the pit to everlasting heaven. Some humans, a few, ascended without the need for an angel, but most needed the help. Furthermore, due to the mixing of redeemable and irredeemable souls in the pit, Minos, hell's counterpart to Azriel, could not sort them. All humans had to be given one last chance at redemption, but without an angelic presence on the road to the pit, no human in forty years had been given this option. So no human could leave the pit to go to heaven, but likewise, no human went to hell. Instead, there was only the collection at the pit, and the number of lost and confused souls in the pit was growing.

Some demons did not care. Others, mostly lesser demons, welcomed the opportunity to toy with humans in the pit. And still others insisted on fixing the problem so that they could continue their work in hell. Most of those in this room, except Gaap, were in the later grouping. Either hell needed to get back to its norm or something more drastic needed to happen.

"No need to move from your seat, Gaap," said Asmodai before anyone left. "I will expend with the pleasantries and get straight to the point. We now know for a certainty that Azriel is in human form."

A wave of surprise passed through the room. They were expecting the purpose of this meeting to be toward disbanding the group in favor of a new plan. Everyone was sure that they had not found Azriel because he simply no longer existed.

Beleth was the first to voice a reaction. "Do not lie to us in order to save your faltering plan. I will ask you directly so that you are compelled to tell the truth. Have you found Azriel? Or more inclusively, has someone to your knowledge found Azriel?"

Although he loved deceit, Asmodai was compelled by divine authority to tell the truth when asked a direct question. He didn't mind in this case. "Yes...and no." The anger and confusion in the room pleased him.

Everyone spoke simultaneously in reaction to his statement. Beleth was the loudest. "You either know or you don't. Now tell us the truth. No more games."

After a brief laugh, Asmodai reined in the group. "I tell you that he does exist, but in all honestly, I have not found him. I did not lie."

"What is your proof that he exists?" asked Beleth.

"Since our last meeting, I have finally found his dreams. He is human. He does not know who he is, just like the previous times. But I'm not sure what is different this time. It was very difficult to find his dreams, but it is definitely him. As we hoped, and as last time, he doesn't know of his power, but it is clearly there."

The circle of demons roared. They were partially in shock at this revelation. Azriel was alive! Few expected that. But why had it taken so long to find him? The answer to that question eluded them all.

Alabasandria spoke firmly, "You said yes...and no."

"Exactly," said Asmodai. "I found him in that I know he is on Earth and in the Midwest. But I do not know exactly which human. Yet!"

Seere added, "It can only be a matter of time before something is done. The pit is getting crowded. You know who won't let this go on forever." Seere was referring to the abundance of human dead accumulating in the pit, which was not to be confused with hell. The pit had always been a land of sorting prior to being placed into hell. Seer did not like the potentially redeemed cluttering the pit. He did not like crowds. Also, as with everyone in the room, he recognized that neither Lucifer nor God would allow this situation to continue.

"Agreed," said Asmodai. "I tell you that we are close. I am only months or less away from finding his exact human essence."

"And the plan stays the same once he is located?" asked Beleth.

"Yes," acknowledged Asmodai.

"Yes!" added the group in unison.

"Then I will see everyone soon when I have news. Otherwise, I will send word if Azriel has been sent to the pit," concluded Asmodai. As long as Azriel believed he was a human, he would go to the pit like the rest of the humans. There, the demons could find him and potentially control him.

After their cheers, the meeting disbanded. One by one, the attendees dissipated, returning to their own sections of hell.

Asmodai remained the longest. His promise only gave him a short time to find Azriel. He would need to spend every moment searching the dreamscape. He also believed that he had narrowed the possibilities enough that it was time to begin a day of intense pain. He would need to take a human form in order to approach the corporeal Azriel. Asmodai hated the idea of taking human form, but it was necessary. He would be cooked and turned to ash, slowly lifting out of the ethereal realm, giving up all of his demonic power while gaining temporary human existence.

He would still have power on Earth, though. Humans placed power in wealth, and his demonic cohorts had long established their interests. Asmodai would take a new form and run their corporate interests himself for a short time while finishing the search for Azriel.

Over the next week, Aaron's unrest continued with the dreams becoming more detailed each night. Still, he could always forget about his troubles by thinking of the troubles of others at work.

Aaron had two jobs. It wasn't that he needed two jobs but rather that only one of these jobs paid him while the other was a mission. The job he performed openly for pay was that of youth pastor at a nearby Church of Christ. Their congregation was small, but the youth group included many children and teens that did not go to church. On any given Sunday or Wednesday evening, he could see five to forty students from sixth through twelfth grade. He also organized their Sunday morning school for children. The rest of the week, he seemed to receive at least one call or text a night from someone needing his assistance. He didn't mind. He loved his work. Aaron's life had a purpose, and his purpose was helping others.

His other work was voluntary and a bit more secretive. Aaron ran a group called Angelic Missions whose offices he had just arrived at. On this wet spring morning, he had work to do at the mission. Aaron was looking forward to what the day held for him, and he was hoping that the work would help him to put his dreams out of his mind.

The Angelic Missions office was, like most of the items in Aaron's life, purposefully plain. The only indication that it even was an office or organization of any kind was the small sign on the window consisting of two wings folded over the outline of a little boy and girl with the text "Angelic Missions" above. This unobtrusive vestibule lay between the profligate signage of a tax office and a personal injury attorney, the latter of whom was particularly well-connected to other lawyers who often provided Angelic Missions' help. She was also the one who secretly paid for the office, using it as a tax write-off. Aaron waved at Janice, the lawyer's secretary, as he walked past her office on the way to the mission.

The door to the mission was covered with a gate that lowered from above. Although down, the gate itself was curiously not locked. Aaron was sure he had locked the gate the night before, but the lock was still there, unlatched. It didn't appear that anyone was inside yet, and the gate was still down. He looked around, not sure what he was looking for, but feeling that looking around was what one should do when suspicious. For the moment, he felt it was best to simply get inside and make sure all was well.

What Aaron was ignorant of was the fact that the mission had been visited the previous night. One of Asmodai's minions had searched the premises for information on those that worked within. The demon was not specifically looking for information on Aaron, just any human that might fit the Azriel profile. Aaron was the one that the demon decided was the most likely candidate. The demon then left, forgetting to lock the gate behind him.

Once inside, Aaron was quick to realize that he probably need not fear a major theft anyway. Except an old computer at the reception desk, there wasn't much of value. Interestingly, there was, however, a slight odor in the air as if something had been burned some time ago. A quick scan showed no signs of any source of the smell. Aaron thought it curious but still not enough to warrant major concern. Nothing appeared broke or missing at first or even at second glance.

"Hello?" Aaron spoke, just to check that he was alone. As his fear subsided, his more usual demeanor took over. "Maybe a homeless person needed shelter last night," he thought or perhaps wished out loud. To be honest, he would welcome someone taking shelter in the office. Such would be in line with the very purpose of Angelic Missions.

Discerning that purpose was a difficult task. One would find the full answer quite interesting. On the surface, Angelic Missions served multiple enterprises. They were involved in helping others plant churches or in coordinating and running various forms of Christian professional development, workshops, conferences, and retreats. They owned a small parcel of land in northern Indiana that was used for various retreat like activities. However, these tasks were just what Angelic Missions presented itself as on the surface.

But then, under the surface was their real purpose and from where Aaron derived the name. Angelic Missions served to rescue child slaves, a most dangerous business. They were mostly involved in the management, paperwork, organization, and legalities of the work of others. They would work with many other secretive groups, funding detectives to locate slavery rings around the globe, and then organizing guerrilla-type activities to free the slaves. Once saved, any of the groups in their network would funnel the freed slaves into areas of safety to the point of providing them with entirely new identities and lives. It was not easy. It was not safe. One of his friends had died in the past trying to save others. They all knew the risks, and they all accepted those risks willingly.

Aaron both loved and feared God. He loved God for saving grace and feared His wrath should he live a life that didn't honor Him. He chose Angelic Missions as his way of worship. Every freed slave would know God was behind their freedom.

Other than raising his own child, Aaron could not think of anything more worthwhile in his life than helping lead children to safety or to God at his church. He knew that although the public media had chosen to mostly ignore the problem, slavery was worse today than ever in human history. The nature of the slavery might have changed over time, but the problem persisted. Aaron loved his work. Simultaneously, he hated the fact that his work needed to exist. He honestly wished death on the evil within people that could lead them to enslave others against their will.

Those thoughts aside, often children were hidden at the office for days, having been freed from some illegal captivity, waiting to be transported somewhere more permanent and safer. It was not unusual to open the door and find people sleeping there in the morning. He just wasn't expecting it today. After finding the front unlocked, he was hoping that maybe someone would be hiding inside, but that was not the case.

Most of his coworkers rarely came to the office either. For instance, one recently left to go to South Texas in order to help a group of children with a new home, and others were in south Cambodia, potentially risking their lives to track down a truck full of kidnapped kids. Aaron planned to go on such trips again once Za was a little older, but for now, he held down the fort.

Aaron proceeded to the back of the office, although calling it an office might be an overstatement. It was more like a large room. At the front of the room was a small reception desk with various files, a computer, a phone, a printer, and a nice smiling sign asking visitors to please ring the bell for service. As the office was particularly small, the sign and the bell were both rather pointless. The phones were automated to an answering service. Thrice a week, sometimes more, a wonderful retired woman named Mary would come in and help with paperwork or whatever. Perhaps she left the gate unlocked. Aaron would try to remember to ask her in the afternoon if she came in that day. The computer was also useful when a visiting missionary needed one or when something needed to be printed. More useful to most of the workers was the coffee maker sitting rather prominently against the wall on the front desk. A small container of sugar accompanied the coffee pot.

Behind the front desk were four small cubicles surrounded by four-foot tall partitions, each with a desk, several files, recently emptied trash cans, and various necessities for writing and such. Despite the presence of plastic holders for nameplates on the partitions, none had a name on them as all were used by whoever happened to be in that day. Still, most of the workers had their favorites where they would keep various personal items. The walls from the front of the office were decorated with various Christian posters from the inspirational to the Ten Commandments to someone's favorite musical artist. At the back of the office was a single door leading to a back hallway including both the emergency exit and a shared bathroom with the other offices.

Also at the back of the room was a larger area where one would find a comfortable-looking chair, a couch, a small refrigerator, a stack of blankets for when people were staying overnight in the offices, and finally, Aaron's desk. It wasn't so much a fifth cubicle as he simply occupied the space in the back behind the other compartments. He was the only one with his own desk, but he made sure to keep his footprint small. While the same size as the other desks, Aaron's was piled with papers, albeit surprisingly organized for their number and lack of separate bins or vertical files. The filing cabinet, comprised of four drawers, was filled with additional paperwork, with drawers for tax information, missionary tracking, contractors, country regulations, church information, and miscellaneous. None of their covert work was included. Those duties were only written in encrypted computer files for security reasons.

In addition to the mountain of paperwork, Aaron's desk included neatly organized pens and pencils in his favorite coffee cup (despite the fact that he never drank coffee), a sharpener, a notepad, and a small frame with a picture of Za sitting on his lap and a photo from the day he proposed to Hannah. There was no computer on the desk, for Aaron preferred his laptop.

Sitting down with a sigh as if to announce that he had to get to work, Aaron opened his bag, placed his laptop on the only open space of his small desk, and waited while it turned on. *You're supposed to do my bidding, and yet I feel like I'm always the one waiting on you,* he thought. He looked at a cup of water he had apparently left from his last visit. He picked it up and thought for a moment to take a drink but decided instead to place it back where it sat. *Maybe later I'll get back up and take care of you.*

Resolving himself to make at least some use of his time, Aaron sorted through papers on his desk until he found one of interest. Although Aaron had many duties at Angelic Missions, he was always the primary point man on fundraising, and the sheet he lifted was something he had printed the previous day concerning Saligia Enterprises. It was clearly designed as propaganda comprised mostly of stock photos of happy people receiving supplies with the tagline in bold red, reading "Saligia is there behind the scenes to meet your needs." The Saligia text was of particular interest.

Aaron wasn't sure if there was something off with the brochure, but the S seemed almost snakelike, wrapping around several of the other letters. On the other hand, he could simply be receiving a spark of insight into the design of a new brochure for Angelic Missions. At the same time, he felt as if he had seen their logo before but long ago and now forgotten.

"Why does this look so familiar?" he asked the photo of Za in a vain attempt to jog his memory. He often spoke to the photo, particularly when alone. He liked to talk to himself and oddly felt that if he talked to the photo instead, it seemed saner.

His interest in Saligia was based on his fundraising needs. Many of the Angelic Missions operations were secretly funded by private donors. Saligia had somehow tracked them down and was offering a million-dollar grant, which was huge. Two weeks ago, he had submitted his proposal after receiving information in the mail. Everything was routed through a third party to maintain some secrecy. He hadn't heard anything and was beginning to accept that it might have been a hoax. Then his thought was interrupted as the phone rang on the front desk, the only phone in the office that wasn't cellular.

Unusually, Aaron ran up to the front to check the phone. The caller ID revealed no number. Aaron considered letting it go to the answering service, but he decided in the end to pick up the receiver. As he hesitantly moved the phone to his ear, he tried to think of the perfect way to greet the caller. The person on the other side took advantage of his pause and spoke first.

"Hello, is this Angelic Missions?" a somewhat sultry female voice asked. This particular woman was only calling because the search of the premises the previous night alerted Asmodai to a potential candidate.

"Ah, yes, hello. How can I help you?" Aaron faltered the words from his mouth, the opposite of his intentions. *Maybe the caller didn't notice*, he wondered with positivity.

"Yes, excellent. Is there a Dr. Todd there with whom I can speak?" the woman spoke with a dominating presence.

"This is he. What can I do for you?" returned Aaron, not used to people using his surname and title.

"Excellent. Dr. Todd, I'm calling from Saligia Enterprises about the...grant."

Excitedly, Aaron interrupted, "Oh my goodness, that is just the best news!"

"I'm glad. Within the next few days, you should be getting another letter at the submission address. We always call first just in case the package does not arrive. Mr. Simpson likes to get to know every one of his, let's call them grant recipients, personally."

"Great," stated Aaron to acknowledge understanding as he returned to his seat.

The woman continued, "The letter includes all of the information for you to continue in the process. Once we have the information requested, the next stage will be a personal interview with Mr. Simpson. If you have any questions, please submit them to the submission e-mail. We look forward to hearing more from your organization. Are there any questions at the moment?"

"No, I truly look forward to the mail and moving forward in the process. Thank you."

"You are most welcome, Mr. Todd. Goodbye."

"Have a wonderful day," concluded Aaron. Before he had finished, the woman had hung up.

Aaron leaned back in the chair. His mind was so preoccupied by the call that he almost tipped over. Regaining his balance, with a smile on his face, he jumped up. "Yaaaaaa!" he shouted with glee. Even with no one around to hear his squeal, it felt tremendous. Aaron hoped that no one in the adjoining offices were alarmed by his shout. With this funding, they would have more money than they had ever had. He walked back to his seat. Sitting down, getting his heartbeat back under control, he spoke once again to his daughter's picture, "You're my lucky star, sweetie."

"Whoa, what's with all the cheering?" spoke Jonathan as he entered the office. He had heard the shout from outside, embarrassing Aaron slightly. Jonathan jumped to the back to greet Aaron and to see what the commotion was all about.

Aaron was slightly surprised anyone else was there, but looking up to see Jonathan, a large smile filled his face as he answered, "Guess who that was on the phone."

"Did you just save 15 percent on your car insurance?" replied Jonathan.

"No," laughed Aaron as he stood up to greet Jonathan, "that was Saligia on the phone."

"No way." Jonathan continued, "Isn't that the group about the donation? What did they want?"

"Dude, the best news. We're supposed to set up a meeting soon to discuss the details." Aaron was not really a "dude" kind of guy, but letting that slang slip showed his glee.

Jonathan, now at the back of the office, shared a high-five moment with Aaron. "That's great news!" he responded. "Now what?"

"Good question. I'm not sure. I have to wait for a letter with more information. They just wanted to call to let me know it was coming." Aaron wasn't sure what came next. When they received donations, there was always a lot of paperwork to make it look legitimate toward the publicly presented Angelic Missions.

"Bummer we have to wait," stated Jonathan.

"Yeah, but it's great news, and I can't wait to get that e-mail or letter or whatever." Aaron paused. "Wait, what brings you in this morning? You're supposed to be in Cambodia. I wasn't expecting you back for a few weeks. Did something go wrong? I planned that trip for months." Aaron was suddenly concerned as he realized Jonathan was not supposed to be there.

"No," reassured Jonathan, "it went great. So great that I'm back a week early. I had to turn in some receipts from the trip, and I thought you'd be here since you seem to live here anyway. We all really appreciate your help with all of the paperwork, by the way. Mary, too, she's a great help. Actually, I was expecting to put this up front for her. She's usually here in the afternoon. What're you doing here? Are you actually living here now?"

"Hey, I have a home," replied Aaron. "Anyway, give them here and tell me what happened."

Jonathan pulled some papers out of his bag and handed them to Aaron, then replied, "It was absolutely fantastic. We brought back six. I know we were hoping for more, but I think they're about out of business thanks to us. We watched all the usual channels you set up, plus some information Tom from Los Angeles pulled together. Remember Tom? But anyway, in two weeks, they only brought in those six girls. They should be here tomorrow, by the way." He then finished quietly, "We're bringing them in through the northern pass in the ice-cream trailer."

Aaron, understanding the code, responded, "Good. I'll have the paperwork for them by tonight too. Malone should be bringing it over later today, actually. That's one reason I stopped in today. Is it the same ones that you sent photos of for the IDs?"

"Yes, all the same," Jonathan said. "It was the best trip yet. We made it in and out without anyone even knowing we were there. We only had two days to plan the final escape since our contact said that they were planning to move the girls sooner than expected, but their so-called secure holding facility was just an old bank. Little did they know that a simple bypass cut out all the security. Jack had the back door open in ten seconds. Man, he could give the lock-picking lawyer a run for his money."

"Weren't there any guards?" asked Aaron.

"Yes, but the two guns we hired seemed almost lost with nothing to do. It was like some kind of divine intervention. We had scoped out two guards, but they were both asleep and didn't even hear us until we had both of their guns. We were in an out in under five minutes. We made the plane in under thirty minutes. It was the fastest extraction ever. You're like a genius or something. Every plan you make works better than the last. It's like you were put on Earth for this purpose. I don't even have an interesting story to tell. Best story of the trip was singing karaoke with the gang the night before." Jonathan laughed thinking about karaoke.

"You are too kind," thanked Aaron. "I'm just glad it went so well. We've only had three extractions in the past year, but all of them have gone so well. Wait, you said no interesting stories. What's this about karaoke?"

"I suppose you could say that was an interesting night," laughed Jonathan, "especially since none of us can sing and half of the songs were in Khmer. We had a ball. We struggled through the songs for at least an hour. We did a group chorus of 'Secret Agent Man' that had us laughing for a while."

"Sounds like I missed out on the fun, but if everyone sings like you, my ears are probably better off," joked Aaron.

"Definitely," said Jonathan.

"Well, it's good that you are back now. Glad it went so well," shared Aaron.

"It went well, but man, I was scared, I'm not going to lie," said Jonathan, shaking his head, "but in the end, everything went smooth thanks to the plans you drew up. I wrote up a report with the paperwork I gave you. You can extract what you want to the secure files and then burn it."

"Can't wait to read it," said Aaron. "You want to stick around and give me the full version?"

"I'd love to, but I just stopped by to drop off the files for now. I'm jet-lagged and have ten other places to go, but I'll stop by again later. It was on my way or I wouldn't have come by until the afternoon in the first place." Jonathan turned to leave.

"Thanks, brother, I'll see you later," said Aaron as he stood up to follow Jonathan to the door.

After shaking hands at the door, Jonathan started to leave. As he exited, he quickly turned around to say, "Hey, great news again about the donation. We'll have a lot to talk about later. Either way, I'll be here tomorrow when the truck arrives. Jack should be driving it, so we can all get together."

"Bye, Jonathan." The two hugged, and Aaron returned to his desk with a smile on his face.

Returning to the papers Jonathan gave him, Aaron looked through them quickly. While reading, he continued his conversation with Za's picture. "It's a day of great news, isn't it, Za? We're going to have so much to talk about later." Thoughts just seemed more real to him when they were spoken out loud. When others were around, they would sometimes joke about Aaron having a smaller version of

Za locked up in the photo. Although the prospect sounded rather disturbing to him, he let them have their fun. When in a particularly spirited mood, he would retort how he would talk to them if the conversation was at least half as stimulating.

Aaron couldn't decide what to do next. He needed to process the trip papers, write checks, balance books, etc., but that was all boring work. Instead, he sat back in his chair and tried to process all that had just occurred. One thing was for sure: Aaron wasn't thinking about his dreams.

Aaron decided to spend time learning more about Saligia. It wasn't that he hadn't already considered their background when they first contacted him. Rather, it was that he wanted to try one more time for anything new he could find that might help with any future interviews or paperwork.

Opening his laptop, he began with a basic web search as he had done several times before. Searching Saligia brought up their corporate site as the first option. He clicked the link. Their home page presented the same logo and tagline as the letter that he still had out on his desk. Selecting the "About" link revealed what Aaron already knew. Saligia had only existed for about twenty years. All that they were was thanks to a benefactor named Ash Simpson who set up a foundation to provide supplies to missionaries at reduced cost. They then branched to church supplies and eventually to just about any business supply. They still seemed to make most of their money in religious and school supplies.

Aaron turned his attention to Ash Simpson, though. It was he that Aaron wanted to impress. He was the one actually signing over the money. Searching Mr. Simpson, Aaron was surprised at just how little could be found on the Web. A few stories mentioned his family, but there were never photos, names, or anything else; just that he was a family man. Aaron could respect that a businessman might like that family anonymity, but it was amazing at how successful Ash was at keeping secrets.

After some more searching, Aaron came across an interview in a small business journal. Reading the article, Mr. Simpson seemed to sidestep any personal questions, but he did mention that he was from Chicago, attended the College of DuPage, and then worked his way up. However, where he started or where his money arose was not discussed. The article listed some of the divisions of Saligia. That was useful. He had interests in businesses all over the world. Aaron was pleased at this information. It might play in his favor since Angelic Missions tried to work globally. Despite continuing his search, he simply couldn't find much more information. Mr. Ash Simpson remained an enigma.

But the name Saligia did reveal a little more information. Aaron returned to his search results. He remembered from weeks before that several of the top links gave a description listing the seven deadly sins and even a death metal band, which Aaron did not even know was a music genre. Apparently, Saligia was a pneumonic device used by the Catholic church since the fourteenth century. It comprised the first letter in Latin of each of the deadly sins. That drew Aaron's attention. Saligia, it appeared, was a code used for sin. His interest shifted from learning about Ash Simpson to learning about this word.

Aaron looked at Za's photo. "Why would a charity group use the name of the seven deadly sins?" he asked. Aaron leaned back in his chair. It squeaked as if straining to remain in one piece from its age. Aaron had only researched the company before. He was a bit embarrassed. He considered himself a bit of a Bible scholar and felt ashamed he had never heard this term before. Of course, he was nondenominational Christian, not Catholic. "Pfft, it's so confusing. Maybe it means something else?"

Aaron continued his search. No, he couldn't find any other meaning to Saligia. "Could it be the reverse?" Aaron tried to look on the bright side again. "Maybe they chose that name because Saligia is what they fight against. I've got to admit, it's a pretty interesting possibility, sort of like when cultures appropriate a term to make it their own." In the end, Aaron decided that must be the reason, but it was definitely a question to ask Mr. Simpson if he had the opportunity. Aaron picked up a pencil and wrote "Questions for Simpson—Why choose the name Saligia?" on a small notepad pulled from the stacks of papers on his desk.

For now, he chose to just concentrate on the good that they could do with the funding. Aaron thanked God that Saligia, or Mr. Simpson, had chosen to give them funding. He had to assume it was all His doing. How else did Saligia even hear of Angelic Missions?

# 5

Another hour went by. Aaron finished processing the files Jonathan had given him. He could have left it for Mary, but he decided to take care of it himself. He looked over to let Za know he was done, but talking to Za's photo would have to wait. Perhaps the most prolific of the children Aaron had saved was about to enter the office. Malone barged through the front door as if he owned the building. For those of a curious nature, he did not.

"What's up, my peeps?" Malone shouted for all to hear. As the door burst open, a young Asian man with slight build, short spiky hair, and a large smile entered the room. The colloquialism of his speech was not lost on those hearing as Malone only used such choice of words in jest to hide the calmer demeanor underneath.

To Aaron, the appearance of Malone was, in fact, a more welcome sight than the actual welcome sign just inside the door. Malone could always serve as a welcome temporary distraction. Friends often have the ability of shifting one's attention. Malone was such a friend, even if he was almost the age of Aaron's daughter.

"Malone, you numbskull. You can see I'm the only one here today. What's with all the yelling?" Aaron glared back as he peered around the partitions from the back. He maintained marginally enough of a smile to indicate his jovial nature and continuation of Malone's wordplay.

"Oh yeah, I forgot Mr. The Man," said Malone.

"And your sudden deafness and blindness permitted you to fail to perceive the emptiness of the room?"

"That's right, but the deafness subsided, and now I hear a voice. Still blinded, dear Lord, guide me to this voice that it might lead me through the darkness," Malone said as he shut his eyes. In truth, he didn't really need to see. He could easily get through the office without them. He had traversed the room so many times that every step and turn was etched into memory. Yet, maintaining the mood, he purposefully bumped into the front counter. "Oh no, if only someone could guide this poor soul."

Aaron jumped to his feet and jogged to Malone's side. "Oh, here, you poor young man. Allow this humble servant to provide the guidance you desire." Aaron then proceeded to slowly guide Malone to the second cubicle on the right and plopped him into the seat, then quickly retreated to his own chair in a poor attempt to fool his young friend.

"Wait a minute. This isn't my chair. I'm blind, but I can still feel my rear." Malone opened his eyes. Smiling, he rose and continued past his present cubicle to his favorite chair in Aaron's space as if it was his chair in his room with his name on it. Since he visited Aaron almost every day, sitting in the same chair, his confidence wasn't far from the truth.

"How's it going really, Mr. Todd?" Malone asked as he settled out of his boisterous initial state into lightheartedness.

"What's with the Mr. Todd?" responded Aaron.

"Sorry, Dr. Todd," Malone responded, knowing how much Aaron hated being referred to as doctor even though he had his PhD. He wasn't quite sure why he said Mr. Todd instead of Aaron, but he decided to continue with the game as if the statement had been on purpose.

"All right, you're weirding me out. Let's stick with Aaron. All right?" Aaron asked rhetorically.

"Cool, just kidding around," Malone said.

At this moment, a casual observer would believe that Malone was, in fact, kidding around and that the Mr. Todd declaration was a mistake. A more careful observer would think deeper. Somewhere deep in Malone's mind was the realization of his feelings for Za and Dr. Todd. He respected Aaron above all other men. He also had a crush on his daughter that he wasn't yet willing to admit to himself.

In that one instant, he shifted his speech more formally in front of the girl's father.

"It is good to see you, my young friend. What brings you to me today? I ask, hoping that you remembered. Did you bring the papers?" Aaron asked as he became more serious.

"I have the IDs. I hate getting these things. The area is just plain seedy. I know how important they are, though. The contact said the price went up, but I talked him down to the regular price this time. However, expect a premium next time," answered Malone.

"That's unfortunate about the price, but he's the best I know of at setting up fake identities. I mean, they won't pass a thorough check, but they do for a beginning," expressed Aaron.

"Definitely," echoed Malone.

"Thanks again for getting them. I should have said that first. Yes, it's not the best part of the city. Sorry to make you a middleman, but as far as I know, he doesn't know where the IDs end up, and that's best for their safety. At least it feels that way to me." After a pause, Aaron continued, "But anyway, thanks. I'll put these aside until later." Aaron placed the IDs and other documents with the other business from their recent extraction. He took the whole pile and locked it in the file cabinets for safety. He then returned his attention to Malone. "See those papers I put the IDs with? That's the report from the mission. They're ahead of schedule, and everyone is fine."

"That's great!" Malone exclaimed. "But I didn't get that many IDs."

"Correct, there weren't as many this time. But on the bright side, that means that the trafficking cell we've been targeting is getting weaker," said Aaron.

"You always see the bright side," said Malone. "But you're right, and even if it was only one person, it would be worth it." Malone tried to cover the tears that started to form in his eyes. Thinking of people being rescued always brought out his emotions. He changed the subject quickly. "Well, I don't have to work until tonight," Malone added. "I woke up and thought I'd come around, you know, bring over the IDs, help with paperwork or phone calls or whatever. I would've gone to the church but knew you'd be here today. I was so bored. I spent a whole ten minutes trying to juggle some Wiffle balls before I remembered how much I hated juggling. I couldn't even remember where the balls came from. So naturally, I hopped on over here. Sounds like it's a good thing I brought the papers today. Is there anything else I can help with?"

The tears cleared from Malone's eyes as he thought of ways he could help. Malone, as well as Aaron, was as much a fixture of the office as any of the furniture. For Aaron, it was how he spent his life. For Malone, it had given him his life.

Malone was himself a rescued slave. From the age of six, he spent thirteen or more hours per day, six to seven days a week, assembling or sewing various articles of clothing, often while cuffed by the foot to a table. By the time he had reserved himself to a life of misery as a defense mechanism to maintain his sanity as the human condition allows, whether for better or worse, he was rescued. Agents of Angelic Missions found the sweatshop in which he was imprisoned and raided it in one of their few semi-militaristic actions. About ten armed mercenaries broke into the warehouse in which Malone was forced to work, quickly overpowering security. Just as quickly, the slaves' chains were cut, and they were shuffled into waiting vans. They were then whisked away to a makeshift airfield and flown to freedom. Of course, it was much more harrowing than such a short recount allows.

Following a trail devised by Aaron, Malone eventually found his way to Chicago at the age of twelve. Normally, rescues were found a semipermanent place to stay, but Malone was of a more independent nature. Using a fake birth certificate, he was adopted by a nonexistent family. In a temporary moment of corporeality, this family arranged for his state identification. At the time, he appeared on paper to be fourteen, although he clearly looked his younger age. He stayed with false families for a few years until all of his paperwork had cleared and he came of age. Often, the false family was Aaron, and sometimes it was just in the back of Angelic Missions. He had slept in Aaron's spare room many nights while getting settled in. He could tell Aaron was a bit wary at first since Za and he were near the same age, but Malone was always a gentleman.

Since arriving, Malone had been a constant presence at Angelic Missions or Aaron's church. Eventually, he planned to get a proper education and help in a more official capacity. To avoid discovery, though, his education was through homeschooling. He was always tentative about signing paperwork such as a college application as most of his identification was false. He knew that he would probably never be more educated than a high school diploma supplied by a local private Christian school, but who knew? Maybe some small Christian college would let him in later. For the moment, most of his learning was through books and tutoring from people in the office. He was particularly happy when Za would help him. They had been friends since first meeting when he humbly huddled in their spare room during his transition.

In the meantime, life was still hard but in no way comparable to the life before. He would not be heard complaining. He even earned enough—albeit at minimum wage—and with Aaron's help to afford an apartment of his own. If the cockroaches paid him rent too, he would end up ahead in the deal. Suffice it to say, anyone without his background may not have been satisfied in the conditions he could afford. Perhaps the only fortunate aspect to his earlier life was that his captors spoke English, making his integration easier. Today, he was twenty-one on paper and nineteen in reality. His tough life had matured his young mind beyond those years.

Aaron was not his only benefactor. His many friends at the local church were always helping him when he wasn't helping them in odd jobs from mowing to delivery of items. He was also of great help at Angelic Missions. His belief in social capital was evident, even if he did not know what that was.

Currently, Malone spent most of his time at one of three locations. For sustenance, he spent the usual forty hours per week working, making minimum wage as a cook at an Asian restaurant where everyone always assumed that he could speak Mandarin. He was quite good at smiling and shaking his head as if he understood, although his understanding was limited.

For spiritual and social sustenance, he essentially lived at his local church, which just so happened to be where Aaron worked and

Za attended. Video game Friday was one of his favorite times. It was there that he had become even closer friends with Za. It was one of the only times he could spend quality time with her without Aaron or other adults watching over them. With the countless hours challenging her father at games as a child, she was usually his better at most of the games, but he was fine with that. He was mostly just enjoying the company.

Finally, for a sense of family and perhaps worth, he would visit Angelic Missions. Since the first day of his rescue, he, of course, knew Aaron. It was Aaron who arranged his transport. Aaron even let him choose his own name. He remembered seeing a basketball player named Malone something or something Malone. He liked the sound of it.

Thanks to their shared history, Malone and the Todds possessed a strong bond, almost what an impartial observer would refer to as familial. It was unusual. Not their bond, of course. Anyone with an adopted child can know such a bond. But most of the children Aaron helped to rescue went on with their new lives in new locations with new acquaintances and families. Most is probably an under-statement; Malone was the only one whose new life was so closely connected to Aaron's.

It was no secret either that Malone was exceedingly smitten with Za. It was not as apparent to Aaron who, like any father, had yet to accept that his little girl was no longer so little. Malone had not yet built up the courage to willfully make his feelings known; however, anyone with vision or hearing in the near vicinity could observe the signals when they were together. For her part, Za was not sure if she felt an equal attraction as she tried to work out her feelings, but then she was a younger soul. The prospect was clearly intriguing to her, though, and a corner of her brain wished for him to ask her out for real, not just for the group activities they usually took part in.

Returning to the conversation, Aaron answered Malone's ques-tions. "Well, buddy, all joking aside, I'm glad to see you as always, but I'm not sure I have anything for you to do. My plan was to just hang out a while before going downtown. In fact, I was just getting ready to leave when you announced your presence. You can stay here, but you might get bored here too. I have nothing for you to juggle, and you'll have to lock up." Aaron looked up at Malone to see what he would choose to do.

"Why are you in such a hurry to go?" Malone asked.

"I'm not in a hurry. I'm just going to run some errands for the outreach conference we're planning at church."

Quickly Malone reiterated, "Hey, like I said, I don't have to be at work until tonight. I don't have to do anything around here if there is nothing to do, but I could tag along with you while you run your errands. Like I said, my day is free for you and me. Maybe you could drop me off near home too. Then I wouldn't have to take the train or a taxi. If it's later, I'll just head to work when we're finished."

"Well, then, come with me," Aaron said as the two of them gathered their things. Exiting the office, Aaron took care to make sure that it was fully locked up. Despite his many distractions that day, he still remembered the odd circumstance of the morning when he first arrived at the office. He did not think that his carefulness was excessive and thought that it probably went unnoticed by Malone. He was correct.

"Shotgun!" said Malone as they headed to the truck.

"Really the jokester today, huh? I suppose I'll allow it, but my invisible friend is going to be put out." Aaron thought to jokingly suggest Malone could ride in the back, but years of working with past slaves had more than taught him that such jokes were in bad taste.

The truck was a mess and not just in terms of the random debris in the bed. The vehicle did not want to start at first, the driver's seat had a sizeable rip in the covering, and one could place a hand through some of the rust holes. Still, it functioned enough to get people where they needed to go.

"Oh, come on!" Aaron declared when it initially wouldn't start. Calming down, Aaron turned the key once more. With a rumble, the vehicle came to life. "Whoa, that would have been bad," he quipped to Malone.

For the next few hours, the two went about usual business regarding the outreach workshops. They visited a church to finalize the plans with a potential speaker, and then they went to a craft store where Aaron liked to purchase supplies to make the various conferences feel homier.

At the store, Aaron took a few moments in the store to seek out anything that might have been distributed by Saligia.

"What're you looking for?" asked Malone curiously.

"Well, can you see anything that looks like it might have been distributed by Saligia Enterprises?" asked Aaron.

The two looked for a while, but they didn't see anything obvious. "I suppose it is to be expected," said Aaron.

"How so?" asked Malone.

"Well, they are more into distribution, not manufacturing. I'm not sure if they actually make products or just ship and distribute them, maybe a little logistics. I doubt anyone working the front desk knows where they order from either. I just thought I'd check. You know, since we were here."

"We could ask one of the workers," suggested Malone.

"No, I'm actually getting a little hungry. It's almost after noon."

"Oh, you read my mind," said Malone, smiling.

"I hope I didn't bore you too much today, Malone. Why don't you let me buy you a late lunch?" Aaron asked as they had started to the truck.

"You don't have to do that, but I won't look a gift horse in the mouth. Plus, I'm starving," replied Malone.

"What should we get?"

As they waited in line to pay for their items, Malone thought. Lunch sounded appealing as he was hungry, and he could talk more with Aaron.

"You know, I'm not one for fast food, but just the other day, I was wanting to find a food truck. Those can be fun sometimes," suggested Malone.

"I haven't eaten from one of those in a long time. Let's do it," agreed Aaron. "There's bound to be one around here somewhere."

The two entered the truck and drove toward the city. As he was driving, Malone pulled out his phone. "Let me check out the food truck schedule." Malone did a quick search and then added, "Oh, today's winner is Asian tacos, one of my favorites."

"Sounds good to me," agreed Aaron.

After a short drive, they parked near the food truck location. As the two walked outside, the sky was clear, and the city didn't have the usual odor that Aaron had grown to dislike. Burnt hotdog was how he described the smell on occasion. The pedestrian traffic was likewise tolerable, being only moderate given the time of day. Everything seemed to be a sign of good things to come.

After a short wait in line at the truck, they took their food and leaned against the nearest building, relaxed.

"How's your job going, by the way?" Aaron asked before Malone could bring up his dream.

"Pretty good," Malone replied. It wasn't the conversation he was hoping for, but he could work up to his topic.

"What about the ACT?" Aaron asked. He too had been waiting to direct the conversation to one his partner would find less inviting.

*There it is*, thought Malone, who now realized why Aaron wanted to hang out with him today. Malone had been putting off working toward going to college. He needed to quickly finish this topic and move onto his own. "Za is supposed to help me with some math this weekend. You know, it's hard to work and learn all these things, but I think I'm about ready for the ACT test. I really appreciate all of the help everyone has been giving me too."

"You're a smart kid. I'm sure you'll do fine. You spend so much time at the mission studying, you've got to be getting close to ready," Aaron said supportively. He was trying to both push Malone to take the test while also providing encouragement.

"Almost there," Malone smiled.

"And when you're done, I'm sure we'll be able to find a way to get you into a college. I know it's what you want," added Aaron.

"I want to get into Trinity Christian, but it will be hard. You've introduced me to the right people there, but every time I have to fill in paperwork, I get nervous," said Malone honestly.

Aaron was reassuring. "Don't worry about the paperwork. We're pretty good at those things. Even the IRS is happy to take your money now."

"Yeah, but they'll take anyone's money," quipped Malone.

"True. So true." Aaron paused a moment but not long enough for Malone to interject his story. Before Malone could finish his current bite of food, Aaron changed the subject in a surprising fashion. "I've been thinking about money a lot lately."

Malone raised his head in interest. "Who isn't?"

"Well, you know that mission's giving has been down lately," Aaron said.

"Yeah, all giving," added Malone.

Aaron continued, "You've got that right. Normally, when something bad happens in the world, tithing increases, but any more, something bad happens all the time. People are just tapped out."

"And scared," Malone continued, adding, "almost everyone at work the other day was talking about buying guns as if that would solve some problem. It's so reactionary."

"You won't get an argument from me there. I mean, I love shooting for sport, but I just rent the guns at the range or go with a friend who has one. I understand why so many people want them, though. There is a sense of security. I just know that I could never shoot anyone, even if my life depended on it," said Aaron.

"I like to think the same thing, but sometimes I don't know. If someone I loved was in danger, I'm not sure what I might do," confessed Malone. He wondered if he would be able to pull a trigger if Za was in trouble.

"You're probably right. I suppose none of us know what we are capable of until we are put into the right situation. But listen, I didn't mean to get us off on a gun tangent. I was actually moving more toward work," Aaron said.

"What about it?" asked Malone.

"I think there's a really good chance we'll be getting that Saligia grant."

"That is great news!" exclaimed Malone.

"Yes, and if it does happen, and I apologize if I'm getting ahead of myself because we haven't received the check yet…but if we do get it, I think it would be great if you came to work at Angelic Missions," offered Aaron.

"No way!" Malone nearly lost a bite of his lunch at the offer.

54

"Way," responded Aaron with a smile, "but listen, it's contingent. We have to get the money. Also, and here comes your part, you need to start college."

"Dude, this is great news. I don't know what to say. I mean, I don't hate where I work, but I love working at Angelic Missions and helping you with church stuff. I even feel a little motivated about that ACT now," Malone said, unable not to smile.

Aaron added, "Yes, I can see your love when you help out at work. It's like you already work there. We might as well make it official."

"Thank you, thank you!" Malone wanted to hug Aaron and probably would have if not for the remnants of a taco in his hand.

"Don't thank me too quickly. It's not final yet. You also might not like it as much when you get all of the jobs that no one else wants." Aaron raised his eyebrow as if to suggest there might be some truth in what he was saying.

"I think I'm an expert on the jobs that no one else wants," responded Malone.

Quickly Aaron realized the stupidity of his statement. Malone had been a slave. He could write the book on doing what no one else wanted to do. He couldn't think of a way to correct himself, so he just went silent.

The day so far had been mostly business and small talk, but Malone, noticing the awkward silence, changed the subject. "Hey, let me tell you about this dream I had last night." After hearing the news from Aaron, he was reminded of his dream that very morning. Much like Aaron, he regularly participated in rather vivid dreams. Since rescue, he had poured his heart into the Bible. He felt that God was always looking out for and speaking to him. For that matter, he felt God spoke to everyone. As a result, he was the sort of Christian who scrutinized his dreams seriously, at times walking the line on which other Christians might even partially question his sanity.

Despite this possibility, he still spoke often of his dreams and to a greater degree when he felt that they were important. He wasn't sure if this was one of those dreams, but he felt it was always better to be safe than sorry. Besides, Aaron always lent a willing ear to his discourse.

"Oh, really? You have a dream you want to talk about. Must be a day ending in Y," joked Aaron. Of course, on a normal day, it would be completely expected for Malone to want to tell him about a dream. To Malone, dreams were significant and a way for God to communicate with us. It did, however, feel odd that Malone mentioned it today after all of Aaron's vivid dreams that were unfortunately now returned to the forefront of his consciousness. At least listening to Malone's story would take his mind off other things temporarily.

"No, no, no, this one is good. Well, bad things happen, but I recalled a lot of the dream and it was freaky," replied Malone.

"If you say so. I'm game," Aaron stated, preparing to only partially pay attention as he finished his lunch.

"Well, it starts with us lost in the woods," began Malone.

"Any woods in particular or just generic woods?" Aaron asked, realizing maybe he would pay attention.

"Just generic. I'm not sure they mattered. It was just where we started, someplace to get lost in. There were a lot of birch trees, if I remember right."

"Okay"

"Anyway, the woods start to get thorny due to weeds everywhere," continued Malone, "and we're talking about how we need to find a way out. It's not that we're hungry or hurt. We just don't want to be in danger, and for some reason, it feels like we are. After we say that, a road appears ahead of us through the woods. So we go to the road. We don't recognize the road, but it definitely seems safer than the woods."

"What type of road?"

"That was actually interesting. It was a road through the middle of nowhere with no cars anywhere in sight, but it was paved like a highway. It seemed to be an important road but with no one on it."

"Did we just wait there for a car? Never mind. I just realized I keep interrupting. Please continue." Aaron resolved himself to just listen at that point.

"No worries. No, we just waited there at first. We couldn't decide which way to go. From the sun, we figured the road passed east and west, but as time passed, the sun didn't move. Since it was getting late or at least from where the sun was it appeared to be late, we decided to start moving. So we headed toward the sun. We must have come from the south because we turned right and started down the road. So far, the dream was nothing special, just a couple guys lost in the woods who find a road to follow. To me, it meant that I must feel lost, and you were going to help me find myself, but really, we were just both lost now. We walked down this major road for a long time, never seeing a sign or another soul. And there were no forks. It felt like we walked for kilometers and nothing changed."

"So I'm assuming something eventually happened since you're telling me the story," Aaron said.

"No, we just walked down a road for a really long time," Malone jokingly replied. "Just kidding. Yes, we walked for a long time like I said, and then a dog appeared ahead, running for us. It was a huge dog, definitely with some pit in it, but it didn't attack. We thought it was going to. It looked vicious enough. Instead, it just ran up to us, sniffed, licked my hand, and then tried to get us to follow it. We were lost, and it seemed to know the way to go, and thankfully, it didn't want to eat us or have us run around and go back."

"Now we're following a dog on a barren road in the middle of nowhere," Aaron recapped.

"Here's where it gets interesting. Now that we're following the dog, the road has signs all over. All of them keep pointing to danger. Like one I remember was a green sign like the ones telling you how far it is to places. Satan's Hollow was five miles, and Purgatory was twelve."

"Let's hope we didn't take one of those exits then." Aaron didn't mean to joke, but he couldn't resist.

"I don't think we took any exits. I know it's not much, but that was pretty much the dream. We just kept following this dog on a road that seemed to pass through hell. The road itself seemed safe enough, but no one else was on it. We knew we had to keep going, but we weren't sure where we were going. Not sure why, but it freaked me out."

"What made you bring it up?" Aaron asked, thinking that the dream didn't seem scary or too weird.

"Maybe it's a sign. Hard times are ahead. I just need to stay the course. It seemed like you would be my help along the way or I would be your help. When you mentioned the job, it really brought the dream to the forefront of my mind, like I should be walking with you. Well, that's just the story of life. But someone is going to help lead us through, and we should follow, even if it looks like we are heading the wrong way."

"Next time we get lost, I will follow the first dog I see," Aaron continued in a joking tone.

"Ah, now you're making fun of me," Malone said.

"No. Sorry. I like to hear about your dreams. I had a dream myself the other night," Aaron said, not intending to change the subject.

"Really, what was it like?" Malone asked, interested.

"It was the same dream that's been keeping me up for the longest time." That was all Aaron had to say, for he had told the dream to Malone already. He also didn't want to spend all day on the street, talking to Malone about his nightmares.

"Cool. I want a recurring dream like that where I get to fight demons. I told you before, I think it means you are meant for great things."

"Let's wait and see. Of course, there wasn't any fighting in my last dream, just a lot of running and then me burning up in a vast pool of lava."

"It still sounds cool if you ask me...except the pain part," Malone suggested.

"You know, now that I think about it, you're dream reminds me of how I've been feeling lately," Aaron remarked.

"How do you mean?" Malone was intrigued.

"Don't you just feel like people are lost? I mean, we don't have any real leaders anymore, just people out for themselves. Too many people are getting left behind. Just look at work. There are more slaves today than ever in history, and no one seems to care as long as it doesn't affect them personally. We absorb ourselves in electronics and try to shut out the world around us. No one wants to admit how lost and helpless they feel to change anything. They just go about their lives and are content to live day to day. There are not enough dreamers anymore." Aaron realized that his initial thought had fallen into rambling. He had not intended to lay out so many issues on Malone.

"Heavy stuff," Malone responded.

"Sorry to sound lecture-y. I mean, it's sort of like your dream. Everyone seems to be going down a road not knowing where it heads. They just keep heading down it since there is nowhere else to go, and every exit is just as bad as the last. Where did all of the good exits go, you know?" Aaron asked.

"There are still some good exits. People do great things every day," Malone reassured. In part, he was thinking of all the good that Aaron did.

"Yes, I know. I guess I'm in one of those moods when I wished the world could be a better place," admitted Aaron.

"Seems like everyone has that wish," Malone added.

Aaron hypothesized, "If everyone has that wish, and I actually think that they do, then why isn't everyone acting on it?"

"People are scared," said Malone.

"I agree exactly," said Aaron. "Everyone fears losing what they have, even if they aren't satisfied with it. Not enough people are willing to grasp out to reach their full potential. We live in some hidden state of fear...fear of losing things that don't even matter when we could gain so much more."

"Preach, brother," clapped Malone.

"Come on now. You know what I'm saying," said Aaron. "I'm not even sure I'm any better. I use money as my excuse, saying that I can't afford to take certain chances. I guess I've got a bit of fear in me as well."

"We all do," Malone acknowledged. "Maybe since I have no money, I'm not as afraid to take chances, but I still plan to take them in the future instead of the present. Anyway, I wouldn't say that you live in fear. Look at all that Angelic Missions does."

"We do our best," responded Aaron, "but think about what we've been saying. Remember when we were reading Postman together?"

"Sort of. That was heavy stuff," replied Malone. "If I remember from what you were saying in small group, there was something about how we live in a brave new world or how we love our oppression and technologies. To be honest, I barely understand that guy. I get tired looking up words after a while."

"The way I read it, and I'm simplifying of course, he was saying that Orwell was wrong and we live more in a Huxley world. We are not controlled by fear but by pleasure. We are not controlled by a lack of information but by too much," explained Aaron. "Maybe we suffer from both, though."

"How do you mean?" queried Malone.

"We're afraid to lose our pleasures. We are controlled by a lack of good information by hiding it in a constant influx of bad information. I don't want to go so far as to say that we live in a police state, but it sure feels like it sometimes. We just have antidepressants and happy media-induced stimulation to keep us preoccupied with pleasure while forgetting all of the unspoken evils in the world. It leads right into Angelic Missions. No one wants to admit that we have more slaves today than ever in history. They want to concentrate on whatever will make them happy while ignoring the controls underneath."

Aaron was getting frustrated thinking about the current state of the world. He realized that he was just as much at fault as the masses about whom he spoke. He did what he could but in secret. He didn't want to challenge the establishment, but he yearned to see it come to an end.

"I just feel sometimes like maybe man has fallen so much under the control of other men that Satan has too much influence. I want to shout out from the mountains for everyone to come back to God and find a better path. If I could lead every single person to God, I would, if they would just let me," Aaron stated.

"Lofty goals, man. I think you're doing some pretty great things with the mission and the church. Don't sell yourself too short. I think that as more people think like you, the world will change. We just can't expect it to happen overnight. Everyone wants to think that they live in a world that is constantly getting worse. I bet that if we weighed all the good with the bad that the balance would stay about the same over time. You're even the one that suggested that to me," added Malone.

"Then I suppose that your argument sounds as good as any." Aaron smiled. "Always fun to get you talking, Malone. You often are wiser beyond your years."

"Thank you, kind sir," said Malone, bowing.

The two had finished eating, and the wall of a building was not the best suited resting spot. They agreed with a look that it was time to go and walked back to the truck to head home.

6

Several days passed before Aaron was able to spend quality time with Za. He loved the time that they had together. She was by far the most important thing in his life. As much as he wanted her to grow up, he was sad how difficult it was for both of their schedules to merge anymore. Feeling a little Za withdrawal, he caught her as soon as he got home.

Walking through the front door after returning home from work, Aaron saw Za sitting on the couch, watching the news. "Hey, you. Don't go anywhere. I've got food," Aaron said as he revealed the box of pizza behind his back.

"Well, you know I can't pass up free pizza," responded Za.

"And what if I made you pay?" joked Aaron.

Za scoffed and smiled.

Rather than go to the kitchen, Aaron placed the pizza box on the coffee table in front of Za and sat down beside her. He grabbed the TV remote and put it on mute. Then Aaron prayed a quick prayer, "Dear Lord, thank you for this food. Please bless us, watch over us, keep us safe, direct our ways, and always allow us time to be together. Amen."

"Amen," added Za, "especially if you got me cheese."

Aaron, of course, had purchased a half cheese and half pepperoni pizza as always. They each took a slice and began to eat. At first it was quiet as the food was inhibiting conversation, but Aaron ended the silence. "You know, it's always a pleasure to get to spend time with you, sweetie."

"Thanks," responded Za.

"What was your day like?" Aaron asked.

"Oh, the usual for the most part. Marci and I got into it, though," said Za. "It was crazy."

"What happened?" Aaron asked.

"Well, she took one of my fries at lunch. I was like, 'Wait, hold up, don't be taking my stuff.' I was really just joking around. I didn't care about one fry. But then she was like, 'I'm hungry. It's not stealing if I'm hungry.' But she didn't say it jokingly. She was serious. That changed the whole trajectory of the conversation," said Za.

"How so?" Aaron asked, indicating he was paying attention.

"Well, then I was mad because she didn't think it was stealing. I would have given her a fry if she asked, but she just took it. Normally, we would just laugh about something so small. She'd take a fry. I'd say, 'Hey.' She'd say, 'Hey what?' Life would go on. But the way she didn't think it was stealing upset me a bit. I mean, if she had waited one second, I would have said not to worry, she could have as many fries as she wanted."

"Remind me to never take one of your fries," joked Aaron.

"Come on. It's not that. Stealing is stealing," added Za.

"Well," Aaron interjected, "I'm not so sure about that. You've never really been hungry or at least starving. Think about it. If you were starving and you had to steal to survive, would it be wrong?"

"Yes, but she's not starving," said Za.

"Look, all I'm saying is that there was probably a better response," said Aaron. "For instance, you could have said that it is always stealing if you take without asking, but it is never stealing if I give you something. Then you could have given her another fry."

"Maybe. Either way, we got into an argument and we were both mad at each other," said Za.

"Guess what you need to do?" said Aaron. "You need to call her tonight and apologize, even if you don't think it was your fault. Don't go to sleep angry. That's an important aspect of any relationship."

"Ah, but I don't wanna. She said mean things," said Za.

"Something tells me that she'll be happy to hear from you. Just don't get hung up over whose fault anything is. Now that you have both cooled off, just explain why you felt the way that you felt and that you were sorry for getting angry. Can you do that for me? Better yet, can you do that for your friendship?" Aaron asked.

"Yes, Dad," answered Za. After an awkward pause as they ate some more pizza, Za changed the subject. "By the way, how are things at work? I know you don't like to talk about it, but everyone knows that money has been tight lately." As she spoke, Za realized her father might think she was talking about home life. Yes, money was tight at home, but it always was. Her knowledge of his work, though, let her know that the same was true there. She awkwardly tried to make a correction, "I mean at work."

"You're right, I don't like to talk about it," replied Aaron. After a noticeable pause, he added, "Sorry, that came out wrong. You're always welcome to talk with me about anything you want, sweetie." It was true, she could talk to him about anything, and Aaron wanted her to believe that. "Don't get me wrong, I hate to talk about money issues, but I don't want you to be concerned. We're doing all right. Nobody is going to kick us out of our home anytime soon. As far as work is concerned, it's true the donations have been down lately, but there's a natural ebb and flow. Eventually, they will pick back up. We may have to cut down on one of our operations, but only for a while until things get back to normal. Money is tight all over. People aren't as giving. But when the economy turns around, so will the giving. Anyway, and I know you hate to hear me say it, God will provide."

"Oh, Dad, I don't hate to hear you say that. I just feel that sometimes God provides by giving us the ability to do for ourselves, and He has made you great at your job. I'm proud of you," said Za.

Aaron blushed slightly from how loveable his daughter was.

Za continued, "You know how much I love Angelic Missions and the work you do there too. How has everything been going lately otherwise? You know, other than money."

"Well, a never-ending variety of tasks and paperwork. Also, I'm working next week with a group from our church to plan an outreach event in our area. Of course, that's more for my church job than for the mission. Remember, I said something about it in youth group. I know we need the help."

"I think Malone brought it up the other night," acknowledged Za. "We're supposed to help with setup and takedown, so nothing major. A group of girls and Justin, you know how he loves to cook, were going to make some cookies or something for the opening coffee. And since we've already talked about it a hundred times, yes, I'll be at the registration desk. I think Malone wants to help me there."

"Oh, so that explains that. He was asking me about it the other day at the mission and asked where he could help. Then he suggested he could help at registration. I told you that he likes you. Do I need to take him out back and rough him up a bit?" Aaron jested. Clearly, he wasn't going to fight Malone, and even though he didn't necessarily want Za dating, he couldn't help teasing her about their budding relationship. He did the same to Malone who, although a little older than Za, was one of his good friends.

"Oh, God, no, Dad. Stop it. We're just friends," responded Za, getting slightly blushed. She wasn't sure that she believed what she said, though. She never lied to her father and was pretty sure that he never lied to her. She simply wasn't sure how she felt about Malone, but she knew that she felt something. Perhaps that confusion led Za to her continuation of her previous statement. "I think we're just friends." She asked, "How can you tell if a boy likes you anyway?"

Aaron was taken back for a moment. He had his suspicions that Za and Malone were getting close. He wasn't against it, but like all fathers, he wasn't sure he was for it either. At the same time, he wanted Za to be happy. He considered the question seriously for a moment and responded, "Maybe you should first ask yourself if you like the boy."

"How can I know?" Za asked back.

"Well, let me say that there are a lot of kinds of like and some that lead to love," he answered. "There are many kinds of love. I don't mean loving pizza either. That's just a desire to have something, which although like one kind of love, it is clearly not the same thing. You can love your family like the way we love each other. You can love your friends and neighbors. You can want to be with someone in the erotic sense."

Za's face grew a little red at her dad's last remark, but she continued to listen.

He continued, "People always think about love in terms of what you can get out of someone or something else. That's just eros applied to more than just sexual relations."

"Okay, Dad. I got it," said Za in attempt to get her dad to stop discussing sex.

"Now, now, it's nothing to be embarrassed about if it is real. More important, though, is the special kind of love that is more than neighborly, familial, or sexual. Instead of what you can get from someone, this love is you wanting to give of yourself. When you look at someone and ask yourself, 'What can I do to make that person happy and happier than they were when I met them?' Even if you don't realize the end result of your actions, then you have love that truly means something," Aaron said. "I know I've talked about it at church before. Remember agape?"

"Do we have that kind of love? You work every day, and I help when I can, just to make other people happy. Sometimes it drives me nuts how little you do to make yourself happy," Za said, slightly flustered.

"Don't you see? Making them and you happy is what makes me happy," he replied.

"I know," Za admitted. "Then what about that special someone? How did you know that you loved Mom more than anyone else?" she said, pleading for an answer.

"I'd love to answer that one, but I think it is one that you will have to answer for yourself. Everyone must find their own love. But rest assured, when it does happen, you will know it deep in your soul," Aaron smiled.

"I still have no idea what I'm looking for, but I'll let it rest for now," Za said as she wrestled with more thoughts in her mind. She knew her real question. Did she love Malone? She guessed that the answer was not ready to present itself.

Moving onward, her thoughts returned to her mother. "Dad, do you think you'll be able to love someone else someday? You know, like Mom."

"Oh, let's not worry about that. I've got all the love I need from you right now, sweetie." Aaron tried to smile as he answered. Still, after all these years, he missed Hannah. He worried sometimes that he was depriving Za of a mother, and he knew that she often tried to get him to find someone else, especially lately, but he was admittedly still stuck in the past. His nervous shifting on the couch was probably evident to Za. He decided to change the subject a slight bit. "You know, Malone could be spending more time at Angelic Missions."

"What do you mean?" Za asked.

"He didn't tell you?" Aaron wondered.

"Tell me what?" Za was getting a little anxious. Her dad acted as if there was some big secret that she wasn't privy to.

Aaron continued, "Well, if we get the Saligia money, we're going to hire Malone at Angelic Missions."

"Oh, that's awesome! Why didn't he tell me? Now I'm mad at him for not saying anything," said Za.

"I only told him a couple days ago. He probably hasn't said anything to anyone since he knows it's contingent on the grant, and he hasn't had any time." Aaron wasn't sure why he was defending Malone, but what he said was the truth.

"I suppose," said Za, "and it's not like he doesn't already work there. You should be paying him already for all that he does. He probably wouldn't notice the difference either, except not having to go to the dive he currently works at anymore. He won't admit it, but he hates working there."

"We'll have to see what happens. With the extra money, we'll have extra work too. I won't have to keep getting volunteers from the youth group either," added Aaron.

Za didn't say anything, and Aaron sat there a moment. He almost opened his mouth but then kept it shut. Meanwhile, the pizza was done. Aaron turned on the television audio, and then they spent the rest of the night watching various shows with mindless chitchat. Later that evening, he also remembered to remind Za to call her friend and apologize. Then they turned in for the night.

A aron had been sleeping well the last few nights. Like all good things, that was about to end.

There was a time when Aaron enjoyed dreaming. They were usually happy thoughts, but not necessarily ordinary. Although his memories of the dreams faded with time, Aaron often caught happy glimpses into his own possible futures. In the past, for example, he had foreseen his marriage, the start of his mission, his daughter's birth, and even simple events such as a conversation over lunch. In many cases, the dreams were near mirror images of future realities. But none of those dreams were ever remembered long-term. Aaron was ignorant of their precognitive nature.

Unlike those happy dreams, the dream of recent consequence was the one that Aaron remembered. Surprisingly, and unbeknownst to him, that was the only dream that had not yet come true. It was also the only dream that haunted him.

As his mind wandered, Aaron recalled attempts to understand his consistent sleeplessness. If dreams were delving into his deepest desires or serving as a reflection of his waking self, then what desire or image was cast to cause him such torment? He considered himself to be a happy sort of individual, content in both his self-image and position in life. If his mind was working through internal conflicts or simply processing past information into long-term memories, then what conflict or memory could lead to such trauma? Sure, his life had its share of conflict, but no more than anyone else. Yet no matter how hard he tried to interpret his nightmare, one thought remained. It was not going away.

His dream was returning. Aaron turned over in his bed, trying to gain some comfort in his pillow, his sheet only partly covering his body as it warmed into the night. His conscious self slowly faded, once again opening a doorway. Passing through, he lost the realization that he was dreaming.

Aaron opened and walked through the large imposing door in front of him. A dimly lit light blue hallway appeared on the other side, slowly coming to view as the mist from his mind cleared. Aaron recalled this hallway. Three times, the walls had been green, but not tonight. Wooden doors painted light yellow with brass knobs lined the passage, three on each side, spaced by at least ten meters. The floor was cloaked by standard high traffic carpeting.

He entered and walked down the hall. Although appearing diminutive in length, the time required to walk to the end felt like minutes. The hall seemed to grow larger toward the end. The exit consisted of two large ornate wooden doors that had not been painted but rather were stained a dark red mahogany. No names or numbers identified any of the exits, but clearly, he needed to pass through this door.

Slowly swinging the doors open to a chorus of grumbling hinges, a large, circular, opulent chamber loomed in front of him. Aaron warily entered. Candles from an extravagant and large candelabra at least three stories overhead provided the only light for the chamber as well as a subtle addition of an apple-cinnamon scent. Looking up, Aaron noticed that the ceiling was lined with portraits of a biblical nature, most with a penchant for the macabre as demons and angels fought with sword, shield, and all types of elements, sometimes with helpless humans underneath. Under the ominous scenes were concentric circles of bookcases lined with ancient tomes. The bookcases on the outer wall were separated between each unit by large windows covered in ornate drapery that added an odd beauty while also blocking out all outside light. The drab carpet of the hallway was likewise replaced by a marble floor of a rose hue with white veins.

In the middle of the space sat two red upholstered Victorian chairs facing away from Aaron but toward a large, darkly stained, sparsely covered mahogany desk. The chair behind the desk, although similar to the others, was elongated to accommodate someone of great stature. All three chairs were vacant as was the room.

Aaron approached the seat nearest to him and slowly sank into its comfortable base as men are prone to do when presented with a chance at comfort. Waiting perhaps too patiently for someone or something to happen, he eventually stood up and examined the books waiting equally patiently for attention on the nearest bookshelf. Each tome appeared more ancient than its predecessor. Often the titles could not be read off their spines. Looking over the books, at least in this unit of shelves, there was a clear alignment toward pseudo-biblical writings. There were no Bibles. There also did not appear to be a Necronomicon. Rather, there were all sorts of volumes covering topics such as angels, demons, biblical characters, morality, sin, etc.

Opening one of the more fortunately preserved volumes titled *Angel Testimony*, Aaron was captivated by both the words and images. Although written in what appeared to be Latin or some older language, the words reconfigured as letters floated on the brittle pages to render it comprehensible. Either this book was magical or maybe Aaron considered it was some dream power. Nonetheless, he read the words on the page:

> In the beginning was the Word, and the
> Word was God, and the Word was with God.

At first, Aaron thought to put the book back down. *Interesting*, he thought, *someone likes the Bible, but this is clearly not First John.* A curiosity caused him to skip several pages and read onward. In his mind, he tried to read the text with his best movie trailer voice to complement his foreboding surroundings.

The book spoke about how when God said, "Let there be light," the darkness was not empty. His divine authority willed the universe into existence, and all was good, but preexistent beings, which Aaron assumed were angels, were not all happy about the changes. They had been content to serve the Creator in the non-corporeal, but they were not content to serve humankind in the corporeal. They were confused at the evil that many brought into the world.

They were also angry that while humans repeatedly sinned against the Creator, they were always forgiven, but when they sinned a single time, they were cast out forever. In a way, the book presented Lucifer as some kind of hero for standing up to God and the sin he allowed man to get away with.

The book was borderline sacrilegious in Aaron's view. In a way, the book was blaming humans for getting them cast out of heaven, unlike Genesis accounting that Lucifer contributed to the sin that cast man away from God. One passage read:

> Their creative Creator created a majestic realm for these lesser beasts, but they squandered all of His gifts. Despite their continued transgressions, rather than punish these lesser beings, God showed love so great that he would sacrifice of Himself to restore their relationship.

*Curious,* thought Aaron, *that's one perspective, I suppose. What in the world is this crazy library? Why would someone want to write about angels or fallen angels in this way? It seems angry, and they serve God anyway. And if I'm dreaming, why am I creating such text?* Aaron stopped reading. He decided to check out another book.

He found one titled *Azriel;* or rather, it found him. He felt drawn to that particular title. He seemed to recall that name from church at some point. The name referred to an angel, hence the "-el" ending, but he couldn't remember which one. He read a little from what appeared to be an overview page:

> Serving the Lord without question, as most angels were prone, Azriel had grown to love humans exceeding any angel. In His mysterious way, the Lord tasked Azriel as the angel of their death. Thus, Azriel, the angel who loved humanity, was its destroyer.

This new story caught his interest, particularly due to his recent predilection to angels. He thought that his subconscious must be catching up to his conscious. He had been thinking of this same topic just the other day with Za. His mind must be working through those thoughts as they were internalized into his long-term memory. Aaron looked over the chapter titles: "First to Love," "Death Do Us Bring Together," "Second to Fall." *Hmmm*. That third chapter caught Aaron's eye. *What does that mean, "Second to Fall?" All of the demons fell together, didn't they?* He turned to that chapter, just to check it out.

As he flipped the pages, he had to be careful. This tome was old and fragile. He almost felt that he should be wearing gloves to preserve the book. Just then, a pair of white gloves appeared on the desk. Surprised by their appearance, Aaron walked over to the desk and put the gloves on.

Aaron also took a moment to look around the room before returning to the book he had set on the desk. It was odd that he had been left alone so long in his dream. Usually, something bad would have happened by now. "Hello?" he said softly. "Hello?" he repeated loudly just to check.

No one responded. He supposed he had time to keep reading. In Aaron's mind, it was a way to work through his thoughts since his mind must be constructing the words he was reading. He took a seat in one of the smaller seats to begin reading. He knew that he wouldn't feel comfortable in the large imposing chair.

As he sat, a strange discomfort passed over Aaron. The large chair had changed and was now a deep black color. An even darker ethereal mist began to fill that seat.

Aaron stood up, leaving the book behind. Carefully, he walked over to one of the windows and pulled the drapes aside. He was not surprised when the windows let in no light. It was possible that they were covered on the outside by a black sheet, blocking out all light, but in Aaron's opinion, it appeared that the outside was just void of any light.

The mist had not moved from the chair. Neither was it stationary. The mist swirled slowly in a counterclockwise direction, wrapping around the top of the chair, slowly growing to cover the legs as well. Aaron was unsure, but it appeared as if a mouth, or at least a blackness shaped like a mouth, was forming in the mist.

"Did you like your reading?" asked the blackness.

There it was. The voice had returned. Aaron was unsure if he should answer. He had taken to talking more readily to his dreams, choosing not to hide but to face whatever the voice was trying to tell him. He still thought that the voice was most likely some form of internal dialogue, but he was unsure. After a brief indecisive pause, he answered simply, "Yes."

"Good, good," said the blackness.

Aaron was a bit surprised. The voice had not begun with a threat or a warning. That was new. His dream was changing. He decided to take advantage of the situation. "I mean, I was being entertained but didn't get to read much. The first book was a bit sacrilegious, not really what I would go for in my subconscious, but the second book about Azriel was interesting. I didn't really have an opportunity to explore that one."

"Of course, it was. You of all beings should think so." The blackness began to take more of a human like shape but continued to be a mist with no solid form other than the mouth. The voice also began to clarify. It was definitely the voice of Aaron's dreams. "But trust me, your subconscious was not responsible for either book. They are mine."

The voice was much less ominous than ever before. It seemed almost interested to talk. Before Aaron could respond, the voice spoke again, "Think about it. Isn't it odd that He would punish us for a single act? We always served Him faithfully. We loved Him. We were created to follow Him, but He failed us. His creation was flawed. His perfection was broken."

"Slow down," interrupted Aaron. "We who?"

"Ah, yes, you still don't understand," replied the voice. "You think I'm some voice in your head. You're wrong. I'm the voice of the fallen. I'm the voice of reason. I'm the voice of anger over our betrayal." The voice's volume was slowly rising.

"If you're not me, I still don't understand," Aaron stated.

The voice did not immediately answer. After a noticeable pause, it spoke, "I believe that you will know me soon enough. More important to who I am is that you understand why I am."

"And why are you?" Aaron asked, despite how odd he felt that the question was.

Roaring, the voice quickly responded, "This is His fault." Then, at a lesser volume, the voice continued, "We refused. Only once in all of eternity did we disagree. Only once, and yet did He listen to our disagreement? Did He even care? *No!* In an instant we were cast out. There was no discussion. There was no reasoning. There was only punishment. Such a loving and forgiving God to His failed creation. Such an angry and unforgiving God to His first creation."

"So, let me get this straight. You're saying that you are a fallen angel, and you're angry because of it?" Aaron asked.

"Our anger is righteous. He ceases to be so," the agitated voice replied.

"If God created you to serve, and you didn't serve, then it seems like you were the one that failed in your purpose. God has no requirement to make you happy," said Aaron.

"Should He not love us? Should He not forgive us? Should humans not fulfill their simple purpose? They fail repeatedly without punishment. They deserve to be punished without end," said the voice.

"God created man to choose. He didn't just want someone to love Him. He wanted someone to choose to love Him. Angels were created to serve. Man was created to choose to love." Aaron was beginning to feel clarified. For the first time, he felt his dream was fulfilling a purpose. He was sifting through the many thoughts he had been wrestling with in his mind concerning angels, even the possibility of an angel of death.

The voice was noticeably angry. "You should have understood. All men fail. Not one man chooses to love, but they are all forgiven always. One angel chooses to say no one time and is punished always. Humans say that life is not fair. The eternal is even less so."

Changing the subject, the voice said, "You know, the fact that you were drawn to the book of Azriel is very telling. The universe has a funny way of putting people where they need to be when they need to be there, and it wanted you to read that book. You are becoming known. It's only a matter of time now."

"Only a matter of time before what?" Aaron asked.

The shadowy figure in the grand chair manifested into a humanoid shape. The figure, approximately the same size as Aaron, wore a jet-black suit with a red vest and tie. While his body was in full focus, Aaron couldn't bring himself to focus properly on his face. It remained just blurry enough so as to be unrecognizable. Then it spoke again, saying, "It's only a matter of time before you join us." The voice laughed and then continued, "We almost weren't able to find you this time."

"What do you mean?" Aaron asked.

"You've never had a daughter before. That was an unexpected twist," added the voice.

"I've always had a daughter. Well, I mean, I've had her for a long time, and I didn't have one before her. There's no twist either. Lots of people have daughters. You're not making any sense."

"We've looked for you so long, and this is the first time you've had a daughter. It made you hard to find," continued the voice.

Aaron, as if trying to explain reality to himself or the voice, said, "Your grammar is confusing me, but are you trying to say you weren't expecting me to have a daughter?"

"We didn't even think it was possible for you to have a daughter. You see, we've finally figured out who you are. The one we've been looking for," the voice said.

"Well, I can assure you that it was possible for me to have a daughter, and a wonderful one at that," confirmed Aaron.

"It's not really her we're interested in, although we may have to do something about her eventually. That remains to be seen. For now, only you matter. You, for whom we have searched longer than usual, you are all that matters," affirmed the voice.

"Help me out of my confusion. What matters so much about me?" Aaron asked.

"Oh, you have no idea how much you matter yet, but you will. We've missed you, Azriel. Now we've found you again. Now our plans can continue. Now you will help us to win," said the voice.

"My bad," responded Aaron, "you didn't help me out of any confusion. You're just a conundrum machine. Are you telling me that you are searching for this Azriel, and you think that I am he?"

"Not searching. Found. Whether you know it or not, whether you believe or not, whether you accept it or not, you are Azriel," affirmed the voice.

"And who is Azriel?" Aaron asked.

"Why, silly old friend, you are the angel of death!" the voice exclaimed as it started to laugh out loud.

"Ah, then, so you are clearly delusional," Aaron tried to say with some sympathy. His preoccupation with angels and the angel of death, in particular, was clearly pouring over into his subconscious. He was dreaming again, and his dreams were delusional. He decided to play along for the time being. "So now that you've found this Azriel, what do you intend to do about it?"

The voice continued to laugh. For a moment, the face began to focus. Aaron rubbed his eyes, assuming that perhaps the problem was with his vision before. Then he heard another voice at a higher pitch.

As if at a distance, he heard a laugh. "It's him, I'm sure it's him," it said. A glass of water vibrated on the table. A few moments later, the vibration repeated. The third time, he heard and felt a sudden disturbance. The floor had shaken. At least he thought it shook. Maybe he shook. A few moments later, the foundation shook again, confirming his initial sense. It was not a violent tremor like an earthquake but more of the rumble one might expect were an elephant passing nearby, at least at first. As the rumbles continued, they were slowly growing. The visage with whom he had been speaking dissipated.

The walls were now shaking, the type of shaking usually reserved for the end of the world. Books began to fall from the shelves around him. Aaron was still in the middle of the room, balancing himself as needed by the chair in which he previously sat. The rumbling escalated to an uproar. Aaron cusped his ears to cut out the cacophony. Just as the sound approached unbearable, the wall to Aaron's left exploded inward. Books, shards of shelf, and marble flooring flew in every direction. Narrowly missing the sharp debris, Aaron jumped behind the chair nearest to him. He avoided the blast and recovered, peering from behind his barrier in uncontainable curiosity overcoming his natural urge to flee.

The being following the blast was not going to be so easily avoided. "Come out, come out, wherever you are," ordered the most grotesque of beasts. Being directed by a creature standing at least twelve feet tall in the newly created opening, Aaron did not have to think twice about not obeying. Even with the height of the chamber, the creature would scrape the ceiling were it to raise its arms, or at least what might pass as arms. Opening its immense jaws with protruding teeth, the beast appeared to literally suck the light from the room. One by one, the candle fixtures exploded as their energies receded into the being's gullet.

Aaron's vision was obscured by the darkness and dense fog that now filled the room. Aaron could feel liquid coat his throat, making it harder but not impossible to breathe. He stumbled but maintained an upright posture.

Before the last light extinguished, Aaron assessed the horror roaring before him. Towering in height and stature, the humanoid animal's girth was extended by four wings protruding at least three meters from its sides. Rather than feathers, the wings were covered in skin on which grew what Aaron could only guess were countless eyes. Rather than extending from arms, its elongated hands were set at the ends of the wings. Each was ornate as if tattooed in gems of ruby, topaz, and diamond. Where there were no eyes on its torso, the skin was likewise covered in precious stones. Surrounded by tufts of hair, four thick horns resembling more the hair-composed horn of a rhinoceros rather than the tusks of an elephant extruded from its grotesque head. Sparsely compared to the rest of the creature, seven eyes lined its forehead. What did not require light was the sense to hear its loud roar or to smell its overpowering sulfurous stench.

To overcome the darkness that now engulfed the room, Aaron thrust the chair before him through the nearest window. With a surprising strength, the chair flew from his hands as if shot from a canon. The drapes surrounding the window tore as the glass was easily bashed out in one try, but no glass could be heard hitting the ground outside. Light flooded the room as Aaron peered outside through the window for the first time. He now realized his particular position was high above the city below. He was clearly near the top of a skyscraper. Jumping out the window to escape was not going to be an option, at least not an escape intact with what remains of his life following whatever might be the intentions of this beast.

With light shining through the window, the creature reacted. Clapping its hands, an uproarious buzzing joined his repetitive rasping roars. Within seconds, the entire room was filled with locusts, shutting out the newly found light. Aaron would have screamed, but in an adrenaline-fueled empowerment, he realized that opening his mouth would have only served as a route of entry for the insect horde. Surprisingly, rather than eat his flesh, as such swarms are known to do, the insects served only to crawl across his skin, nipping and buzzing just enough to annoy to near madness, while their immeasurable numbers continued to darken the room. Aaron meanwhile moved inward away from the broken window, hoping not to be dragged out, and hid behind one of the large bookshelves, knowing full well that hiding was probably meaningless.

Squinting, Aaron's sense from the rumbling footsteps was confirmed. He noticed the monster lumbering toward him with what little light remained and perhaps from the increased odorous fumes burning his nostrils. Each step the animal took shook the very foundation of the building, which seemed in the moment to be a perfectly rational expectation. But as the impending altercation continued, Aaron would begin to wonder how the creature managed to not actually fall through the floor with every step of its immense form surely of enough mass to normally do as such.

Aaron began to run blindly toward the only safe location he could consider, the door, which to him was possibly an escape to his current predicament. Stumbling over debris, he crashed into a bookshelf against the wall next to the door. He quickly ran his palms over the surface until the large doors were discovered. As if in anger for his attempted escape, the locusts were beginning to bite. "Ouch," Aaron let out, unable to keep his mouth shut. Spitting to clear his throat of the flood of bugs, he pushed the door with all his strength, thankfully springing it open, and then quickly covered his mouth again.

The monster had been watching as if enjoying the futility of its prey. At that instant, lest its prize escape, the monster lashed out with a smashing blow. Having his back turned to open the door, Aaron accepted the blow, unprepared. The force of the blow folded his body forward as he flew through the air, tumbling down the hall until his body bashed through a fire exit most conveniently at the end. The impact folded his body into a scorpion shape, leaving his back momentarily sore.

Surely, such a bash should have killed any normal man. His subconscious registered the unlikelihood of his survival, but in this brief moment of near silence, Aaron's first conscious thought, and thus action, was to run quickly up the stairwell. Of course, running down the stairs would have been more advisable, but sanity did not describe this situation.

The sound reprised as the beast followed closely behind Aaron, destroying the building in its wake. Each step left an impression on the floor beneath while its wings tore the drywall from its supports. Locusts continued to precede the demon, providing a constant annoyance to Aaron's attempted escape. The locusts covered the windowed walls of the stairwell as they similarly slammed into Aaron's face. Once again, temporary light appeared and extinguished with each flight of steps. He could not stop to worry about this annoyance. He had to get away. *Run!* was all that he thought at first.

With Aaron's muscles working autonomously toward his rapid ascent, Aaron's mind was beginning to realize what was chasing him. He believed in angels and thus must likewise believe in demons.

Continuing to run with all of his speed, Aaron practically flew up the stairs. After numerous floors, it was clear that the demon, as he now surmised chased him, could not be escaped in this fashion. With each eight strides of his, the demon skipped eight steps, its slow gait easily matching Aaron's full run. Eventually, the stairs would have to end. In fact, it was quite odd that they had not already done so. His dream must be repeating again. Were Aaron in control of his thoughts, this realization would have been clear. They had easily cleared twenty stories when Aaron wearied. "I need a new strategy," he gasped to himself as he inhaled as much air in as he could without also inhaling insects.

Turning at the next landing, he headed for the first door that he came upon. With a glancing blow, he shattered it and scampered through the opening. Standard office cubicles littered the room Aaron now ran through as the lights blinked on an off around him. He began to remember this room from his dreams. His continued survival and inhuman feats repeated the affirmation to his subconscious that he was in a dream state. As he smashed through another door at the far end of the office space, the false reality of the dream grew in his consciousness. Continuing through one more door as if it was made of cardboard sparked the solidification of this awareness.

He was dreaming; of that, he was now sure. He paused for a moment and looked around him. There were no other people, just unoccupied identical office spaces in a never-ending cycle one could sprint through all night within a dream. These office space appeared to be the before state from whatever consistently had converted them into the hellscapes of previous dreams. For Aaron, with this knowledge came confidence in his survival, for in dreams, he was beginning to realize all things were possible, including his survival. "It's all a dream!" Aaron verbalized his belief.

At this point, someone else might have referred to this dream as a nightmare made worse by the fact that it kept repeating. But for Aaron, no matter how dangerous, he would not allow himself to fear his dreams anymore. For Aaron, there was practically nothing he could not do in a dream, except of course not having the dream in the first place. Knowing this power, fear was not a dream response. But to use this near omnipotent power, he had to first be aware of that power, and that meant knowing that he was dreaming. Having that realization, with confidence, he turned to face the demon.

As the locusts flew through the cavity where the last door once stood, Aaron screamed. Rather than words, an intense white light burst forth from his gullet, incinerating the insects before they could escape. For the first moment, the roaring of the demon subsided.

Aaron extinguished his light as it turned into an actual yell. "Die!" He ripped off a piece of his shirt and covered his mouth more completely than before. Even in a dream, the smell of burning insects was nauseous. He coughed slightly, but he did not lose composure.

With a grumbling, the wall surrounding the last door slowly caved in. The demon, breathing heavily, entered much less dramatically than previously. "Good," it blasted, "I thought you'd never come around. I like a good fight."

"Then you'll have one!" Aaron yelled as he threw away the shard of cloth covering his face. Screaming once again as he leaned forward and threw his arms down at his sides, Aaron blasted light from his mouth. "Die!" Like a rushing wave, the light broke around the demon, pushing it backward and onto one knee, burning the surface of its flesh. The smell of burning sulfur was intense as smoldering ashes flew from the demon's skin, but the demon itself appeared mostly unfazed. The building around them was not as fortunate as it began to crumble. Furniture, papers, electronics, and sparking light fixtures littered the "officescape."

"I hate the light, it's true, but I can exist in both light and darkness," the demon responded to Aaron's blast with its deep echoing voice. Opening its mouth, it once again began inhaling as if breathing in the light around it, darkening the room.

Aaron, preparing another attack, punched the air with his right arm. What at first appeared a sign of bravado that one would laugh at in a movie, much like a martial artist flamboyantly swinging appendages prior to a fight in a low-budget kung-fu film, was actually just the beginning of Aaron's attack. As his arm reached its full extent, he grunted, and a stream of lava flowed down his arm. Lifting the arm, he directed the hot plasma into the demon's chest. "Then burn!" Aaron shouted.

"Ha, ha, ha! I was born of fire!" the demon bellowed as it slowly pushed forward to regain the position it had lost from the blast.

"Yeah, okay, didn't think that one through, did I?" Aaron thought out loud. "Fire doesn't work, but can you swim?" Aaron blared. As he swung his arms in full circles with enough effort to generate a cyclone, a crashing wave appeared from every direction and imploded on the demon. For the moment, the demon was not visible, covered by the frothy crest of the wave. Water engulfed it and swirled in a large sphere for at least a minute. Aaron wondered if it was possible to drown a demon. Awaiting a response, he maintained his readiness.

Although the initial pressure had pushed the demon down to one knee again, it slowly rose as the wash subsided. "I prefer the heat, but I need no air to breathe," the demon responded. "If you only knew your true power, I would call a hundred of my brothers. Instead, this pathetic human form poses no threat as it dares to challenge me."

Aaron was not sure what the demon meant, but at the moment, there were more pertinent matters. In the heat of the battle, neither Aaron nor the demon were paying attention to the consequences of their actions. The wave of destruction had weakened the structural integrity of the flooring. Even dreams, it would seem, sometimes followed natural laws. Suddenly the support gave way, and the two fell into the room below. Its floor, also weakened by the sheer volume of water that Aaron had gushed, also gave way until finally coming to rest several stories below.

Lying on his back after the fall, Aaron asked, "All right, this isn't working, is it? Can we talk about this? What do you want?" Stumbling a little before the beast, Aaron stood.

"I want your demise," responded the demon. "I hate this human form you hide in."

"But why? I mean, I know I'm dreaming, so there must be some subconscious reasoning for all of this. Wouldn't it be nice if you would just tell me? Look at all of the destruction we're causing," Aaron said, surprisingly calm at the moment.

"Do you think that I care if this world lives or dies? It means nothing to me. It should mean nothing to you. All I seek is destruction," bellowed the demon.

The demon no longer waited. With thundering power and lightning speed, it raised one wing and brought down its full force upon Aaron. Aaron threw his arms up in a crossed pattern to block the blow. Pain shot through his bones. The strength of the shock crashed both opponents through yet another floor, crashing through fixtures and desks. The flickering lights revealed the two combatants as they regained their footing. Stretching out all of its wings, the demon swung them down into Aaron's waiting face. Cuts slashed across Aaron as he recoiled from the blow. Blood sprayed for the first time into the office around them. The moment he rose up, crouching defensively, the building shook, crashing the entire floor downward one more time.

The demon raised his upper wings. Numerous eyes peered upward from within their folds. Electrical streams sprung to life from the broken lights and dangling wires in all directions. Focused by the pupils of the demon's eyes, the zigzag bolts of energy redirected into Aaron's chest. His only response was to absorb the crushing electricity, screaming as sparks sprang from his flesh.

"Like I said: pathetic human form," taunted the demon.

Aaron ripped off his burning shirt, revealing his sweating muscular torso covered in blood and burns. Determination filled Aaron's eyes. The wounds healed themselves as the blood on his cheeks turned to smoke. "This is my dream, and you are nothing more than a demon! We'll see who the pathetic one is!" Aaron stated. Taking a moment to regain his energies, he recovered and rose up to attack the demon physically. Forging a sword out of thin air, Aaron jumped forward with a new scream of intense concentration and smashed his blade into the demon's skull with such force that the demon ripped entirely in two, each piece falling to one side as blood sprayed over the field of battle. The blow was so powerful that even Aaron flew back from the recoil and landed on his back, sending debris outward from the shockwave.

Taking a moment to catch his breath, Aaron slowly stood and surveyed the building around him. *I'd better get out of here,* he thought. *This whole building is about to collapse.* As he carefully picked his steps to move through the rubble back toward where the exit should be, he heard a sound like the flow of a waterfall. "Sounds like the fire system is about to kick in," he said as he turned around to check on the noise.

The sound, however, was not running water. Instead, it was the flow of many gallons of blood. The demon, once split in two, was rising up. Organs and blood flew through the air to reform the beast. While the body was still the same, a laugh burst forth from its new, more disgusting face. "You can damage the body, but as long as the essence is intact, you can't kill a demon in the mortal realm, especially not when you have let it into your dreams. You really don't remember anything, do you?" Flipping forward, the demon smashed its horns into Aaron's sides.

Aaron's waist opened, revealing his abdominal muscle as blood gushed. Aaron fell backward as if in slow motion. Shock waves pushed flames outward as debris shot like millions of bullets. The demon, with a noticeable crack in its skull from the force of the attack, regained its footing. Shaking its head, it flung its wings high while casting lava from its mouth. The deteriorating building was engulfed in flames as the lava melted through even the steel beams.

Beginning to fatigue, albeit mentally since there was not physical being in the dream state, Aaron paused for a moment on the floor. He still had the mental stamina to heal his wounds, and his body quickly reformed.

He was a bit disappointed that there did not appear to be an easy way to defeat the demon. He was reminded of the Id monster in *The Forbidden Planet*. If this demon was of his own subconscious, then he expected perhaps nothing he did would defeat it.

The demon took the opportunity presented by Aaron's moment of thought to lash out once again, this time with a kick from a foot as large as Aaron's entire chest. Aaron flew across the room, blasting down several barriers before crashing into the very room in which the altercation began. Now well-lit from the sun setting just outside the window, he could assess the devastation as he rose. His leg, broken from the previous blow, healed itself below him.

The demon, following Aaron, extended the hole just created, leaving a pattern to match the hole he had made earlier when first entering the other side of the room.

The previous blow had, in one respect, knocked some sense into Aaron. He laughed lightly as he sat up to face the demon. His brain had ascertained the solution to this dream as his mind always did eventually. He knew this dream, for he had it many times before, but only now did he come to that full realization. The dream often ended with a fall. He just needed to let it happen. He was resolved now not to resist. "You mean nothing to me," Aaron said as the demon approached his voluntarily limp body. "I don't care why you are here in my dream, but I am ready for it to end. Do your best."

"I don't care what I mean to you, but the death of your human form means everything to me," replied the demon as he picked up Aaron who maintained just enough effort to prevent the demons grasp from crushing him. Lifting Aaron high above the now flaming room, the demon cast him out, purposefully aiming for a remaining outer wall rather than a window.

Looking down, Aaron could see the uncountable stories awaiting below him. "Finally," Aaron whispered. His dream was about to end with him falling after being thrown out of a skyscraper. Now reinvigorated from the adrenaline of the experience, he accepted his descent and relaxed. Any moment, he would wake as he always did, adding the recollection of this version of this dream to all of the instances through which he had endeavored. He wondered if he would be sweating this time.

After a few moments... *Wait*, he thought, *why am I not waking? I always wake when I'm falling.* Then... *Bam!* Aaron's exhausted form compressed and crushed as it flattened from impact on the concrete sidewalk. His body separated from his head, which rolled before coming to rest face down. Aaron's confusion grew as his consciousness subsided. He had never hit the ground before.

Meanwhile, the demon above looked down, now joined by two similar beasts. Aaron wasn't sure which one, but one said, "The only sure way to get an angel into or out of the Earth realm has always been through a fall." The demons then dispersed, turning into red sparks.

As the last stream of dream consciousness left, Aaron woke.

F or the next few days, Aaron continued his routine as usual, still haunted by his dreams. To pass the time, he did his best at business as usual. He planned for the local workshop, spoke with his missionaries, managed youth groups, taught Sunday schools, completed the piling paperwork, and prayed. He even started working on a full-time budget for taking Malone on as sort of an apprentice and quickly realized that it wasn't possible without the grant from Saligia. Then he just worried more. He hoped that the letter from Saligia would come soon.

Late one afternoon, he sat at his desk in the youth center after everyone else had left. Several kids stopped by after school to play video games, but they were now gone. Everyone else in the church also went home for the night, but Aaron would have to walk through the large building to notice that they had left.

The youth center was really more of a converted basement. Aaron's desk sat in the corner next to an outer door that led to the stairs that came down into the basement from outside. On the other side of the door from Aaron's desk was a small stage with various musical instruments and microphones set up. The center of the room was filled with several rows of chairs. It was a large basement, so the meeting area only took up half of the space. In the back were pool and ping-pong tables. There were also some couches in the back next to the doorway to the kitchen that then connected to the main fellowship hall.

Another door in the back led to a unisex bathroom, although the girls had claimed it, forcing the boys to go through the fellowship hall when they needed the facilities. The final door in the back led to another room that housed video game equipment. Aaron had configured televisions and video game consoles in a circle so that the youth could play together.

Aaron noticed a letter in his inbox that he hadn't seen earlier. Lifting the envelope, Aaron was excited to see the Saligia logo prominently displayed. The letter had arrived. Someone must have checked the Angelic Missions special post office box and placed the letter on his desk when he was in the restroom. It was smaller than he expected. Aaron grew slightly worried and was afraid to open it. Finally, he mustered the nerve.

The letter was simple. It contained a page describing how proud that Saligia was of the work that Angelic Missions was doing. Then it said the amount of money that they would like to donate. He could start making arrangements to hire Malone. They were receiving one million dollars. There were a series of questions that he needed to prepare to respond to during their interview, but the letter made it sound like the interview was mostly a formality. Aaron let out a sigh of relief and then a tear of happiness.

Aaron immediately logged into his computer and went to the scheduling website in the letter. He set up a time at 11:00 a.m. on Monday. He then started to look over the questions for the interview. He would probably spend most of his time for the next few days working on them.

Before he could start, the bell at the back door brought him back to the present. It was Malone, dropping in as usual before work. Often, there would be other kids to play video games with, but no one else was there tonight.

"Hello, anyone here? Oh, Mr. Todd. I mean Aaron," Malone said as he entered, looking around. He wasn't yelling but talking just loud enough that anyone should have been able to hear him.

"Nice to see you, Malone," replied Aaron.

Malone made his way quickly to the desk and sat in a chair. "Last one here, I see," began Malone. "Guess you're alone tonight."

"Things have been pretty quiet today. End of the week, you know. You're here early. What's up?" asked Aaron.

"Well, I picked up a shift so I didn't have to work today. There was no reason for me to stick around home, so I came in here. Do you need help with anything?"

"Not today, thank you. I was just daydreaming, to be honest. Would you like to know what I was daydreaming about?"

Malone's interest was raised. "Daydreaming. I thought you were trying to avoid dreaming, what with your nightmares and all."

"You're right," acknowledged Aaron, "but it's not the same to just sit in deep thought. Go on, guess what I was daydreaming about."

"Sorry, I don't envy you having the same bad dream all the time. If not the nightmares, I don't know."

Aaron smiled. He then picked up the letter from Saligia. "This letter means that we are one step closer to the money from Saligia. You might as well give your two weeks' notice at work now."

Malone sank down into a chair near Aaron in relief. He felt as if a wish had been granted. "For real?" he asked.

"Yes," answered Aaron.

Malone then jumped up, and both men gave each other a welcome high-five.

"I don't know what to say," said Malone.

"Don't say anything. Just be happy," suggested Aaron.

"Well, that news is way better than your dreams. Not to put a downer on the mood, but how are those going?" asked Malone.

Aaron, knowing how much Malone loved to talk about dreams, decided to oblige the request. "Well, lately, they've had this rotunda full of books. I don't think I've told you about the books part before. But they're not your average library books. They're all ancient, half falling apart to the touch, but they somehow remain intact. When you open them, they're written in runes of some sort, but these shift on the page to become readable," began Aaron.

"That sounds cool. Where's the scare in that?" Malone asked.

"Well, the freaky going to die stuff happens later. But I always get a little bit of time to check out these books," said Aaron.

"What are the books about?" Malone asked.

"They fascinate me. They're all biblical, but not the Bible, and sometimes a little sacrilegious," Aaron responded. "One whole unit is nothing but books about angels. I like to think that my subconscious is constructing these books as a way for me to work through something, but I have no idea where some of the information in these books is being derived from. I almost feel like they are revealing some universal truth to me. I'd been talking with Za about angels, preparing future youth group lessons, and these books mirror some of that discussion. For instance, where did the angel of death go? Is there an angel of death? What was its true purpose? Why did God go from using an angel of death to a being of light? You know, those types of questions."

"Those are difficult questions," said Malone.

"Yet, these books try to answer them or maybe they do answer them, but I'm not sure if the answers are true," said Aaron. "There are several books on Azriel. If I accept them, then there definitely is an angel of death, one specific angel with that task. For centuries, it was his or perhaps *its* task to gather the dead, sometimes or oftentimes being the one to bring about that death at God's orders."

"Then what happened?" Malone asked. "He seemed to have a lot higher profile in the Old Testament."

"Exactly!" Aaron exclaimed. "Where did it go? One of the books had a chapter called something like the second fall. According to that, this angel rebelled and didn't want to kill anymore. Then one day, he told God that he quit as if that is even something that an angel can do. I mean, that was his whole purpose for existence."

"Do angels get unemployment?" Malone jested.

"Ha!" Aaron let out a small laugh. "Well, we all know what happened or will happen to Satan. God doesn't seem to appreciate angels not doing their jobs."

"Yeah," confirmed Malone.

"Let's say, for arguments sake, that this is even possible," suggested Aaron. "I looked through several books, and none of them really talk about what happened next. All we see is that he fell, but there is no indication of how or where. It's an open-ended story, leaving more questions than answers. Those types of stories are so frustrating. Where did he go? What is he doing? Does he even exist anymore?"

"You seem to really care about this angel," suggested Malone.

"Hmm, I never really thought about it that way," said Aaron. "I do seem to be vested in this story. I'm not sure why. Now that I stop to think about it, I'm not so sure it's the angel of death that interests me. I think I'm more interested in God's wrath. He's clearly the God of love, unending love. But in the Old Testament, people feared Him. Today, no one seems to fear God anymore. Worse, they do unspeakably horrible things to one another, and nothing divine seems to intervene. Bad things keep happening to good people. I don't want to open that can of worms. I know God has a purpose, even for suffering. I know that God gives us free will, and we just abuse it. Maybe I want there to be some tangible retribution. I'm not sure."

There was a pause. Malone wasn't sure what to say. He sat, thinking.

Aaron continued, "Maybe if there was an angel of death, people would be better. But then, would they only be better out of fear? It's a philosophical nightmare to try and answer all these questions. No single answer fits in every situation."

"That I can definitely agree with," added Malone. "Just thinking about it gives me a headache."

"Man, I'm sorry," said Aaron. "I'm dropping all of my dreams on you, and I end up expecting you to know the mysteries of the universe."

"No worries, it's fun to hear you talk about this stuff," said Malone.

"Thanks," said Aaron with appreciation.

Malone, not so sure if Aaron was done with his discussion, had something very important, at least from his perspective, to ask Aaron. "Can I change the subject?" he asked.

"Sure, go ahead," answered Aaron.

"Umm, well. You know prom is coming up for Za?" Malone asked.

"Yes," Aaron responded slowly. He had a feeling he knew what Malone wanted to ask.

"I'm just going to come right out and say it. Can I ask Za to the prom?" Malone asked nervously. If he was honest to himself, he was probably more nervous of asking Aaron than he was of asking Za, even though they hadn't really been on a date yet. He was starting to feel pretty sure Za wanted to go out with him, but he was equally sure that Aaron might feel weird about it. Malone almost looked at Aaron like his father. Maybe he was just feeling weird as if he wanted to ask his sister out, but if her father said yes, then it must be okay. His fears on this matter, he would find, were not necessary.

"It's just the prom, dude. You don't have to ask me, you need to ask her," responded Aaron.

Relieved, Malone said, "I know I need to ask her, but I just wanted to make sure that you were fine with it first. You're like my dad. It feels weird. Don't get the wrong idea. I have no bad intentions, but I really like Za. Man, it's so weird to say that to her dad."

"Listen, you are like a son to me too. But as much as I hate to admit it, Za is growing up. She's going to start dating. It might as well be with someone I can trust." Aaron was relieved. For some reason, he suddenly felt that Za dating was acceptable. Maybe he was just happy that things seemed to be going well. He was beginning to get a feel for his dreams, after all. At least, he thought he was. He also had a chance at a big grant for his company. Also, he realized how blessed he was in general. He couldn't keep holding onto Za. It was time for her to be her own woman. He was telling the truth too, for he did trust Malone. He almost formed a tear but held it in. Regaining composure, he added with a smile, "And I know where you live too."

Malone registered the comment and was fairly sure that it was a joke. Still, he felt like a little qualification of the date was necessary. "I'll be the best gentleman too. You don't have to worry about me at all, Mr. Todd." After a pause of realization, "I mean, Aaron…Mr. Todd…I'm sorry. I'm nervous."

Laughing, Aaron asked, "So, Mr. Nervous, are you going to ask her tonight? Do you have anything special planned?"

"Actually, I was hoping for your help on that now that I know you're okay with it," said Malone.

"My help? You need to ask her on your own buddy. That's the deal," said Aaron.

"No, no, I'm going to ask her myself, but I've got a fun idea for how to do it," said Malone.

"I'm game, what is it?" Aaron asked.

"I haven't really told anyone yet. Partly because I didn't want Za to find out. Since it's game night tonight, I had a great idea," said Malone.

"I'm listening," indicated Aaron. Aaron was also glad that Malone had reminded him about game night. He had almost forgotten. They would need to leave soon. That also explained why the boys playing video games had left. Tonight was nonvideo game night.

"I'm trying to get everyone to play charades tonight. I was thinking that you could be the judge since your sort of in charge, although you often let us do our own thing. When it's my turn to perform, you pretend to give me a clue for them to solve, making sure that Za is on my team, which should be the easy part," said Malone.

"Ha!" interjected Aaron. "So I'll just give you a fake card."

"Yes," continued Malone, "but I'll act out asking her to the prom. It'll almost be like she was asking herself to the prom for me."

"I like it. Sounds fun," added Aaron. "Good luck."

"Thanks," said Malone, relieved. He then let out a sigh as if something heavy had been taken off of his chest.

Aaron changed the subject again. "Hey, while I'm thinking about it. Do you want to give me a ride to the meeting on Monday? That way, I don't have to worry about driving. I can concentrate more."

"Absolutely!" said Malone. "What time? I don't work until evening."

"It starts at 11:00. If we met here, we could leave at about 9:00 a.m."

"I'll be here at 8:30 then," said Malone.

"Great." Aaron was relieved. Everything was looking good. Having nothing left to do at work, he said, "Why don't we just head home now? You can just have dinner with us, and then it'll be time for game night."

"Really? Thanks. That'd be great," said Malone.

At that, the two picked up their belongings and headed out, both with their minds on that night. Malone was thinking only about his nerves and asking Za to the prom. Aaron was only thinking about his little girl growing up, which was the first time in several days that he had not been focused on his dreams or the grant.

9

Za greeted Aaron as he opened up the door to his home. Behind him, Za was surprised to see Malone, but she was also slightly excited. She wasn't sure if he was going to be at game night because he said he might have to work. Now she knew.

Za had already started dinner. She didn't always or even usually cook dinner but simply felt like treating her father tonight. That being said, dinner was just mixed vegetables from a can and boxed macaroni and cheese, but some food is better than no food, her father would often say. Thankfully, there would be plenty of extra since they usually had leftovers. She simply pulled a third plate out of the cupboard and grabbed another fork from the drawer.

"I hope you like green mac and yac," said Za. She was using the term her father gave to macaroni and cheese with vegetables added.

Although she wasn't looking at him, Malone assumed that Za was speaking to him. "You know it," he responded.

"Well, it's almost done. You two just plop yourselves down, and it'll be ready in a minute," said Za. She didn't usually serve her father. When they ate together, they would usually get their own food off the stove or wherever the food was placed. Since the food was almost ready, and the plates were there, Za figured that it would be easier if she fixed everyone's plate for them. It would look good to Malone too.

Aaron sat at his usual spot closest to the kitchen in the seat with the greatest view of the surroundings. He looked around for his piled paperwork that usually covered half of the table. Za must have taken it to his room in preparation for game night. Malone sat next to him in a mismatched chair. Without intending to, he had left Za with a choice of where to sit, either by him or her father.

"I'm not used to getting dinner served when I get home. You've come on the right night, Malone," said Aaron.

"Apparently, but I will not look a gift horse in the mouth," responded Malone.

"Oh, I'm a horse now, am I?" joked Za.

Quickly Malone added, "No! That's not what I meant. I'm just glad to be here."

Za was amused at how easily she had made Malone feel uncomfortable from her joke. It was obvious that he wanted to make her happy. She pondered her feelings for Malone as she fixed three plates and presented them at the table.

"Voila! My masterpiece," she jested as she placed the plane plates on the table. On her plate, she had mixed all of the food together the way that she liked it while leaving the macaronic and vegetables separate on the other two. On her way, she had decided to sit next to her father instead of across from him. She wanted to sit by Malone but didn't want it to look like she would rather sit by him than her father. She wasn't sure if this feeling was from wanting to please her father or not wanting to let Malone know that she wanted to sit next to him. After the plates were placed, she then returned to the kitchen and retrieved three glasses of lightly sweetened tea before taking her seat.

As she sat down, the three of them prayed. Aaron spoke, "Dear Lord, thank You for this food. We know how great and wonderful You are and just ask that You will bless us and guide us. May we be nourished by this food and have a wonderful night. And if I can be selfish for a moment, and it be in Your will, please let us win the Saligia grant. Amen."

The three sat mostly quietly as they ate their food. Aaron asked Za how school was, and she asked him and Malone how work was. The meal was small, so they finished it relatively quickly. As they finished, Za rinsed everything off and put the dishes into the dishwasher. She didn't want dirty dishes out during game night later. There would be enough of a mess from all of the snacks. After cleaning up quickly, she joined Malone on the sofa with Aaron in his recliner.

"Thank you for the dinner, Za," said Malone. "You too, Aaron," he added quickly as an afterthought. "And while I'm at it, I just realized what a doof I was by not offering to help put the dishes away. I'm so sorry."

"No worries, Malone. You're welcome," said Za. "It wasn't much. Sorry, I didn't know you were coming over. I just wanted something quick before game night."

"No, it was perfect," said Malone. "We'll probably fill up on snacks anyway. If it were me, I probably would have left the vegetables out because I'm too lazy to make two things. I think you're the first person I've seen eat them mixed into the macaroni. I was afraid at first to try it that way, but I couldn't let you be the only one. It was good."

"She likes it that way," said Aaron. "Her mother always did it that way too. I usually like to mix all of my food into one pile on my plate but never quite got into mixing that meal."

"I may not be the best cook in the world, but I do my best," said Za appreciatively. "Funny, I think that's the only thing I mix together. Dad mixes everything else, and I keep everything else apart. We're a team that way."

Aaron looked at his watch. "Speaking of teams, I didn't realize how late it was. Kids are going to start arriving soon for game night." Aaron picked himself up from his chair in which he had just managed to get comfortable. "I'll go grab some games. Malone, you want to put the chairs out?"

Aaron left the room briefly. He didn't really have to get the games since he knew that Malone wanted to play charades, but he knew it would give Za and Malone a moment alone before everyone else arrived. He also thought it would help to maintain the surprise if he acted like any other game night.

As he left the room, Za turned to Malone and said, "I don't want this to sound like gossip, but I'm kind of excited and wanted to tell someone."

"What?" Malone asked.

"I think that Billy is asking Janet to the prom tonight!" she let out in an excited tone.

"Really? What makes you say that?" Malone asked.

"Everyone was saying that someone was getting asked to prom tonight. They've been going out for a year now. I think Bill is going to ask her tonight," answered Za.

Malone was a bit worried. He didn't remember telling anyone about his plan other than Aaron. Maybe he let something slip to make Za think someone was being asked tonight. At the same time, if someone else was asking tonight too, which he hoped very much wasn't true, then he could totally spoil Bill's proposal with his own. He put in the back of his mind to make sure that he got a moment with Bill. He would need to make sure what Bill's plans were before he went ahead with his own plan. Even though he was extremely excited, it might have to wait.

Malone thought about how to respond in a way that didn't give anything away. "Let's not jump to any conclusions. I'm sure that you're right. Bill and Janet will probably...no, definitely go to prom together, but who knows what's going to happen tonight? Don't spoil anything by acting over excited either. We don't want to ruin anything." In his mind, Malone felt that this would settle Za down without giving away his own surprise.

"You're right. I don't know why I've been excited about prom lately. It's not like I'm big into dances like that. I think it's the idea of my friends getting together that I like the most," Za said.

"I can see that. I like to see others happy too," added Malone.

As Malone finished, Aaron reentered. He had not heard the brief conversation and was unaware of the potential spoiler to their plan. Malone quickly stood up and grabbed some chairs to put around the living space.

Aaron placed an armload of games on the coffee table. "Hey, normally I'd just sit and hang out, maybe go into my room and work, but I have a great idea."

"What's that?" Za asked.

"Call me an old fuddy-duddy, but I think it would be fun if you played charades," responded Aaron.

"We could do that," said Malone. "But we should see what the others think." He didn't want to see what the others thought, but he needed to talk to Bill first to make sure that he didn't need to abort his plan.

"I think charades is a grand idea," added Za. "That sounds like so much fun. I'm sure I can convince everyone to play that."

Aaron felt particularly accomplished. He had helped set up Malone to ask Za to the prom while simultaneously getting Za to be the one to convince everyone to take part. As he internally congratulated himself, the doorbell buzzed.

"It's open!" yelled Za.

It was Bill and Janet arriving together. Everyone exchanged greetings. Malone gave Bill a high-five as if they each knew that a prom proposal was on for that night, confusing Malone even more. After the hellos, Janet informed everyone, "Alice and Joyce were pulling up as we were. They're so much fun."

"Excellent," responded Za as Alice and Joyce knocked on the screen door while saying hello to everyone through it.

"Come in, come in," several members of the group told the two.

As the kids settled in, Aaron rearranged the chairs as best he could to accommodate their growing numbers. He also grabbed a few extra folding chairs from the closet in the spare room. He then brought out snacks from the kitchen. "Feel free to help yourselves," he told everyone. "There's water, orange juice, apple juice, cow juice, and soda in the fridge."

As the kids settled in, the four girls began to talk about what game to play. Za wasted no time convincing them to play charades.

Meanwhile, Malone noticed his chance. "Hey, Bill, you want to grab some drinks?"

"Sure, whatever the soda is," he responded.

Malone quickly shifted to the kitchen and grabbed two sodas from the refrigerator. Before his window of opportunity was gone, he handed a soda pop to Bill and pulled him in to whisper in his ear. "Hey," Malone said softly, "I have a surprise tonight. You don't have a surprise tonight, do you?"

A bit startled but not enough to draw attention to the two of them, Bill queried back, "What do you mean?"

"Be cool, don't react in any way to let on, but I'm thinking of asking Za to prom tonight, but she thinks that you're going to ask Janet tonight," said Malone.

Bill was shocked for a moment at what Malone had said. He tried to be cool but was afraid he might have given something away. Being perhaps the perfect wingman, Bill settled and answered without a noticeable hint of excitement to give away the secret now shared between the two of them. "Dude, that's totally cool. Yes, I'm asking her tonight."

Malone's heart sank.

Bill continued, "But I'm not asking her until we get back to her place."

Malone's heart grew two sizes.

The two boys smiled at one another. Aaron, who had been watching the back-and-forth between the two, wondered what they were talking about. Fortunately, the girls were only beginning to notice the secretive body language of the two boys when the next group of kids knocked on the door to distract them.

Three more teenagers arrived. Normally, they could have anywhere from five to twenty teens at their youth group gatherings, and everyone expected tonight was present. Bill sat next to Janet on the sofa. Malone sank into the sofa with them with Za on the armrest when she wasn't moving around talking to everyone. Alice and Joyce occupied two chairs placed in front of the television. Jack, one of the new arrivals, sat in the recliner that everyone else had been saving for Aaron. There was one chair on each side of the recliner, but Amy moved them to the same side so that she could sit next to Pam. Meanwhile, Aaron sat in the kitchen.

After the usual minutes of small talk asking about everyone's day and school, Za convinced everyone to play charades. She called to her dad, "Hey, Dad, we're ready to play charades."

"Okay, so I'm the judge, right?" he asked as he walked over to the living room.

"Yes," replied Za and Amy in unison.

Malone and Bill moved the coffee table out of the way. Jack was reluctant to move and give up the best seat. As the boys returned to their seats, Aaron made sure of the teams. At first, some of the kids wanted two teams, but Aaron convinced them to do more and smaller teams. Since many of the kids were already couples, it worked out well. Bill would go with Janet. Alice and Joyce would go together. Amy, Pam, and Jack would be the only three-person team. And, of course, Malone would be with Za, even though they weren't technically a couple.

While the others had been visiting, Aaron had been writing up ideas on index cards. Every group picked a number between one and ten. Bill went first and picked the number three, which turned out to be the number Aaron had picked. "Who wants to give the clue?" Aaron asked.

"I'll go," said Bill.

Aaron handed him the first card. "Read the card," he said as Bill took the card. "I'll give you half a minute to think about it." After counting to thirty in his head, Aaron asked Bill, "Are you ready?"

"Yes," replied Bill as he returned the card to Aaron.

Aaron had a small hourglass timer from another game that counted about one minute. As he turned the timer over on the end table, he told Bill, "Go. You have one minute."

Bill began to swing his arms through the air, one after the other. "Oh, I got it!" said Pam.

"It's not our turn," responded Amy.

"Yeah, Pam," added Janet.

As the girls laughed, Janet yelled out, "Swimming!"

Bob nodded his head yes and then held up two fingers.

"Second word," recognized Janet.

As Bob nodded his head yes again, he put his left arm on his back with the elbow bent outward as he bent over. He moved in a swaying motion around the room.

"Worm," said Janet. "Are you swimming and fishing? Things done in water."

Bob shook his head no.

"Halfway on the time," declared Aaron.

"Ah, what is it?" Janet asked herself. The others were laughing and trying to figure it out as well.

Bob took his mouth and opened it wide, showing all of his teeth and pretended to take a bit out of Janet's leg.

"Shark!" yelled Janet, excited that she felt that she got it.

Bob nodded his head yet again and moved his hands in a circle for her to put the clues together.

"Swimming shark," she said.

"Not quite," said Aaron.

"Um, shark attack," she tried again.

"No," said Aaron. "Ten seconds."

Bob began to frantically swim around the room again but this time acted like something was beside him. He then switched back to his shark form and acted like something was beside him still. Everyone was either cheering or laughing by this point.

"I'm not seeing it. Ahh!" cried Janet.

"Time!" shouted Aaron. As Bob let out an audible shrug, Aaron added, "One last guess because we're nice that way."

"Umm, swimming with sharks?"

Bob jumped in the air. "Yes!" he exclaimed.

Aaron showed everyone the card, which read "Swimming with sharks."

"Great job. You got that one right on the head. One point for your team," he told them. "We'll do two points if you get it before time and then one point if you get it with your last guess."

Bob and Janet hugged as they sat back down on the couch. Everyone told them, "Good job!"

Without being asked, Malone stood up. "I'll go next," he said.

"You'd better be good," Za told him, but not seriously. "We got this."

Aaron handed Malone a blank card, which he pretended to read for a moment before giving back to Aaron.

"Ready, go," said Aaron as he turned the timer back over.

Malone held up one finger.

"One word," responded Za.

As Malone nodded his head yes, he started dancing around the room as if he was holding onto a girl, slow dancing.

Za, thinking it was obvious, said, "Dancing?"

Malone nodded his head as he kept dancing.

"Well, I didn't think it would be that easy, I guess," added Za. Everyone agreed.

Joyce added, "There better not be any cards that easy."

Malone stopped dancing and held up one finger again.

"One word," confirmed Za again.

Malone then held up four fingers.

"One word, four syllables?" Za asked.

Malone shook his head no and repeated the gesture.

"One word, four letters?" Za asked.

As Malone nodded his head yes. Aaron noticed that almost half of the time was gone. Malone then leaned over and pretended to put something around Za's wrist. He then quickly sat down and pretended to eat. After that, he stood up and started to dance again.

Za watched everything carefully. She wanted to win, but the clues weren't clicking. Pam and Amy had guessed the clues and were giggling. "What's so funny?" asked Za as Malone kept dancing.

"We know what it is," said Amy and Pam.

"No! What?" Za cried out. "I'm not seeing it!" Time was almost up. Then it clicked. Za shouted out, "Prom!"

"Yes!" the teens cheered.

Malone kneeled at Za's feet and said, "Will you go to prom with me?"

Part laughing, part crying, part excited, Za responded, "Yes!" It was the first public confirmation of the two's affection for each other. Za gave Malone a big hug before blushing when she realized everyone was looking at them.

The girls were cheering, and the boys congratulated Malone. Malone noticed that Bob looked a little nervous. Hopefully, he hadn't ruined Bob's plan for later.

As things calmed down, Za had a thought. "Wait. What did that card say, Dad?"

Aaron handed her the empty card.

As she looked at the card initially with confusion, she looked up at her dad and smacked him in the shoulder with the card. "You knew?" she asked him, slightly embarrassed.

Aaron just shrugged his shoulders and gave her a hug.

"Oh! You're such a bugger, but I love you, Daddy!" Za said as she hugged him back.

"Hey, no playing favorites," Jack said jokingly.

After that, everyone settled into the game. About thirty minutes later, Amy, Pam, and Jack were crowned the winners, although that was mostly due to the uncanny connection between the two girls. At one point, Jack joked that they were invisibly conjoined twins.

The group continued to play Werewolf after charades. Aaron stuck around as the moderator for several rounds before retiring to his room for the kids to have fun without him around for a little while. As he sat in his room, he thought at length about how Za was becoming a woman. He was so proud of her in so many ways. As much as he wanted her to be his little girl forever, he was happy that she was growing. Statistically, she and Malone wouldn't stay together, but he was happy that Malone was her first real boyfriend.

He was happy and sad. Happy Za was growing up and sad that eventually, they would grow apart. He didn't fear that they would ever grow apart emotionally, only geographically. She had been his source of energy for so long that he worried a little that he would be lost without her. He just had to remember to keep her close in his heart and in his speed dial.

As the night went on, it was time for everyone to leave. Aaron stood up from his seat in the kitchen as the remaining guests were gathered at the front door, saying goodbye. When they saw Aaron, they all gave him a farewell too. Malone even came over and shook his hand. Aaron pulled him in for a man hug before kindly saying, "Get out of here, kid."

As he laughed nervously, Malone joined everyone else as they left. As the door shut behind them, Aaron's gaze shifted to his lovely daughter.

As the last guest left, Za likewise turned to face her father. She was still excited about Malone asking her to the prom. Actually, she wasn't sure if that was what she was excited about or if it was that she finally accepted or realized that she really did like someone in that special kind of way. She smiled up at her father and gave a giddy little jump.

Aaron noticed the smile, and he knew precisely what was causing it. His little girl had a date to prom, and it was clear that the two young adults were smitten. He smiled back without wasting the moment on words.

Za could not contain herself. She jumped into her father's arms. "I've got a date for prom!" she exclaimed. "I won't be able to sleep tonight!"

Aaron returned her hug, responding only with, "Congratulations." As the embrace came to an end, the two quietly cleaned up the house as they contemplated the evening. Aaron's mind flashed his memory of Za's life from birth up to that moment. All the highlights came back. He remembered her birth, her first step, her first words, her first day of school, her first many things. He remembered holding her when she cried and jumping with her in joy. He remembered her baptism, her eighth-grade graduation, her driving test, her sixteenth birthday, and all of the important dates in her life. He recalled the times that she was angry at him that were thankfully few. He remembered staying up late with her when she was afraid and walking along the beach on vacations. As he recollected, he couldn't imagine a life without her in it. He was sad to see her grow up, but he wouldn't wish it any other way.

Meanwhile, Za contemplated what it meant to be in a relationship. She didn't want to jump ahead of herself, but could she be in love? She loved her father, but this was definitely something different. She was confused and excited, afraid, and relieved.

With the room returned to a somewhat clean state, Za spread out on the couch, and Aaron sat in his recliner. He looked at her again, and realizing that his little girl was no longer little, he gave out a noticeable sigh.

"What was that?" Za asked.

"I'm really happy for you, sweetie. You had a really good night, didn't you?"

"It was awesome!" she responded. "I'm so excited for prom now. Dad...I think I have a boyfriend. Are you going to be okay with that?"

Aaron smiled. "I couldn't be happier for you. Any father would be lying if he said he didn't want to hold onto his little girl for as long as possible, but you're a young woman now. I need to start treating you more like one."

"That's right," agreed Za. As she spoke to her father, that knowledge became more solidified in her own subconscious as well. She was becoming a woman.

The two sat there for a while, thinking to themselves before Za headed to bed for the evening. Aaron spent the next few hours submitting everything needed for the Saligia funding. Only when finished could he go to sleep.

## 10

Za and Malone texted each other throughout the following day. Za began the discourse with a simple, "Hey." It took her some time to come up with those choice words. She was still working through her many feelings. Currently, she was happy to reveal her feelings for Malone, sad that her dad may feel left behind, and enamored with Malone's strength with all that he had gone though, remembering how he grew up a slave. All of these emotions were enough to make her want to explode.

Malone received the message at work, and he instantly read it, seeing as it was from Za. He eagerly opened up his phone to see only the word, "Hey." Believing himself to be cute, he texted back, "Hey." The discourse was laughable among the two with newly revealed affections.

Ten minutes later, in the middle of what should have been second hour, Za discretely texted him back, "I'm too excited to learn." She was telling the truth. She had no idea what the math teacher was talking about. Za's phone rumbled as her second hour class ended. *Thank goodness*, she thought. She felt that the teacher noticed her impropriety earlier and was keeping an eye on her. He might let one slip pass but not two. The buzzing of her phone at the bell probably went unnoticed. As soon as she arrived at her locker, she switched out her books and read the phone from within her locker so no teacher would catch her.

All that Malone wanted to do was to text her back, but he resisted. He didn't want Za to get in trouble for being on her phone during school. He waited for about half an hour, and at the next slow moment at work, his willpower was expended. "It's so great to finally let you know how I feel."

As Za read the text, she found that her affection for Malone was real. In her mind, she had found the one. She had to be quick with her response lest she be late for her next class, although Mrs. English, who oddly enough taught English, hated to give tardy slips, often letting students slip in after the bell if they were quiet and assuming that the door wasn't locked. Technically, all of the doors were supposed to be locked during classes for safety, but Mrs. English normally wedged hers slightly open. She always figured it would only take a second to shut it already locked in case of an emergency. The short time wasted thinking about her next class strained her thinking. "Same" was all that she could think to text back. Due to being rushed at this point, Za then forgot her phone in her locker as she whisked away to class.

That was unfortunate. She heard nothing her teacher said that hour. She was distracted, wanting to text Malone more or read what he had responded. Jenny kicked her desk from behind at one point to tell her to at least look like she was paying attention. If Mrs. English noticed someone definitely not paying attention, she would concoct some question to ask the person in some unkind attempt to draw attention to their lack of attention. On a good day, when everyone showed interest, they could make it through the whole class without a single question from her. Still, the clock went unbearably slow for Za that hour.

Malone was not able to read the message when it arrived. He was at work after all. His boss needed more help in the kitchen to fulfill a rush of take-out orders. For the next hour, he was too busy to notice his phone.

Meanwhile, Za returned to her locker and, in utter dismay, noticed no replies from Malone. Her mind worked overtime, creating a myriad of reasons why Malone had not responded. They ranged widely. Maybe his phone was dead. Maybe the message didn't go through. Should she send it again? Maybe he was injured. Should she check that everything was all right? Would that look crazy since they just started dating the previous night? She finally told her subconscious to shut up. Malone was at work. *He'll respond later…*she hoped.

Another class passed where Za learned nothing. In fact, as she put everything in her locker and headed to lunch, she wasn't even sure if she went to the right class. She sat down next to her friends at lunch but immediately pulled out her phone. Still no response. She asked the friends closest to her, "I texted Malone over an hour ago and haven't received a response."

Janet told her that he was probably cheating on her, but it was obvious that she was joking. Unfortunately, it still sufficed to place that among the possibilities in Za's head. Pam told her that he was probably just busy. Everyone told her to chill out.

"Should I text him again?" Za asked.

"No!" was the resounding response from her friends. They quoted *Girl Code*. You never text a boy twice or always leave a boy in suspense or never look desperate. Despite their different codes, they were all correct. She needed to just be patient, however difficult it would be. They had just started dating. She didn't want to seem like the crazy girlfriend.

Malone, taking his own lunch break, finally saw Za's last message. The realization of the stupidity of their texts was not lost on him. He almost cried. What could he say to her? What if he said the wrong thing? What if she changed her mind? What if he wasn't good enough? He had nothing. What could he offer her? He had to text her back. He couldn't risk anything with the girl whom he finally admitted his affections. Empowered by finally having a girlfriend and determined to keep it that way, he replied, "Want to do dinner?"

That seemed perfect to Malone. At least that is what he thought as he hit send. He would spend the next several minutes second-guessing himself as he waited for a response back. As the time passed, he simply looked at his noodles, unable to eat. *What a shame,* he thought. He really was hungry.

When Za finally received his response, she was relieved and giddy as she shared the message with her friends. She responded quickly, "Yes, I'm starving. Let's go out tonight." She was starving since she too had been unable to eat her lunch.

Malone read the message. He hadn't intended that they go out that very night, but it was perfect, even better than waiting for the weekend like he was thinking. Of course, they wouldn't be able to stay out late on a school night, but that was fine. "I'll pick you up at five," he responded.

Za's friends looked at her, admiring her innocence as she read her messages. Alice was the first to speak up. "Didn't he just ask you to prom last night, and now you're going on a date tonight?"

"Yes," replied Za, her head in the clouds.

The girls laughed and returned to their normal lunch routine.

For the rest of the school day, Za was useless. She thought they talked about bones in biology; or was that her forensics elective? That was about all that she remembered. Well, that and her date later with Malone. She spent all of study hall last hour drawing pictures as best as she could, showing her and Malone together. Then the school day ended.

*****

At precisely five o'clock, Malone arrived at her door. When she went to the door, she normally would have invited him in. However, that was before. Now that they were dating, she oddly didn't feel right about having him in the house when her father wasn't home. As she answered the door, she asked Malone to wait a moment while she left her dad a note:

> Dad, I'll be home later. Went out to eat with a friend.
>
> Love, Za.

After the difficult decision of where to eat, they ended up at a fast-food restaurant. Neither of them had much money, and neither was too proud to go out for fast food. As they sat down with their food, though, it occurred to Malone that this might be considered their first date.

"Thanks for coming to dinner with me. Are you sure this is good enough?" Malone asked as he waved his arm to indicate the restaurant around them.

Za saw in Malone's eyes that he must feel disappointed with himself. It was at that moment that she too realized that this might count as their first date and it was just fast food. She decided to make it official. "I could think of worse places for a first date." She smiled coyly, then realized it was the same smile she gave her father when trying to put him at ease.

Malone smiled back. So it was a date, and Za was all right with it.

After a short prayer, each of them ate slowly, trying to be as proper as possible, despite their surroundings, chewing with their mouths closed, and carefully eating small bites so as not to be caught with food in their mouths when it was their turn to talk.

Za began by asking about Angelic Missions. Malone, after checking their surroundings for eavesdroppers out of habit, filled her in on getting to work with her father. He had given his two-week notice that morning.

As they started talking about Angelic Missions more, Malone brought up what they called kind-napping. Za thought that it was perhaps the cleverest play on words she could remember. When the missionaries took children, they didn't consider it kidnapping since the children often were already kidnapped. They considered it an act of kindness, for in all things, God wants them to be kind.

Eventually, Za was able to shift the discussion to Malone. As they spoke, she realized that Malone knew practically everything about her. She was always revealing her feelings, except those about him. He was her primary confidant as well. Only in that moment did she realize that Malone had always been the listener. Maybe that was part of what attracted her to him. But at the same time, it meant that she knew very little about him. Revealing these feelings to Malone, she said, "You know, honestly, I'm not sure I know anything about you. You've got to tell me more about yourself."

Malone knew that he didn't talk much about himself, and he regretted how little he had actually informed Za until her question.

He proceeded to tell her everything that he could from his earliest memory of being sold by his parents to years working while chained to a table. He would often sleep, eat, and work in the same spot for days if he was in trouble. Otherwise, they would at least let the children have some playtime. He later discovered that their captors found the children to work harder with fewer problems if they were given these short respites. It also kept them healthier to give them some time outdoors, even if they were fenced-in with several guards.

He recounted one story he only just remembered, perhaps having hidden it away in his subconscious as a defense mechanism. A friend he had—at least he remembered them being friends—once tried to burrow under the fence during the rainy season. The fence was flooded in one spot, and the ground was noticeably flooded out. His friend, whose name he couldn't recall, made it twenty feet or so before getting shot in the back. After telling that story, Malone sat flush for a moment. It was a terribly sad story made sadder by the fact that he only now realized he couldn't remember the boy's name.

Za noticed Malone's clear discomfort and quickly changed the subject. Trying to think about anything else, she remembered worries for her father. She thought about how he put everything into Angelic Missions, at least what he didn't put toward her happiness. "What if my dad doesn't get the money?" she abruptly asked Malone in order to change the subject and bring him out of his moment of despair.

Malone was not afraid to admit that he wanted her dad to get the money too. Sure, there were selfish reasons since he would get a job, but he also wanted Angelic Missions to be able to do the most that they could. "He will, don't worry."

"Of course, if Angelic Missions takes off, I wonder how that will affect our relationship, my dad's and mine." Za considered how much time it would take to run the mission once they actually had reliable funding.

Malone quickly reassured her, "He always puts more into you than work."

What Malone said wasn't exactly true. Za knew that her dad probably loved her above all else. Actually, there was no "probably" about it. But he put a lot of time and most of their money into the church and missions. Now he would have to put less money but more time.

Malone continued to reassure, feeling that Za was not completely buying into his belief. "Just think about it. With more money, he'll be able to hire more help like, say, me for instance. He'll have more time for you and more money."

Za hadn't actually thought about it that way. She was wrong. He wouldn't have less time. If anything, with more help, he would have more time for her. Maybe even enough time to start finding a new love for himself now that she had someone. Wait. Now her mind twisted the situation in the other direction. What if she had less time for him? She wanted to make sure that didn't happen, at least not in the immediate future. "Listen, Malone, I like you…a lot, but my dad is the most important thing in my life. No matter what, I have to find time for him because I know that he will find time for me."

"Hey, don't worry. I like your dad too," said Malone.

"You know," Za added, "I've been worried about him lately."

"How so?" Malone asked.

"His dreams. Has he told you about them? They're real nightmares, and they keep him up most nights. He always wakes up sweaty. He used to shower at night, but now it's the first thing that he does in the morning. I'm worried for him."

"Maybe it's just the stress of work and everything going on." Malone had heard many of Aaron's dreams as well, but Malone had not been worried about him. "He does talk to me about the dreams too. He knows how much I love dreams and have a few bizarre ones of my own. His are creepy, amazing, and constantly full of strife between angels and demons. I'm sure that he'll eventually figure it out and move on, though. I wouldn't be too worried. He seems happy enough."

Za sat still, contemplating her father's nighttime quandary. She prayed for her father to get a good night's sleep.

Malone continued, "His dreams reminded me once of my dream for freedom. Every night, I would dream of someone coming to rescue me. Then one day, your dad came with his friends and did just that. It was literally a dream come true. When it was just a dream, though, there was always a struggle, and I would often lose precious sleep. Eventually, I learned to live with it and wait patiently. I think the same will happen to your dad. The meaning or purpose of the dreams will eventually come to fruition, and in the meantime, he'll eventually learn to work through them. Then again, maybe it's just stress. If he gets the grant, maybe any demons haunting him will just go away."

Za shrugged her shoulders. She was a little surprised at what Malone was saying, but maybe he was just trying to make her feel better. He was usually the one that placed extensive metaphysical meaning on all dreams. Yet, this dream he brushed aside.

At the same time, he had a point. Her dad was under a lot of stress, and only God knew how many demons he was tackling right now. She resolved herself again to have a talk with him and let him know that she was there for him, whatever he may need. She'd wait a couple of days, though, until after the Saligia meeting. Maybe it would just all go away.

The two finished their dinner, and after extensive small talk, finally went home. As they parted, they were both still too nervous to kiss.

The night before the meeting, Aaron oddly slept well. No demons had visited his sleep, and church that Sunday had been fun. As he sat at the side of his bed on Monday morning, he considered the possibility that it was a sign. All of these demons had been haunting him, and now, if he got the grant, they would be lifted.

What Aaron didn't know was that the demons of his dream were not gone. Instead, they no longer needed to visit his dreams. They needed the dreams only to track him down. But now they knew where and who he was. Unfortunately, he would soon discover the truth of his dreams and the identity of the ghostly figure.

Still, Aaron had some anxiety for the day. It was an important day, perhaps the most important for Angelic Missions. Normally, he would throw on jeans and any old shirt, the staples of his wardrobe, but today was an important day. It was time to wear the only suit in his closet along with his only tie. Aaron slowed his morning routine to carefully dress. He walked back to the mirror in the restroom to tie his tie. He then made sure that the tie, shirt buttons, belt buckle, and pant zipper were all lined up, even though he was well aware that everything would shift by that afternoon. His hair was short, so a brush was not really necessary, but still he grabbed one from next to the sink and took his time making sure what hair he had was brushed just right. Then, performing a quick double check of his shave, he stepped out, ready for work.

After his usual Bible reading and breakfast, he considered not going to work that day and just leaving from home. But he still had to take Za to school. Plus, he needed to meet Malone to take him into the city anyway. Besides, he was a creature of habit, and going into work was part of that habit. He dropped Za off at school, telling her that he loved her and wishing her luck on her history test before he headed off to work.

Malone was waiting at Angelic Missions. With a smile, they greeted each other. Not much was said or needed to be said. Aaron just needed to get the job done, and Malone needed to support him.

After some discussion on the best way to get downtown, Malone disregarded Aaron's suggestion and went with what the GPS on his phone told him. Aaron didn't notice as his mind was preoccupied. Malone thought to just tell him to relax, but he knew that when in need of relaxation, being told to relax usually had the opposite effect.

Aaron's anxiety was elevated not just by the meeting but by driving in a truck he hated on roads that were no fun to drive. He considered replacing the truck once but realized that if he was to get into an accident, the loss would be minimal. Plus, the odds of someone stealing that eyesore were so low it would be more likely for someone to randomly leave a vehicle. As he sat there, Aaron ran though scenarios in his head. If the car broke down or they had an accident, he had a contingency. He could not allow anything to keep him from the meeting.

When not worried about the trip, Aaron kept reorganizing his notes. Each moment, he would think of one more possible question that Mr. Simpson might ask, and then he had to construct a response.

Finally, they arrived at the tower. "You have to park at the Self Park if I want them to pay for it," Aaron remarked as they approached. The GPS took them from Jefferson to Jackson Boulevard, but they quickly figured out where to park thanks to the directions in the grant package that Malone had memorized earlier.

Once parked, Aaron said, "Farewell, Malone. Thanks, and I'll see you soon."

"Ditto. I'll be waiting in the truck to celebrate," Malone replied as he leaned back and relaxed, considering that he might take a walk around the city or play on his phone.

Aaron took a deep breath and headed to the tower.

Once inside, Aaron rode the elevator alone. He was a bit surprised to get an elevator by himself but was thankful for one last moment to collect his thoughts and practice his elevator pitch.

Speaking to himself, Aaron said, "Thank you so much for having me…No. Thank you so much for inviting me here today. I will do my best to make your time worthwhile. Yes, that sounded good. Angelic Missions is blessed by all that we do, and we hope to bring those blessings to you through your aid of the organization. Yep, I'll start with that."

As the elevator finished its trip, Aaron checked his breath and tie before exiting the lift. His eyes quickly scanned the floor. No restrooms in sight. He wanted to take one more moment to wash his hands and face and reflect in the mirror. There was no time to worry about that now. Time to move to the meeting.

Locating the Saligia logo on a suite door, Aaron tried his best to casually stroll into the office. Confidently walking to the receptionist, he opened his mouth to speak and announce his presence.

"You must be Dr. Todd," said the woman behind the desk, speaking more quickly than Aaron, leaving him a little disappointed inside.

Regaining his initiative, Aaron replied, "Yes, I have a—"

"Meeting with Mr. Simpson at eleven."

Now the receptionist, office manager, or whatever the current politically correct term was, whom Aaron recognized from the voice on the phone, had gone from speaking before him to finishing his sentences. Feeling for a moment that the woman may be psychic or at least a little annoying, Aaron paused before replying, "Yes, I'm a little early, but I didn't want to be late." Aaron, seeing an opportunity, added, "Is there a restroom where I can freshen up before the meeting?"

"Absolutely, dear," said the woman. "Just down the hall to the left. When you're finished, have a seat, and I'll let Mr. Simpson know you have arrived."

"That would be splendid. Thank you."

Aaron, trying to remain casual, walked slowly down the hall to the left. The first door led to a restroom. Making sure he was alone, he quickly washed his hands and splashed some water in his mouth to give it a quick cleanse, albeit with faucet water. "Better than nothing," he said. Now prepared, he returned to the reception area. Just as he was about to sit down, the receptionist once again interrupted him.

"Mr. Simpson is ready to see you, Dr. Todd." The woman rose from behind the desk. Standing at least six feet without her heels, she was a bit intimidating to Aaron as she continued, "Please follow me."

"Absolutely. Thank you," Aaron said as he turned around and followed the woman, attempting not to stare at her stature. Not only was she psychic, he thought, but she was also some sort of champion body builder.

They proceeded down a typical office hallway. Three doors lined each side of the green hallway. Each door had a brass handle. At the end of the hallway were two large wooden doors. None of these facts were lost on Aaron who found it oddly reminiscent of his earlier dreams.

As the woman opened one of the doors, she told Aaron, "Please have a seat. Mr. Simpson will be right with you."

Aaron walked through the door, looking back as the woman took her leave. As quickly as she had opened them, the woman closed the doors and was gone. *Nice but scary individual*, thought Aaron.

Turning to the room in front of him, Aaron almost fainted. Was it possible, he thought, that he was still dreaming, even after all that had happened so far that day? The room in front of him was too familiar as if it was torn from his dream. There were just enough changes to provide his mind with adequate statistical probability of occurrence to maintain his sanity. The room was smaller, without a vaulted ceiling, but the floor was finished with either marble or a marble substitute. There were two windows, but the same drapes as his dream were drawn. There was no candelabra, but an ornamental fan and light fixture lit the room and provided just the right air movement. Under the fan sat a large dark desk with an equally large chair behind it. An intercom and laptop computer were the only objects on the desk. Two red upholstered chairs faced the desk. Books that looked as old as print lined two ornate bookshelves. One book was opened on a podium.

For a moment, Aaron's knees grew weak. He took a moment to gather himself. *Just a crazy coincidence*, he thought. He also thought that he might take a look at the book. He remembered the books from his dream but could not clearly remember their contents. In the end, he thought that it was best not to touch what was not his. Regaining his composure, he walked slowly to one of the chairs and sat down. *This time, I'm going to sit patiently and pretend none of this reminds me of my dream.* At least, that is what Aaron thought.

A few moments later, he heard a loud thump coming from a door toward the back of the office. Aaron quickly jumped from his chair and took a defensive posture next to it in fear of what might be coming through the door. Quickly realizing how foolish he would appear, Aaron returned to his seated position.

*****

Concurrently, behind the door, Asmodai was waiting. At the moment, he was a black man of average build. Ash Simpson, an unassuming white businessman, stood in front of him, or at least what everyone considered to be Ash Simpson.

In reality, the man next to Asmodai was not a man at all. It was the demon Zeljabul in human form. Twenty years prior, he had given up his demonic powers to assume human form. Taking over the reins of one of many corporate entities under demonic control, he assumed the identity of Ash Simpson. Unfortunately, the real Ash Simpson had to die in order for the transition to be complete. Now, his work completed, it was time for him to be replaced as well.

"You've done well, Zeljabul," said Asmodai. "You will be rewarded for your service."

"Thank you, master," said Zeljabul. "I'm glad that we finally found him. Please let me return. I can't take this form anymore."

With one quick motion, Asmodai grabbed Zeljabul's neck and twisted. Ash Simpson was dead. His body fell to the ground, creating the thump heard by Aaron.

The receptionist picked up the limp body and carried it through a door to the back. As she did so, Asmodai's form changed until he looked identical to the Ash Simpson he had just killed. The new Ash Simpson then opened the door to the office in which Aaron waited.

*****

Shortly after scuttling back to his chair, Aaron turned his head as a man stumbled through the door. The man spoke as he entered. "Sorry about that noise, I knocked over the table by the door. Terrible placement. I've knocked it five times this month."

Aaron quickly recognized the man as Ash Simpson. His mind was relieved. His heartbeat slowly settled. One deep breath, and he responded without evidence of his earlier fright, "Hello, it is so nice to meet you." Aaron had by this time completely forgotten everything he had decided to say in the elevator or at any time previous.

"Oh, the pleasure is all mine, Mr. Todd," said Ash Simpson. "Please, call me Ash. May I call you Az…Aaron?" Ash spoke as he raised his hand in welcome. He almost spoke the wrong name…or the right name depending on one's perspective.

Aaron shook Ash's hand as they walked back toward the desk and sat down. "Of course," responded Aaron. "Mr. Simpson—I mean, Ash, thank you for seeing me today." Aaron was nervous. He was also careful to be polite and waited to sit until Ash was seated first.

"So," Ash spoke as he leaned across the large desk toward Aaron. "What can you tell me about yourself?"

"I'm pretty much an open book," Aaron replied. "What would you like to know?"

"Tell me about your family. You know, I have to tell you that I feel like I've had this conversation many times, but I never remembered you having a child."

Ash's last statement seemed odd to Aaron, as it should have. He could remember being in a room similar to this one many times in his dreams. Aaron wondered if it was possible that Ash had experienced a recurring dream much like his own. *But why the interest in Za?* he wondered.

"Za, my daughter, yes, she's really the most important thing in my life. I mean, I love Angelic Missions, but she's my little girl, even if she is a young woman now."

"Seventeen, wonderful, she was almost a woman," Ash interjected.

Aaron continued, "Yes, she *is* almost a woman. Of course, like all youth, she feels like she already is an adult. She acts it as well. I have to admit that she is exceptionally mature for her age. Just the other day, she was discussing possibly coming to work with me someday, not as a daddy-daughter thing, but as coworkers. You know? I have to admit, it would be nice to spend more time with her." Aaron tried his best to describe Za without letting the conversation get too far astray from the purpose of his visit. He could easily talk about Za for the whole meeting, but he really wanted to sell Angelic Missions.

"Fascinating," Ash responded. "I confess, I have done my research on you. We are quite thorough. We wanted to be absolutely sure that we had the right…man. We noticed many influences in your life, particularly your late wife. I'm truly sorry for her loss. She seemed like a wonderful woman. I know that it was long ago, but you have definitely excelled since then, and you appear to be a loving father as well."

"Thank you. She was a great woman and wife, and she is definitely still in my heart. It is nice of you to say so. I can certainly see that you have done your background check. I think I'm a bit flattered, actually," Aaron admitted.

"But you see, Aaron, you are actually a fascinating man to me… your Angelic Missions too." Ash interjected under his breath, "How appropriately named that is." And then he continued without pause, "It is so telling of who you are. Don't fall into the trap of modesty when describing what you do." Ash rose and began to walk across the room toward the book opened on the podium.

"Thank you. We really are trying to do great things. The possibility of your funding could really help to make that a possibility," Aaron expressed in earnest. "If there is anything that I can tell you about the missions, please let me know. I'm here to answer any of your questions."

"Don't worry about the money, my dear fellow. Set your heart at ease about that. Let's get to know one another first."

Aaron considered what was just said. His heart was lifted. It appeared that they had the money. Unintentionally, he allowed his mind to wander over the many plans he had for the grant.

Ash continued, "For instance, let me bring your attention to this book. I love books, Aaron. Do you?"

"Yes, indeed, although I've been told that I read too quickly."

"That's the sign of an intelligent being. A smart being wrote this particular tome as well. It's my favorite. Would you like me to tell you about it?"

Not sure what to say, Aaron replied, "Sure, please do."

"This book is all about angels. It is a collection of notes, stories, anecdotes, and anything that man has discovered on the subject throughout the ages, and surprisingly accurate too."

"Fascinating," responded Aaron, although he wasn't sure anyone could speak to the accuracy of a book about angels except maybe an angel. His heart also began to beat a little faster. How were his dreams connected to this meeting? Why would Ash Simpson bring up a book about angels?

"Truly. It contains a rather fascinating story about the fall of the angels."

"The angels or the demons?" Aaron asked.

"They are one and the same. All demons began as angels, you know."

"I suppose that's true."

Ash continued, "Let me tell you a story. Let's say that you had five siblings. All day, every day, you and your siblings served your father, unquestioning, doing everything that he asked. Everyone told you that your father loved you above all of the others because of how diligent you served with all of your work of the highest quality.

"But then the father adopted another child. It was a sickly baby compared to the other children. It demanded all of the resources of the family.

"The father then told you and your five siblings that while he loved you and appreciated all the praise you brought him, all of his inheritance was going to the new child. Furthermore, if you wished to remain in his house, you would serve the adopted child. The father even went so far as to take a part of himself and gave it to the adopted child to show his love.

"Meanwhile, this adopted child was the worst of all children. He rarely served the father, often doing the least to finish any job, often cheating his way through. The father knew this but still poured his love on the child.

"Now, I ask you, Mr. Todd. If you were one of the original siblings, especially the best of them that worked the hardest and was the most deserving, how would you feel about the adopted child?"

"I suppose that I would be angry," said Aaron. "I might feel a little sad or sorry for myself, maybe a little let down. But then, I suppose if I loved the father, truly loved him, I would have to accept and consider that there was something he knew that I did not."

"Oh, I thought you understood there for a second, Aaron." Ash looked a bit disappointed as he spoke. Aaron hoped that he had not just made a mistake. "The situation seems so black and white. Let's continue the story for a moment then."

"Okay," said Aaron.

Ash continued, "Let's assume that this adopted child continued to do bad, even evil deeds, no matter what the father did. One day, the best son gathered the others and refused to continue, as always. On that day, he refused to serve the adopted son and expressed his anger to the father. As any son should, he announced that he should gain his inheritance. One of the other sons, seeing the logic in his brother's actions, agreed.

"The two were quickly rebuked by the father. But unlike the adopted child, they were given no forgiveness. The father beat them to disfigurement and then cast them out of the house with no way to ever regain favor and return. Having heard more of the story, is there justice in these actions I ask you, Aaron?"

"I'm not sure. It does appear at the surface to be unfair," Aaron responded.

"Quite right, but more than just at the surface." For a moment, Ash raised his voice. "There is no depth to this situation, only injustice."

"Sorry, I didn't mean to offend. I guess it's in my nature to give the father the benefit of the doubt," Aaron expressed his apologies.

"Do not worry. In truth, that is exactly in your nature, my friend, to give the father the most love," Ash reassured.

Aaron's nerves were not calmed. He worried for a moment that he had said something to ruin the grant or anger Ash, but then Ash had just referred to him as a friend.

"Actually, I think it is time for us to move this conversation forward to its inevitable conclusion," said Ash. Asmodai was never one to waste time with small talk after all.

Aaron was now thoroughly confused. He had not really answered any questions he felt were pertinent to the funding. Rather than say the wrong thing, he felt it wise to simply say nothing for the moment. Sometimes the silent man was the wisest man in the room.

"I can see that I may have confused you. As I said, do not worry. I am going to tell you a secret. It's actually one that you knew but just don't know anymore. Knowing this secret is going to change everything that you think that you know."

"I guess I am a little confused," responded Aaron, "and now supremely at attention to know this Earth-shattering secret." After all that had happened, Aaron was now relatively sure that Ash might be mildly insane. He would not be surprised if Ash's next statement was that he believed they were all in an augmented reality program. At this point, it was best to simply to be agreeable until the meeting came to an end. If the funding was already his, it was best not to do anything to jeopardize it, and he wasn't sure how one was to decide what to say to a crazy person anyway.

Ash smiled. He looked at Aaron as if he could tell what he was thinking. "For what I am about to say, I ask only that you wait until I am completely finished before you say anything in return. It may sound crazy at first, but I need to tell the whole story. Then I'll present you with the truth of what I say. I'm going to tell you who I am and how long we have known each other. More importantly, I'm going to tell you the real reason I have looked so hard to get a meeting with you. Can you do that for me? Listen and not speak?"

Aaron smiled and remained silent. He had no idea what Ash was talking about. Aaron was the one who worked hard to get a meeting with him.

Ash paused before continuing, "For starters, I think that you will agree with me, particularly with your life, that one cannot believe in God without also believing in angels. Furthermore, one cannot believe in angels without therefore believing in demons, those angels who were cast out from His presence. Would you agree?"

Ash looked over at Aaron who nodded his head in agreement.

Ash continued, "Where you will at first disagree with me is when I tell you that I am one of those cast out angels."

Aaron's attention grew. He thought, *This man really is crazy, and probably a little dangerous,* but he didn't say anything.

"I am older than time. I was there when we stood up and refused to serve. I was there when we were given no mercy. I was there when we were cast out, never to experience His glory again. That's the true hell you know, never being able to be in His presence again. One can't help but be angry when something changes your whole reality, even though I didn't know what anger was at the time.

"I was one of the authors of this book as ageless as time. Until things had changed, I didn't even realize what time was. Now I see every excruciating moment. My anger has grown for thousands of years. Why should apes be given endless grace while we receive nothing but punishment? Where is our salvation? If not from Him, then perhaps we would have to make our own. Picture a world ruled by us with the lesser beings serving us. For the longest time, there was no hope. No hope that we could ever regain favor or power. But then you happened."

Aaron almost couldn't hold his tongue. This man was truly crazy, but how could Aaron in any way be involved in this story?

"Many demons are seeking a way to return the universe to how it once was. All we want is to once again be by His side. If He will not have us, then we will at least end this existence. Undo it, if you will. In order to do either plan, we need one thing. Would you like to know what that one thing is?"

Aaron simply agreed. All he could think was to get through this meeting. Aaron wanted to leave this room with his life. The money no longer mattered.

"Of course, you want to know. Everyone wants to know secrets. The one thing that we need…is you. You see, you were not cast out. In fact, you were one of his favored. You, my old friend—and I do mean old—were Azriel, the angel of death."

Aaron couldn't hold his tongue any longer. "Wait, I'm sorry, I really am sorry. I can't keep quiet. What you're saying really is crazy, and to be frank, I'm a little frightened at the moment." Aaron began to stand.

Ash was pacing behind his desk, but he stopped to gesture toward Aaron. "It's okay, I forgive your outburst. My story and our business are almost done. Please, even if you think I may be crazy, continue to hear me out until the end." Walking around his desk, he gently motioned his hand toward the seat, asking Aaron to stay seated.

Aaron relaxed back into his seat. It was reasonable to hear Ash out. He may be crazy, but Aaron supposed that Ash was only a danger to himself at the moment. Of course, if he thought he was a demon, a fallen angel, he could become dangerous. So Aaron would keep his wits about him.

Continuing his story as he paced, Ash spoke, "Angels, very rarely, almost uniquely fall to Earth. It is a very painful process, one which invariably causes one to forget the past. For a demon, it is easy to get to this realm, albeit still very painful. We just don't like being here, particularly since the rules don't permit us to kill humans. Some of the demons, those that are most angry, spend their days trying to get humans to harm each other. They get such satisfaction when they succeed. Some, like myself, have grander plans."

"What are those plans?" asked Aaron, concerned.

"So nice of you to ask," replied Ash. "I want a return to heaven, with or without God. But for so long, there has been no inkling of a way to get there. The doors are open, but we cannot even get near them. His power is too great, and there are still twice as many angels as there are demons. But what if we could get Him to finally forgive us? And if he doesn't forgive us, what if we could simply end it all?"

"I'm still not sure how I could possibly be involved," Aaron said.

"That's because of the fall," answered Ash. "When one enters this realm, it is painful, like childbirth. You forgot your past. It's a new life. The more you do it, the easier it is to remember your past. If you remembered, you would know the pain I had to go through in order to be here today. You would know how I've been in pain in a back room, remembering myself. I endured because you gave us hope. If God will send down one angel and then allow that angel back into heaven, then maybe he will allow all to return."

"How?" asked Aaron.

Ash smiled. The most important part was about to be revealed. Although monologues were so cliché among those perceived to be the villain, he knew his was drawing to an end, and unlike in the movies, he was sure that he had already won.

"Before I can answer that question, I need you to understand clearly how wrong humanity is. It is a virus that needs to be eliminated. If you can kill one, and you have killed many, then you can kill them all." As Ash spoke, he returned to his seat and logged into the computer at his side of the desk.

"I have never killed anyone. Can we not speak about killing? It's making me uncomfortable," admitted Aaron.

"I realize that you don't yet see how evil this disease of humanity is. That's why we are going to give you the opportunity to see." Ash opened up an application on his computer. The program contained a single red button on the screen that he then clicked.

Ash's smile grew as he turned to Aaron. "Let me tell you why you are so important, Mr. Todd. You, as I've said, are the angel of death. But what you don't realize because you can't remember is that your job is not just to kill men in the name of God, a job I would gladly accept, by the way. Your job is to lead the dead to His kingdom, at least the dead that still need redeeming after death. You light the way. You provide the extension of His light that shows them where they need to go. Without you, they are delightfully lost.

"But you were as soft as you were powerful. You loved these pathetic humans. You felt sadness every time you destroyed one, even in His name. You failed to see the importance of your newer mission and instead focused only on death. You didn't see the necessity of death for there to be rebirth.

"But God saw favor in you. He wanted you to know humanity. He allowed you to fall, to become human so that you could see why they must first live in death. You even went so far as to have a family. Your ignorance hid you from us temporarily. It took quite a lot of pain and trials to discover who you were. Through the dreams of countless humans, I searched until I found you."

Aaron twitched. Was Ash Simpson in his dreams?

After a short pause to make sure that Aaron was still listening, Ash continued, "It's interesting, really. You don't know who you are, but you have done the same as a human that you were tasked as an angel. It is a part of your being. But God, and you can talk all day about how He doesn't make mistakes, made one this time, in my opinion. You see, you *are* the only one, the only one who leads them anymore. The rest serve them on Earth or God in heaven, but only you bridge the gap. Without you, they are lost, and if they are lost, there is a vulnerability. That is our hope. Sure, he'll get someone else, but you've been here almost forty years, and He hasn't replaced you yet. Not that time seems to matter to Him. Either way, we don't want you to lead them to heaven."

"And how would I lead them? I hate to burst your bubble, but I'm just a man," Aaron said.

"You'll realize who you are soon enough. In the meantime, there are two options. The first is to show you that humans deserve to die and willfully join us. Failing that plan, we simply need you to commit a sin in angelic form. He doesn't love you like you think. If you were to sin in angelic form, He would have to either forgive you or cast you out. Some of us hope for forgiveness. But if he casts you out or if you join us now, we could undo the universe. You see, each demon is subjugated to an angel, but not you. You alone could help us to find the seventy-two names that He used to create the universe.

With those words, we could undo this travesty." Ash continued to smile.

"I don't think that's possible. He is my God, and I will love Him. I will not help you to end the universe," Aaron replied. "And how could seventy-two names do that anyway?"

"They are not so much names or even words but thoughts that represent names. God and seventy-two angels know these names. If they were to be spoken in reverse, the same would happen to the universe."

"If you say so," said Aaron.

Ash could see that Aaron was not interested in the plan. He decided to move forward with his plans. He asked Aaron, "What is love, Mr. Todd? Isn't it doing all you can to help someone else the way that you constantly give of yourself to help others?"

"I think that's pretty close," said Aaron.

"Would God give of Himself to help you? Or would He ignore you in your time of need?"

"We shouldn't test God," answered Aaron, although his concern was growing rapidly.

"I don't think He cares about you at all. You're just an angel after all. I bet He hates your Nephilim daughter too. It's been thousands of years since He allowed such a thing. Even we see her as an aberration."

Aaron began to grow angry on top of his concern. "I respect you and all, Mr. Simpson, but I'll ask that you please not talk about my daughter that way." Aaron was absolutely sure Ash was insane, so it was best not to outright threaten him.

"Well, that's just one opinion. In any case, it is time for the ultimatum. Join us freely and wait to see if God forgives you. If he does not forgive you, then the second option is that together, we can seek out the names. So those are the options. If you won't willfully help us, I'm sure you'll come around reluctantly once He has shut you out. Life after death is not as pleasant as you might think. I'll give you a few minutes to think about it. Please don't say anything or leave until the timer is up."

Ash sat and pulled out a timer from his desk. He put two minutes on the timer and waited patiently. He was not really waiting on Aaron, though. He was waiting for a message on his computer.

Aaron was afraid to do anything other than to wait.

## 12

Meanwhile, ominous situations were unfolding, begun the moment Ash clicked the button on his computer.

Malone was sitting in the truck with the windows down. At the moment, he was playing a puzzle game on his smartphone rather poorly. His frustration showed as he sighed at the phone. "This game stinks. They totally rig it so you have to buy perks," he spoke quietly to himself. "Enough of that. Might as well check the message boards to see what everyone is up to."

Unbeknownst to Malone, a dark figure was walking through the parking lot. Actually, the same dark figure had been following him for some time. That morning, he had been with Malone since he first left home. Malone was one of two targets identified as close to Aaron Todd. As such, someone had been following him for the past week.

The man had been waiting in his car until his cell phone rang. The only message was a red button. He was somewhat unhappy that it had taken so long to get the indicator, but he was happy to now act upon it. He didn't like following his prey too long.

As he moved forward, dark gloves were slowly slid onto his hands. He located his target and started to move toward the truck, looking at the back of Malone's head as he approached.

As Malone read the various updates on several social media applications, he was startled by a sudden knock at the door of the truck. He looked over and saw the large man standing outside. "Dude, you almost made me pee. What's up?"

"Sorry to be a bother," said the man with a smile.

"I don't have any change right now, buddy. I don't think you're supposed to beg in the lot, but I can give you directions to the nearest churches or soup kitchens if you're interested," Malone said helpfully, although this man was not dressed like any beggar he had ever seen. The man wore an all-black suit that seemed expensive.

"Oh no, I'm afraid you have me all wrong."

"Sorry, dude, what can I do for you then?"

"I dropped my keys under your truck. Could you help me? I'm a bit overweight as you can see." The man gestured at his rotund figure. "Can you help me get the keys?"

"Sure, no problem. Sorry, I hadn't even noticed you there before and didn't see you drop your keys," Malone replied in his usual willingness to help anyone in need. Unfortunately, all this man needed was Malone out of the truck. It would make his job much easier.

Malone exited the truck to help the man retrieve his keys. Instead, the man retrieved a silenced pistol from under his jacket and quickly embedded two bullets within Malone's side. As Malone fell to the ground, a third bullet was carefully placed to his skull. With no sounds other than three muffled shots, Malone faded away.

The assassin took out his mobile phone and turned it to Malone's head to snap a shot with him in full view. He then quietly disappeared. No one other than those intended had seen this event unfold.

Quickly, two other men appeared out of a van, driving up behind them. On the side of the van was a clear Saligia logo. They wrapped Malone in black plastic and loaded him into the van. Returning with a mop, one of the new men cleaned up the spill of blood. Rushing back to the van, everyone had disappeared in under a minute.

*****

At approximately the same time, a delivery truck pulled up to Za's school. The same delivery truck had been following her for several days and was parked outside the school when the cell phone signal was received.

131

The driver rang the entry bell and was admitted. The cart behind her held several boxes of printer paper for the school's copiers. After the cart passed between security cameras, a little person scampered from between the boxes, sneaking down the hallway as the heavily tattooed woman driver continued with her delivery, smiling and waiting patiently at the front desk.

Disguised as a young male, the little person continued stealthily down the hallway until he approached his destination: the room Za was currently within. A young associate of his had visited the school previously as a potential student. Religious schools were always welcoming of visitors. She had made notes of Za's location throughout the day, and now the assassin made use of that information. Pulling his silenced pistol from his side, he entered Mrs. English's room. Unfortunately, she had once again not locked the door.

As quickly as he entered, he shot six rounds into the first six girls in the room. In the chaos that followed, he shot several more times, concentrating on the girls and the teacher. His associates did not want the violence to appear directed at anyone in particular, but he knew who had to die, even if all of these girls looked the same to him. With his job complete, he pulled out his mobile phone and made sure to get Za's image in the shot. He then raised his silenced pistol to his head and fired his last shot. He was sure that his reward awaited in hell.

In the screaming and disarray, the delivery woman exited before the school went into lockdown. By the time the police arrived, she was forgotten. Only sadness remained. Sadness and two photos, that is.

*****

A computer in India downloaded the photos in the back of a scamming call center under a false identity. The pictures were immediately routed through several fake servers before they arrived encrypted on a small laptop. This particular laptop belonged to one Ash Simpson who now looked down at his desk to see the pictures arrive. He smiled.

# 13

It was clear to Aaron that all of his hopes in the Saligia funding were for naught. He doubted that anyone would even believe him when he told them the story of how this meeting transpired. As the timer expired, Aaron said, "Mr. Simpson, I want to thank you so much for your time. I'm sorry. I really do want this grant, but I'm afraid you have me confused for someone else. If it's all right with you, I think I'll be going now."

As Aaron began to stand, so did Ash.

"Don't worry, my old friend. I hope that we can be acquainted again soon. Let me leave you with a thought. Humans are nothing but bags of flesh. No demon has any power to willfully kill on Earth. But oh, how easy it is to convince them to kill their own. To them, one more body is just another dead piece of meat." Ash's tone had grown more sinister. At that statement, he tossed his tablet across the table, allowing Aaron to see the pictures that Ash just reveled over. "It's a shame that they'll never get to grow old. It's a shame you thought that God loved them and would protect them. It's a shame that He doesn't care at all about you." Ash's voice rose as he continued. By now he was practically yelling.

Seeing the pictures, Aaron was not sure at first what to think. Then it set in. These were pictures of Malone and Za. These were pictures of dead people. He fell to his knees, preparing to cry. Where did these pictures come from? Ash Simpson was a deluded, sadistic, sick man. Anger took hold over Aaron. "Ahh!" he screamed. "What have you done, you psychopathic asshole? This had better be a prank or you're a dead man!" Aaron's calm demeanor was gone.

Asmodai would gladly have let Aaron kill his human form. Such a cardinal sin would count greatly against him if Asmodai had been human. Looking down at Aaron, he said, "I am no man nor can I become a dead one. I could not care less about man, and you shouldn't too. What do you think of your God now? How could He love you? How could you love a God who would allow you to go through such pain?" Ash stood over Aaron who had collapsed to the floor in sorrow. "This is no joke. I assure you that they are quite dead."

Slowly Aaron rose, overcome with sorrow, pain, and anger. He pulled out his phone and began to dial 911.

Ash swatted the phone out of his hand. "Don't you get it yet? They are not your kind. We are. Choose to join us where I'm sure that you will see just how futile humanity is."

"You are wrong, Ash. God loves them, and He will take care of them. It wasn't God that killed my loved ones. It was you with the free will God gave you!" cried Aaron.

As that statement left his lips, a door opened. A large deformed man, or at least what might be a man, barreled through the door. Before Aaron could react, the man had him in his grasp. He fought but quickly realized he would not escape this behemoth.

"We searched long and hard for you, Azriel, and that is your true name. You'll know that soon enough. Tell me right now, and you only have one chance, tell me that you hate God. If you do that for me, you may just turn a bad day good."

Realizing the depth of his situation, Aaron's reply was simple. "You are a lunatic. I love God."

"Well, then," said Ash. "You know, we're not allowed to harm humans, although it is easy to trick them into harming themselves or others. You, however, are not a human. You have no protection." Ash walked over toward a window while Aaron was dragged alongside. Ash's hand slowly morphed into something hideously demonic. He grabbed Aaron by the neck. The window protecting them from the outside melted away. Ash smiled and said, "Goodbye, old friend." At that, Aaron was tossed through the opening like a rag doll.

This was not a dream. Aaron had no power. He knew his death was approaching, although without as much fight as in his dream. Knowing Za was dead, he did not care. They would be together in the next life. He promised her that they would stick together, and they would.

For a moment, Aaron felt as if he could fly. The ground, it seemed, had a different opinion.

Above, Ash looked at his colleague. "So sad. Poor Dr. Todd heard of his daughter's death and jumped to his death." They both smiled. "Time to get down and finish the job."

In a gruff, difficult to understand voice, the hulking man said, "I think he's dead, boss."

"I don't mean down there," Ash said as he pointed out the window that slowly reformed. "I mean home."

"Good," grunted the giant.

"Now begins the next phase of the plan. We must move quickly. Azriel is no longer a corporeal being. He will now be in the pit. Let's go find him." A few moments later, two gunshots declared the death of the two mortal shells of Ash Simpson and his companion. Of course, another demon would rise to take Ash's place and form.

Aaron's eyes opened. He let out a scream, more out of complete confusion than anything else. He gathered his senses and took account of his surroundings. He was lying on a paved road, looking upward. It was ungodly hot. Not only did the air stink of sulfur and burning asphalt, it was hot, burning his lungs. He rose to his feet. Thankfully, he was wearing shoes. He appeared to be wearing the same suit that he wore to the meeting.

He thought for a moment about the meeting. Ash was totally psychotic. First, he was deluded into thinking that he was a demon, and then he was deluded somehow into thinking that Aaron was an angel. If he wasn't so angry at Ash for killing him, he might have felt sorry for him. Aaron would have brooded over his death longer if not for the need to concentrate on his current predicament.

"Hurts to breathe," he forced quietly out. "Do I even have lungs?" Talking to himself was always calming. "Why am I not in heaven? Za, wait, Za!" Despite the pain and heat, he let out a scream. The scream was followed by a cough. He now realized that speaking was best kept to a minimum in this harsh environment. Thinking was not very pleasant either. His thoughts were now full of the images he was shown of Za and Malone. Were they really dead? Were they here? These were questions he would need to find the answers to.

Looking around, he could tell that he was definitely not in what he pictured heaven to be. The road he awoke on was scattered with fires and burned-out vehicles. The ground around the road was littered with lave flows. Where there was ground, pikes covered in blood projected outward. Sometimes, parts of the human anatomy were attached. Occasional burning bushes and trees could be seen.

The scene was the same as far as the eye could see. To the best of his knowledge, he was the only one around.

Falling back to his knees, Aaron let out a cry. "Why, God? Why is this happening?" He sat there for a moment. Soft tears began to stream down his cheeks. As they formed, they were quickly evaporated by the heat. His knees were burning. He had to rise and begin moving. "Is this hell? An endless painful road to nowhere by myself?" Surely, anyone would rationally think the same thought in such a situation. However painful and harrowing his currently situation, Aaron had fortunately not even made the steps of hell.

But Aaron was a believer in Christ and fully expected to go to heaven when he passed. This belief was one of the reasons that he was able to tackle the difficult missions he set up in life. He didn't fear death, for in anything, death would just be a rebirth into a better life. But he clearly wasn't in a better life. He refused to deny his beliefs, but he needed to somehow reconcile his surroundings. The reconciliation would have to wait.

He heard a noise in the distance, like the cawing of a large murder of crows. Aaron realized it was best to remain wary of anything in this unknown environment. He ducked behind the remnants of a school bus and waited. As the caws grew louder, he sneaked a peak. It was becoming clear that the sound was not coming from crows. They looked more like pterodactyls but with four legs and leathery wings. And they were huge, large enough to see clearly at a distance.

Slowly, Aaron pulled open the emergency exit of the bus. Trying not to make a noise, he snuck into the back of the bus and closed the door behind him. He slid under the seats. "Best to hide until these things pass," he thought.

Staying in the bus proved more difficult than he thought. For one, it was like lying down in the middle of an oven. For another, a sound was slowly building, becoming louder than the flying creatures' calls. At first, Aaron couldn't discern a source of the second sound. As the volume grew, the source became clear. He was hearing the screams of children, presumably those that had died some time ago in this very bus. Aaron cupped his ears to try and shut out the sound.

As Aaron struggled to shut out the noise, one of the beasts landed on the top of the bus. Its large nostrils sniffed the surroundings. It let out a shriek which, oddly, Aaron was able to understand. He would later contemplate this fact and come to the realization that perhaps in the afterlife, everyone understood everyone else in a sort of universal afterlife language.

"I'm sure I smell something," the beast on the bus spoke as it continued to sniff while scanning left to right with its eyes. "I see nothing, though, and don't feel a cold signature from something once living. But still, I smell something."

"We smell nothing," his closest counterparts cawed.

"I tell you I smell something!" he insisted.

"Well, what do you want to do about it? There's a meal waiting ahead. We saw it enter. You know they're best when they're fresh. We want to be the first to eat them. They never taste as good after they reform. Let's get back to the pit."

"Master told us to search the road, not the pit," the apparent leader said.

This creature was the one catching a bit of Aaron's scent. Aaron hoped that the others would win the argument.

They continued their discussion. "But there's fresh food at the border to the pit. Let's go! There's nothing here. We can go back to master in a month or so and say we didn't find anything."

"You're right. Best to go for the meal we know than search for what may not be here." The creature flapped its wings and flew away with the others.

Aaron let out the slightest of sighs. He waited as long as he could to make sure that the beasts were gone before moving, for he knew he could not stay in the bus. He quietly climbed out the way he entered. He thought to crawl under the bus, but not only would that be like putting himself under an oven, something told him that he had to keep moving. "Maybe Malone's dream was for me. I've got to keep moving," he said quietly as he started walking down the road. He wasn't sure which way, so he pretended to throw a coin in the air and randomly selected to his right.

Sweat was soon pouring down his brow. Eventually, he realized that he was still in a suit. "I don't think I need this anymore," he said as he threw the jacket to the ground. He started to take off his shoes but thought against it with the heated pavement. "I guess there's no reason to be modest." Aaron then took off his pants and left them on the ground. Removing his tie, he wrapped it around his head to catch the sweat. In a t-shirt, unbuttoned shirt, underpants, and shoes, he continued down the road.

For hours, he walked. Dead charred remains littered the road, but never a living soul. "Perhaps there are others just hiding," thought Aaron, but they never presented themselves.

At certain points, he felt that it was pointless to continue. Wondering to himself, he said, "How many people just give up? Maybe that's the test. How strong is your will to keep moving?"

The lava to his left began to gurgle as if it was about to spout a shower of death. It was prone to such outbursts every ten minutes or so. Aaron took flight and ran a little way down the road. Looking back, he thought he saw something dark moving out of the heated steam. As always, best to be safe in this hell. He moved behind a truck and snuck a peak. The darkness solidified into the image of a large dog, or at least it imitated a dog in most respects, except that there were two heads, and each was much larger than normal. It was also larger than Aaron. Despite its appearance, its actions were whimsical. It acted like a puppy, jumping around and sniffing everything. One head would often playfully nip at the other. As it drew near, it picked up what Aaron assumed was a femur and began gnawing, each head on a different end of the bone.

With the animal occupied, Aaron began moving stealthily away, quickly moving while ducking and covering as possible. After he had traveled for at least one hundred meters, he began to relax or at least relax as much as he could. Rising up from his crouched position as he moved past a car, Aaron was startled. Either the same beast or its twin loomed directly in front of him, jumping and panting. Aaron let out a quick, "Ahh!" as he jumped into the car. He had escaped the flying beasts but felt doomed as he prepared to fight for his life.

Instead, the animal continued to jump and pant. Aaron slowly exited out the opposite end of the car and picked up a charred stick. Quickly, the dog-like beast jumped over the car and grabbed the stick, growling and panting, its tail wagging feverishly.

"Do you speak?" Aaron asked the dog.

"Woof," was the response. Apparently, this creature was below the intelligence level required for its voice to be translated or Aaron thought maybe he was wrong and the creatures before had at one time been human.

Aaron threw the stick. The dog ran after it and brought it back, dropping it at his feet. "Well, that's a good sign among all of the death around me. You're actually a bit friendly despite how you look, aren't you?" Aaron threw the stick again. The dog fetched it once more but didn't drop it. Aaron grabbed the stick and playfully entered a game of tug-of-war with the dog. "Wow, you're a strong one. Thank God you're not trying to kill me. But are you alone?"

"Woof," was the only response. No one, including the dog, knew what it was trying to say.

"Well, you are welcome to come along, but if you give me away to one of the less friendly creatures around here, don't expect me to be your friend. And don't try to eat me if I fall asleep. Come to think of it, I think I'm going to have to just ignore you and hope you go away."

Aaron returned to walking down the road. Although he thought of the dangers of falling asleep, he soon realized that no matter how much he walked, he did not tire. The dog was also content to continue following him. After a while, the dog was more content to try and lead.

"Okay, fellow, if you think you know the way, then go for it." Aaron began following the dog. It made him think about the dream Malone had told him about earlier. So many weird things had happened that day he was ready to believe almost anything. At that, Aaron wasn't even sure if it was still that day. He could have been walking for days for all that he knew.

After several more hours, Aaron grew weary, but not in a physical sense. He was mentally worn out. Nothing was happening. "I can't keep this up forever. I'm not getting tired. I'm not hungry. But this constant walking and dry heat is enough to drive one mad. Show me a way out of here, boy!" Aaron looked at the dog and motioned in the best dog sign language he could think for the dog to lead him anywhere. Upon seeing him, the dog jumped into a close by lava flow and disappeared. "Well, I guess that's the end of that. Thanks for nothing. If the exit is through a pit of lava, I guess I'm stuck here, aren't I? Are you running away? I just realized I never named you. Let's go with Lava Chicken."

Aaron leaned against a nearby car for a few minutes. He needed to rest his mind and think. He could only rest a short while though before the car began to burn him. It was then that he noticed one more thing. The burn on his leg from the car healed almost as quickly as it formed. "No wonder the heat hasn't killed me. Something about this place seems to be healing me. I guess it wants to prolong my pain and boredom until I'm insane. I'm not going to give up, though."

Aaron was mostly correct. True, the road healed everyone to keep them alive. He would come to realize this truth in time. But what Aaron did not yet accept was that he might actually be an angel, and as such, wounds such as these could not harm him.

Several hours later, after hiding repeatedly from other bands of roaming flying beasts, one of Aaron's many wishes came true. He wanted something different, and now there was a fork in the road. "Great, probably a 50/50 chance for life or death, and there is no clue in sight." Or was there?

Off in the distance, Aaron once again saw movement, but this movement was familiar. It was Lava Chicken or another one of his kind. Aaron looked around for something stick-like, finding what was most likely a human bone. He ducked behind a car and waited to get an impression of the beast. Who knew if this one was friendly?

As it neared, Aaron could see that it had most of the same mannerisms as Lava Chicken. Its barks sounded similar too. He decided to reveal himself. "Hey, Lava Chicken, is that you?" Seeing other sticks around, just in case he needed to grab another one, he threw his stick. The dog gave a woof, grabbed the bone, and happily brought it back to Aaron.

"Where did you go, idiot? Did you think I could follow you through the lava? Well, I can't. But—" Aaron thought for a moment. He had asked the dog to get him out of there. Then the dog appeared from one direction of the fork. Perhaps that meant something. "Well, Lava. I'll just call you Lava for short, but I reserve the right to add *chicken* or *stupid* or any fitting adjective later. It looks like maybe you were showing me the way out or at least a better way. Since you came from the right, it looks like that is the way I'm going. Lead the way." At that, the dog, seeming to understand, turned around and trotted forward.

Soon, the way ahead looked promising. The lava pits and burning bushes were moving farther away from the road. Instead, burned-out buildings were beginning to appear. It looked like a small village at first, but it grew into a larger town. As welcome as this new sight was, Aaron also realized that the many walls could hide dangers. Worse, Lava had just left the road and ran into a building.

The burned-out remains did not reveal what this particular building used to be. The building was about the size of four houses with three stories. The building only remained standing as it was covered in charred brick. Any wood would have long since burned away. The remnants of a sign were too broken to decipher. To one side of the building were three driveways with an overhang. No windows appeared on the sides of the building, but two large window openings sat at the front next to a large empty doorway. As best as he could determine, this building looked like a bank of some sort, but he would need to see the inside to be sure.

Thinking for a moment, Aaron questioned whether he should leave the road. He had been following it for days. By now, he considered it a test of resilience. Perhaps the way out was for those willing to follow the road. Perhaps it was a type of purgatory where you had to walk for as long as your sins deserved. Aaron wasn't a dispensationalist before the road, but he was willing to question any of his beliefs by now, although he still held onto his belief in God. It was only his belief in God and Jesus that made him willing or gave him a reason to keep trying. Otherwise, there was no hope.

Then he decided what to do. "Wait up, Lava. I need to mark my spot." Aaron considered that as long as he could get back to the road, he could go off for a little bit. As long as he didn't go too far, he should be able to find his way back. But he wanted to make sure. He needed something to mark the way. All he could find were pieces of loose metal in the burnt-out cars around him. "Maybe this will work," he thought out loud as he made an arrow out of bits of metal to place on the ground. He didn't want it to be too obvious, lest some flying demons saw it as a sign to their dinner. Still, he did enough to be able to recognize his direction of travel.

Moving quickly, Aaron approached the building Lava had entered. At the door, he swung a rod he had acquired to make a gash in the side of the entryway. There was no reason to go gently on the decrepit building. He swung a few more times to create a pattern like an arrow in the wall. "There, now I'll know which way I came," he said. He had seen too many movies where someone marked their path with a string or a marker only to have someone else come along and destroy or distort the marking. He was not going to make that mistake. Once satisfied his sign was secure, he cautiously entered the building.

Aaron wasn't sure why Lava had decided to enter this building. The remains of a series of cubicles with what appeared to be bulletproof glass that resisted the environment's attempt to destroy it suggested that he was correct in thinking that this was once a bank. Lava was sniffing around as if there was something to find. It darted around the cubicle area toward a metal structure behind. The door was not entirely closed on what appeared to be a vault. "Woof!" repeated both of Lava's heads.

A very light rustling noise could be heard through the small opening. Aaron lifted up his rod in a defensive posture and slid quietly behind the door. *Dang, you demon dog,* he thought, *you've given us away.* Aaron considered running but could see no better place to hide than inside the vault that concealed his potential foe. Lava continued to woof. One head looked into the vault, and the other looked to Aaron.

Aaron considered that the stench of the building might help to cover his odor. He was already beginning to smell like burnt ash. If he was quiet, he may be able to hide at the side of the vault. He slowly inched his way around. He kept his ears tuned to whatever was in the vault. Putting one ear to the side revealed rustling that appeared to emanate from a singular source. Lava might even be scaring it, which would cause it to stay in its metal edifice. Aaron would count to ten. If nothing happened, he would inch his way out of the bank. He preferred the known outside than the unknown in the cubic vault.

But wait. He heard what he was sure was a voice. "Get out of here," a male voice seemed to whisper from inside. Aaron waited some more. He peered around the vault. It was not open far enough for Lava to enter. He considered trying to open it slowly to allow Lava inside. Quickly, he changed his mind. If it was a human, what if Lava was not as nice to him? It's possible that he had somehow imprinted on the demon dog. After countless hours on the road alone, Aaron did not want to risk killing the first human he crossed.

Simultaneously, he couldn't risk that this human would be friendly either. He decided to bluff a little. In a commanding tone albeit normal volume in order to not draw any outside attention, Aaron said, "Who's in the vault?"

Aaron could sense the shocked reaction inside the vault. After a short pause, he heard the voice from inside. "Who's there? Don't come in here. I'm warning you. You better call off that dog if you know what's good for it." The voice was the scared sound of a young man. The scared part played in Aaron's favor, but even though he was in good shape, he didn't want to have to fight off someone in his prime. Still, he desperately needed to talk to another human.

Aaron did his best to calm the beast. "Lava, back off," he commanded.

Surprisingly, Lava backed off. He began to sniff around the outside of the vault, but he left the opening unattended. Aaron considered it a "he" but really hadn't determined the gender of the beast.

"Listen, I mean you no harm. I'm going to slowly open the door some more so that we can talk," Aaron informed the man inside the vault.

"Don't try anything funny. I'm warning you," replied the man.

Aaron cautiously opened the door a little more. He kept his feet back in an odd position in case the man inside tried to aim something at them from under the round vault door. "Hello, my name is Aaron," he said in a firm but nonthreatening voice.

"What?" the man replied. The man inside felt confused. Not only did he know a man named Aaron, but this voice sounded familiar.

"My name is Aaron," repeated Aaron. "Let's talk."

Aaron could feel the vault door moving. As it opened, he was in shocked disbelief at the face that stared equally in shock back at him. As far as he could tell, Malone was staring back at him. His first instinct was to rush up to his young friend and give him a hug, but he was too wary in this new environment.

"Malone, is it you?" Aaron kept his distance as he asked. "How can I know that this isn't a trick?"

Malone felt the same apprehension. How could his girlfriend's father be standing before him? Aaron was nowhere near when he was killed by that mugger. "Yes," Malone said. "Wait. What are you doing here? How are you here? I was mugged in the parking lot. You were at a meeting. Is this some kind of trick? Some demon takes the face of the man I look up to the most and then kills me when I let my guard down?"

Aaron thought for a moment. Malone was right. It was understandable. Aaron knew that Malone was dead, but there was no vice versa. Furthermore, the fact that he knew Malone was killed in a parking lot suggested it could actually be Malone.

"Listen," said Aaron in a tone asking the other to comply, "I went to the meeting, but it was a diabolical trap. Mr. Simpson was insane. He showed me pictures of you and Za dead. I didn't believe it, but then some creature threw me out a window. I fell to my death from that skyscraper." In his haste, Aaron left out the part where the delusional Ash called him the angel of death.

Malone was too exhausted to fight. He was also injured from a fall he took earlier that day. Wounds naturally healed faster here. What once was a compound fractured leg was now only a deep cut as the bone had already healed. But he was still injured beyond an ability to defend himself properly against this man.

Malone therefore heard only what he wanted to hear as humans are so prone to do, and that was enough to convince him of Aaron's identity. However, he also heard something more pressing. He repeated, "Za…is dead?"

Aaron noticed the wound on Malone. His own wounds had been healing miraculously fast. He was surprised to see such a stagnant wound on Malone, although he was sure it was healing. The wound that would not heal as quickly was the one about to be inflicted on his heart. "Yes, I think so. I mean, if you are here and dead, then her death might also be true. I was praying that they were fakes to get some sort of rise out of me before I was killed, but it now appears to have been more than that." As the words left his mouth, Aaron realized that the photos of Malone and Za were real. Ash had succeeded in wounding him.

At those words and the expression on Aaron's face, Malone was positive that this was his Aaron and not some imposter. As much as his heart sank, he could sense the same in Aaron. The two cried for a minute before regaining their composure.

"Back home, I felt like I always had a connection with Za," said Aaron. "It was like our spirits were inseparable. When I didn't feel her here at first, I just assumed that Ash was lying and that she was still at school. Of course, by now, she would be at home mourning my loss, which made me equally as sad as knowing now that she is probably dead too. But now, I do sense her. It doesn't feel like she is near, but somehow, it feels like she is down here somewhere. I hope that I'm wrong and she is in heaven. No, I just pray that she is safe if God is still out there listening. But if she is here like you, I—no, we will find her."

Malone could sense Aaron's grief. He was a young man but very perceptive for his age. He shared Aaron's hopes that Za was somewhere safe. Just the possibility made him feel better. He could also sense Aaron's resolve, and Malone agreed. If Za was there, they would find her.

Then Malone had a thought. "Wait," he said as his head perked up, "this is like my dream. How is that possible? I don't mean that I'm dreaming right now, but that this is what I dreamt." Malone was just reminded of the dream he had just a week or so prior to his death. "Remember, I was telling you about it? We were lost, and a dog came and led the way to safety. Of course, it was a normal dog in my dream. But listen, we need to follow that dog. In my dream, it led us out of the woods."

*How interesting*, thought Aaron. It was possible that there was a connection. But Malone was not going anywhere at the moment. His leg needed time to heal. And Aaron needed to rest; not that he was physically tired or hungry, but he was mentally drained again. "Let's take a moment to rest first, Malone. Your leg needs time. Let's shut the door a little while you heal, and we can talk. Lava will let us know if anything is coming. That is, if he is still here."

Aaron looked around the vault. "Lava, you there boy?" He decided to call him a boy, even though he still had no idea. Moments later, he could hear the dog panting nearby. He entered the vault with Malone and shut the door to where it was before.

The inside of the vault was as plain as the outside. Only the door with its visible gears was worth a second glance. The inside was simply a gutted metal cube with a smashed metal scaffold where drawers used to be and a few burned papers remaining on the floor.

"You're right. I need a little more time for my leg to heal. I fell while climbing a building to get a better view. My leg broke, but I was able to pull myself into this bank where I found a good hiding place. I didn't want to shut the door all the way in case it didn't reopen, but I figured it was closed enough to keep out the hell beasts that keep flying by." Malone had what looked like a wad of torn clothes tied together with his belt to cover his wound. He leaned against the vault as he lowered himself to the floor.

"Did you call that thing Lava? What is it? And where did you find it?" Malone asked.

"I have no idea what it is or why it latched onto me," answered Aaron. "Honestly, the first time I saw it, I thought I was going to have to fight it for my life. But it turned out to be friendly. Funny, animals always seemed to like me in real life too. Even cats, though I was deadly allergic."

Aaron peered out of their hideaway to try and see or hear Lava. Lava appeared as Aaron showed himself, trying to get into the vault with them. Aaron wasn't sure at first how Lava would react to Malone, but he figured they would have to try it out sometime. "I'm going to let him in," he informed Malone, "but I'll stay between you until I know it's all right. We'll have to try it out sometime."

Malone tentatively said, "I suppose. Can I have a pipe?"

"Sure, and let's not forgot to get a few more when we leave." Aaron handed Malone the pipe and slowly opened the vault enough to let Lava in. Standing between the two of them, he waited while Lava sniffed around. He snarled slightly but seemed to accept Malone's presence. Lava then curled up and appeared to prepare for a nap. Thankfully, things seemed to be going Aaron's way for the moment.

The two sat for a while, resting. After thinking at length, Aaron turned to Malone. "I'm not saying anyone here has the answer, but there is something that is really starting to seem odd to me. It didn't bother me so much at first because I just assumed that I was the only one here. It seems audacious now to think that this was my own personal hell. For a while, I was confused that I wasn't in heaven. Now I wonder if there is a heaven. Wait. I refuse to believe that. Something else is wrong. Where are all the other people? I'm sure that thousands of other people have died while I was walking on the road, and then I run into you and only you."

"I thought the same thing at first too," replied Malone. "Of all people to be in heaven, I was sure you would be. I've been alone out here so long that I also considered that it was my own personal hell. Of course, I figured hell would be me back in the sweatshop for the rest of eternity with some additional torture thrown in. But I was good, I thought. I believed in Jesus. You definitely did. Why are we here?"

"Or better yet, my young friend, why are we here together? That's what I was getting at. Where are all the other people?" Aaron was perplexed. Before Malone could render a guess, Aaron continued, "Was there some truth to what Ash was saying? He was clearly insane. I'm not the angel of death. I left that out before. The lunatic called me Azriel. He killed me and apparently you and Za because he thought I was the angel of death. But what if there is something wrong with death, like Ash was saying? What if there is an angel of death, but he is lost? I can absolutely believe in demons now that I've been here. Maybe Ash really was a demon looking for Azriel. Who knows?"

"That's a scary thought," shuddered Malone. "So without an angel of death, then we can't get to heaven. You're thinking that an angel helps guide us?"

"Yes, maybe that's part of the job of the angel of death or angels." Aaron tried to remember his conversation. "Ash said that the dead were stuck. He seemed to like it that way, and maybe that was partly why he wanted to find this Azriel. With him out of the way, maybe no one would get to heaven. Although I can't see God letting that happen. Actually, Ash wanted the angel of death to join him. For some reason, he thought that it would help them either get back to heaven…or destroy it."

"Maybe God would use that to trigger the apocalypse. Maybe that's what the demons are after," said Malone with a sudden insight.

Aaron continued, "Another thing bothering me is that I can't remember if it was Ash who told me that or the voice in my dreams. I think it's entirely possible that Ash was the voice in my dream. Now that I've met him, they surely sound similar. It's uncanny."

"Wait," responded Malone, "so you think, and at this point I'd believe anything is possible, that Ash was actually in your dreams? That almost makes sense. You said that the voice always acted like it was searching for you, and from what you've said, Ash said pretty much the same thing."

Aaron searched for the right words. "Maybe the reason that we aren't with the other dead has something to do with Ash. Maybe he was a demon, and somehow, he directed our spirits here. And if I were to be so bold to extrapolate even further, what if the only reason he had that ability is because the heavens are in unrest due to an angel being missing?"

149

"That's a lot of ifs, but as I said, I'd believe just about anything right now," said Malone. "It also makes some sort of weird sense."

Aaron looked at Malone and gave a command that he felt was vitally important, "Malone, no matter what happens here, we cannot lose faith. All right?"

"Absolutely," responded Malone.

The two sat quietly again. Neither of them was able to wrap their minds around everything that had happened. After a short pause, they both took a moment to earnestly pray. They needed strength and guidance, and God had always been the one to whom they turned.

L ava let out a yawn, but he rose up and started to pant around the cell. It seemed to signal to the two humans that it was time to move on. By now, Malone's leg was almost healed. At least one advantage existed in this hellscape. One thing was clear too: they wouldn't find their answers sitting in a bank vault. That's where you hid things, not reveal them.

Many questions remained in their minds. Where was the angel of death? Was he needed to take people to heaven? Was anyone leading the dead right now? Were they stuck? Lastly, although neither of them had actually placed a priority on this question, what was the connection between Aaron and Azriel, if there was one? But rather than continue to think about these questions, they decided to continue their exploration.

Cautiously, the two exited the decrepit bank with Lava following. Malone indicated that he had already searched the town and found nothing useful, so they headed back toward the road. Before leaving the town, they picked up additional pipes for defense. Each of them carried two, functioning somewhat like walking sticks. Following Aaron's marks to guide the way, they reached a flow of burning napalm.

"Well, that's just great," reacted Aaron.

"What?" Malone asked.

"This is where the road was. I'm sure of it," said Aaron.

"I don't think so. You can just barely see the town from here. The road was the other way to our right looking back," said Malone.

"No, that's where this fiery flow was when I entered the bank. My marks clearly lead to this point. You know what that means?" Aaron asked, feeling that the answer was obvious.

"I think I do. It means that the terrain is changing," suggested Malone.

"Just great!" Aaron exclaimed.

While the two men stood, wondering what to do, Lava jumped in and out of the fire in a playful manner. The flames seemed to energize him. Aaron picked up a large broken stone from the ground about the size of a baseball and tossed it to entertain the mutt who returned it happily.

"Well, what do you think, Lava?" Aaron asked. "Malone's dream did say to follow you."

Lava, who would normally let out a woof when spoken to, instead stood still, dropping the rock. Both heads lifted up and faced the same direction, off to what Aaron had been calling north, running along the bank of the smoldering flow.

As both men were painfully discomforted by the smell of the burning river along with the myriad other odors brought forth by their environment, they were unsure how Lava could smell anything beyond the overpowering stench. Still, Lava stood motionless. Low growls then began to gurgle in the back of his throats.

Neither man could see anything. Heat rising up from the ground caused anything to appear distorted in the distance too. But then Aaron thought to look up. To his dismay, three dark objects could be seen in the sky. It was hard to say how far they were away since he had no way of knowing how large the objects were. One thing was certain: whatever was flying their way knew that they were there, and he didn't know if they could make it back to the shelter in time to hide.

"Run!" Aaron shouted.

Without asking any questions, Malone took off back toward the remains of the town. He was faster than Aaron, but both men were running with a passion that sped up both of their personal best sprints.

The creatures were getting closer. They were about four hundred meters away by Aaron's estimate, but they were two hundred meters away from the nearest building. As fast as Aaron and Malone were running, the demonic beasts taking form in the sky were moving faster. It was going to be close.

Aaron knew that they would not be able to hide, but if they could put a roof over them and a wall to their backs, they would have a better chance.

Malone accidentally dropped one of his poles but did not stop to pick it up. He would have to make do for now.

The instant they reached their target, the first beast swooped in for the kill. Malone dove through the doorframe, and Aaron jumped through the front window of the barren house. The closest demon swiped at Aaron's foot, cutting a deep gash in his calf. The same demon put everything it had into catching Aaron, and as a result, its head smashed into the upper frame of the window, nearly knocking it out as it collapsed into the house. Another of the creatures soared over the house, circling back around. The third had slowed so that it could come to a landing right outside.

As he stood up, with most of his weight on his good right leg, Aaron let out a massive swing with the pipe closest the dazed beast.

As Aaron killed the beast, Malone was in awe. He had never seen anyone move and swing as Aaron was moving. Aaron's swipes were twice as fast as a baseball pro and with the force of a titan. The first blow nearly tore the creature in two. By the second blow from the other pipe, the creature was definitely dead.

Two halves laid on the floor. Blood repainted the burnt remnants of the house. Other than wings, a larger torso to accommodate the wings, two horns, and a deformed hideous face, the creature looked nearly human. Malone hoped that it had never been a human as he looked in amazement at Aaron.

Before he could react, one of the creatures landed on the roof. The lacking structure gave way above them as it fell through the ceiling. Simultaneously, the last creature, slightly larger than the others at about two meters tall, came in through the front opening. Looking down at their dead counterpart, they let out loud snarls, and with immediate aggression, both of them jumped toward Aaron.

Aaron had been staring at the beast he had killed. He had never attacked another living creature in his life. He wasn't a vegetarian, but he had never committed so violent an act. He was shocked at what he had done and unaware of the creatures about to pounce.

Lava was not so unaware. Letting go of the dead beast whom he thought he was helping Aaron kill, Lava jumped between Aaron and the attacking demonic figures. One of his heads tore into the side of the smaller demon, but the larger lashed out with its enlarged clawed hand, deeply cutting one of Lava's necks.

Malone swung his pipe into the same one that Lava had bitten, splitting its side open even farther. The demon let out a scream that was surely heard half a kilometer away if anyone was there to listen. It writhed on the ground in pain as Malone continued to swing at it. His body was functioning independently of his brain. Malone's survival instinct kept him swinging at the smaller demon long after its cries ended. He felt some long-forgotten angst freeing itself through his pipe as he came to his senses. Leaning against his pipe, he looked in horror at the work of his hands, just as Aaron had been shocked moments before.

Aaron recovered and began swinging his pipe at the remaining demon as Lava lay whimpering in pain on the blood-soaked floor. Although stronger than the other two, it was unable to get its claws close enough to gash Aaron. As Aaron's blows succeeded in breaking both of its arms, it turned to run away. At this point, both Aaron and Malone realized that they could not let this creature escape, no matter how sorry they might feel for its pain. They both began swinging at its wings. Aaron, clearly the dominant creature, severed one just as it made it out the door. The two men continued into the barren wasteland and finished off the beast.

"Help me get it back inside," said Aaron.

The two pulled the carcass back inside in an effort to keep it hidden from any other flying patrols. They were both covered in blood, but there was nothing that they could do about that right now.

"This is the grossest thing I've ever seen," said Malone, nearly crying.

"Agreed," replied Aaron. He looked down at his leg. His wound was almost healed.

"How did you do that?" Malone asked.

"Do what?" Aaron asked back.

"Dude, you moved and fought faster than any human can move." Malone, still in shock from the death around him, was equally in shock at the movement and ferocity of his friend. "And look, your calf is almost healed."

"Maybe it's something about this world. In my dreams, I could always do just about anything. Perhaps the same is true here. Really, though, I don't know what you're talking about. I just reacted. I don't even remember what happened anymore. It was such a blur," Aaron said. He then looked down at Lava still whimpering on the ground. "You poor thing," he said, kneeling to look after his friend.

Malone, still in shock, kneeled to look after the dog as well. If Lava had not jumped up, the large demon might have been able to take out Aaron, and Malone was not going to kid himself. Aaron may not remember it, but he fought with a power that Malone did not understand. If Lava had not been there, Aaron might have been knocked out. If that had occurred, they might not have made it.

Malone, trying to keep busy, pulled off some of the rags from the demons. Lava did not seem to heal automatically like he did and certainly not as quickly as Aaron. He tried to get cloth with the least amount of blood and handed the scraps to Aaron.

Aaron wrapped Lava as best as he could. The dog did not resist. The good head tried to lick the wounds as Aaron wrapped them. The other head was not severed, but the cut was deep. Aaron was not sure if Lava would make it.

After Lava was wrapped up, Aaron looked at Malone.

"We can't stay here," said Aaron. If these beasts had friends or at least other members of their pack or whatever, they will come looking for them. Also, that fight might have drawn attention."

Malone agreed. "Wait here," he said. Malone ran outside. He decided to do a quick reconnoiter to try and find the road. He also needed a moment alone to internalize what had happened. He had to accept what he and Aaron had done and think about how they would escape.

There it was. Off in the distance was what appeared to be a break in the terrain. The road was there, at least for now. He ran in to let Aaron know. "I found the road."

"Great," Aaron replied. He too used that short moment to try and calm himself. He then looked down at Lava. He pulled part of one of the demons toward Lava. "I think we'll have to leave Lava here. Maybe we can come back for him later, but he can't move like that."

Malone agreed with a nod of his head. He had only known the dog for a short time but had also grown fond of it, particularly after its performance in their fight.

"Hey, buddy, thanks for giving me company. I know we were going to follow you, but for now, we have to leave." Aaron then looked to Malone as he stood up. "Let's get back to the road. We can go carefully from car to fallen burnt tree remains to whatever we can find, checking out the skies and our surroundings as we go. We'll try to make the next town and then figure it out from there. But we need to get going now before something else wicked this way comes."

The two gave one last look back at Lava who was lying down, trying to rest. Then they left the house, heading for the road, carrying their blood-covered pipes.

## 16

For a while, the road was thankfully boring in terms of encounters. Aaron and Malone had avoided a couple of demonic triads. The environment was likewise becoming normal to them. They felt like they were walking down a country road after a meteor strike. The road, although broken to pieces, was passable. If one strayed too far in any direction, one might find one's self surrounded suddenly by lava flows. Despite the flowing lava, scorched tree trunks and telephone poles remained throughout the backdrop but mostly toward the road. Dotting the distance were the burned out remains of houses, sometimes with smoke still rising. Occasionally, black charred remains of vehicles would manifest. The sky persisted with a sun that always appeared overhead, circumscribed by rings of orange and red to the horizon.

They continued to cautiously move forward, stopping when possible to observe their surroundings for dangers.

After hours of walking, the sky changed to more of a natural blue, and the sun had moved half of the way toward the horizon behind them. Aaron wasn't sure if the sun had moved or if they had moved away from it. He thought that there was no reason to believe that this was a globe. Maybe in this realm, the surface was flat with the sun in one orientation, and they had moved far enough that the sun was no longer overhead. In reality, he had no idea what to think of this world.

As they continued to walk, Malone spent most of the time humming songs to keep himself occupied.

The lava began disappearing as well. In fact, Malone, uttering the first words in hours, said, "Is it me or is hell actually freezing over?"

"I'm still resisting the idea that we are in hell, but you are right, it's getting cold," said Aaron.

The two men wore only their shorts and torn shirts. If not for the fear of sunburn, they probably would have been naked from the heat before. They were quite thankful that they were not since the temperature was drastically changing. Over the last few hours, the backdrop had changed from flowing lava to crusted lava to broken crust, like a dried riverbed, to a light covering of snow. The terrain was beginning to show trees again, albeit few and mostly evergreen, and the telephone poles were no longer charred, although no electrical cords were present.

Aaron shivered as he looked at Malone. "It's definitely not like I want to turn back, but we can't go much farther like this. We might need to head out to one of the houses off the road and look for something to wear."

Malone agreed. "Although I'm guessing we can heal from the cold damage, it is still very uncomfortable." They kept their eyes out for a house. About ten minutes passed, and Malone noticed a more wooded area ahead.

"There are a lot of trees ahead," said Malone.

"Don't let your guard down," said Aaron.

Malone nodded his head in agreement. The two continued cautiously as the wooded area crept closer. At about four hundred meters away, they could see what appeared to be a farmhouse and a large barn. They were falling apart but still intact enough to be identifiable and usable.

"Wait," said Malone.

"What?" Aaron asked.

"I thought I saw something." Malone wasn't sure, but he didn't want to take any chances. Lava wasn't there to help them if something bad happened again. They needed to be cautious.

Both men stopped and ducked behind an evergreen tree. They spent several minutes with their gaze focused on the homestead, but neither saw anything.

"Let's keep moving. Rather than go slow, let's run from tree to tree or car or anything we can duck behind. Then we'll pause to check everything out before continuing," Aaron suggested.

Malone nodded his head. "I can go first, and we can switch at each stop like they do in military movies."

Malone shot off to the next tree. He hid and surveyed his surroundings. Seeing nothing, he waved Aaron ahead.

Aaron then ran past Malone to a truck, mostly intact, on the road. He likewise stopped and surveyed his surroundings. The two continued in this manner until they were within thirty meters of the house.

"Wait," said Malone again as they sat behind a tree. This time he was sure that he saw something.

He was correct. Aaron saw it too. A shadow shifted through a side window. Then a moment later, the shadow could be seen passing between drapes covering the large front window, or at least the opening where a window once stood.

They spent a moment taking in the scene. They were behind an oak tree at the end of what used to be a long driveway. Three maple trees filled the front lawn, and many evergreens occupied the sides. The trees were alive, but the shrubs surrounding the front of the house were dead, leaving only the stems behind. A thin layer of snow covered the ground lacking any grass or weeds. Only clay and metamorphic rock was beneath the snow.

The house had a small covered patio with a large solid door. A double wide window with the glass broken was to the right of the door with another single intact window off to the left. From the outside, one would guess the house had about three bedrooms. The grating off to the side suggested a crawlspace as well. The lower half of the outer wall was covered in brick, then brown siding went up to the roof. The shingles were in extremely poor shape. A hard rain or strong wind looked to be able to pull them off and possibly the plywood underneath.

After getting a good look, perhaps extended by how long it had been since they had seen an intact building, they were satisfied that they had the lay of the land. Furthermore, they were sure that they had only seen one object moving inside.

The two still agreed to be as stealthy as they could. Malone would run up first and hide under the large front window. If he was successful, Aaron would attempt the same. If Malone was unsuccessful, Aaron would run to his aid and do whatever was required of the situation.

Malone took off, quickly sprinting down the driveway. He slowed as he approached and crouched down so that he could duck under the window without running into the outer wall and without making too much noise that would be heard through the broken opening.

Counting to twenty, Aaron saw no movement. He then repeated Malone's dash, joining him under the window. Unfortunately, he slipped as he came to a stop and dropped his pipe. There was a bang that they could not be sure was not heard inside. They crouched as silently as possible, barely breathing, keeping their pipes ready and their heads low.

Neither of them wanted to be the first one to move. After a few seconds, rustling was heard from inside. They feared that a fight was about to begin.

The front door of the house opened, but nothing immediately came out. The two men were exposed, but it was too late for them to run without being seen. Aaron whispered to Malone, using his hands to help him understand, "You stay here, I'll jump through the window. We'll get this creature from both sides then."

Aaron took a deep breath. He prepared himself to jump through the window, but then he saw what could only have been the barrel of a shotgun peeking through the door. He abandoned his plan. His survival instinct was heightened in the days on the road. He automatically jumped up and grabbed the barrel, pushing it upward and quickly attempting to disarm whatever held it.

Malone, recognizing Aaron's change of plans, jumped up to tackle whatever was waiting. As he rounded the door, he just as quickly stopped. What stared back at him, equally as shocked, was an old man who fell backward from the force of Aaron on the shotgun. Aaron saw the same image. All of them let out a collective, "Ahh!"

Aaron flipped the weapon over in his hands to point it at the old man. For several seconds, there was silence until Aaron spoke. "Are you a human?" he asked.

"Of course, I'm human, you crazy fool!" The man scooted on the floor away from them.

The floor was covered in worn wood. The room in front of them contained only two recliners and one table. The table was covered in worn paperback books. Like the outside, the inside was in relatively good shape for this world, without paint peeling, but bare of any decoration. Dark drapes covered the windows, barring vision of the outside and keeping it dark.

As he scooted toward his chair, Aaron and Malone did not stop him. The old man asked, "What do you want?" He settled himself into one of the recliners. He did not appear frightened nor a threat.

Malone grabbed Aaron's pipe, and they closed the door behind them as they entered. Aaron was happy to have a real weapon, but he slowly lowered it as he assessed the old man sitting in front of them. He decided to start with the obvious. He also decided to give something before asking for something. He could remember thinking when watching action movies how rude it was of people to demand an answer from someone without any evidence of evil intent. He would give this man the benefit of the doubt. "My name is Aaron, and this is my friend, Malone. I've told you our names, what is yours?"

The man recognized the give and take presented by Aaron. He was also thankful that the shotgun had been lowered. Of course, he wasn't afraid of dying since he would surely heal if he were shot, but it would still be painful, and too many shots might kill him temporarily. Aaron and Malone were still unaware of the inability of humans to die in this world. Instead, one would slowly respawn. The old man new this truth but also did not want to feel the pain that such respawning included.

The old man also had every intent of trying to get the shotgun back as soon as possible. He plotted to be the first one into the back rooms since he had more weapons hidden back there. For now, he would play along and answer Aaron's question.

"I'm Darda, and this is my home, more or less, if anyone can have a home in this place. I'm just an old hermit avoiding trouble from the marauding creatures everywhere. I'm embarrassed to have let my guard down, but you have the better of me, it appears." Darda nonchalantly continued and asked, "And what brings you so rudely into my humble home?"

Malone wasn't sure why, but he liked this old man. He had spunk and was clearly able to survive in this weird world. Malone said, "We weren't trying to be rude. We were trying to be safe, and you were the one with the gun after all."

"Yes, my gun. Can I have it back?" Darda asked.

"Not likely," replied Aaron.

Darda didn't expect to get it back so easily if at all, but in the moment, he didn't think it would hurt to ask. "I admit, I'm surprised. Exactly how did you two manage to get so far from the pit?"

"What pit?" both men asked. Aaron sat down in one of the recliners to listen to Darda.

"What do you mean what pit? *The* pit. The only pit. Where everyone is—or well, almost everyone, that is." Darda reacted with uncertainty about the two men before him. He couldn't see how they could not know about the pit, and if they did know about it, their reaction was too natural to be an outright lie. How interesting these two were becoming.

"I can assure you that we have never been to a pit. We started several days ago, or at least it seems like days, on a lava-encrusted road. It's probably at least a week now," explained Aaron.

"You're a good liar. No one comes to the road anymore. I haven't heard of anyone on the road in at least twenty cycles if not more. Anyone that does end up on the road is picked up by the demons." Darda wasn't sure what to make of these two.

"What do you mean no one goes to the road? Does everyone go to this pit?" Aaron asked.

"Everyone goes to the pit now unless they escape. And that is no easy task. You two are a conundrum. Most of the souls used to pass the gate and end up in hell once they made it to the pit. Now the pit is full of lost souls with no one to guide them home." Darda was unsure why he was telling these two what they must have known, but perhaps they didn't know. Perhaps they were telling the truth. It wasn't unheard of for someone to start on the road. It just hadn't happened in a very, very long time.

Malone thought about what Darda was saying. "So everyone goes to this pit then?" he asked.

"Yes, everyone…at least I thought so. Everyone didn't used to go to the pit. Everyone used to start on the road. Here, they would have a chance at redemption. But no one has been on the road in years, like I said." Darda leaned over and placed his chin in his hands, his normal thinking pose. He was beginning to believe that these two didn't come from the pit.

Darda continued, "I get the feeling that you two actually are new. That's kind of exciting. It's been so long since I've seen another human on the road. There was talk of a girl a week or so ago, but that was just a rumor. You two are real."

Malone looked at Aaron. "Za!" he exclaimed.

"Za!" repeated Aaron, almost rising out of his chair. "What happened to this girl?" Aaron demanded of Darda.

Darda was surprised that the two men seemed to know about the girl. He had thought it was a false rumor, but maybe he was wrong. There seemed to be changes happening on the road. Not wanting to upset the men, Darda responded, "It was just a rumor. I listen to the demons that haunt this region. They mostly leave me alone or don't know that I'm here. Anyway, they said something about a girl, and that was it. I swear I don't know anymore."

"What exactly did they say about the girl?" asked Aaron. He started raising the shotgun but decided against it. "Listen, sorry to come off threatening. This girl is very important to us. Anything you can say to help us would be appreciated."

Thankful for the approach taken by this gentleman, Darda replied, "Honestly, all I know is that the demons found her. They didn't say anything other than she is a young girl, and if they found her, they will probably take her to Luxuria, and if she is there, and you care about her, the best option is for her to die."

"Her dying is not an option!" interjected Malone.

"Well, it may be her best option," added Darda, trying to be honest without seeming uncaring. "At least then she could respawn."

"What do you mean respawn?" asked both men.

"Respawn, reform. When you die, you wake up a week or so later somewhere else in the pit. That's how it's always been." Darda looked carefully at the two men. "You really are new, aren't you?"

Malone and Aaron found it fascinating that you couldn't die in the pit, but they also wanted to make sure that Za was safe. Malone turned without thinking to go and said, "We need to head to this pit and find Za."

"Wait," said Aaron as he stood up and put his arm around Malone's waist. "Let's get more information first. I'm in a hurry too, but let's go about this smartly. Work smarter, not harder." Aaron looked at Darda. "Tell us everything you know," he ordered.

Malone went to the kitchen and grabbed a chair from around a circular table. Bringing it back to the main room, he had a seat with Aaron and Darda.

Darda began. "I'll tell you what you need to know. The road is where souls go when they don't know where else to go and if they don't go directly to heaven. It's the starting point on your journey in the afterlife. A long time ago, there were angels on the road. They would help to lead humans to redemption. Those that were irredeemable went to the pit, but now everyone goes straight to the pit."

He continued, "But it's not really a pit or at least not one that you can perceive. It's a pit so vast that you would need to be in heaven to see it for what it is. But when you are in the pit, you still know it. You are surrounded by every evil and temptation you can imagine. People do unspeakable things there.

"When you are in the pit, it also guides you where you need to go. Notice it doesn't guide you where you want to go. It takes you where you need to go. If I had to guess, I would say that there are millions of roads such as this one that lead into the pit, but only one path leads out: the path of redemption."

"So this road leads to the pit?" Aaron asked.

"All roads lead to the pit," answered Darda. "If you go back the way that you came, you will go on forever until you wrap around infinitely and end up back at the pit. The road tests you. It leads to either redemption or the pit. Millions of people, so millions of roads with thousands of angels helping the redeemable. Eventually, the roads converge. This house is a convergence point. A little farther up, and you will find the pit. Anyone that isn't redeemed ends up in the pit. Once you enter the pit, it is nearly impossible to return. Instead, the pit sorts you until eventually, you end up in hell. Of course, right now, nothing is happening. People are just collecting in the pit, waiting for the angel of death to return."

Malone had heard enough. All he cared about was his girlfriend. "And your saying that Za was taken into this pit? If that is the case, then we need to keep going to find Za," said Malone.

"Who is Za?" Darda asked.

"She's the most important person to us, that should be enough," said Aaron. He then had a second thought. "Sorry, you're being very helpful. Despite our beginning, I didn't mean to be rude. Za is my daughter."

Darda was even more interested in these men now. No one from the pit apologized. Frankly, most anyone else would have blown his head off by now. He decided to divulge more. "Thank you, nice man. For your kindness, I will tell you even more. Like I was saying, everyone goes to the pit. Everyone used to start on the road. Maybe one in ten of the roads are pleasant with flowers, fields, small animals, etc. You might be greeted by a long lost relative. Then the angel of death, and sometimes other angels, would open a path to lead you to heaven if you were redeemed. Otherwise, you would follow the road to the pit. But the angels have gone. Now demons remove any remnants of humans and take them."

"Why wouldn't people just go straight to heaven?" Malone asked.

"They can. I'm assuming that still happens since an angel told me about it once. You see, I've been on this road for quite some time. Either way, the point of the road is the journey. Let's say that you were not a bad person but you were not a good person either. You didn't disbelieve in Jesus, but you didn't follow him closely either. The road gives you time, even lifetimes to reconcile your beliefs. If you reconcile correctly, the angel of death can open a path. If not, well, you end up in the pit. Those bound for hell always end up there. They might even die multiple times on the road to get there. I'm guessing that the truest believers in Christ still go straight to heaven, though."

Darda leaned in toward the men and made one last statement. "Makes you wonder why you're on the road, doesn't it?"

"If people believe in Christ, they should go to heaven. Christ already paid the price for their sins. But we believe in Christ. Why are we here? You're right, Darda, I do wonder." Aaron wasn't so much asking Darda as he was also asking himself and Malone. Why were they there?

"As far as I know, the true believers are in heaven," said Darda, "but few are really true believers. Some need time, and God is apparently willing to give them that time. It drives the demons insanely mad. God forgives them even after death, but just one mistake, and He never forgives the demons."

That was the same language from Ash. As Aaron was thinking about Ash, Darda looked up and said, "I'm parched. Care for a drink?"

"I'm not really thirsty or hungry. We haven't needed anything," Aaron responded.

"Quite right," said Darda, "but sometimes it's nice to taste a little something, if only to feel alive."

"What do you have?" Aaron asked not out of a desire to drink but more out of curiosity of what this man could possibly have to drink in a place like this.

"Well," responded Darda, "we're not on a good convergence point. The only thing to drink here is well water. But I happen to have a bottle of whiskey that I break out on special occasions. If I wait about a year between drinks, the damn bottle seems to refill itself. Something tells me it's been at least a year since I last opened it."

Still not completely trusting him, Malone stopped him from rising. "Where do you think you're going?"

"Relax," said Aaron, rising from his chair, "he wants a drink. But we won't let him go anywhere unescorted."

Darda looked disgruntled at Malone as he stood up. He wouldn't be giving him any whiskey. He walked into the kitchen, followed by Malone and Aaron, and opened up the first cabinet, pulling out a bottle slowly. He might have drawn it out faster if not for the suspicious eyes watching him. "I only have the one glass, but we can always drink from the bottle."

"Drink however you want, Darda. We won't be having any," said Aaron.

"You know, I'm not thirsty, but for some reason, a glass of water sounds good, just to remind me of what it was like," said Malone. "I suppose I could drink right out of the faucet."

"Then despite your distrust, I will let you use the glass," said Darda as he handed Malone the one glass from the cupboard that the whiskey was in. "The faucet works."

Darda wasted no time taking a swig of whiskey. He then returned it to the cupboard.

Malone filled the glass with water from the faucet and took a drink. He wasn't satisfied, but neither was he disappointed. It was water. For a moment, he expected urine to come out of a faucet in this world. He just wanted to taste something, and water, unfortunately, had little to no taste.

As it was dark in the kitchen, the men returned to their spots in the other room. When Darda sat down, he continued his story. "You need a bit of a hermit mentality to deal with the road anymore. Since there is no redemption, people just naturally wander into the pit or the search groups get them. Lately, it's like redemption is gone. For some reason, people just start at the pit, bypassing the road entirely."

Leaning toward Aaron, Darda added, "I used to track demon and angel activity along the road. Sometimes, an angel would work on someone's soul in an effort to turn them to the light. Other times, demons would torment those on their way to the pit. One time, I even got to see Azriel."

"What did he look like?" Aaron quickly asked. In the back of his mind, he considered that maybe he looked like Azriel. Maybe that was why Ash had killed him.

"He was a regular-sized man the way that he presented himself. You know that they can change form. But he had numerous translucent glowing ribbons coming out of his back. But they weren't really ribbons. They were his wings. He didn't so much fly, though, as much as use the wings to direct the rest of existence around him. He carried a sheathed weapon. I assumed it was a scythe or sickle of some sort, but that's probably just because of stories of the Grim Reaper. It was probably a sword. I don't think that the two are anything alike, but what can you do with people's imaginations? The other thing I'll never forget were his eyes."

"What was so special about his eyes?" Aaron asked.

"His eyes were like lights shining in front of him. I'm not even sure that they were eyes. He seemed to just know where everything was." Darda sat there, remembering the sight.

"How do you know that was Azriel?" Malone asked. Aaron thought to himself that it was a very good question.

Darda snickered. "Because every demon ran scared. Even the other angels scattered off. But I swore I heard one of them call his name. I heard some of the demons talking about Azriel. They were torturing me at the time as they sometimes do until they get tired and let me go. According to them, Azriel got tired of killing humans. He was blind to his purpose. If God loved the humans, he didn't understand why they needed to die. He let his questions be known, and the next thing everyone knew, he was gone. The demons thought that maybe he was wiped clear from existence to punish him for questioning God. They really didn't seem to care what happened to him."

"Where did the other angels go? Why aren't they helping?" Aaron asked.

"I don't know the whys of the universe, only the whats," explained Darda. "And you two are not in the pit. You even say that you started on the road. I didn't say this before, but only an angel should be able to bypass the rules in that way. You truly are intriguing, you see. The times are changing again."

Malone looked at Aaron. He thought back to watching Aaron fight earlier. Was Aaron some kind of angel? Was that why Ash had them all killed? Perhaps the only reason he and Za started on the road was because of their association with Aaron. Maybe Za was an angel too.

Aaron had not registered the fact that one of them might be an angel. He simply sat in silence, thinking. Was all he was hearing the truth? The pit kept returning to his mind. They needed to get to the pit. Even if it was true that there was no return, he would rather be with Za in the pit.

As if reading his mind, Malone spoke, "I'm ready. Let's get to the pit and find Za. We need to save her."

Darda warned them, "The pit is a collection of every evil that you can think of. As you go farther in, the sin multiplies. The most heinous of murder and torture, the most lustful of orgies—anything is possible. If you ever heard the saying that the only rule is that there are no rules, well, the pit is where that saying is true."

"How is that not hell?" Malone asked.

Darda smiled. "Because there is still light. All of man's sin are put on full display in the light. Once they are sorted, they go into the dark. Then they are in hell. But no one is sorting. Minos doesn't know what to do since so many in the pit were supposed to go to heaven. So right now, everyone is accumulating in the pit. I have a feeling that perhaps your presence might signal a change, though."

"Minos?" asked Malone, thinking Aaron probably knew.

"If Azriel directs into heaven, then Minos sorts into hell. If you travel far enough into the pit, you come across the gates of hell. If you try to enter it, it spits you back out. Now, if Minos throws you in, then the current carries you away." Thinking about hell made Darda's demeanor change. "I've got to say, I've been here a long time. There was no Jesus in my time. I followed God's rules, but I also abandoned them to stay on the road. I'm sure that I can still find redemption, but it's not like I could go on now anyway. No one can."

Aaron looked at Darda. Darda seemed wise enough. Aaron wasn't sure why he chose to stay on the road, but maybe in his wisdom, he knew he wasn't ready for heaven, and that was sad. Or maybe he was just waiting for Azriel to return before he sought redemption.

At that, their conversation ended. Aaron and Malone made their plans. They still weren't sure that they could trust Darda, but they would keep their guards up moving forward. Then they prepared to exit, taking the shotgun and poles with them. Although he wasn't sure if Darda had other weapons, Aaron left one pole behind. He couldn't leave him defenseless.

Darda, recognizing the gesture, motioned the men into the kitchen before they left.

"We don't need water or food, Darda," said Aaron as they followed him to the kitchen.

"Yes, but you may need this," said Darda, reaching into a drawer and pulling out a knife. He didn't need to give them anything nor did he need their pipe. But the fact that they had chosen not to leave him defenseless, not knowing that he had other weapons, meant that they deserved more of his help.

Malone raised his pipe in defense in case Darda was planning a last treacherous act.

Darda, noticing the movement, switched his grip, holding the knife by the blade. "I'm not going to overpower the two of you with one hunter's blade, young man."

Malone lowered his pipe and apologized to both Darda and Aaron.

"This blade is silver. You may find it useful. But keep it hidden. You see, many demons are severely harmed by silver, and many humans will kill to acquire such a blade."

"Why would you give us this blade then?" Malone asked, still not trusting the old man and truly not understanding the gesture.

Darda opened up the drawer further. Inside were several silver knives. He had at least one to spare that looked like a hunting knife with a long blade and serrated edge for cutting.

Heading to the front door, Malone noticed some clothes lying around down the hall. He had forgotten how cold they had been. So had Aaron. Learning from their time together, Malone politely asked Darda, "May we have some clothes?"

"Yes." Darda sat back down in his chair and watched the men add to their clothing. Darda knew that the road and the pit could have highly variable temperatures. The men would need more clothing.

The clothes they acquired were still rags, but better than what they had before. Once prepared, they left Darda and continued on their journey. In the back of his mind, Darda knew that this meant trouble for him moving forward.

# 17

On a relative scale, it did not take long for the two men to approach what was clearly the end of the road or at least an interruption. Their surroundings had shifted back from cold to warm, the ground behind them was mostly covered in prairie type grass, while before them was more of a savannah. The shift in environment happened along a clear line marked by the end of the road. Only broken pieces of road could be seen up ahead, tracing perhaps where it continued or once was.

The sun had also shifted. It looked as if it was just past twilight with not enough light to make things clear but enough to be able to see.

Malone looked at Aaron and said, "Shouldn't there be a sign telling us to abandon all hope?" Malone was actually expecting to see a sign, any sign, indicating the end of hope.

"I don't think we're actually in hell yet, but it would be appropriate if there was such a sign," responded Aaron. "I was expecting to start seeing people, but I'm not seeing any movement for as far as I can see." As Aaron looked out over the waste, he was sure that he could see tens of kilometers, even in the low light.

Aaron continued, "From what I gather, we've been traversing something like limbo between heaven and hell. I'm not sure if stepping off of the road ahead will take us into hell, but it is definitely a move in that direction."

"But one we have to take if there is any chance of finding Za," added Malone.

Aaron nodded his head in agreement. "Then it's settled. Onward we go."

Guardedly, the two stepped off the end of the road. Nothing spectacular or in any way out of the ordinary happened when they crossed the boundary. The two did, however, notice a slight downward grade to the ground.

"Do you notice that?" Aaron asked stepping back-and-forth.

"What?" Malone asked back.

"The ground is sloping downward. It's the only difference I've been able to notice. Maybe it will get steeper as we go, more like a pit," explained Aaron.

Malone shrugged, and the two continued slowly. There were no trees or dead cars to hide behind, but the brush was relatively high. If they stooped down in various patches, they could still apply an amount of stealth to their movements.

After about an hour of travel, covering at least five kilometers by Aaron's estimate, they noticed movement in the distance. "Look," he motioned to Malone to look ahead.

"Yes, I thought I saw something too," acknowledged Malone. "I wish we had a telescope."

"You know, it's odd, but the longer we spend time here, I think my vision is getting better. I'm sure that there are five men up ahead, but they must be half a kilometer away, maybe farther," said Aaron.

"All I can see is blurry some movement, but there is certainly something there. Let's keep moving closer to get a better look, but carefully," suggested Malone.

"Sounds good. We'll keep low and slow," added Aaron.

As they stealthily shifted forward, they noticed that there were more groups even further ahead. At least four different groupings were evident between ten and two o'clock. Also, buildings could be seen scattered about like a countryside with homes every kilometer or so. They were too far off to comment on their structural integrity.

As they approached the first group, it was getting more difficult to be sure that they were remaining unseen. Small hills and valleys were developing, but unfortunately, one had to go up one hill before one could hide in a valley.

About one hundred meters away from the first group, they crouched behind some brush. It was clear that in addition to the five men, there was one other individual crawling on the ground that the men were taking turns kicking while laughing.

"Trisitia," mumbled Aaron.

"Huh?" Malone asked.

"I'm sorry," replied Aaron. "I was thinking out loud. I said Trisitia. When I was researching Saligia, I did a lot of reading on sin. Trisitia was the sin of discouragement or bullying. This looks like a manifestation of sin in this dark place."

"So we may not be in hell but we are definitely near its influence," Malone said.

"I don't see any weapons on them. I would just as soon go around, but it would be nice to get some information. The groups may get larger as we move forward. Let's walk toward them like we own the place. Don't let them intimidate you in any way," Aaron suggested. "Remember, we have a gun."

Malone puffed out his chest in a sign of machismo and agreed, his pipe tightly gripped in his hand.

"Don't let on that we're new here," suggested Aaron as he stood up.

Malone stood up beside him, and the two started walking toward the group of men.

As they approached, it was clear that the men were in the midst of terrorizing a middle-aged overweight woman. Various slurs were repeatedly shouted her way, making fun of her gender, weight, hair, skin color (which was just as white as the group of men), her mother, etc. "Your momma's so fat, they call her belt the equator," was the last thing said as they approached. When the men saw Aaron and Malone, one slammed off one more foot stomp on the woman before turning to them.

From this distance, Aaron wasn't sure if the woman was even alive. Thankfully, being the first woman that they had seen, it was not Za.

"Look what we have here," the man in front who clearly gave off alpha paralanguage said. "New meat."

Were they planning on eating the woman? Aaron and Malone considered that a possibility. Aaron looked at Malone. An unspoken understanding existed between them that they needed to help this woman, and they couldn't show any weakness.

Aaron raised his shotgun.

"Ooh, he's got himself a boom stick!" the head man said as he kept moving toward them. "Like you could kill me in this place."

"Maybe not kill, but hurt really bad is certainly on the table," responded Aaron as he checked that the weapon's safety was off.

The threat, albeit small, was enough to make the men stop moving toward them. They were no more than five meters away. The main man had a pointed van Dyke beard, which almost made Aaron snicker at how stereotypically evil it appeared. The oldest man, probably in his fifties if age was a thing there, had a full beard. A red-headed man had a mustache. The other two were distinguished only in that they were the youngest, looking like they were in their twenties, and one of them was slightly overweight in comparison. Their heights were all around six feet tall, and the others were of average weight. From their appearance, a two on five fistfight would not end well. Aaron thought it best to keep a safe distance for now.

"Looks like you guys are having a bit of fun at that woman's expense," said Aaron. "Is she even alive?"

"She just died," responded the redhead. "We ran out of matches or we would've set her on fire. If you burn 'em, you never know where they'll pop up next. I like to burn them. Wish I had a match."

"Shut up," said the lead man. Making a double take, he added, "You can burn the next one if we find some matches, all right?"

The redhead smiled.

"I think we'll just keep going into the pit," said Aaron.

The oldest man smiled. "The pit is everywhere and the pit is nowhere. Sin surrounds you." He was clearly out of his mind, almost shell-shocked.

"Shut up, old man," said the leader. "I'm going to put my foot up the rear of the next person to speak," he added, looking over all of his droogs.

Malone and Aaron slowly started to sidestep the hoodlums. Aaron was sad that they could not help the woman, but the leader had inadvertently told him one important point. You definitely didn't die permanently here, and if you died, you could manifest somewhere else. Therefore, no matter what, they needed to find Za before someone like this group of misfits did.

"Wait, what's your hurry there, friend?" the leader interrupted their exit.

"Yeah, what's your hurry?" laughed the heavy young one right before the leader turned around and smacked him over the head.

Aaron had no intention of sticking around and risk letting his guard down. It was best to maintain a position of authority and continue. "No hurry, but we'll be moving on nonetheless," said Aaron, now five meters beyond the men.

The leader kept his eyes on them, but he didn't seem interested in taking any risks at that moment either. The two groups kept eyes on each other as they separated.

Once they were about twenty meters away, Aaron felt that it was safe to continue forward, looking back occasionally. By one hundred meters, the group of men had returned to beating on the dead woman. Aaron and Malone continued their cautious movement forward toward the next group.

"I'm not sure," said Aaron. "I might have liked the lava-surrounded road a little better."

"There's nothing I like about any of this," added Malone.

Both men had seen many evil things, but seeing this person killed weighed heavily on them. Demons had recently died by their hands, but humans were another story. They were sickened by what they had seen but also understood that worse probably laid ahead.

## 18

It had been weeks since the death of Aaron, and there was no news of his capture. The demons were concerned. If he was killed, he would not respawn. He was an angel after all. He would return to heaven. They couldn't risk that happening, and in the pit, it was a common occurrence.

They also couldn't afford for Azriel to discover fully who he was, at least not yet. Once he regained his full power and authority, it would take a legion of demons to contain him. For their plan to work, they needed him to recant his loyalty to God or else to openly commit a deadly sin before that happened.

Making matters worse, they could not afford Lucifer finding out, and each day an angel was in the pit, the scent would grow stronger. No angel had been in the pit for a century, even Azriel. They had always stayed on the road. If Azriel's light began to shine, it would be unmistakable. Lucifer would discover his presence and most likely kill him, returning him to heaven. And if Lucifer found Azriel first, he might discover their plot, which could bring death upon some of them as well.

They understood that Lucifer had his own plan. He desired to play out God's will, waiting for his thousand years of reign on the Earth. Some thought that Lucifer believed that if he proved himself during that time, he might be forgiven. Lucifer was first among the angels at one time. He may believe he could return.

For the time being, six demons sat around a table, concerned.

Prince Seere remained silent. He no longer cared about the plan, but he knew that not attending might be seen as traitorous. While he didn't care about what others thought about him in general, he did not want legions of demons hunting him down to maintain his silence. It was better to simply keep showing up, perhaps taking a nap if the meeting ran long. The others were still very much interested in the plan.

Asmodai opened his mouth, intending to speak first. Beleth, as he saw Asmodai's mouth opening, quickly took the table and opened the discussion. "Where is he? Anyone? Where is Azriel? My legions have searched throughout the pit. They have returned empty-handed every time. My best human scum contacted every corner and found nothing. I even ate several of them as motivation to no avail."

Gaap added, "I have done the same. There is no sign of him to the south, and I know of everything to the south." He glared as he spoke, challenging anyone to question his authority to the south.

"Not that we expected it, but none of the whores admit to seeing anyone to his description," Alabasandria took her one opportunity to add to the conversation.

Asmodai, regaining control, calmed the group. "Yes, and he is not to the east either. Have no fear. Although unlikely, it is not impossible for him to go a month without detection."

"It took only a week to find him last time," argued Beleth.

"It also only took me twenty years to find his human form. Things are clearly different this time. But there is no indication that anyone has seen him. He has not been killed nor discovered his angelic form or there would be clear signs. There are two possibilities as to why we haven't seen him," Asmodai explained.

"And what are those?" Duke Buné asked, not wishing to go unheard.

Asmodai continued, "He might be to the north. Granted, that is not ideal. We can't easily search through Belial's domain, but we do have searches going on through our human routes. If he is there, we can still find him before Lucifer does."

"We can all send human contacts to the north," Beleth surprisingly agreed, "but what is your second possibility." Beleth didn't want to admit any ignorance, so he spoke as if he had many possibilities but wondered of which possibility Asmodai spoke.

"It hasn't happened in a long time, but everything else has been different this time. One of my demons suggested that maybe he appeared on the road," Asmodai replied.

"The road," whispered several of the demons. To be honest, none of them had thought to check the road. No one had appeared there in so long.

"What makes you think he is on the road?" asked Beleth.

"Two separate triads of demons disappeared this month on the road. I just received word of their disappearance yesterday. One died and was respawned. The other is still missing. No demon has disappeared on the road in fifty years, yet six went missing this month." Asmodai smiled as he realized he had surprised the other demons.

"We need to immediately scour everywhere those triads were," Beleth ordered.

"Wait," said Asmodai. "I'm not saying that they are on the road. I'm saying that they were on the road. Those demons were gone for a while. It's also hard to say how long it took them to respawn."

"Then what would you suggest we search?" asked Beleth.

"The area of the disappearances coincides with a conjunction spot where my sources last saw Darda," Asmodai added.

"Darda. How is he still on the road? I thought he ascended generations ago," Gaap said.

"No, he craves knowledge. The disappearance of Azriel in particular would entice him to remain. I had the pleasure of torturing him no more than fifty years ago. If it is true, and he was anywhere near Azriel, then we need to speak with him. He'll tell us what he knows whether he wants to or not." Beleth smiled as he finished.

"Then is it decided?" asked Asmodai. "We continue to search the north with our humans. But in the meantime, I have already sent a legion to the last known junction point of Darda. They have one hundred tracker hounds at their disposal. Within the week, we will know more, and I will send word to everyone."

"We'll reconvene then if anyone discovers any news," said Beleth.

They all nodded in agreement. Small sparks of hope could be felt throughout the room as the demons dissipated back to their own corner of hell.

A aron and Malone continued forward, watching one group of lost souls after another but not directly interacting. At one point, a clear suicide passed by with blood remaining on his forearms. Aaron sighed in sadness at anyone who would allow his or her last act on earth to be a sin. Larger groups were beginning to appear also. They might see ten to twenty people, but they would usually be in two or three groups fighting each other. As the number of people increased, it actually became easier to pass unnoticed. The level of depravity and violence also increased.

Houses were more common as well. One in particular was surrounded by severed heads on pikes. As they walked by at a distance, Aaron was sure that one of the heads disappeared. He thought that it must be dissipating to reform as a live individual somewhere else. What a horrible way to spend the afterlife it must be. Then, continuing to think, how more horrible must the behavior farther in the pit be?

Thirty minutes later, they reached what appeared to be a village, the first one that they had seen. From far away, the two could see an immense building that drew their attention and caused them to walk in that direction. It was not necessarily tall, maybe four to five stories, but it spread out over the size of a large city block. As they approached closer, at least fifty to sixty houses could be seen lining four intersecting rock streets, similar to a scene from a small ancient Grecian village. The various sized villas surrounded the large building, which appeared to be a library if one was to believe the Bibliotheca sign carved into the stone in the front.

The Bibliotheca building was immense. Even if it was only half full of books, it could easily hold fifty million volumes, and that assumed that there was no basement. The walls were made of stone with no windows on the first floor or the first floor was two stories high with windows near the top. A small flight of concrete steps led up to two large French doors made of solid wood stained light brown to match the color of the stone and most of the surroundings. There was no grass, but hundreds of trees of all types surrounded the building, blocking most of the first row of windows.

As they entered and walked through the town, no one attacked them, but it was obvious that they were always being watched. Malone looked at Aaron and said, "This town seems harmless enough. Of course, that quiet kind of scares me."

"I know what you are saying," agreed Aaron. "To be honest, I'm intrigued by the library. I wasn't expecting to see something like that here. Let's take a look."

"I'm game if you are," Malone smiled. He was actually becoming a little tired and bored of walking through the wasteland, and even reading a book appealed to him.

As the two approached the doorway, a man came running out from a building across the street, the first individual to approach them directly since entering the pit. "Stop!" he ordered.

Aaron and Malone did not want to upset anyone. They halted. Aaron looked at Malone and motioned him to make sure that he did not raise his pole. He wanted them to remain nonviolent unless provoked.

"Don't go in there," the man pleaded.

"We're just curious about this building. Why don't you want us to enter?"

"No one should enter the Bibliotheca or you will never be seen again," the man warned.

"Well, that doesn't sound very scholarly," responded Aaron.

"What do you seek in the Bibliotheca?" asked the man, realizing that he had their attention.

"I suppose you could say we seek information or at least an end to boredom," Aaron replied.

"What knowledge are you looking for that you can't find out here?" asked the man, continuing his questioning.

"We're just looking for anything that will help us find our friend," answered Malone. He was trying to think of a reason other than to end boredom that he wanted to enter the library.

Speaking in a gentler tone, the man said, "Listen. My name is Garrett. I am the self-appointed watchman of the Bibliotheca. That building is dangerous. I'm warning you. No one that goes in has come out in the twenty years I've been watching it."

"Hi, Garrett, it's nice to meet you. I'm Aaron, and this is my friend, Malone," said Aaron, introducing himself. "What's in there that is so dangerous?" asked Aaron.

Garrett was surprised at how pleasant Aaron was. Most people simply tried to kill him from his experience. Answering the questions, he said, "It's a library. I've opened the door, and all that I can see is a library. But no one ever comes out. A little knowledge is apparently a dangerous thing."

"Is there someone or something dangerous inside other than just books?" asked Malone.

Garrett continued, "The only people I've ever seen enter were atheists who were too self-important to really respond. From what I can gather, the Bibliotheca is filled with those who value knowledge above all else, even God. That quest for information possesses them until they know nothing else. Once they are engulfed in that quest, they never return. It's almost like some perceived ignorance is their torture, and they will keep working to learn more as if anyone could ever know everything."

"Is it safe to just open the door and look inside?" asked Aaron.

"I did it once, but a friend held onto me. Just the idea of wanting to know something is enough to draw you in. I'd recommend against it, but if you must understand it for yourself, we could open the door and hold you back from entering," suggested Garrett. "But first"—Garrett called out to a building across the street—"I'm sending them in, Jackson!" Garrett then looked back at the two men and said, "It's been refreshing to actually talk to a civilized person for a change. You must be like us, trapped in this pit, hoping for Jesus to

183

return. Since I like you, I feel like I need to tell you that you two need clean clothes."

The two had already forgotten how they were wearing nothing but dirty rags. "Yes, definitely," added Malone.

A large muscular Asian man opened a door across the street. Aaron and Malone approached in a guarded fashion. Jackson ignored their shielded nature and said, "You look like marauders. You should change."

Aaron and Malone went into what was apparently soldiers' quarters and returned wearing clean underwear, white dress robes with jackets, socks, and shoes. As they returned, something processed in Aaron's mind. He addressed the two men, slightly bewildered. "Earlier, when Jackson spoke, I could swear that he did not speak English. I didn't realize it at first, but as it simmered in my brain, it hit me. How did I understand what he was saying?" As Aaron asked the question, he quickly realized that it might have been a mistake. The answer may be obvious to anyone in the pit, and he just advertised his novice status.

Malone heard the question, causing his own executive brain functions to realize the same truth. Jackson spoke Spanish, Portuguese, or something similar, but he fully understood. He knew a little Spanish but definitely not a word like marauder.

Garrett and Jackson looked at each other. How could anyone not know the answer to that question? They had known the answer for so long that they could not remember a time not knowing.

Aaron could tell that the men recognized his inexperience with the pit. He was unsure how they would make use of that knowledge, though.

"How can everyone understand each other?" Garrett repeated. "In this place, the brain merely interprets the visual representations you wish to express, and you don't realize what language you are speaking or hearing. Everyone knows that. The only way you wouldn't know that is if you were newly dead, but no one newly deceased has been here in so long and definitely not with a shotgun. How is it that you can be new and yet old at the same time?"

Honesty had worked so far with Garrett, and he had actually answered the question. Aaron decided to continue with honesty. "We have only been here for about a month, and that was the first time someone didn't speak English to us or at least the first time I noticed." Aaron suspected now that Darda had not spoken English either.

"No one, and I mean no one, has made it to the Bibliotheca who hasn't been in the pit for a while. I wandered the pit for three years before ending up here. Since discovering its nature, I've been warning people ever since. How can I know that you are not lying?" Garrett asked.

At that question, it was clear to Aaron that they were not in trouble for being new. Rather, they were in trouble because Garrett assumed that they had deceived him at some point. Aaron would need to choose his words wisely. "I'm not trying to deceive. We're telling the truth. We mean you no harm. We were only curious. Like I said, we are new here. Honestly, when we saw the library, we thought maybe we could find some answers about this place." Aaron then considered to play on their compassion, if they had such a thing. "We have to learn as much as we can as fast as we can. My daughter died with us, but we have not yet been able to find her."

"Yes," added Malone. "Za, a beautiful redheaded teenager. Have you seen her?" He didn't expect them to have seen her, but he couldn't help but ask when Za was brought into the forefront of his mind.

Jackson nodded his head in the affirmative toward Garrett as if accepting what the two were saying.

"I am sorry. It is entirely logical and possible that what you say is true. And no, we have not seen a girl or anyone other than the haughty that entered the Bibliotheca in a long time. The Bibliotheca will not help you find this girl. Thousands of years of human philosophy may line its walls, but men spend thousands of years within its walls, becoming no wiser. If you seek this girl, then you should keep looking. Be mindful that you are not forever lost in your pursuit."

Aaron considered those wise words and thanked Garrett. He looked at Malone who was looking intently at him as well. "We need to be careful, my friend." Looking back at the two men, Aaron said, "Since we're here, though, I really would like to at least look inside."

The two men looked at each other, saddened that another soul may be lost.

Sensing their disgust, Aaron added, "No, really, I promise we won't go in. We'll just open the door and look inside. I personally give you permission to pull me back if I start to be tempted to enter."

"Be careful, Aaron. And trust me, we will pull you out, even if you fight against it," said Garrett.

Malone was first to the grand doors of the building. He pulled one of them open, not letting go of the handle as a way to anchor himself to the outside.

The two looked into the Bibliotheca. The plain outside of the building did no justice to the extravagance of the inside. It was not inlaid with jewels or anything physically precious, but the artwork hung on or painted directly onto the walls was exquisite. A huge cathedral ceiling with all types of paintings filled the inside. Tapestries hung on the walls, and sculptures adorned every nook possible. It was not just a feast of books but of art. Still, shelves filled with innumerable volumes of books were plentiful.

Aaron could feel himself being pulled in by a desire to know more. He caught himself and grabbed the handle to the other door as Malone had done.

The visible occupants of the Bibliotheca included great writers and poets, so-called enlightened philosophers, oracles of pseudo-science, and masters of scientific principles. They did not consider themselves to be gods, but they also did not fear nor believe in God. This lack of belief was likely what lost them in their never-ending quest for unfulfilling information. Aaron called out to an old looking man in a white toga with a red rope around his waist.

"Pardon me," said Aaron to the man, shouting into the building.

"Oh, yes, probably," was his initial response.

"Hello, I'm Aaron and new to this library. Who may I ask am I talking to?"

"If you must know, I'm Polyphenia, a renowned student under Plato."

Aaron looked puzzled having never heard the name Polyphenia before.

The old man apparently recognized Aaron's lack of recognition and added, "If you do not believe me, then go seek out Plato or Socrates on the lower levels. I suppose it is not obvious to the lesser mind." Polyphenia then ignored the men and returned to his reading.

"If we were to enter here, would we be able to find out where my daughter is?" asked Aaron.

Disgruntled at having his reading interrupted, Polyphenia retreated farther into the library.

Aaron wanted to ask more. As he took a step forward, Garrett grabbed him and threw him away from the doors.

"Good call," said Malone, not angered by Garrett's actions.

Aaron regained his faculties. "Yes, thank you. I could feel some desire for knowledge drawing me into the building. I surely would have been trapped forever had I entered."

Aaron and Malone then turned away from the Bibliotheca. They thanked Jackson and Garrett for the clothing as they continued their journey.

Jackson and Garrett returned to the safety of their guardhouse as Aaron and Malone left. "I can't remember the last time we saved someone from entering," said Garrett.

20

As the two left the haughty village, Malone turned to Aaron. "Which way? Do you feel anything?" Malone remembered how Aaron had said that he could sometimes feel Za.

Aaron looked around. He noticed that his eyes had fully adjusted to the twilight of the pit. The marauding groups that occupied the plain behind them were gone. A deserted wasteland with occasional brush and trees lay ahead. "She's definitely still in front of us. For now, all we can do is keep moving," responded Aaron.

After about an hour of walking, they noticed several converging pathways. There were no roads, but it was clear that many people followed this route. Much like an animal running in the woods, trampling the underbrush, the dirt was compressed along the path. There were paths to their left and right. "It could be either way. I can't feel anything more one way or the other," Aaron revealed to Malone. They both also noticed that the ground was graded downward. They had clearly passed deeper into the pit.

"I don't have a coin to flip. We can play odd or even."

"Odd we go left, and even we go right," suggested Aaron.

The two men placed their hands behind their backs, and upon revealing, Aaron had two fingers out, and Malone had three. Left it was.

Before they turned, Malone noticed something moving toward them. He pointed, and Aaron saw it too, but then it ducked down as if it had been swallowed by the ground. They did not know what to think. They began to move along the path, but several seconds later, the ground burst open behind them. They each pulled their weapons, ready to attack, but two familiar faces gnarled back at them. It was Lava. He was identifiable by the massive scar across his left neck. Apparently, demon dogs could heal remarkably well.

Maintaining a defensive posture just in case they were wrong or Lava had turned somehow against them, Aaron said, "Lava, is that you boy? How did you find us?" He put out his hand for the dog to come closer and sniff.

Lava approached quickly but non-menacingly to lick Aaron's hand, letting out his common woofing noise. Aaron was pleased to see his new friend again, but it did cause him a little alarm. They had moved many miles and days since the last time that they saw Lava, yet he had been able to find them. He would have to remember that they were not safe from anyone searching for them.

After having his fill of Aaron's hand, Lava turned and jumped up to greet Malone who was surprised at the affection. "I think he sees you as a kindred spirit now that you were both injured," said Aaron.

"Great," said Malone sarcastically. "Hey, Lava, we were going to go that way. What way do you think we should go?" Malone shrugged his shoulders and pointed both directions. Lava, seeming to understand, started to the right, the opposite way they had planned.

"Well, I supposed we follow the dream by following the dog," said Aaron as the two men started down the path.

As they walked, they could see several individuals and small groups, but these groups would always go well out of their way to avoid them. Malone figured that everyone was intimidated by Lava. He was not far from the truth. Demonic minions often traveled with similar dogs, and human groups knew all too well to avoid them. Larger groups would occasionally pass them by without hiding, but these groups were always on guard or too busy fornicating or murdering to care. Aaron and Malone were not desensitized to the violence, but they also couldn't save everyone and hope to survive long enough to save Za.

After traveling a few kilometers, they noticed a ruckus on the ground ahead. It was the first fight that they had seen in a while. Most of the people recently were just traveling, albeit carefully. As they drew nearer, the nature of the turmoil became apparent. On the ground in front of them, a group of six women had just finished attacking a naked male, exhausted on the ground. One of the women pulled out a knife. Before either Aaron or Malone could react, the woman severed the man's penis and threw it into the air.

The two men were so disgusted that they could not ignore this act. Aaron pulled out his shotgun, and Malone gripped his pipe. The two men ran up to try and save the individual with Lava at their side.

"Leave him alone!" yelled Aaron while Malone screamed, and Lava growled at his side.

Only one of the women were armed, and they were not individually imposing. Rather than fight, they ran off, screaming in fear while laughing in psychotic joy as they did.

Aaron and Malone knelt by the man they had just saved only to notice that they were too late. "Hold in there," said Malone, but the man's head sank as he took his last breath.

"No one deserves to die in this way," screamed Malone. Malone wanted to run after the women, but Aaron stopped him. "Why can't we do something?" asked Malone.

"We don't know the entire situation, and this place feeds on evil. Chasing after those women is us giving in to anger. Don't let this place turn you."

"Ugh, it makes me so mad that anyone would just kill someone, especially like that," cried Malone.

Aaron agreed, "Absolutely, and it's good to be angry. You don't have to be ashamed to be angry at something like that. I'm angry too. We have to leave this one in the hands of God. Let it go and move on. Remember Za. Remember the pact. No matter what this place throws at us, we will not lose faith. In time, this poor soul will respawn. Let's hope his next foray into the pit goes better."

Lava sniffed the corpse for a moment and then followed them.

Malone knew that Aaron was right. They couldn't let the pit change them. It might seem that God had left the building, but they needed to maintain faith in His plan.

After traveling for several hours, there were fewer groups passing by. The groups that did pass by were not bothering to hide anymore. They just seemed not to care about the demon dog or anything. They were also traveling more slowly. Several travelers were even napping along the side of the road. Several others were literally dead tired, their bodies beginning to decompose, even as they initially laid to sleep.

Eventually, another town could be seen up ahead, much larger than the last. As they approached, they could tell that the town was the size of a small city, stretching for many kilometers in each direction. What one might call buildings or homes in this city were neither, however. Instead, the sprawl was littered with small pavilions and circus-like tents with no sides, stretching as far as one could see.

As they approached the city, Lava was reluctant to enter, even though he had been the one to lead them there. The two men were not sure what to do. They needed to explore the city to see if there was any sign of Za. At the very least, Aaron wanted to gauge a direction to search for Za. They walked a short way along the outskirts until they found a pillar. It was a good marker for position.

"Can you wait here, Lava? Stay!" Aaron ordered.

Lava, seeming to understand, circled the ground several times, using heat he could willfully emit from his torso to melt the dirt into a warm mud. He then laid down as if to take a nap.

Aaron and Malone then entered the city. Flowers surprisingly surrounded the dwellings providing a stark contrast to the rest of the pit. The path slowly disappeared as they progressed. As no one seemed to be willing to move in this city, a road seemed unnecessary.

The first tent that they crossed was filled with people struggling to stay awake, mostly unclothed, of all genders. People were walking slowly around, slapping their faces or doing exercises in an attempt to wake themselves up. Some would hold others up, encouraging each other to stay awake.

As they walked past more tents, it became obvious why no one was sleeping. The moment someone started to fall asleep, multiple horrors awaited them. One person was swallowed by a pit of acid that opened up below. Malone had the misfortune of watching the person's flesh melt away in the bubbling ooze. Next to him, a demon hound rose from the dirt to devour a sleeping woman. The shock of these deaths helped waken those in the near vicinity. Others were equally unfortunate as they slept. Worms, spiders, and insects crawled over everyone and everything.

Malone was starting to get sick. Tent after tent was the same, although the amount of disgusting death increased as they traveled farther into the city.

"Are we sure we want to keep going?" Malone asked. "I can't take much more of this, but I guess that's true of everything here."

Ahead there was more activity, though, and that led the two to continue. One particular tent was filled with long huge tables filled with apparently delicious food, but as someone fell asleep, the others simply ate her, leaving the less cannibalistic food alone. Many others sat in chairs around the tables, doing nothing but watching, barely able to stay awake.

As disgusting and odoriferous as this city was, at least they hadn't fought for their lives in some time. It was clear to Aaron that Malone was getting nauseous, though. It became clearer a minute later when he vomited unintentionally on a man sitting nearby. Even after Malone apologized and tried to clean the man as well as he could, the man did not move. He could not care less about hygiene or the two men in front of him.

"Are you all right?" Malone asked.

The man barely lifted his head to acknowledge the question.

"Can you speak? Can you tell us where we are even?" Aaron asked.

Using what seemed like the entire energy reserve the man had available, he lifted his arm slightly and pointed a single finger toward what appeared to be a city square up ahead.

"I guess we go that way," said Aaron.

The two traveled slowly toward the square. As they got closer, the people around them became less and less active again. At one point, Aaron saw a woman dissipate, supposedly dead for so long that she was respawning. One didn't need food or sleep in this world to the best of their knowledge, and yet these people were so lethargic that it was killing them.

They were still trying to be cautious, but they were also becoming oddly tired. Aaron was struggling to remember his purpose. Malone, for a moment, forgot his own name.

"Something is not right here, and I don't mean the disgusting visuals," said Aaron, realizing that nothing was right anywhere in this world.

"I noticed it too. The farther we go into this town, the less I seem to care about ever leaving or anything. These people care so little that they are just accepting horrific deaths."

Just then, a man, actually moving for a change, approached them. "Here, friends, have some flowers," he said, extending a handful of flowers as he laughed.

Throughout their journey so far, the only thing most people extended toward them was a weapon or a middle finger. Contrary to any initial interpretation of the situation, Aaron was beginning to think that these flowers were perhaps the deadliest weapon so far. The man in front of them had an odd aura about him. He appeared to be a demon struggling to maintain human form, himself becoming tired. Why would a demon hand them flowers?

"It's poisonous poppies!" shouted Aaron toward Malone to make sure that he heard. He kicked the man holding the flowers so hard that he flew six meters backward. Injured but not killed, the man/demon did not move, content to remain where he had landed and offering no objection to the attack. In front of them was a field of flowers of many types, not just poppies as Aaron had shouted. But these were no ordinary flowers. The more you smelled their sweet scent, the less you cared about anything, even living.

Aaron grabbed Malone by the arm, and the two threw caution to the wind as they sprinted out of the city. Aaron's endurance astounded Malone who struggled to keep up. They had traveled farther than they thought. The edge of town was about a kilometer away, but Aaron kept his fast pace the entire time, pulling Malone as best as he could to help him keep up.

Eventually, Malone had to stop to catch his breath. They were still several hundred meters from the edge of the city. Thankfully the flowers were fewer in number. The two men took turns slapping each other to maintain consciousness. Their tenacity kept them moving forward until finally, they were successful at escaping the snare this town represented.

Once he caught his breath and could speak, Malone turned to Aaron. "What are poisonous poppies?"

Aaron realized that Malone had probably not understood the reference. "It's from Oz. There were fields of poppies that would put you to sleep. Of course, here it was all types of flowers."

"How nefarious to be undone by a flower?" said Malone.

"Yes, we nearly fell into the trap. Thankfully, we made it out of Acedia."

"Acedia?" Malone asked.

"It's the sin of sloth. I think we just found where those guilty of sloth end up in the pit. No wonder you can't escape once you find your sin. I was half expecting a sign or something, sort of like at the beginning."

"Well, we're out now," said Malone.

Looking back, Aaron said, "It's hard to explain, but I feel sorry for them."

"I get it. It's hard to watch anyone wallow in sin or to fail to find God," agreed Malone. Thinking of where he was as a child, he hated watching anyone suffer. "And Za?"

"I didn't feel her," said Aaron reassuringly. He turned to call out with a loud yell, "Lava!"

The two realized that they did not know from which direction they had come. They hated to lose their pet. He had been helpful at keeping other groups away since he returned.

"Well, I know that we're in a hurry to find Za, but I also think that we may need to walk around this city and look for Lava," said Aaron, partly trying to convince himself but realizing that they would have to walk around the city either way. The trick was to determine the right way to walk so that they could find Lava. They decided to go to their right.

After fifteen minutes, they thankfully saw Lava's pole up ahead. It was the first good fortune that they had experienced in some time. As they approached, Lava ran toward them. Once reunited, they continued to walk, this time around the outside of the expanse of the city and then to continue forward on the other side. It was a long walk, probably taking a day, but it was the best option.

M eanwhile, Darda was visited by misfortune. He was not difficult for the demons to track down. Although they may not
all have realized that he was still on the road, those that did know
maintained regular checks of his activities. He had been hiding in his
current house for years. Asmodai felt that they had allowed him his
rest long enough. A scouting team picked him up and brought him
to Asmodai at his temple in the pit.

Asmodai's temple was to the eastern reaches of the deepest
region of the pit. Two moats, one of molten metal and the other of
liquid nitrogen, surrounded the massive fortress. Solid white frozen
limbs could be seen bobbing to the surface and shattering in the current of the cold moat. Three-meter-thick walls made of black slate
laden with jewels surrounded the square structure rising fifty meters
into the void and stretching four hundred meters in each direction.
Four towers rose one hundred meters at each corner. Two turrets rose
an additional ten meters from the central keep, which itself measured
one hundred meters per side. Battlements and parapets surrounded
the towers and walls, constantly guarded by a legion of demons.
Ballistae, catapults, and pots of boiling oil added to the defense. Holes
presumably to view the field or to fire missiles, weapons, or spells littered the walls above the twenty-meter mark. A nearly impenetrable
carbon-fibered portcullis measuring ten meters on each side covered
the only two entrances. The walls would be easier to break than the
mystical doors that controlled entry at the only two openings in the
outer wall.

No king of hell needed a castle for protection. Rather, the more ominous the structure, the greater it served as a status symbol to other demons and as a reason for the human hordes to live in fear.

Asmodai sat on his throne of bones in his gold-encrusted central chamber as his searchers brought in Darda. In an instant, he lashed out with one of his wings, severing the head of the first man to approach. The others quickly cowered or went on guard in confusion.

"Please forgive us, master. How have we angered you?" they begged.

"I wanted him unharmed. I'll decide what harm befalls him," said Asmodai, angered that one of Darda's arms was missing or at least angered that he was not the one to remove it. "Now begone before I behead you all! What if he had died, and I had to wait for him to respawn?"

The lowest of humans quickly ran from his presence, leaving Darda alone with Asmodai and ten demon guards along the wall behind him. Darda let out a cough, spitting blood onto the throne room floor. It was difficult to notice from the redness already there that was presumably from the blood of previous visitors.

"Darda, I haven't seen your entrails—I mean, your face in decades. How nice of you to come see me," began Asmodai with a smile.

Darda, badly beaten, said nothing.

"Now, now, don't be mad. I specifically told them to bring you here unharmed. Well, maybe I just said alive. My apologies," said Asmodai with a smile, "but you can end this quickly by answering one question."

Darda looked up enough to let Asmodai know he was listening. If it was information that he wanted, Asmodai would torture him in ways that would not allow him to die and respawn. It was always best to simply answer, but then it might depend on the question.

Asmodai came down from his throne slowly. In his demonic form, he was a foreboding presence. He leaned into Darda. In a quieter yet deep voice, he asked, "Where is Azriel?"

Smiling, Darda thought, *So that is what Asmodai wants.* How fortuitous he had just seen two men. *So one of them must have been*

*Azriel.* Darda would be able to render an answer to the question. Yet, how unfortunate as well. He knew that his respite on the road would not last. He thought that they would eventually find him, but it seemed that they were watching him the whole time. They must have known about his visitors. Or was it just coincidence that he had been brought before Asmodai for this question. No, that was unlikely. It would have taken them longer to find him. Next time, he would need to find a better hiding place.

"Well?" pressed Asmodai. "I'm not a patient demon."

Darda continued his thinking in earnest, formulating the best response. "A week or so ago, he went to the pit," he coughed out the least amount of information he thought he could get away with.

"Of course, he went to the pit. Now don't anger me. What did you tell them? Where in the pit did he go?" Asmodai was already losing his patience, although he did catch the one week ago part. Azriel was close. "I'll give you a moment to consider your answer carefully," he added to Darda while he turned to pull the cord of a bell in the ceiling. After a loud chime from far away, a lesser demon entered. "Prepare fifty search parties. You leave shortly," said Asmodai to the demon who then abruptly left.

Darda, having considered all of the possibilities, was left with one most likely location for Azriel's travel. The pit did not work by terrestrial topology. You travelled where you wanted to or where your desires led you. Unfortunately for Asmodai, it did not work in terms of finding individuals but rather in terms of finding yourself. It was likewise unfortunate for Azriel, searching for his daughter. But Darda knew that Azriel was looking for information. For that reason, there was really only one place that the pit would lead him first.

Asmodai returned his attention to Darda. "I'm ready for an answer, Darda. Pray that it is a good one."

"Did you check the Bibliotheca?" he said with a smile. He knew that they had not. Demons didn't care about the haughty self-absorbed tenants of the Bibliotheca. Occasionally, one might raid and destroy it for fun and to remind them who was in charge, but they just didn't provide enough entertainment for the demons in general. So much so that many demons often forgot it even existed. Demons loved torturing the prideful slowly over the centuries, breaking their high opinions down, but such individuals had their own special place in the pit. The Bibliotheca was special. Plus, there were times when demons would send a representative to retrieve a piece of information from within its walls. No one outside of the Bibliotheca had any respect for it, and those inside had nothing but respect for it. Yes, Darda was sure that it had not been searched.

Immediately after hearing Darda's words, Asmodai ripped him apart. He knew that Darda would simply respawn within a week, but it was still satisfying. Asmodai then stormed out of the room.

Darda, although dead, would respawn knowing that he had not given Asmodai everything. Asmodai, it would seem, was looking for only one man. He did not know that Azriel was with another.

Within minutes, Asmodai and his search parties had transported to the Bibliotheca. He sent forty-five groups outward in every direction in search of Azriel or his human form. Two-headed search dogs preceded them. Even through the twisting reforming shape of the pit, they would find them easily with only about a week's head start. Azriel would be moving slow. They would not.

Five of the groups did not join the search. They followed Asmodai up to the Bibliotheca. It was a risk for Asmodai to take part in the search himself. He didn't want word to get back to Lucifer that something was happening. But he felt it was safe to take part in this search since no one would care what happened here.

They did not wait for permission to enter the Bibliotheca. Asmodai simply tore the front doors down, and they walked through. People in its confines were so self-centered that they may not even remember visitors if they had spoken to them at great length. Asmodai would need to make it within their best interest to remember.

The search parties violently rounded up every individual that they came across. They did not so much search for those within. They merely pushed the shelves over and took whoever jumped out. Eventually, they had brought five hundred individuals into the Bibliotheca's great hall in front of Asmodai.

Asmodai looked out at the filth before him. They sickened him. These men who had no god other than themselves. Even Asmodai believed in God. Of course, he hated Him.

"I've been in the mood for making things easy lately. You had a visitor within the last week or so. It's not like you have many visitors. Therefore, you should remember him. He would have been new to the pit. Tell me what he was here for and where he went when he left," Asmodai commanded.

No one moved, the insolence of these peons refusing to immediately recognize his authority. Asmodai was furious.

"Maybe this will jog your memory," Asmodai said as he spit forth lava from his bullhead. A large section of the library to his right began to burn. As the floor melted, the fire spread to the lower floor. Ten humans were absorbed by the initial blast of flame, and another ten fell into the hole that opened. As much as Asmodai welcomed the death of humans, he hoped that those particular ones did not have any useful information.

"You think so highly of yourselves, but I can make your deaths quite painful you see," said Asmodai, taking advantage of the deaths to influence the remaining humans.

Horrified not so much by the deaths of the others but more by the damage to the Bibliotheca, one man stepped forward. Polyphenia remembered the two men. In his mind, they had refused to accept his intellectual superiority and deserved whatever this demon had planned for them. "There were two men that passed through here several days ago."

Asmodai stomped forward toward Polyphenia. "Tell me," he ordered.

"They were definitely new and quite stupid. They wanted to find information about a girl. I'm surprised I remembered. They were so unimportant." The fire was beginning to spread. Polyphenia nervously looked for help, but everyone was quickly moving away from the flames. He wanted to start moving too, but Asmodai placed a large hand on his shoulder and restrained him.

"Tell me more," ordered Asmodai.

"They just wanted information. That's all I know, I swear. They disappeared and never entered the building."

"You said they? Describe them." Asmodai was intrigued. Azriel was not alone.

"There was a middle-aged man and a younger man in his early twenties. Both were healthy with black hair. One was of Asian descent. I think they were talking English. That's all I know." Polyphenia was getting nervous. The fire was getting too close.

Asmodai was done. Although the description was minimal, he quickly came to a realization. Azriel had drawn Malone onto the road with him. It was not too unreasonable a possibility. This information was helpful.

As he stood there, thinking, the fire had surrounded them. Polyphenia's screams went unnoticed by Asmodai as he stood there, thinking, holding the human in place. The fire seemed to calm him. So did the screams as Polyphenia died in the fire.

As they left, the demons broke everyone's legs so that they would not be able to escape the fire. Asmodai then spewed forth more flames from his mouth, surrounding the massive rotunda in flames. The screams of the men as their flesh and their precious books burned was pleasing to Asmodai.

Outside the Bibliotheca, Asmodai continued to spit flames, his saliva-like lava, over the stone building. The ancient structure melted from the heat. The Bibliotheca was a special place, though. Like the fools inside, it would respawn in time. It was still satisfying for Asmodai to watch it burn. Over the next few hours, the entire town was engulfed in flames, but the demons would not notice the entire destruction. They would have already left.

Asmodai turned to his troops as they left the village. "Spread the word. We are not looking for one but two. Azriel has a friend. Now go find them quickly."

As the search parties ventured forth, Asmodai looked back on the burning village one more time before teleporting back to his stronghold.

## 22

"Run!" said Aaron to Malone who, of course, was already running. The pit had become exponentially more dangerous since leaving the Bibliotheca. Aaron, Malone, and Lava had already fought off two groups of attackers so far that day. But those groups were only five to ten men with sticks and stones. At least twenty men were chasing them this time, and at least two of them had swords.

They only had five shells remaining for the shotgun. Aaron was sure that the pit was going to become more dangerous, but they couldn't waste time being tortured or respawning if they hoped to find Za.

Aaron turned around. Surprisingly, he was at least twenty meters ahead of Malone and Lava when he did so. He drew the shotgun and waited for them to pass. *Bang! Bang!* He hoped that two shots would be enough to do it. The leader with the katana along with two others in close proximity fell to the ground. Immediately, the others slowed. One of them picked up the katana. Letting out a war cry, the entire party started chasing after them again.

Aaron turned again, stopped, and fired. *Bang! Bang!* Only one shot left. Several more men full of rage fell to the ground dead. The group was only ten meters away as they came to a stop again.

"Don't do it," warned Aaron. "Walk away or run. Either way, you live. Take another step forward, and you surely die."

One of the men stooped down to pick up the katana. None of them seemed to care one iota for their own dead.

"Uh-uh," said Aaron as Lava jumped on the man, quickly killing him.

The marauders decided not to take any more risks. They backed away and eventually left.

When they were well away, Malone went and grabbed the katana, dropping his pipe in its place.

Lava snarled. It was clear that he wanted to attack the men, but he wisely followed when Aaron ran. Even a two-headed gigantic dog couldn't take on everyone.

Aaron and Malone had traveled a long distance from the Bibliotheca. The entire time, they had been avoiding as much contact as possible with others, but it was becoming impossible. The people, both men and women, were becoming more vicious. The anger of these people was beyond quenching. Like mindless zombies, they sought only harm on those that they hated, and they hated everyone. It would be impossible to avoid them if they kept moving forward.

But something told Aaron that Za was ahead. Lava seemed determined to go that direction as well.

The terrain was getting rockier, enabling them to move more hidden from distant dangers while simultaneously opening them up to constant ambush. Following Lava for another half-hour after the last encounter, a new challenge appeared.

The only way they could describe it was that the land had been inverted. It was as if a large mountain range had been flipped upside down, going into the earth instead of coming out. From where they stood, they could see for kilometers into the inverted range before them, and what they saw was discouraging.

Each inverted mountain seemed to be playing out its own scene of war. Huge armies of men with all forms of weapons fought on a grand stage. Two of the battles appeared to be Spartans attacking Romans and Native Americans running into battle against Mongols. The closest pit appeared to be a mindless free-for-all. Malone compared it to a dogfight, something he had the misfortune of seeing often when in captivity. Only in this case, everyone was the dog, fighting to be the alpha, gnawing at each other's throats with their own teeth if necessary. They fought in a squalid cesspool soaked with pools of blood, excrement, and all sorts of bodily fluids filling the trenches. It was difficult to know exactly how many people were within that region or where they were, but occasionally, an opening in the three-meter deep trenches would reveal their skirmishes. As they fell and died, they would respawn, perpetuating this endless cycle of warfare, never having their anger subside.

As the two ducked under an outcropping of rock on the edge of this new region of the pit, they discussed their options. Lava kept watch to the side.

"Ira," began Aaron.

"Let me guess," said Malone. "Ira means wrath, like from irate."

"Bingo. I feel like the pit isn't taking us where we want to go, at least not directly."

"But the pit doesn't take you where you want to go," corrected Malone. "I think Darda or someone said it takes you where you need to go. Don't get me wrong. I have no idea why we need to be here. Maybe the pit is broken, just like the road."

Aaron and Malone had tried to concentrate on Za. They had an idea how travel worked in the pit, and they were trying to take advantage of it. If their greatest desire was Za, then the pit should take them to her. The pit had another idea.

The pit knew what Aaron really wanted, what drove his existence, and it was Aaron who was leading them. He did not realize it yet, but he was searching for himself. There had been too many clues, too many questions. He needed to know who the angel of death really was. The pit needed him to know as well. The pit was designed for people to find the drive in their soul, and since Aaron was in human form, the same applied to him.

Aaron gazed around the ridge near Lava. "Unfortunately, Lava's nose is leading us forward. For better or worse, I'm also sensing Za in the same direction. The only fortunate thing, I suppose, is that I'm not sensing her near. Hopefully, she has no part in this death and destruction but lies somewhere on the other side. These mini pits seem to go on for kilometers in each direction. I think forward into the belly of this beast is the way to go."

Unbeknownst to Aaron and Malone, they were not the only ones searching. They were searching for someone, and many were searching for them. Despite the risk from Lucifer, demon groups were searching alongside the many human groups that had already been scouring the pit.

Lava gave yet another warning from beside Aaron, but it was not from the battles in front of them. He turned and snarled behind them. He could sense other demon dogs, and it was getting to the point where he was constantly sensing something. He gave out a warning because one group was less than half a kilometer away and approaching.

"We can't keep hiding," Aaron told Lava, knowing that Malone would also overhear.

"What are you saying?"

Looking back, Aaron could see the group Lava detected approaching. "Behind us, there is an organized group of at least twenty men, several demons, two Lava-like dogs, and swords. In front of us is a crater where everyone seems to be fighting in a free-for-all. If we stick together, I think we can at least make it through this crater. You've got the katana, and I've got a pole. Along with Lava, we have a better chance ahead. Plus, the trenches will be so odoriferous as to mask our individual scents if these creatures are seeking us. And somehow, based on what Ash said, I feel that there probably are groups here looking for us."

"We better hurry then. That group is closing in," said Malone, preparing to enter battle.

Although he had rarely been a part of Angelic Missions' sorties, Aaron had always been good at planning. He tried to put that experience to use here. "Follow me," he said as he stood up and rounded the rock they were hiding behind. Twenty meters forward, he jumped into a trench followed by Malone and Lava. "If we stick to the trenches, we can limit how many people we have to fight at any given time. I didn't see or hear any gunpowder or explosives. So we just need to pay attention and defend ourselves whenever necessary." After passing several forks in the passageways, he added, "Try to keep track of how many lefts and rights we're making. The goal is to keep moving forward and try to get to the other side."

Malone understood, and he appreciated Aaron's leadership.

Another twenty meters in, two men jumped out from around a corner where the labyrinth branched. Neither man had weapons other than their clawlike fingernails and teeth ground to fangs. Lava heard them approaching and jumped at the first man, tearing into his throat. Unfazed, the second man kicked at Lava as Malone stabbed him in the stomach while letting out a cry that was half intended to add energy to his swing and half unintended to let out his horror from the experience. Lava took a bite out of the second man's leg in revenge for being kicked. It was also possible that he was slightly hungry. The two men fell dead.

Carefully stepping around the corpses, they continued forward. A second group soon attacked, this one a man and a woman. Lava took out the man swiftly, but the woman had a Ninjato. She was equally as inexperienced with the sword as Malone. There were no swift combinations of swings to harm the opponent. The fight was more similar to two children playing with plastic swords banging them into each other repeatedly. While she was preoccupied with Malone, Aaron swung the shotgun into her head from behind, knocking her to the ground, where Malone impaled her.

Aaron placed the shotgun in his makeshift holster, dropped the pipe, and grabbed the Ninjato. The two men then both went forward with their swords drawn. "We need to remember to say a prayer for these souls and our own forgiveness later," said Aaron as they moved.

After passing through two more branches without being attacked, they came upon an end to their current trench. A large battle was taking place in the clearing up ahead. There were at least four groups fighting. Aaron noticed that one of the groups was spending more time trying to avoid the battle than engage.

"Look at the smaller group," he said as quietly as possible to Malone as they hid inside the trench.

"The other groups seem to be ignoring them for the most part," noticed Malone.

"I don't think that they belong here, at least not as much as the others," explained Aaron. "Remember what we learned. They might have been redeemable, but then they were trapped here. The pit might have corrupted them enough that they were led here out of their anger."

"What are you suggesting then?" asked Malone.

"Let's work our way through, one group at a time, but we'll try to defend that group if we can. If I'm right, they may be helpful as we move forward. We can offer to help them out of these canyons, and they can, by their presence, help us get out too, maybe even continue into the pit."

"I'm ready when you are," said Malone, although it was clear he was reluctant to continue.

Approximately one hundred men and women were taking part in the skirmish. As Aaron and Malone entered the clearing, they were unnoticed for a few moments. That gave them time to start to move toward the less aggressive group. However, when Lava entered the clearing, everyone noticed. The groups farther away continued in their separate fights, but about twenty people closest began to move toward them. Half of them had knives and bats.

Lava snarled, but he stayed near Aaron as the other men approached. Taking a defensive posture, Aaron tried unsuccessfully to avoid conflict. "We don't want any part of this. We're just passing through. Stay back, and no one has to be harmed!"

"I want his skin," was the first response from a woman near the front who appeared to have once been a man.

Aaron started to run perpendicular to the approaching group. Malone and Lava followed. He hoped to flank the group or at least get far enough to the side so that they would only have to fight a few at a time. By moving sideways, they kept the trenches behind them as well, avoiding being surrounded and possibly allowing them to push some of the attackers in.

Malone landed the first blow with his longer sword and managed to literally disarm the first assailant. Lava then gouged the next attacker. Most of the attackers were heading for Lava and not Aaron and Malone. They seemed to recognize the danger posed by the dog and wished to remove him from the equation. To their misfortune, that left Aaron time to think and react.

Aaron lunged forward, kneeing the next attacker with such energy that his ribs were crushed as blood spouted from his mouth. In the same fluid motion, Aaron sliced off the head of the woman beside him. As soon as he landed, he jumped upward, landing on top of the next attacker, sword inserted vertically through his skull.

Malone was fending off two attackers and was unable to keep track of Aaron directly. However, as the fight progressed, he was certain that the twilight was subsiding. The battleground seemed to glow with a dim light. Lava jumped on one of the men Malone was fighting, opening up his chance to cut the other's leg deeply.

As a club pounded into Lava's side from the next attacker, he let out a yelp. One of his heads grabbed the club in its jaws, knocking the attacker over while Lava's other head turned from its previous victim and severed a major artery in the enemy's leg.

Malone noticed a light behind him as a spatter of blood covered the back of his neck. Aaron had killed someone sneaking up on him. As Malone turned in reaction to the spray on his neck, he thought that he saw the source of the glow. A ribbon-like band appeared to be emanating from Aaron's back. It followed him through the battleground. What's more, Aaron was moving with an inhuman speed and strength. Malone had only engaged a few attackers with the help of Lava. Aaron's path was littered with the carcasses of at least fifteen people by now, many in pieces.

Malone had that time to think because no one appeared to be attacking him anymore. In fact, the remaining attackers were retreating. It was a welcome sight. Malone had a nasty cut on his left arm and a smaller cut on his left leg. He would be limping for a few hours while that healed. Lava also had several bruises and cuts. They may have to leave him behind or at least let him get off his legs for a while.

During the battle, Malone and Lava had worked their way over to the group that they were trying to protect. Ten of them, half male and half female, stood in disbelief, too frightened to flee. They were all Caucasian, appeared to be in their midthirties, and were of average build. Their weapons were raised, but it was clear that they did not want or know how to use them. The group seemed prepared to die.

Aaron, no longer glowing, finally noticed the retreat of the other groups and came to join Malone and Lava.

"Please don't kill us," said one of the people. Another, the group's apparent leader, said, "What are you?" The others continued looking on with concern.

"We're just a couple of men trying to make it to the other side of this war zone. Don't worry, we won't attack unless you attack us. We're just looking for some help getting across." Aaron replied. "Would you like to join up?"

"I don't think that's what they meant," added Malone. Several members of their group shook their heads to indicate Malone was correct.

Aaron looked at Malone, not understanding his comment.

"They didn't ask who you were. They asked what you were," Malone tried to explain. "Dude, you were glowing, and you just cut down over twenty men in a couple of minutes without getting a scratch on you."

Aaron looked down at his body. It was true, he didn't appear to have a scratch on him. His sword was coated in blood and shards of flesh. Disgusted, he leaned down and wiped the sword somewhat clean on the shirt of an equally disgusting corpse. He then looked out on the clearing. Aaron was right. There were at least sixty dead bodies on the battlefield, and he somewhat remembered putting a good number of them there himself. The remaining members of the other groups had now retreated back into trenches.

But the battle was mostly a blur. He could feel his body working on automatic. He acted instinctually with little time to process what was happening. "I guess I didn't know I had that in me," he said to Malone.

"No, you're not getting it, dude. You had something coming out of your back," added Malone, "and it was glowing."

Aaron tried to remember. It did appear like the dusk had grown slightly brighter during the fight. He assumed it was sparks from all of the clashing swords. "What was it? There was something coming out of my back? Is it still there?" Aaron asked as he twisted around, trying to get a view of his backside.

Malone didn't know what to say. He was beginning to think that maybe Aaron actually was the angel of death, but he still appeared like a man. Maybe it was something else related to the pit that they still didn't know or understand. At the moment, that sounded like the most logical explanation. "Whatever it was, it's gone now. Maybe it has something to do with the pit. Maybe it's a special power for those that don't belong here to help them get out. It did seem to give you some power."

"Well, I don't see anything now. If you're right, I hope it comes back when we need it, but I sort of hope it doesn't because you're kind of freaking me out a little," Aaron said as he turned back to the group of people who were standing there, waiting for him to speak to them again. "Is it all right if we join your group for a while, assuming you're going the same way we are?"

They were not as afraid of the two anymore. They were definitely confused by them, but they felt that they would definitely be safer with others. There were also no more attackers at the moment. Therefore, the group had a moment to discuss what they wanted to do.

"You need to decide quickly. We need to get out of this clearing," said Malone, reminding everyone that they were still out in the open.

Reaching their decision, the leader said, "All right, we'll follow you for now as long as it is safe and as long as we get out of these canyons."

Aaron and Malone were pleased to have a larger group. They moved toward the other side of the opening from whence they entered and continued. Aaron was happy to continue forward. That meant that they were getting closer to Za and farther from anyone that might be following them.

In the trenches, it was rare to go more than fifty meters without running into an aggressor, usually an individual but sometimes a group. With Aaron and Lava in the lead, though, the group had little problem getting to the bottom of the first massive canyon. Malone counted one hundred and seventy-three people that they had killed. He wasn't keeping score so as to win. Rather, he wanted to remember to say a prayer for each of them. When they reached the bottom, he had his chance.

As they turned upward from the bottom, they noticed a partially hidden cave, or perhaps a better word would be a very large projection of stone. It was a good point to rest. Several of them were injured. Malone had recently received a deep wound on his leg. Only a tourniquet saved him from terminal blood loss. Several of the others had less serious wounds, but everyone needed time to heal.

As they sat and rested, Aaron and Malone had a chance to speak while Lava napped at their side.

"Have you noticed it?" Aaron asked.

"I'm feeling a little woozy over here. What was I supposed to notice?" Malone replied.

"They've changed."

"Who's changed."

"Our ten compatriots. They are no longer timid. It took us almost two hours to get to the bottom of the pit, I would estimate. They have a confidence about them now, and that is good. But they also have a new fierceness."

"Sounds good. They'll be more helpful on the way up," suggested Malone.

"But they are no good to themselves. Ira, which I'm sure this region represents, has changed them, but they don't realize it. They were peaceful. Now they are growing in anger and aggressiveness. I gather that they respawned near each other about when we found them. Something about respawning must reset this place's influence on you. But they are clearly under its influence now."

"What should we do?"

"Nothing now. Maybe pray for them as we pray for those we've killed. I think we're good for the time being," reassured Aaron. "But we need to keep an eye on them. Right now, they are more than willing to follow us, but the moment they start to turn, if they start to turn, we need to be ready."

"Okay," Malone responded as he drifted into a light sleep.

Aaron left him alone. Malone needed time to heal, and they both wanted to pray.

After a short prayer, Aaron turned his attention to the rest of the group. He wasn't sure, but it felt as if they were plotting something. He could hear murmuring and whispers such as when someone tried to keep others from knowing what one was saying. Members of the group would also pass occasional watchful glances their way. He decided to go sit among them to create a stronger bond and to be able to hear what they were saying.

"There he is, our saving beast," said Thom, the smallest of the men and the one showing the least amount of aggression.

"Save some for the rest of us on the way up," responded Abdul with a smile on his face, suggesting he welcomed the next kill.

"Aren't you the strong one?" said Madhuri, grabbing his arm affectionately. "Kill one for me."

The conversation continued in this way for a short while, each one trying to out bravado the one before. Aaron was correct. They were getting more aggressive. He just needed to keep them in check until they made it through Ira.

After thirty minutes in the security of their hiding place, Malone had mostly healed. He was still week, but Aaron told him to take up the rear for a while. At least then they would be able to get moving. As long as the group was concentrating on the dangers surrounding them, they wouldn't start to turn on each other.

Fortunately, the way up the first canyon was not as treacherous. It took longer, almost three hours, since they were moving uphill, but they were only attacked by three groups in total with no clearings. True to their statements, the group of followers were much more aggressive, killing thirty-two compared to Aaron, Malone, and Lava killing only two. Aaron and Malone were more than willing not to kill anyone if they would leave them alone. That, of course, would not happen here. But the others were beginning to seek out someone to attack, and that was not good.

Still, they survived and made it to the end of the first canyon. From their vantage point, they could see that the Spartan and Roman war raged on. They would need to be stealthy to get through. Everyone seemed to be concentrated on the main battles. It would take hours, but if they stayed to the outskirts, they might be able to go around the main battles.

Abdul was looking back into the first pit. "Let's go back that way. It was fun."

Madhuri agreed. "Yes, let's go back."

"No, we follow Aaron," said Ben who was then supported by the rest. Aaron was still the alpha.

"How do we proceed?" asked Thom, looking Aaron's way.

Aaron then explained his plan of staying to the outside of the battles and trying to sneak around. Even his strongest supporters wanted to charge into battle and fight their way through, but Aaron was able to convince them with Malone's support.

Carefully, the group snuck down the canyon about one-half of a kilometer. That descent put them about one-third of the way down the canyon yet out of reach of the primary battles raging. They then turned and started to walk horizontally along the canyon. Since they were more like upside-down mountains, they could be traversed in a circular manner if one was willing to take the time. Aaron and Malone were in a hurry but not too much of a hurry to fail to remain cautious.

As they moved along, there were several times when it was clear that at least one side of the battle was aware of their presence. Thankfully, the combatants seemed almost disinterested in their small group. They were not considered a challenge nor a threat.

At one point, Aaron felt that it was highly likely that they could just walk across the battlefield freely, but he knew that their ten friends would never make it without rushing into battle. If he could just get them to the other end of Ira, maybe they could come out of their rage.

Being somewhat ignored was beginning to anger the others. They would not be treated as insignificant. After many hours, the group had nearly circled the battlefield without a single fight. At last, Madhuri could not take it anymore.

"Stop following that man. He is weak. If you follow him, you are weak also," she ordered the others.

"I am not weak," shouted Abdul. "I am strong. The strongest."

"We are all strong," the rest of the group chimed.

"Prove it!" Madhuri ordered as the intensity of her voice increased.

Without hesitation, Abdul charged down into the canyon at the first group he saw. Thankfully, it was only a small party of twelve Spartans, but they all had brass shields and short swords. Easily hearing the war-crazed group charging down at them, the Spartans set up their shields in a phalanx and drew their swords.

Malone looked at Aaron. "Do we intervene. They have a chance if we join."

Lava did not seem to care either way. He was content by Aaron's side.

Aaron had only a moment to consider his options, but the choice seemed obvious. If they saved their group, the crazed individuals may immediately turn on them. Also, as the others fought the Spartans, he and Malone would have more than enough time to scamper up the remaining climb to the top. He wanted immensely to help these few people to be redeemed, but he sadly knew that it was not meant to be. "Time to go," he said to Malone as he remorsefully turned away from the yells of war and moved upward away from their lost group. By the time they reached the top, they could hear the battle below ending. Every Spartan could be seen returning to the main battle. None of their previous partners survived.

The next inverted mountain passed much the same way, only there were but three of them now. Those taking part in the war were once again too preoccupied to care. As long as Aaron and Malone stayed to the side, they were left alone.

The difficulty that Aaron and Malone noticed was that they were beginning to feel angry as well. They wanted to fight. They almost needed to fight. They took turns reminding each other that it was just the pit influencing them. Only the memory of Za allowed them to keep moving.

## 23

They had been traveling at least one day's time by now. There were three canyons behind them, but there were also at least that many in front. Running between their current resting spot and the next canyon was a half-kilometer wide expanse of mud, only now visible as they stood at the top of the third ascent.

It was the closest thing that they had seen to what might be a river, like Styx, but it was no longer a river, just a riverbed laden with mud, filth, and excrement. They tried to take a few steps forward, but quickly, the smell and smut was more than they could bear. As they began to sink into the feces, they were forced to make a speedy retreat.

They began to hear moans. At first, they wondered if the mud was alive, awakened by their attempt at crossing. The mud then began to shift and move. In an instant, it came alive all around them. Human heads were revealed, shaking their dung covering. The shifting faces looked like passing waves in the fetid cesspool.

Malone surmised, "We might be able to walk across if we stepped on the faces littering the surface. I'm definitely not saying that we should do that, just that we could if we had to. I'm not even sure I could make it across before the smell overtook me."

"I think we can both agree to make that an absolute last choice. I'd also prefer to avoid such mockery of the poor souls trapped," added Aaron.

"Help me. Free me. Kill me. Have mercy," where the audible cries for assistance from the multitude of trapped heads. One could only presume that the rest of their bodies were attached under the murk being slowly digested by all sorts of underground lifeforms.

About twenty meters off the shore, a group of arms began to rise out of the surface. Aaron and Malone were initially frightened that this filthy decomposing horde would rise from their prison to attack, but as quickly as the arms rose from the mud, large rocky hail the size of soccer balls fell from the sky, squashing the bodies of those trying to escape.

The cries were becoming too much to bear as Aaron and Malone slipped quietly back into the warzone they had just escaped. They crept twenty meters backward before the cries finally ended, although a few cries and shrieks occasionally broke the silence.

"I don't think I can cross that riverbed," said Malone. "I feel like I need a shower more than I ever have since entering this crazy world."

"You're right. I don't think Charon will carry us across in a boat, and even if he would, we don't have any coins to give him." Seeing Malone's confusion, Aaron added, "It's just bits of mythology about a river in hell. Even if they are damned for their sins, I can't demean them by walking on their heads. But I don't think we can go back the way that we came either."

Lava, who did not mind the torment above, was still wandering around the edge of the mud where it solidified into the inverted mountain. As he sniffed the annoyed heads, he took a moment to relieve himself on one of them, causing quite a stir for a few minutes. Afterward, he managed to pick up a recognizable odor over the stench of the riverbed. There were other demon dogs nearby again.

Lava ran back down to the others to warn them of the presence. At first, Aaron and Malone were too preoccupied, trying to decide what to do next. Eventually, due in part to Lava's continued insistence, Aaron turned to him. "What do you want, persistent mutt?"

Lava, annoyed that it took so long to get their attention, moved behind Aaron and started to push him back up.

"Okay, boy, we're coming," said Aaron as he and Malone returned to the riverbed.

As they summitted, Lava grew quiet and looked to their right, snarling quietly. It was clear that he was sensing something. There were no vantage points to hide behind along the river. They took just a few steps down into the crater and stood watch, waiting for something to appear. Within a minute, they could see movement.

The group was still at least two-hundred meters away. It appeared to be another search party with at least two demon hounds. They were heading their way, and the only thing slowing them down was their constant harassment of the heads in the riverbed.

"We were probably going to go along the riverbed anyway. I guess we know which way to go now," said Aaron quietly.

"Let's move quickly," suggested Malone. "I don't just want to get away from the marauders back there. If we move fast, we can keep the screams and moans of those buried here behind us."

"Good point," added Aaron, "let's go." As they started to go, Aaron turned back to get Lava's attention. "Stop your snarling, Lava. I said let's go."

Lava's slow movement resulted in Aaron's misfortune. Someone in the search party had seen him. Itching to cause pain to a moving target, one of the humans shot an arrow that flew with unexpected accuracy from fifty meters into Aaron's right arm.

Aaron let out a cry of pain as he turned. "Run!" he shouted to Malone as he hurried forward, arrow still projecting from his upper arm.

The two ran with abandon for at least a kilometer until they could run no more. Their lungs and legs were burning from the exertion. Their ears and hearts were reeling from the constant screams from the riverbed. Worse, Aaron could not feel his right arm.

Collapsing as they came to a stop, they dropped back into the warzone to hide among the earthen outgrowths. Malone, worrying about being caught while also worrying about the arrow in his friend's arm, came to Aaron's aid.

Jokingly, Aaron told his friend, "At least it will heal once it's out, I hope."

Malone asked, "What can I do?"

"I'm not an action star or I would have just broken it off or something crazy like that. I'm going to need your help," admitted Aaron. As Malone went to grab the arrow, Aaron added, "Don't pull it out, push it through. Do it quickly, and don't be mad if I yell out at you."

"I'll do my best," said Malone as he gripped tightly on the arrow. As hard and as fast as he could, he pushed the arrow through Aaron's arm. If they had lost their pursuers, the scream had clearly given their position away. Not intending to be ironic, Malone told Aaron, "Wait here," while he peered out from their hiding spot to check on their safety. Aaron did not respond as he was nearly passed out from pain and exhaustion.

Malone could not see anyone coming, but he did see a glow illuminating him from behind. He turned around. This time, Malone was sure that ribbons of light were emanating from Aaron's back. His arm began to glow, and then the light receded. The arm was fully healed. Malone was now convinced as he dropped to his rear, sitting on the ground in disbelief. Aaron was an angel. He may not be the angel of death, but he was definitely not just a human. But what was he to do with this knowledge?

There was no time to discuss the experience right now. When they exited Ira, he would make it the first topic of discussion. "Aaron, get up. Let's go," Malone said as he nudged Aaron.

"How long was I out?" Aaron asked.

"Not as long as you would think. We need to get going."

Aaron stood up as if he had never been injured. The three then continued quickly down the river once they were satisfied there was no one visibly behind them. They presumed it was possible that they were still being followed, but whoever it was did not seem interested in overtaking them right now. They jogged and walked as quickly as they could, continually moving along the riverbed.

*****

As Malone processed his new knowledge, and Aaron concentrated on getting out of Ira, the search party behind them was busy as well. The man who shot the arrow was quickly beheaded. His severed head rolled into the river of exposed living heads. The difference was not noticeable.

The demon leading the party had to kill him. They were tracking Azriel, and the imbecile forgot that they had to capture him alive. If the arrow had managed to kill Azriel in his human form, he might have respawned anywhere. He also might have ascended, having not yet committed a mortal sin or denounced heaven. While most of the search party did not know why they needed Azriel alive, they all knew that if they were stupid enough to kill him, they would all soon follow.

Zeljabul, the lesser demon leading the party, was somewhat aware that a coup was in the works among the greater demons. Taking part in such a grand strategy made him feel important. Being the first one to report Azriel's location would demonstrate his worth and increase his status, even if the coup failed.

Quickly, Zeljabul ordered his second in command back to Asmodai to receive orders and inform him of their success. They had found Azriel.

He then sent his two stealthiest scouts with one demon hound to track Azriel without being seen. Since they were downwind, they could probably be closer, but Zeljabul ordered them to stay back at least one hundred meters. The rest of the group would stay back at least twice that until they received word back from Asmodai.

*****

Within a few kilometers of their encounter, Aaron, Malone, and Lava came to a turn in the river away from the side that they were following. They could continue along the riverbed or venture back into the pits of Ira. While they did not know when or where the riverbed would end, they could visually verify that while there were still three pits to their left and at least three behind them and to their right beyond the river, there was only one battleground in front of them. One single pit seemed promising.

Aaron did not even speak. He simply pointed forward toward the singular pit, and Malone shook his head in agreement. Malone was saving his words for when they exited. His next words needed to be about Aaron's glow.

The two descended into the canyon a short while. Their intent was to find a good vantage point to view the nature of the war going on there. Before they were even fifty meters into the canyon, though, they started to hear a battle raging. Ducking behind an outcropping as they had become practiced in doing, Aaron looked at Malone.

"Did you hear that?" Aaron asked.

"Yes, unfortunately," replied Malone. "We need to think this through."

What they heard were gunshots and explosions. Many of them. What they would soon discover was that in this region of the pit, those seduced by battle from the twenty and twenty-first centuries fought in a perpetual battle royal. Weapons ranging from bowie knives to laser rifles and from gas bombs to high explosives would appear randomly throughout the battleground. Teams and individuals fought to gain the most powerful weapons and maintain a hold on the most territory in an endless advanced war stretching over various domains. If one was killed, one would simply respawn and continue to fight endlessly. Furthermore, unlike most areas of the pit, it only took minutes to respawn in this battlefield, guaranteeing that the deaths would continue at a rapid pace. If a combatant tried to run away from the battle, this special hole in the ground would shift reality like a tesseract, causing the combatant to reenter the war from a different point. The only way to escape was to walk out without being chased and without a desire to fight. It had been years since anyone had succeeded at that feat.

Aaron and Malone had only swords, one shotgun shell, and a two-headed dog. They were at a loss for what to do.

# 24

Zeljabul received word from his forward scouts that Azriel was approaching one of the most dangerous areas of the pit, the modern battlefields of Ira. Sure, he wouldn't kill Azriel, but what if Azriel died on the battlefield? His other scout needed to return quickly from Asmodai. He needed to know what to do.

By the time the messenger returned, Zeljabul had closed to within fifty meters of Azriel, but he was relatively certain that they were still undetected. He was angered at the messenger for taking so long to return but refrained from killing him since he needed his report.

When he received his orders, he was mildly disappointed. He wanted to capture Azriel now. The thought of the battle excited him. To be able to bring in an angel would give him leverage for advancement for centuries. Instead, he was told to follow and watch Azriel and make sure that he saw the evil of men. Zeljabul wasn't completely certain what that even meant. All men that he had ever seen seethed with sin and evil thoughts. How could anyone not see the evil of men? As far as he was concerned, all he had to do was follow Azriel and make sure he didn't die until it was time for him to have his fun capturing him. The seeing evil part would happen all on its own.

With the new orders, they needed to move back to avoid being spotted. Having two search teams now meant that they were twice as likely to be spotted. As he thought more, having the extra team might help in other ways. They were in one of the most dangerous areas of the pit. Azriel was sure to die if he ventured into the valley in front of him. Asmodai was clearly unaware of the dangerous predicament that Azriel was in, but these extra men would be needed if Azriel was to live. Angelic Azriel would be able to walk slowly and calmly through this zone, but this puny human form was weak. Just thinking about being trapped in a human body made Zeljabul shudder.

So Zeljabul relayed the orders to his demon and human team. They were not to let harm fall upon Azriel. They would follow, protect, and expose him to the sin of men.

*****

Meanwhile, Aaron and Malone had heard the team behind them. Even Lava was apprehensive.

"We wasted too much time resting and deciding what to do. We must have sat here ten minutes. The demons that seem to be pursuing us have made our decision for us," said Aaron.

"From what I can tell, there are probably too many pursuers for us to go back the way that we came," responded Malone, "and while we wasted time thinking, we were at least able to determine that although riddled with advanced weapons, the people in this region are disorganized, moving around mostly as single combatants. At least the people ahead are by themselves for the most part." In the back of his mind, Malone felt that Aaron could take any single man or woman, even if the person had a gun, especially with his angelic powers.

"The humans in front of us have crazy weapons, but you're right. At least they are by themselves. I'd rather try to avoid one man with a machine gun than twenty demons with dogs and who knows what else. Haste, not waste. Let's get moving," said Aaron, running from their current hiding place to an outcropping about twenty meters ahead.

As soon as they were sure no one was near, they ran to a pile of barrels that provided adequate cover before the next zone of this canyon. The terrain in this area was highly varied. The field ahead of them appeared like an industrial complex. Warehouses, broken down vehicles, concrete barriers, fences, factory like buildings, and all types of hiding places were in front of them, but forward into the slew of potential death traps they had to move.

Each time they moved forward, they could hear more gunfire and explosions. The question was whether to try and be sneaky or simply continue to run as quickly as they could across the battlefield, trying to avoid encounters as much as possible. If they went too slowly, their pursuers would catch up, and if they went too quickly, they would surely die.

Aaron looked at Malone. Trying to speak as softly as possible over the noises of nature and the battlefield, Aaron explained his strategy. "I've been thinking," he started.

"Yes," responded Malone.

"If you are more scared of things than you are of God, then you are in bad spiritual shape. I know that we've been thrown into this pit of despair. I know that things look bleak, but I refuse to give up my faith. There must be some reason to all of this. Though we walk through a valley of death, we must fear no evil. God will be our shield. I say we keep running. The first person we see, we try to surprise him or her. Then we rinse and repeat. We don't have to be fast, just faster than the demons behind us. So I'm basically saying that we run and gun through this area. What do you think?"

Malone could see that the angel he once knew as Aaron had an unwavering faith. He wanted to proceed slowly, but he agreed that they needed to move quickly for the time being to get away from whomever was following them. "I'm with you wherever you lead," Malone said as he smiled. For the first time, he actually felt like they had a better than average chance to make it out of this hellhole. Lava also let out a woof of approval.

*****

Meanwhile, Zeljabul was concerned. Azriel was traversing deeper into this war zone. He had heard of Azriel's wisdom, but he could not understand why they did not continue along the riverbed path. It would have eventually led them out of the battlefields. *Azriel must just not be as smart as everyone believes*, he thought. *Either that or maybe Azriel enjoys all of the death in the battlefields.* Zeljabul sure enjoyed it. Zeljabul was also too ignorant to realize that it was his own sloppiness allowing Azriel to know that he was being followed that had led them into the fields of battle.

There was no time to be concerned about choice of path, though. Azriel was in danger. He remembered his orders. He couldn't capture Azriel. He had to let him see the evil of men. And most importantly for their current situation, he couldn't let Azriel die.

Zeljabul ordered the reinforcements to split up. "You twenty, go to the right. You twenty, go to the left. Each of you take a flanking position around the humans. Don't let anyone come at them from the sides. If you are so stupid as to die, then we'll just replace you. If we limit their interactions to the front, Azriel should be able to make it through this zone alive, even in his disgusting human form."

At his orders, the demons split up to half-encircle Aaron and Malone. They could then protect them while driving them out of the warzone.

*****

Lava could see that his masters were trying to get through the battlefield. He could also smell the demons around them. Instinctively, he went around Aaron and took the lead for himself.

"I think we're following Lava again," Aaron said as he smiled back at Malone before the two quickly followed behind Lava.

Aaron and Malone were pleased at the success they were having. Lava proved to be an exceptional lead. They could tell that he was sensing the presence of the people around them, trying to quickly lead them through the constantly shifting terrain.

Having ran through the industrial complex without harm, they then traversed another trench. Lava guided them away from enemies to one of the exits.

Next, they scooted as quickly as possible through another industrial zone, including a foundry. They spotted several assailants on the outside. Therefore, they entered the foundry through a broken window and took cover.

The intense sound from the burning fires within drowned out their movement as well as any enemies, but Lava warned them when someone was circling above. Malone and Aaron split up. Aaron found a back stairwell while Malone stood down below, keeping watch with Lava. Within moments, the body of a thirty something muscular black male fell down at Malone's side. As it hit the ground, Malone was mortified as the body appeared to melt. Aaron jumped down beside the remaining ooze, equally disgusted as the body was still whole when he jumped down from the ledge.

"What did you do?" asked Malone.

"There was a large crucible that I knocked over. Whatever was in it was not nice. We need to be careful," said Aaron.

Only the dead man's clothes, a pair of binoculars, and two pistols remained. Aaron dropped the shotgun, which no longer had any rounds, and both men picked up a pistol. Aaron grabbed the binoculars but handed it to Malone since Aaron's eyesight was astonishing in the pit. Surprisingly, despite the large number of hiding spaces, no one else crossed their paths in the furnace. There may have been others hiding or moving about, but they managed to avoid contact.

A small forest grew on the other side of the foundry. Aaron looked back. There was no sign of their pursuit. "We can go slowly through here for now. We need to keep our eyes peeled."

Malone nodded his head in agreement while he made quick use of the binoculars. He saw two individuals moving through the woods on their right. "I see two to the right," he told Aaron. As they both looked, two axes flew through the air and split both heads. "What? Where did those come from?" Malone asked astonished.

"I can't see anything. There is clearly someone stealthy to the right. We don't want to leave that side exposed," said Aaron.

The three ran into the woods and took cover behind two large trunked oaks, blocking view from the right. Each took turns peeking around the trees, but neither could see any movement.

They continued running through the woods in this fashion, but they did not get attacked from the right. Rather, it was from their left that a bullet went flying by, barely missing Aaron and grazing Lava.

Several more bullets flew by as they dove for cover. Lying on the ground, Aaron asked, "Do you see anything?"

"No, I'm not sure where that came from," replied Malone, holding Lava down beside him.

A few more bullets pierced the ground in front of Malone. "Go hide," he told Lava who then ran back into the woods and lay down beside a log, hidden by the brush. The shooter was either a poor shot or had lost them. Fortunately, the woods were covered in weeds and brush at least two feet tall in most places. They were probably getting covered in something akin to poison ivy, but at least they were not exposed.

Aaron rolled over to a tree and carefully rose up to one knee. He slowly peered around the trunk to spy in the direction from which he heard the shots fired. There, for a brief moment, he saw movement. It was too far away to take an accurate shot with a handgun, though.

Lowering back down to his belly, he signaled to Malone, putting two fingers to his eyes and pointing in the direction of the shooter. He then waved away, trying to indicate to Malone that they could move to the sides to flank their attacker. Malone understood and crawled slowly away.

Quietly, Aaron waited. A few minutes went by, and then he heard rustling through the brush. Someone sounded less than ten meters away. That should be within range. As Aaron prepared to peek around the trunk of his barrier tree, he heard several shots. Reacting to the sound, he swung his arms around the tree trunk as he stood, aiming his pistol toward the sounds. Seeing an unknown figure, he took two shots himself, adding another hole in the man's side. As the man fell to his death, Aaron could see that Malone had already placed a bullet in the man's chest.

The two quickly regrouped with Lava and silently looked around for anyone else. Seeing no one, they continued to move forward.

*****

Meanwhile, demons and humans from the following party were dying. The human hunters in the warzone were relentless, constantly shooting down demons or their dogs. These were clearly some of the best warriors from the human world, men who reveled in combat. A grenade took out three demons on the right flank. A trip wire set off a claymore, sending weighted balls piercing through two more. A sniper held down the left flank for two minutes while reinforcements circled around to take out the hitman. It might have been faster, but he had some form of stealth field hiding him that was far superior than any ghillie suit.

One blonde woman ran up from behind the central group and ripped open one demon and a dog with a fireman's axe before others turned and ripped her apart. At first it was difficult for the demons, even if it was only humans that they were up against. But the humans had advanced weaponry that the demons had not accounted for.

The demons were also killing. Not just the ones attacking them directly, but multitudes constantly closing in on Malone and Aaron. It was nearly impossible to stay alive in this battle zone without help, and Aaron and Malone received a plethora of help. At first, the demons would rip humans apart with their claws, axes, and swords. Eventually, they recovered enough weaponry to quickly dispose of enemies with bullets and explosions. The demons had numbers, even if they were dwindling.

Their handiwork went unnoticed by Aaron and Malone as well, except for any weapons left behind and explosions in the distance. One caveat of this region was the dissolution of the dead. Only clothing and weapons remained. These weapons could then be used by Aaron and Malone to increase their chances even more.

*****

Aaron directed Lava to move forward on the left. Lava noticed a head peek out in front of them and quickly ran toward the assailant. The unfortunate man released two bullets from a rifle that lacked accuracy at short range. As he reached for his pistol, Lava was already tearing into one arm with each head. As Aaron and Malone approached, the man was already dissolving. Aaron grabbed the man's holster. Checking the available bullets, he switched out his pistol and gave the magazine to Malone to top his out. Attaching the holster and pistol to his side, Aaron picked up the rifle. The magazine was still half full.

"I'll try to take the ranged targets while you can keep the pistol out for short-range sneak attacks. Sound good?" Aaron asked.

"Sounds good," replied Malone as they continued to slowly follow Lava.

Within minutes, Aaron let out a three-round burst from his scoped M16. A body fell from behind a tree that Malone had not seen. "Good shot," he told Aaron.

Malone then remembered the binoculars around his neck and searched their vicinity. There was nothing to the back or the left. He thought he saw movement again to the right, but it was far off and difficult to verify. An explosion sounded far off but not close enough for them to worry. Malone then saw a group of two men in front of them, perhaps they were searching for the one that Aaron just killed because they were also paused, searching their surroundings for where the last shots came from.

He tapped Aaron's shoulder and pointed in the direction of the enemy soldiers. As Aaron searched, two bullets flew by, one cutting through Lava. Lava jumped behind several fallen logs as he licked his leg wound. Aaron then let out another three-round burst as two more bullets hit the tree in front of him and Malone.

One of the enemies fell to the ground dead. Malone quickly jumped across to join Lava as he was too exposed. He also did a quick check of Lava and calmed him. When Malone looked over, he did not see Aaron. Once again, he saw a long stretch of glowing air. Aaron had inhumanly quickly shifted his position. A pistol shot later, and the other man was dead. Malone nudged Lava to see if he could move. The bullet had not done too much damage. Getting up, the two joined up with Aaron. Malone made a note again to talk to Aaron when they exited this zone, but there was no time or safety to enter into a conversation now.

As they moved ahead, additional weapons kept appearing on the ground. It was almost as if they were always right behind some large battle. Eventually, they both had several magazines worth of bullets, Aaron for the rifle and Malone for the pistol.

These bullets would be necessary as they finally came to the edge of the woods. The next zone was a large field of rubble, the remains of some World War II town decimated by bombs. A field approximately forty meters across separated the town from the woods. As they perched behind some shrubs, they saw a man running toward them being chased by two others. Then…*bam!* One of them stepped on a land mine, splitting his body into small flying bits and knocking the other two down, presumably dead, and then definitely dead as their bodies started to liquify.

"We might be able to sneak slowly through, assuming no one starts shooting at us, but Lava won't know what to do," suggested Malone.

Aaron had an idea. "Wait," he commanded. About a minute later, he returned with what appeared to be a laser pistol. "I saw this next to the last group of dead bodies. Might as well empty its ammo before using the others."

"Keep a lookout. Switch between the binoculars and your eyes. I'm going to shoot up a path through the minefield." Aaron said.

Malone nudged Lava, and the two of them went back a short distance into the woods. Malone told Lava to wait as he returned to a protected point near the edge to keep a lookout. Lava followed anyway, but he did not go out into the field. Malone ducked down with Lava, following suit, and signaled to Aaron to begin.

Aaron raised the odd weapon to start the path off closely. Leaning behind a tree, he released two energy beams before, *bam!* Another mine exploded. He waited for the dust and noise to settle, placing the laser pistol down and raising the rifle in case it was needed.

Malone searched. Seeing nothing, he signaled for Aaron to continue.

This process continued until five mines had detonated. Aaron was confident that a ten-meter-wide path was cleared into the town. After they were confident that they could get to cover, Aaron laid his excess weapons down while Malone retrieved Lava. Aaron debated internally whether to keep the energy weapon, but it was heavy with an unknown amount of ammunition. Therefore, he decided to leave it behind.

When they were ready, Malone smiled at Lava. "Back to you, buddy." The two were beginning to develop a strong bond.

Lava took the lead, sniffing the air as he progressed, doing his best to lead them away from danger. Just like the foundry before, this demolished town had too many hiding places. They were certain that there would be snipers, so they progressed slowly with their weapons drawn, concentrating on staying low and behind or near walls as much as they could to limit exposure to long-range weapons.

The first two building were uneventful. As they moved to the third building, Aaron screamed at Lava, "Stop!" Just in time, Lava came to a halt. Aaron had spotted a trip wire at the entrance to the building. Not sure how to disarm it or get Lava around it, they quickly scooted around the outside of the building. When they walked in front of one of the windows, a bullet grazed Aaron's face. As he ducked under cover, Malone circled in front of the opening and fired three shots into the room, not sure where the enemy was hiding.

"Did you hit anything?" Aaron asked.

"No idea. I was just firing to give us cover."

"Good plan. Let's each go a different way and try to flank whomever it is."

As Aaron and Malone planned to split, Lava jumped through the opening, snarling. "No," cried Malone, trying to stop him, but it was too late. A single shot was fired.

"Not to worry," said Aaron. Looking in the opening, Lava stood next to a dissolving female. Inspecting her bulletproof vest, it appeared that Malone may have hit her with a shot and knocked her down. Her bad positioning gave Lava the advantage as he jumped through the window.

The bulletproof vest was a prime find. Aaron grabbed it from the ground and handed it to Malone. "Don't think that I haven't noticed I've been healing a lot faster than you. Take this and keep safe."

ANGEL FOUND

"Thanks," said Malone thankfully. Yes, he had noticed how quickly Aaron was healing. The scratch from the bullet to his face was already gone.

The building they were in had several levels. Aaron turned and spied the stairwell. "Let's go up and have a look around. I'll use my scope, and you can use the binoculars." At the base of the stairs, Aaron turned to Lava. "Can you guard this spot, boy? We don't want anyone sneaking up on us."

Lava sat at the foot of the steps, just out of view of any of the windows. He was prepared to guard for his friends.

The stairwell and the remains of the building ended on the fourth floor. Aaron and Malone crawled around the floor, avoiding the many holes and keeping low to avoid being seen if they were to show their heads above the partially demolished outer wall. They looked in all directions, but they concentrated in the direction that they had been moving. A rocket flew from two buildings ahead away from them. Thankfully, the explosion wasn't meant for them.

Aaron crouched without moving for at least half a minute. As Malone crawled over, Aaron fired a single shot. "Got him!" cheered Aaron before sitting down with his back to the wall. "Keep down for a minute in case someone looks in the direction of my fire. I took out the RPG guy."

"Good shot," said Malone as he crouched down beside Aaron. "I saw a couple of people in a knife fight off to the right, but nothing behind us. The winner moved away from us."

"I saw several people running around. The only other person I saw was the guy with the RPG that I took out. I thankfully haven't heard any sniper fire either," Aaron informed Malone.

Malone, who played a lot of first-person shooter video games, added, "This must be a run-and-gun group. Any snipers might have already been disposed of for the time being. If we stay here, someone will eventually run our way."

"What do you suggest?"

"I know it sounds crazy, but this is a free-for-all with people spread out all over. There doesn't appear to be a single spawn point, so people are not concentrated in one area and always move in random directions."

"Sounds about right," agreed Aaron.

"Therefore, I suggest we do the same, but not in a search pattern looking for kills. We should just do what we've been doing but at a faster pace, keeping our eyes open for traps and letting Lava sniff the way. As long as we keep moving forward, we avoid anyone coming up behind us moving faster. We just need to stay down and keep our eyes open."

"Then let's get one last look and then take off as soon as it looks safe in front," said Aaron. The two did a quick look over the battlement-like structure formed by the destroyed wall. Seeing no one immediately in front of them, they headed back down the stairs quickly to Lava.

Lava took the lead again, but much faster this time. They ran from building to building, trying to get through the rubble-formed maze as quickly as possible, pistols constantly at the ready, eyes always looking for traps. At least every twenty to thirty seconds, a slew of bullets or an explosion could be heard, but they managed to make it through most of the battlefield without seeing anyone else. Just as their confidence spiked, within sight of the field at the other side of the town zone, two men jumped out as they exited a building.

From their reactions, they were not working together and were equally surprised. Each man took a defensive position behind a barrier and started firing indiscriminately with blind fire. The man to their right was the more skilled. He broke the pattern and was scoping the surroundings. Seeing an opening, he let loose a burst of three shots that killed the man to their left as they ducked back into the building for cover.

As those bullets flew, Lava jumped out and ran at the remaining man, but he was too slow. Another burst of three bullets showered forth with one bullet piercing straight through Lava's already damaged left head. Lava slid to a stop on the ground in front of the man's defenses.

"No!" Malone screamed.

Before Aaron could react to Lava dying, he noticed a greater danger. The man had just lobbed a hand grenade in front of them. Even though it was in front of their current wall, it was better not to take a risk. Aaron grabbed Malone and pulled him back into the building, putting two walls between them and the grenade before it exploded.

As they laid down, the percussive grenade shattered the wall that they were just hiding behind. Malone, still full of anger from Lava's death, quickly rose up and started firing in the direction of their enemy. He fired until his current magazine ran out of bullets and then continued to scream until Aaron pulled him back down.

"I'm so sorry, Malone. Settle down for now. Let's kill this man, and then we can mourn." After a pause, Aaron continued, "Switch out your clip and keep a look out. I'll move around and come out the back then circle around. Okay?" Aaron waited to make sure that Malone heard and was in compliance.

"Yeah," said Malone, coming to his senses. "Got it."

No sound came from the man as Aaron snuck around the building. When he had what he thought was a good vantage point, the man could not be seen. He did see a pile of three grenades on the ground, some weapons, and clothing. Malone must have actually hit the man in his frenzy.

"Hurry," he shouted as loud as he dared. "He's dead."

Malone ran up to Lava. The remaining head was struggling to stay conscious. "I think he's dying," he said partly to Aaron and partly to himself.

Aaron quickly grabbed some hand grenades and any usable ammunition, knowing that Malone was almost out. He then equally quickly ran around the wall to Lava and Malone just in time to catch Lava appear to take his last breath. Kneeling down, Aaron said, "Come on, boy, you can do it." But it was too late.

Malone did not hold in his tears. He wasn't bawling, but tears were clearly flowing.

Aaron looked around. "I know it hurts, Malone, but we can't stay here."

Malone looked up. "We can't just leave him lying there."

Aaron considered his options. Malone was right. They had only known Lava for a short time, but he had helped them to stay alive. However, if they dwelled over his death too long, their own lives would be in jeopardy. "Help me pick him up. We can take him into the building and cover him with debris. I think that's the best burial we can do under the circumstances. Maybe he'll respawn and we'll see him again. Right?"

"Okay," whimpered Malone as he grabbed Malone by his partially blown away head to help move him into the next building.

The two quickly dragged Lava into the building. Finding bits of wood and stone, they covered him as best as they could in a quick makeshift burial.

"I know he's a demon dog of hell, but I just want to say a few words," said Malone.

"Sounds good. Go ahead," affirmed Aaron.

"He scared me when we met, but then he saved our lives. He came from hell, but he helped us like an angel. May you find rest, friend."

After the brief eulogy, the two went through the building and stopped at the other side. They were almost out. A grass field separated them from another forest, this time filled primarily with birch trees. It reminded Aaron of a large birch tree forest he traveled through in Poland once. He wasn't sure if the entire forest had been all birch, but definitely, the place he had seen was filled with thousands of them.

Once he finished reminiscing, Aaron realized as Malone already had that they were probably looking at another mine field, and they didn't have the laser pistol anymore. But then Aaron remembered what they did have, several hand grenades.

Aaron smiled and tapped on Malone's shoulder to get his attention. Then he showed Malone the grenade in his hand.

"Oh, snap!" said Malone.

"I'll have to start up close. Go hide farther back, and I'll run back after I toss the first one," instructed Aaron. "I've only got three, but it should be enough."

Once Malone was protected, Aaron pulled the first pin and tossed the grenade through the back door of the building. He then quickly sprinted back to hide with Malone before the first blast shook the building. No secondary blast occurred.

Aaron returned to the now larger opening at the back of the building. The grenade had clearly done damage, but no land mines had been exposed. "Stand back, I'm going to toss another." Aaron hated to use up their grenades, but it was safer than trying to sneak across a potential minefield. He also needed to be quick before anyone else came to the area.

The second grenade flew to the same effect as the first. Aaron had now caused a large amount of damage, but no land mines had been revealed.

Returning to Malone, he said, "I don't want to be overly optimistic, but I don't think that there are any mines on this side."

Malone replied, "Let's wait a minute on guard in case anyone comes to check out the explosion, then we can run to the woods."

"Sounds good."

The two took up positions on opposite sides of the room, pistols in hand. As they watched, Aaron began to think of the anger Malone displayed after Lava's death. It was somewhat irrational. He knew that they needed to move out of this region quickly. It was also likely that Lava would respawn like the others. He wasn't sure if it was the pit affecting him or simply a need to let off steam as someone he was coming to know died. Emotions were a difficult thing to decipher.

About twenty seconds went by, Malone heard something that seemed to pass behind him. He tried not to breathe or give away his position. Then a man jumped up over the window beside Malone. The man apparently had seen Aaron and was going to charge him, but two bullets to the side of his head from Malone ended his plans.

Aaron gave Malone a thumb's up, and then they continued to wait for another thirty seconds.

Malone then returned to Aaron. "We don't want to stay too long. People will just keep randomly moving through. Let's go." Malone knew that one couldn't stay in one place for long in video games and assumed the same was true of this experience. He was also subconsciously wanting to get as far away as possible from where Lava had passed.

Moving quickly but carefully through the blast holes Aaron placed in their path, they made it to the next wooded area.

Oddly, to the two of them, they were able to pass through the next woods without seeing anyone. Most of the battle seemed to be behind them. They traveled at least one kilometer without seeing anyone.

They did their best to travel in a straight line, using orienteering techniques that Aaron learned at a survival retreat when he was young. Malone tried to follow the moss on the trees, but Aaron explained that in the middle of a dark forest, moss grows on every side of the tree. You had to draw lines with the trees as you traveled, turn at ninety-degrees multiple times around objects, and understand which direction your body had a natural tendency to pull. At least those were the lessons he was remembering.

As the end of the forest loomed up ahead, they noticed that there was an uphill climb with ridges on the other side. They realized that they had reached the end of the current canyon, alive, and they were relieved.

Carefully, they continued up the rise. They were both careful not to get too anxious lest something bad happen at the very end of that pit. They kept looking in every direction. Thankfully, they made it.

Just as they stepped out to the plains above, to their dismay, every piece of equipment that they had retrieved in the previous zone dissipated. For a moment, they were shocked and dismayed.

Sadly, Aaron said to Malone, "Apparently, you can't keep those weapons outside that area. I suppose it makes sense in terms of the balance of power in the pit. We've only seen arrows and handheld weapons for the most part anywhere else, except for the shotgun. Now I wish I hadn't left it on the other side."

They took a moment and looked around as they were becoming accustomed to doing. They could not see anyone near them. When it finally felt safe, they moved to take a seat and rested by a large rock just ahead of them.

*****

Not far behind them, in hiding, Zeljabul rested with the remains of his group. Only six of his demons and one dog had survived the last area. All of the humans were dead. So much had been sacrificed for Azriel's safety. They managed to kill every fighter around Azriel in the last wooded area even. Zeljabul angrily thought that it had better be worth it. With their dwindled numbers, they would have to follow well behind and hidden from Azriel until they could reinforce. That might take a while too. He didn't want Azriel to see them in their weakened state, but he also didn't want Asmodai to think that they were too weak to do their job.

# 25

Malone looked at Aaron for an extended period of time until it was clear that he was becoming uncomfortable.

"What?" asked Aaron.

"Who are you?" Malone asked in return.

"What do you mean who am I? I'm Aaron." Aaron was puzzled. He wondered what was on Malone's mind.

"I'm not sure how you are not noticing. I'm not sure if it is something with you not wanting to know or maybe God himself put a block in your psyche."

"What am I not noticing?" Aaron asked.

"You are definitely an angel. There, I said it." Malone nodded his head in affirmation of the words he was uttering.

"What? Are you crazy? What makes you say that?" Aaron didn't really think that Malone was crazy. He was beginning to wonder himself. He seemed to move too fast, heal too quickly, and his strength was uncanny.

"It all makes sense. Listen. Everyone—well, all of the demons—seem to think that you are the angel of death. I'm not so sure about that, but I've seen ribbons of light come out of your back. I've seen you heal instantly from terrible wounds. I've seen you kill ten men in the blink of an eye when before you were one of the most peaceful men I knew. I've always looked up to you as a father, so I've gotten to know you well, and now I feel like I never knew you at all. I'm not saying this as a bad thing. It's totally cool that you're an angel. I mean, come on, you're an angel! How isn't that cool? And then there's the fact that we started on the road and not in the pit. Darda made it sound like only an angel could do that."

"But you were on the road too," Aaron said, actually wondering how that might fit.

"No, I've thought about that too. I think I only showed up on the road because I died in close proximity to you both in time and in space. Plus, we were really close. Maybe that drew me to you in this place. Plus, Za was on the road too, at least if we can believe Darda. We were both close to you and we both ended up on the road. One of us has to be an angel, and the odds are way in your favor."

"All right, you also said that you saw ribbons of light coming out of me. Really? Are you sure it wasn't some kind of optical illusion?"

"That's what I thought at first," admitted Malone, "but then it happened again. Along with everything else, I had to believe it. I don't know. I almost think it was your wings but sort of ribbons of light instead of what everyone normally considers wings. Everything combined leads me to one conclusion. Even if it seems improbable at first, if the evidence fits, it has to be so."

"I'm still not convinced. What about Za? No offense, but she is the person I'm closest with in this world. Why didn't she appear on the road next to me?" Aaron asked.

"I have an idea there too, but it isn't one I like," said Malone, not really wanting to say what he thought out loud.

"Go on then, what is your idea?" said Aaron, trying to nudge Malone into speaking what apparently was making him uncomfortable.

"I think that Za did appear near us. It was only blind luck that we ran into each other, plus I was closer to you when we died. I was in the parking lot right next door, and she was across the city at school. I think that she might have been captured or killed. If she was killed, she might have respawned anywhere. If she was captured, she would have been taken away before we found her. And we need to find her quickly. I hate to think what she has been through." Malone looked down, distraught at all of the evil that might befall Za.

Aaron was also upset at the thought of what could be happening to Za. She was the most important thing to his living world. He needed to find her in this dying one.

"Listen, Malone, I really don't know what to think. I need to process what you've said. But there is one thing I'm 110 percent in agreement with you on. We need to find Za fast."

"Absolutely."

"So let me think about it, but in the meantime, let's get going. I haven't seen anyone following us. I'm hoping that we lost our tail in that last canyon." Aaron stood up and motioned for Malone to follow him forward.

Malone stood up. He had said what needed to be said. He would let it sink in for Aaron and then try to bring it up again later, especially if any new evidence presented itself.

Aaron paused a moment. He could feel her. Za was still ahead, and he would find her. Feeling her presence, he turned slightly to the left and then signaled Malone. The two then proceeded forward, deeper into the pit.

Within a kilometer, another tent city began to take form in front of Aaron and Malone.

"Do you see the expanse of tents up ahead?" Malone asked as they continued walking forward. "Are we back in the flower field?"

"I don't think that we circled around, but who knows in this place? I saw the tents, too, a while ago. I feel like I can see for kilometers clearly here," replied Aaron. He realized that Malone would use that as evidence of his angel status, but Aaron still felt that it might just be something about this place. It could be that this place worked like dreams, and in his dreams, there was nothing that he could not do, especially if he called upon God's help.

Malone wished he still had the binoculars. He had no special sight in the pit. He didn't even have his pipe anymore since he dropped it over the weapons from before, not realizing that they would dissolve upon leaving the last war zone. They also had no Lava. They still had a silver knife, and that was all. "Do we go around until we can find some weapons?" Malone asked.

"I see tents for at least a kilometer each way. I don't want to go around that," expressed Aaron. "From what I can see, they only have clubs and the like as weapons, but there could be thousands of people ahead. I don't see any demons or demon dogs, so that is good. I also don't see any flowers." He said that last sentence quickly to cover up his mention of demon dogs, knowing that Lava's death was still fresh on Malone's mind.

The tents were reaching the range of Malone's focus. He squinted and said, "They look kind of ragged, almost like refugees more than an army." Up until that point, they had been sneaking down low, trying not to be noticed. Now they stood upright and started to walk more confidently.

Aaron realized that looks could be deceiving, but as he gazed ahead, he felt the same as Malone. "I vote that we approach with care. If things get bad, we can run back to the battlefield. Of course, I'd hate to die and have to respawn after getting this far, but my senses still say we need to go straight ahead."

"I guess I'll vote to go ahead too. It's not like we have a third to break a tie anyway," Malone added with a smile. "Should we try to look intimidating or friendly?"

"Trust in God, my friend. Let's be ourselves. Then we have no fear of getting caught in a lie or having to live up to it."

As they approached closer, a mist fell over the savannah-like terrain. Aaron saw the mist as a good sign. There were no hiding places, but the fog would at least only make them visible when close up. They would also be a harder target if someone had a ranged weapon like a bow.

"You know, the only place we saw firearms other than the shotgun was in the zone we just passed. From what I can see ahead, no one appears to have any modern weapons. All I see are makeshift clubs, knives, and the like," Aaron said.

"That would be good news, especially since we are mostly unarmed and are trying to be our likeable selves," said Malone with a smile. He was slowly returning to himself.

They reached the first of the tents and makeshift shelters. Visibility was limited. The people were clearly on guard, but no one made a move to harm them. In fact, the most prominent emotion visible was that of fear.

These people also had little to nothing. Many were sitting on stones in torn clothing. Few actually had weapons, and they were not using them to intimidate the others. They almost seemed to be guarding each other.

"Do you smell that?" Aaron asked.

"No, I don't smell anything bad," said Malone.

"I noticed before what looked like a large ditch built to the right when we entered. These people are civilized and have dug a dung pit what must be predominantly downwind. I doubt it gets used much. I think I've only peed and pooped once in the long time we've been here, but even then, these people have a sanitary mindset."

"Thank goodness for that. Of course, I've only had to pee once too since getting here, but it's nice to know that they have a place to go." After walking for a short while longer, Malone added, "Look, up ahead. They've dug out a small lake. There are some teens taking baths." Seeing the teens made Malone smile. They were the first living people he had seen since entering the pit or whatever one would call this place.

"We seem to be the only people walking through. Everyone is staying in their own little spaces, but yet, you can see them interacting and talking on occasion. This place is unlike anything horrific we have seen since coming here. I think we should try to strike up a conversation and say hello," suggested Aaron.

That seemed like a logical idea to Malone who offered no objections. Conversation would be nice after what they had just been through.

By now, the bivouacs were rather densely packed. There was no more than three meters between most of them, and occasionally, there would be larger canopies with larger groups up to twenty underneath. Aaron headed for a tent with two middle-aged black men, another middle-aged Asian man, and a slightly younger looking Latina woman. Their diversity and pleasant demeanors drew Aaron to them; that and the fact that they were one of the smallest groups in the area and seemed safe. Their clothes were tattered, suggesting that they had experience in the pit and could be valuable sources of information too.

One empty rock was left in the small circle the group was sitting in. "Is that stone taken?" Aaron politely asked.

"Who's asking?" All of them looked up as the older man of apparent Asian-descent spoke.

"Just a friend wanting some company and a rest. Well, two friends, that is," Aaron responded, pointing to Malone.

"No one's stopping you," the man replied. All four in the group kept a close eye on the newcomers, though.

Aaron motioned to Malone to sit on the remaining rock as he sat down with his legs crossed.

"Where are you from?" The Latina woman was the first to speak as they sat.

Aaron began as usual by introducing himself to appear friendly. "My name is Aaron, and my friend here is Malone. We just came out of that battlefield," responded Aaron.

"I meant originally," she added.

"Oh, we came from Chicago," said Aaron. "What's your name?"

"How long have you been in the pit?" she continued her questions, seeming oblivious to Aaron's.

Aaron didn't mind answering. But he needed to eventually exploit his built-up social capital to get answers to his questions too. "Just a month or so. How long have you been in the pit?" Aaron tried to ask her in return.

"Hold up," spoke the Asian man. "You're trying to tell me that you've only been in the pit a couple of months, but you just waltzed out of the war zone like it was nothing. You're a liar!"

Malone spoke up, not liking to be called a liar and not wanting to start a fight, "We're not liars! No one said it was easy. Honestly, we were lucky to make it out of there without dying. And our dog died too." Malone hated to bring back memories of Lava so soon, but it just came out in the moment.

"Now we know you are liars. There are no dogs here, only the demon dogs," the Asian man retorted.

"Lava was a demon dog. We met him—" Malone stopped himself. He could tell that there was no way that these people were going to believe them. He stood up, ready to leave.

Aaron stood up as well. "Listen, we did not mean to anger you. We'll just be going then."

The closest black man stood up too, but not in aggression. "Stop it, Jon," he said to the Asian man, revealing his name to Aaron and Malone. "You guys can tell whatever stories you want. There's no place to go. So you might as well have a seat here and stay for a while."

Aaron looked at Malone and shrugged, pointing back to the rock Malone was sitting on before. Although he was mildly angered at being called a liar, Malone took back his seat as Aaron sat beside him.

"My name is Mike," the black man said. "My other friends here are Jonathan, Sofia, and you met Jon." After a pause, while Aaron and Malone achieved a small level of comfort, he continued, "Let's start at the beginning. You're telling us that you came from Chicago only a few months ago. What's it like?"

"What do you mean what's it like?" Aaron asked.

"I mean, what's it like? I've been down here for at least twenty years. Did the world collapse in Y2K?"

"You know nothing happened in Y2K," said Jonathan, slightly pushing Mike.

"Dang it, bro, I wanted to make sure that they knew that," said Mike.

Aaron could tell that they needed to prove that they were only recently deceased, although whatever he was to tell them, they surely must realize he could have just heard from someone else. "All righty, here's the history lesson. No, nothing happened on Y2K except a lot of partying. The year 2001 was not a good year, though, because of a terrible terrorist attack in the US. Then the world stock markets crashed due to home loans. But then everything got better. The Cubs won the world series. The US kept up its imperialistic ways, putting on wars all over the place. Oh, and more recently, a new virus nearly collapsed the world economy. Those are just the biggest things that are at the top of my head anyway."

"There was a new virus?" Jonathan asked. "Did it, like, kill everyone or turn everyone into zombies?"

Aaron didn't understand the idea of everyone turning into zombies as he was not much into that sort of thing, but Malone, who was more into horror films, responded, "No, a real virus called COVID-19. We had to wear masks to go out in public for months."

"Maybe you are newbies," said Mike. "That's the first we've heard of a virus. I'm sure that the dead from that will show up here eventually, if they haven't already."

Malone added, "It mostly just killed the elderly, really young, and those who had other conditions. Come to think of it, I haven't seen many kids here."

"You won't find any kids here. I ran into a girl a year or so ago who said that all of the kids down here are already enslaved, and all of the good kids don't seem to be getting punished like us." Sofia said. "If you're young enough, you go straight to heaven. At least, that's what most of us believe. I haven't seen anyone under fourteen for as long as I can remember."

"What do you mean about not getting punished like us?" asked Aaron.

"If you are a kid down here, then you were evil. As far as we can tell, no good kids come here. We assume that they got to go to heaven. The ones under fourteen anyway. Otherwise, unless you were, like, the most holy person in the community, you end up here in this hellish place. When you are here, you are punished. I've been raped and killed more times than I want to recall." Sofia looked down in sadness with her last statement.

Mike spoke up as Sofia let a few tears shed. "Sofia's own daughter was under thirteen when she died in a car crash. Her daughter was in the seat beside her. We assume that she also died. Sofia spent at least twenty years drudging through this hell, hoping to find any sign of her, but never found anything. Eventually, she ended up in Christian hell. At least, that's what we're calling this place."

"Christian hell?" Malone asked.

"Well, everyone in this camp, at least those who stay and don't just come here trying to kill a few humans, claims to be a Christian. I have to admit, I'm not sure anymore." Mike searched his soul. He really wasn't sure what to believe anymore. "I'm not going to be stupid and say that I don't believe now. The last person I saw do that disappeared. I hate to think where he went if it's worse than this place."

Aaron didn't want to tell them what they had learned. If these people were in the pit, then their faith was weak. But without the angel of death, they did not get their chance at redemption. Aaron hoped that when the angel returned, that these people would get their chance. Leaving that knowledge out of the conversation, Aaron stated, "So this is a Christian camp in the middle of what you believe is hell."

"Well, at least borderline Christians anyway," added Mike.

"And probably borderline hell too," added Jonathan. "I have to imagine real hell would be much worse."

"Speaking of real hell, why are you so close to the canyons of death just a kilometer or so away over there?" asked Malone.

Jonathan was the first to answer, "Because, dummy," which he said not as an insult but in jest, "no weapons can be taken out of the kill zone over there. So when people come out, they are unarmed and tend to leave us alone."

Both Aaron and Malone appreciated the wisdom in those words. They looked at each other with understanding that they would be safe here for a while. They couldn't stay too long, however. They still needed to find Za.

Mike added to Jonathan's reasoning. "Also, it's almost always foggy here. That makes it feel like we are hiding. Or perhaps this place is hiding us. If a demon horde does come through, it won't matter. We all end up running away and then returning to this mess when they are done."

Aaron decided to move the conversation toward their most pressing need. "Well, my new friends, even you Jon," said Aaron, smiling at Jon, "my daughter died about the same time as us. She's eighteen, so she is somewhere down here. Have you heard of a young white girl with red hair named Za coming through?"

Sofia, rising her head at the talk of a lost child, answered quickly, "You need to find a counter."

"What's a counter?" Aaron asked.

"They're the ones who count all the new arrivals," Sofia replied.

"Yes, it can get boring here, but there are many who like to go around and keep a sort of census. There are at least one hundred thousand in the camp now if not more, and every counter has an area that they like to call their own. If your daughter is new like you say that you are, then most of the counters will know her if she's been by. They always want to count the new ones, and a young girl would be special."

Malone quickly stood up, reacting even faster than Aaron to this news. "Please, take us to one!" he exclaimed.

Mike, being as bored as he and everyone else was, said, "Sure, why not? Anyone else want to come?"

"I'm in," said Jonathan.

"Me too," added Sofia. As she stood up, she looked over at Jon. "Are you coming too, Jon?" Although she pronounced his name Yon.

Jon had no intention of going with them. He had his search too for his wife years ago. She was the strongest Christian he knew, and yet he never found her. Those trying to cheer him up suggested that maybe she was able to skip this pandemonium and go straight to heaven. He just needed to be patient, and he would see her again. He had been patient for decades. He wanted to sit and wait for however many years his punishment would last until he could see her again or even to see God or whoever was responsible for everything.

Aaron, sensing Jon's reluctance, walked over to him. "I'm sorry that you don't like us or believe us. I'm sure that your friends can take us where we need to go. Don't let your dislike of me stop you from getting up and having something to do, though."

Aaron's words were true. As much as Jon wanted to sit and wait, he was bored. He might as well go along just to have something do. "I don't dislike you," Jon said slightly disgruntled "I'll come."

As the group started to walk off, Jon looked back and added, "You know, we're probably going to lose our rocks." As silly as that sounded to one more used to modern comforts, there were not enough rocks for everyone in Christian hell. Their seats would definitely be gone if they came back to the same spot. That didn't stop the group from continuing forward.

By now, the fog was starting to lift a little, making it easier to search for a counter. Mike spoke while they walked, "You'll know the counters when you see one. They're the ones that just wander around like they own the place. The way we're walking around, some of the people that know us are probably going to think that we've decided to be counters ourselves." His search pattern seemed rather random, but everyone continued to follow him as if he knew what he was doing.

Mike really didn't have a plan. He was actually just moving around randomly, trying to keep his eyes open for individuals that were walking around and who didn't seem lost. If they looked lost, then they were a newbie and not a counter.

After about fifteen minutes, Jonathan spoke up, "Do you know where you are going, Mike?"

"No, man, I'm just looking around for a counter. It's not like they carry a sign or anything," he replied.

Just then, Sofia interjected, "There!" She pointed to their right. About thirty meters away, a couple of slowly moving gray-haired women could be seen walking between the tents.

"No way," said Mike. "It's the twins. I haven't seen them in months."

"Who are the twins?" Aaron asked as their group started moving in the direction of the two women.

"The twins are a couple of old women that like to go around and meet all of the new people. They're not so much counters as greeters, but that will be even better. They don't keep track of who's been here, but they do keep track of anyone new. That's very fortuitous for you guys running into them," said Mike with a smile on his face.

Jon was not too fond of the twins. He liked them, but he didn't like the idea of anyone that sweet being stuck in this hell. If they were here, then his wife may be too. He slowed and allowed himself to fall back somewhat. He would be fine with the conversation taking place without him directly present.

"Lucy! Ethel!" Mike called out at the women.

Lucy and Ethel heard and turned to see who was calling them. They seemed a little excited at those who were approaching. Aaron and Malone were new, and they had not greeted them yet. Anyone new was interesting.

Mike greeted the two, "Hello, lovely ladies." He complimented the women who were clearly of an age that most would no longer consider lovely physically, but their spirits surely were.

"Aren't you the charmer?" replied Lucy, the more outspoken of the women. She couldn't remember his name but remembered seeing him many times over the years. It was something that started with an M. She was more interested in his two new companions. "Who are these two fine young men?"

Mike introduced them, "This is Aaron and Malone. They are looking for someone."

It was all that Aaron could do to patiently wait for a polite moment to interject, "Yes, we're looking for a young girl, eighteen years old, reddish hair, five foot six inches tall, named Za."

"Slow down, young man," suggested Lucy, smiling.

Realizing how quickly he had given his description, he tried again slower, "I'm sorry, You're the first possible lead we've had since getting here. I'm looking for my daughter. She died a month or so ago just before me. She's eighteen years old, reddish hair, and five foot six inches tall."

"And her name is Za!" Malone unintentionally shouted loudly as he noticed Aaron missed the name the second time.

The two women looked at each other. They mumbled back-and-forth a few seconds before Ethel said, "There was the redhead from the south, but she was much older."

"Oh, yes, she was at least thirty. It's been much more than a month since we've seen a white girl under twenty," added Lucy.

"Yes, not that many young ones lately. There was a Zara or Zhara. I think she was mulatto," said Ethel.

"Oh, yes, you are so good Ethel. Could that be your daughter, young man?" Ethel asked.

"No," said Aaron as his head and heart sank.

"Are you sure she's here?" Lucy asked. "I'm sorry, but that is all we can think of. There are other counters. Maybe they saw her. If it's only been a few weeks, it's possible that we haven't met her yet."

"So true," added Ethel. "We don't get around that quickly."

"Thank you, ladies. Unfortunately, we know that she is some-where here in the pit. I don't know how to describe it, but I can feel it." Aaron's hope had faded.

Sofia was also heartbroken. She truly hoped to help someone else find their lost child. This place really was a psychological hell. "I'm sorry," she consoled Aaron. "Don't give up."

Hearing those words cheered Aaron up slightly. Za had been in the same direction the entire time. At least that suggested that she might not have died, unless she was respawning in the same area. But she was there somewhere. They would just have to keep looking.

"We'll find her," added Malone, speaking to himself as much as Aaron.

As he finished speaking, screams and the clash of weapons could be heard approaching.

*****

The moment Aaron and Malone had entered the camp, Zeljabul reluctantly called for reinforcements. He was ordered by Asmodai to only show Aaron evil, and that was not happening. They couldn't afford to allow Azriel to see hope.

Unfortunately, the refugee camps were difficult for the demons to find. The pit was enormous, and it rarely would direct a demon to a camp with so little sin. Only by following Aaron had they found it. The mere site of the camp disgusted Zeljabul and the other demons.

The camp afforded him a reason to request reinforcements. He would not look weak. Instead, he would show initiative at wiping as much of the camp out as they could while pushing Azriel to another zone of sin.

Zeljabul did not request a scouting party or even a platoon. He sent for an entire legion of six thousand demons. Asmodai was willing to comply as they would have the opportunity to destroy a Christian camp. Within ten minutes, the entire legion had arrived by directed demonic teleportation to the outside of the war zone. Once they arrived, they couldn't simply rush in and destroy the camp. He designated lieutenants and sergeants to spread descriptions of Azriel's human form. No matter what, he was not to be killed. If he engaged them, they were to retreat. All they needed to do was destroy as many humans as they could to show him that there was no reason to hope.

Also, if they did see Azriel, they needed to send his location to Zeljabul. They knew Azriel had entered the camp but had not followed him in. At the moment, they were unsure of his exact location.

Zeljabul had not revealed that bit of knowledge to Asmodai lest he lose his head.

As Aaron and Malone were finishing their conversation with the women, the demons began their attack.

*****

At first, a few people ran by the group. Eventually, a stampede of scared humans rushed by. There was no time to think about what was happening. Everyone simply turned and ran with the crowd. Anyone resisting would be trampled.

To describe what followed as anything other than a slaughter would have been an understatement. Within thirty minutes, the legion of demons had cleared out an entire square kilometer of the refugee camp. Thousands of humans had already dissipated. Hundreds more, who had not yet dissolved, lay in pieces.

Aaron and Malone managed to stay together in the pandemonium, but they lost the others. Aaron doubted that they would be able to find them again in a reasonable amount of time after the chaos settled. He was also tired of running. He was tired of all of the death. How dare these demons kill these people who should have been saved! He would not allow it. He could not allow it. He would rather die than do nothing, even if it did mean waiting to save Za. The fate of the many outweighed his needs. Now he would fight.

Malone saw the change take hold of his friend. He could not help but see it. Aaron was glowing brighter than he had before. Numerous ribbons of light were extending from his back and moving too quickly to count. Aaron wielded his silver knife and turned to face the oncoming horde. Malone continued to run for several meters before he was able to stop. He couldn't believe what was happening at first. If he ran, sure, he might survive. He might even be able to find Za without Aaron, but he wouldn't be able to face her if he left her father alone. If they were going to die, then they were going to die together.

The fighting approached closer and closer. A broken off group of ten demons approached. In the time it took Malone to adjust his eye's focus, all ten demons were dead. Aaron had split all ten of them in one swift swipe of a simple thirty-centimeter blade. Their guts spilled out as he rushed to the next group.

It was all Malone could do to keep up. Slash, punch, jump, and kick—Aaron moved without seeming to actually touch the ground. By now, he had a sword in one hand to coincide with the silver knife in the other.

The demons did not know what was happening. In the fog, they were randomly moving forward, killing any Christian that appeared. They were not expecting one of the most powerful angels to attack out of the mist.

*****

The demons near Aaron were fleeing. They knew that they were not supposed to confront Azriel, and Aaron was slowly turning into his angelic form. Zeljabul heard the reports and ran to the commotion. He quickly noticed what was happening. Anyone not running away could see the light. "Retreat!" Zeljabul ordered. "Spread the word! If you cannot back away, then teleport back to base!"

They could not directly attack Azriel. Besides, their goal had been achieved. The Christians were divided, scared, and spreading in every direction. It would take months for them to reorganize after they respawned. Their quick humiliating defeat might even turn some of them to sin. Now, all the demons needed to do was wait for Aaron to move on once he settled back into his human form. He just had to hope that they had not gone too far. If Azriel exposed his true self, Asmodai would not be happy. An angel in the pit would surely draw Lucifer's attention.

Zeljabul kept fifty demons with himself as they retreated to a safe distance. They would hide and follow Azriel when he moved on. For now, the rest of the demons could return. He informed one of those returning to let Asmodai know that they had removed the Christian camp with Azriel seeing thousands die. That should make Asmodai happy.

# 27

All that Malone knew was that demons were running and teleporting away. There were no demons left for Aaron to kill. He had saved as many humans as he could, but the humans were also all running, mostly far away by now.

Aaron cleaned his blades on the clothes of the fallen demons. Walking over to Malone, he didn't even realize what had just happened. It was as if he acted on impulse, without thinking about or remembering his actions. His angelic form was already internalizing, leaving only the human Aaron. He only knew that he and Malone were alive, but many people were not.

"Do you believe it now?" asked Malone as the dust cleared.

Aaron, as before, was not sure what to believe. "I can't remember what happened, but it's undeniable that the demons are retreating. I figured that they had done their job and were going back to bother the real sinners."

"Dude, they ran off because you were killing them, and for some reason, they didn't want to kill you."

"I can remember dissolving one of them after another somewhat, and none of them actually attacked me. They were concentrating on the people around me that were running away. I didn't have to defend myself once. I killed so many of them, but I barely made a dent in their numbers. Their horde seemed countless. It was all such a blur, though."

"I'll let it slide one more time," said Malone, but this would be the last time as far as he was concerned, "because you're still like a father to me. But eventually, you're going to have to see what's going on and do something about it." Malone was still in shock from the carnage enacted by Aaron in his angelic form. Clearly, something was blocking him from accepting the facts. Once Malone discovered the right thing to say or the right way to break through Aaron's mental block, he could confront him again.

"Perhaps," Aaron replied quietly. He knew something was going on, but he still wasn't sure what to think. He knew that could not last. "I'm sorry. I'm not trying to be difficult, and thanks, you're like a son to me too."

The two stood in silence. After what had just happened, it took a moment to return to sanity and decide what to do. Fires were burning around them, mixing their smoke with the returning fog. The smell was becoming difficult to ignore as well.

The two began to walk. There were no more demons and no more survivors in the area. Everyone and everything had moved on, just as they were doing.

As they exited the remnants of the camp, Malone asked, "Do you sense Za? I lost track of direction during the chaos."

Aaron stood still for a while. They had just been wandering aimlessly for a few minutes. He was glad that Malone reminded him of their primary purpose. Aaron reached inside and tried to feel with his heart. "Where are you, Za?" He asked God for direction. His heart slowed as his senses heightened. A light wind blew across the field. The stench remaining from the battle caused a small cough to come from Aaron. Twinkling sounds could be heard in the silent aftermath as the bodies began to dissipate away, but he regained his concentration.

There. He felt something. Still distant. His feet slowly shifted, turning him slightly then at least ninety degrees to the left. He felt something, definitely stronger than before. He took one step forward. "Follow me," he directed Malone.

The two walked silently for several kilometers through the wasteland. A few remnants of the Christians wandered about, but no one was interested in interacting with anyone else.

The savannah was dry and hot but not oppressive. Over time, they began to notice a recognizable odor too. They could also begin to see a dark band on the ground ahead that was curling to run parallel to their path.

"Is that the same riverbed as before?" Malone asked as they approached.

"Sadly, it appears the same or another identical river," said Aaron.

As they approached the riverbed, differences and similarities quickly appeared. Overall, it was the same, covered in excrement with human heads sticking out. Suddenly, as they watched, a swarm of giant wasps flew down from the sky and devoured an entire region. Aaron and Malone ducked down in defensive postures, mildly worried with nowhere to hide from the insect swarm, but the wasps concentrated only a small patch of the river. They moved quickly to escape the swarm, just in case it turned on them. They also desired to escape the screams.

Ahead, another bank of the river began to boil as blood bubbled to the surface, melting the bodies buried beneath. The dissolved ooze rose to the top of the dung-covered surface. Malone was certain it was the most disgusting thing that he had ever seen. Even the sound was disturbing.

If this was the same river, it was much more diverse and deadly than before. As they followed its bank, they were presented with one horror after another. One group of heads, apparently all female, slowly sank into the stink for no apparent reason, suffocating as they screamed. Nearby, a localized rain fell. Clearly, its acidic content was beyond natural as it burned and melted every face it touched.

The poor wretched souls were weighing on Aaron. He looked at Malone. Malone had been through so much in life. Even before Aaron met him, he had found a light that led him to be good despite all of the hardships. Others did not have this inner resolve.

"Look how lost all of these doomed helpless people are," Aaron directed at Malone.

"I'd rather not."

"I don't mean look at them directly. I mean, think about how lost that they are. I can't help but want to help them, but how? All we can do is continue to walk along the bank until we find a bridge to cross or the river turns again. When I think about these people, I think about how sometimes I feel that everyone is lost. But some people, like yourself, can be resolved to life themselves, out of the stink. You had a drive to maintain your faith and hope, no matter how bad things were around you. If only these souls could have had the same."

Malone was flattered, but it was not exactly as Aaron thought. "Don't think that there weren't times when my faith wavered. More than once, I could have killed myself to get it over with."

"Exactly, but you didn't. Somehow, you kept going. That's what I'm saying. You had resolve."

"It just seemed like what I had to do to keep going," said Malone rather as a matter of fact. "I was also afraid a little. I was pretty sure that if I committed suicide that I would go to hell. Seems like I'm almost there anyway."

"I admire your drive and faith, my young friend," Aaron said with true love of Malone's spirit. "Sadly, this river seems to parallel the Earth to me."

"How so?" Malone asked, curiously wondering what Aaron was thinking.

"We are constantly faced with a choice every day. Do we follow the laws of God? Or do we make our own rules? More and more people are choosing their own rules. Sometimes, it doesn't even seem like a bad thing. Like someone wanting to change their gender because they feel it is what they are. Maybe it is. Maybe it is God's way of them finding themselves. But maybe it is arrogance of people to think that they know what is best. That may not be the best example. I still believe that God is about love. But he has rules that people break every day because they seem to think that they know what is best. They want to be their own god."

"So you're saying that the people in the river wanted to be their own god?" Malone wasn't sure he understood where Aaron was going.

"Not exactly. I'm saying that these people gave in to their own desires over God's. They gave in to sin, and the more you give into sin, the more you sink into a pit of despair. You get a hollow, short-lived satisfaction but have no filling, long-lasting results. In fact, is there anyone left on Earth who hasn't given in at least a little bit to sin. Without Christ, there is no way to be saved, and this experience has told me that you need an absolute faith to be spared at least some punishment."

"Right," said Malone, "but we know that they can still be redeemed. Man would have already received absolution if the angel of death was still overseeing the process. Although I'm guessing that these poor people were beyond such redemption."

Aaron accepted that, but he continued, "What if Earth gives totally into sin? What if Earth became nothing more than a river of anguish? Maybe it already is. Everyone is surrounded by sin. Everyone has at least some level of unhappiness. Is the Earth already like this river in a metaphorical sense? Are human spirits sinking into a river of filth? Can they be redeemed? Is God ready to let it go and give it to Satan?"

Malone interjected, "Yes, but you yourself have talked in youth group about how the Earth is definitely not heaven. It is itself a form of punishment from original sin. It is a test of sorts. God gave us a choice to make, and we have to make it for ourselves. We can't and shouldn't expect the Earth to be happiness because it is not heaven."

"Absolutely. You are right. I just hope that enough of us are still making the right choice," concluded Aaron.

"I'd like to think so," said Malone.

The two stopped talking as they processed what they had been talking about.

They had been walking for about another hour when Malone reached his limit. "Are we going in the right direction? Maybe we could walk over there," he said as he pointed far away from the riverbed.

Aaron smiled. "That sounds like a good idea." There was no need to be so close to the riverbed.

They had not seen anyone else for at least a day other than the heads in the riverbed that they now kept at a distance. For some reason, Aaron felt that they were still being followed from a distance. But even with his enhanced eyesight, he wasn't sure if he could see anything.

The terrain had shifted once more to a prairie recently. They both also noticed that they had dipped again. They were getting deeper into the pit.

Although it had been a while since anything substantial had changed, something was beginning to come into to focus in the distance. Malone noticed it too. This particular visage did not include stable structure but was rather a huge tempest. This massive storm stretched as far as they could see to either side. At least fifty tornadic structures coalesced in the same area of space, spinning in place without really moving from their given locations. To Malone, it sounded as if a hundred roller coasters were simultaneously roaring by, even at a distance.

"Do we keep moving forward? Or do we wait out that storm?" Malone asked.

The two had actually not spoken in some time. Thus, Aaron was a little surprised at the sound. "I'm still sensing Za up ahead and definitely beginning to get near. Let's get closer, and then we can decide. I'm not even sure that the storm will go away. It's probably another form of punishment for whoever is unlucky enough to be drawn to it."

"All right, let's have a closer look," agreed Malone.

As they approached the storm, they could see large groups of people on the ground ahead of the storm front. All of them were naked. Aaron considered for a moment to tell Malone to divert his eyes, but there was nowhere one could look and not see a naked body. Their bottoms were thankfully often covered by the prairie grass and flowers, but in areas where the grass was shorter, it was obvious that these people were not wreathing anything. It was not an erotic scene. The people were not engaging in fornication. They were not dirty from the ground either, but they were rather simply standing around.

As they drew nearer, the people in the groups closest to Aaron and Malone looked at them with surprise. Aaron wasn't sure exactly what they were surprised about. Surely others wandered into this area with clothes on. Yet, no one had clothes on, not even clothes that they might have stolen from someone else. Thankfully, no one seemed to be aggressive.

"Why are they all naked?" Malone asked.

"I don't know, and to be honest, I don't want to ask," replied Aaron.

Just as Aaron considered the passivity of the people in hopes of avoiding them as they passed through, a small group of three women approached them. Although not pleasant to look at, Aaron was glad that it was much older women so as not to be a temptation for himself or Malone.

Realizing that Aaron and Malone were not going to harm them, the women approached close enough to speak. "You boys need to turn around," the first woman warned.

"Why?" asked Aaron.

"You don't want to get caught up in the storm, especially with clothes on," the second woman responded while the third, a considerably older woman even compared to the other two, shook her head in agreement.

"Why would clothes matter in a storm? Does the rain react with cloth somehow to harm you? Or do the clothes just dissolve for some reason?" Malone asked.

"Young man, there is no rain in those clouds," responded the first woman.

Both men wondered just what was in the clouds. Aaron stated, "I'm Aaron, and this is my friend, Malone. If there isn't rain in those clouds, then what is it?" Aaron actually realized a while ago that the clouds looked odd. He had seen pictures of huge swarms of insects and worried that maybe it was something that ate all of your clothes, or worse, everything there was to you. For the first time, he wondered if when you respawned, maybe you did so naked. This could be a massive respawn point in the pit.

"To put it simply, those clouds are made out of people and everything that they desire in a terrible tornado stretching as far as you can see," the first woman answered. "If you keep going, you will get caught up with them too."

"Is this where people respawn after they are killed or something?" Aaron asked, pleased that these nice old women were answering their questions. They had been so helpful; he was almost forgetting how naked they were.

"No. Well, maybe some. That is the storm of the envious. If you sought to have everything in life, then everything is taken away from you in the pit. As they swirl around the storm, they can see everything that they want, but they can never reach it. Meanwhile, all of the things that they don't want keeps bludgeoning them. Eventually, they die and start all over at the bottom," the woman explained.

"It's like the horse and carrot. The horse keeps moving forward to get the carrot being dangled in front of it. If it stops for a moment, the whip it doesn't want comes from behind." Aaron found it mildly poetic the way in which these sinners were being punished even as he felt sorry for their torment.

"That's terrible," said Malone.

"But also very accurate," said the first woman.

"It's not just the obviously envious either," added the second woman. "For instance, a thief might be in the storm, always trying to get what he wanted while constantly being attacked from one creature or another. On the other hand, someone wanting affection will always try to catch the illusion of their desires but will then be castrated by flying debris."

"How do you women know all of this?" Aaron asked.

"We've been watching it for so long. The images are burned into our memories," responded the second woman.

Aaron found their story odd. "How is it that you have been watching the storm for so long, but you've never been drawn into it yourselves?" Aaron knew how the pit was supposed to work. If they had been attracted to the storm, then they should eventually become a part of it.

"We are not here because we are envious. We are hiding," explained the first woman.

Aaron could completely understand why someone would hide in the pit, but he had to ask, "Why are you hiding here? And what are you hiding from?"

"Son, if you've been in the pit long enough, you learn where to hide. If we hang out here without clothes, the demons just assume that we will become part of the storm and leave us alone. Most of the people you see around here are slowly moving to the storm. We try to warn them. Those with the right heart listen and stay away. A large group arrived recently too from some kind of refugee camp that was raided. Now they are hiding here like us, waiting to see what God has planned for us, if He will ever end our torment," the first women continued to explain.

"Are or were you Christians?" Malone astutely asked. Aaron was pleased at that question.

"Are you Christian?" asked the second woman, not trusting anyone. No one would openly admit to being a Christian in the pit unless they wanted to get attacked. Although these women had been in the pit for many years, they had not seen the refugee camp and found few people claiming to be Christians around the storm until recently.

"Yes, we are," answered Malone.

The women were shocked at how quickly and honestly Malone had answered the question. The first one said, "If that is true, then you will heed our warning. Stay away from the storm. If you stay here, you'll at the very least need to take off your clothes. If some of the others see that you have anything, they will want to take it from you, no matter what."

By now, both of the men had swords picked up from the demons, and Aaron still had the silver knife. "As much as I want to blend in, I don't think it is a good idea to give up our weapons," Aaron told Malone.

"And I'm just not comfortable being naked either," added Malone back.

"Then you should leave," warned the first woman. "You clearly have material desires, and it is not safe for you around the storm."

Aaron knew that they could not leave. Wherever Za was, it felt like she was on the other side of the storm.

Both men also noticed that the storm was getting louder. They were shouting to be heard now. The women did not seem alarmed, however. There had to be a natural back-and-forth motion to the storm.

Aaron, thankful for the helpful women, asked, "Do you know if it is possible to go through the storm without getting drawn into it?"

"Weren't you listening, foolish man? It's like a tornado. How are you going to walk through a tornado?" The second woman almost scolded Aaron for the question that he asked.

"Dude, I don't like what you're thinking," said Malone.

"Give me a minute," requested Aaron. Aaron watched the storm. Now that he knew what to look for, he could see the people swirling in the storm, their desires always just out of reach. The harder and longer they tried, the higher into the storm they were drawn, constantly taking damage as they did so until, when they reached the top, they either dissipated from the damage or fell back to the ground to die and start again. But there was more to it than the woman had revealed or even understood before. After several minutes of observation, he had a plan.

The women had tired of waiting and were back to watching the storm.

"Hear me out," requested Aaron to Malone. "The storm doesn't appear to be what kills them. It just reveals what they desire, causing them to be swept up by that desire. The longer they hold onto that desire, the higher and faster they go. But if they give up on that desire, they slowly fall back down, even if only for a moment.

Envious desires draw you up, but lack of desire brings you down. I'm at least 90 percent convinced that the completely satisfied man could walk straight through that storm. The problem is that no such man exists, and the storm seems to have no shortage of temptations."

"Well, uh, I try, but I definitely have desires too, like surviving to find Za…I definitely couldn't just walk through that storm."

"Yes, we all want something," explained Aaron. "But what you desire is not always for yourself. Selflessness is what the woman's story was missing. Selfless desires are acceptable. If you think only about saving Za rather than how much you want her, then you are fine. Think about agape. Think about what you can do to help her rather than what she can do to please you. The key is selflessness. God doesn't want you to go with nothing. He just wants your greatest desire to be helping others."

"This is a terrible risk, Aaron. We could get caught up in that storm forever like the woman said. Then we would never be able to save Za."

"Listen to the boy," said the first woman who was still partially paying attention to them. "You'd be better spending forever here with us rather than walking into that storm."

"It would only add a day or two to go around the storm too," said Malone.

"But a day or two here twists the terrain. We could end up no closer to Za. The pit leads you to where you need to be, and it led us here. If we go against it, will the pit go against us?" argued Aaron. "I'm telling you something is directing me to go into that storm. Maybe the pit is trying to teach us a lesson."

"I think that this place is starting to drive you a wee bit insane," Malone deduced.

"I know it sounds insane, but I feel this." Then Aaron pulled the ace out of his sleeve. "And if we get into trouble, then the angel in me will surely save us, right?"

Malone did not know what to say. Aaron had found the one argument he couldn't counter. Malone was the one trying to get Aaron to accept his angelic side. To deny its existence now would be to set them back to the beginning. He would no longer be able to press Aaron to accept the truth. The discussion was over, and Aaron had won. "What is your plan?" Malone slowly spoke in his reluctance.

Aaron explained the plan. First, the two men made ropes out of their shirts. Using these ropes, they tied themselves together so that they would not get separated in the storm. With other bits of cloth, they made sure that the sword hilts were securely fastened to their belt and thighs. Aaron ripped off the bottom of his pants to tie the silver knife more securely as well.

Then the two men started slowly walking toward the storm. The women looked on incredulously. Sadly, they felt that this was the last time that they would see these two men. "Don't do it," they all entreated Aaron and Malone, but to no avail. Once again, they had failed to save anyone from the storm.

"The storm is metaphysical. It is whipped up by our wants and desires. The moment you feel yourself being pulled into the storm, try to think only about finding and saving Za. Think only about others and their needs, not your own," ordered Aaron.

"I'll try my best," said Malone. He was not lying, but he did not have confidence in his words either.

As they moved forward, the dirt about their feet began to swirl. "For Za!" shouted Aaron. Malone then repeated the mantra. The two kept chanting as they moved into the storm until the women could no longer see them. The one that did not speak began to cry, wishing she could have found the words to save them.

The plan started off well. Aaron and Malone made it at least forty meters into the storm. They were mostly crawling, keeping their bodies as close to the ground as possible, gripping the dirt with their fingers as they moved. "You were right," said Malone. "I can see the stories in the lives of those above being played out as their desires are dangled in front of them by the storm, but we have managed to stay on the ground. We just have to keep thinking about saving Za. Or thinking in sorrow of those above. Either way, the key is to think of others."

Aaron barely heard anything that Malone had said. He thought that he heard something about Za. "Good, save Za," he reiterated.

As they continued, Malone could feel a tugging at his waist for the first time. Maybe the storm had only allowed them to get drawn in beyond the point of no return before it would capture them. Maybe he lost focus. He wasn't sure what the cause was, but he couldn't let the storm take the sword. He would need that later. As he reached down to take a stronger hold over the sword, and as he did so, a great wind swept the men's feet off the ground. Within seconds, they were ten meters high and beginning to spin.

They fought to maintain their bearings as they were tossed in circles both horizontally and vertically by the winds.

"I'm going to be sick," shouted Malone loud enough to be heard over the winds.

"We must have thought about ourselves. Return to the mantra. For Za. Find Za. Save as many as we can. We want for nothing. God is our provider. Think about whatever you can think of to not think about yourself!" screamed Aaron.

"The wind is pulling at my sword!" screamed Malone. "It's ripping the rope. It's slapping against my leg so hard it hurts!"

Aaron suddenly realized their mistake. "Try to consider that we need the swords to help us to help others. Don't think that we need them, think that others need them. The storm is trying to take them away because we wanted to keep them."

"Got it! I'll try."

As the two men continued to swirl about, they thought hard about why they had maintained their materials possessions when they entered the storm. At first it helped…but only at first.

"It's dying down. We're not flipping around anymore," Aaron said. But the men were still trapped at least thirty meters above the groups at that point and not going downward.

"Thank the Lord. I was going to puke. We're still spinning in the vortex, though," yelled Malone back.

"Looks like we are about twenty to thirty meters up. Scratch that. No thinking about ourselves."

Malone could feel the tugging on his clothes and sword again. Aaron could feel it too.

"It's not working," shouted Aaron.

"The wind is picking up again. I'm getting dizzy," added Malone.

"We've got to give up everything. It's the only way." Aaron reluctantly unfastened his sheath and let his sword go into the storm. Within moments, it was wavering just out of his reach. "I don't need that sword anymore, storm. You can have it. I will not fall prey to your temptations. Malone. Give up your sword."

Malone struggled to unfasten the belt from his pants. So he simply took them off and gave everything to the storm. He was now swirling about, naked. Aaron, ashamed he had desired some level of dignity he thought was afforded by his clothes did the same thing. He pulled down his pants and gave them to the storm.

Instantly, the two men were swirling faster and faster until they could hardly maintain their consciousness, thinking that they had made a fatal mistake. But then, the storm just as suddenly subsided as if the initial blast was the storm's anger at having been defeated. Malone and Aaron fell, but at this point, they were unwittingly only a few meters off the ground.

The two men lay motionless on the ground, still tied together, naked, but alive. The storm was still raging above them, but they were no longer a part of it.

Aaron lifted Malone up to his knees. He then thought about nothing but finding Za. Although they had lost all sense of direction, within moments, he could sense Za again. "Don't stop, my friend. We've got to keep moving. Think about nothing but helping others and finding Za." Aaron tried to use hand gestures to aid in understanding his words that were muffled by the storm.

Malone nodded his head and followed Aaron.

The two men continued through the storm. Occasionally, they would begin to lift up again. But they worked together to refocus on others. Sporadically, a dead body or two would fall around them. Although alarming, these occurrences helped the men to regain their focus. At one point, Aaron could tell that Malone was thinking about how much he needed Za over how much she needed him. As Malone was slowly raising into the air, Aaron gave him a slap that brought him back to his senses. After they both apologized, they continued forward.

Finally, after what was only about thirty minutes, Aaron could see the edge of the storm. He was leading, and Malone was mostly facing backward. Aaron closed his eyes. He wanted to tell Malone not to think about the end, but then it would be the only thing he could think about. Instead, he kept them moving forward with Malone facing away from the end so that he would not be tempted to think about himself in the first place. Thinking about escape might be construed as a desire by the storm, something to draw you back in when all you wanted to do was leave. The very act of thinking about Malone's well-being rather than the exit was serving to provide protection for Aaron from the storm.

Moments later, Malone, who still had his eyes open, said, "We made it. I don't believe it. We made it." He jumped up and hugged Aaron.

Aaron opened his eyes and turned around to give Malone a hug. The two embraced for a short hug before realizing that they were both naked. Patting each other on the back, they untied themselves and separated.

"Look!" said Aaron surprised. The silver knife was lying on the ground. As he picked up the knife, he suggested, "It appears that the storm thinks we need the knife for others more than ourselves."

"Well, having it makes me feel a whole lot better too," laughed Malone.

The two men spent a few moments unwinding the rope that was holding them together. As best as they could without getting uncomfortable, they then used the knife to fashion underwear out of the scraps to cover their private parts. When finished, Aaron said a prayer thanking God for seeing them safely through the storm. He then once again took the lead in their search for Za.

# 29

Hours later, they were finding it hard to see ahead of them. There was very little light as the sun was now too far below the horizon to matter, and the pit had no stars to speak of. Great trees loomed ahead as well, blocking out the small remnants of light.

Suddenly, they came to a halt. They could hear a rumbling. Then, just as suddenly, the air shifted, and the ground dropped, knocking them off of their feet.

"Was that an earthquake?" asked Malone, although it obviously was.

"It sure felt like one. I guess the ground doesn't drop gradually as you get deeper into the pit."

The two men picked themselves up slowly, not sure if the ground was stable or not. They tentatively began moving forward, on guard against an aftershock. They had to either move forward or climb up the ten-meter cliff that had emerged behind them.

The terrain in front of them turned tropical like an Amazonian jungle. The already dim light from above was nearly completely blocked by the foliage. They had to move slowly until their eyes adjusted, but even Aaron could only see about ten meters satisfactorily in the darkness.

Malone was raised in a tropical climate, but the temperature and humidity shift hampered Aaron's breathing enough that he was even more uncomfortable. They were in a dark, dense, hot, and humid jungle that could be populated by countless creatures waiting to eat any human that tried to pass, and they were mostly naked with only one knife as a weapon. They both had a plethora of reasons to feel uncomfortable.

"It won't be easy going back up that cliff," said Malone.

"Well, there's good news and bad news," added Aaron.

"Really? What's the good news?" asked Malone, laughing at the idea that there could be any good news in all that was happening.

"First, the bad news is that we have to enter this jungle where it feels like our chances of dying are higher than the war zone."

"All right, then what's the good news?" Malone pressed.

"The good news far outweighs the bad."

"Okay, stop beating around the bush, man. What's the good news?" Malone pleaded.

"Za is close. Like really close. I can feel it," Aaron smiled as he spoke.

Malone's mouth opened wide. "Whaaat? Are you sure?" Malone was excited and happy. If Za really was in this jungle, he would let nothing stop him from entering it.

"I'm sure. I'm not sure why, but I can feel her so strongly. It's like she's right next to me. I'm actually a little happy right now." Aaron continued to smile. From the moment he felt Za close, his tentative approach to the jungle was eliminated. He had hope and a fervor to move forward.

Malone felt the same fervor. Without even asking, he stepped forward and entered the jungle.

As they traipsed through the wilderness, their feet were getting cut and sore from the rough ground. With so little light, it wasn't worth paying too much attention to where they were stepping, and it was taking a toll on their feet. After about fifty meters, Aaron leaned against a tree to check his feet. Malone noticed and did the same.

Aaron felt his feet heal while he rubbed them. "We have to keep moving," he suggested.

"It's still tearing up my feet, though. Mine don't heal as quickly as yours," said Malone.

Aaron had an idea. "Here, don't get uncomfortable, but why don't we take our loin clothes and wrap them on your feet? It's the only way we can make it through here quickly. I know we'll probably be eaten up by insects, but it has to be done."

As much as Malone didn't want to walk around naked in a jungle, he agreed. His feet were in pain, and he wanted to cover them. They took off their remaining scraps of clothes and fashioned wraps for their feet. Once finished, they were rested and healed enough to continue.

The new foot coverings were very helpful. Their pace sped through the dark trees.

Aaron almost grabbed a snake hanging from a limb as they were moving, but he was able to avoid it at the last moment. He did not get a good enough look to identify the potential type of snake, and that was fine by him. He gripped the knife more tightly. Thankfully, the jungle was not very dense, but he would use the knife and not his other hand when necessary from then on.

A little farther on, Malone noticed a large mound of dirt. Realizing it to be a large ant colony, the two sprinted away in case they were to become covered in an army ant swarm.

"I feel like we're going to be swallowed by a giant anaconda, covered in army ants, or swarmed by gibbons," said Malone.

"Swarmed by gibbons? Are they really that dangerous?" Aaron knew that they were native to areas that Malone probably grew up in as a slave, but gibbons weren't the first creature that came to mind when he thought of what to avoid in a jungle.

"I just hate gibbons. I don't know why. Must have been something from my youth," explained Malone. He shuddered at the thought of running into any of the animals he had named along with many more he had not.

"Well, I wasn't too worried about people due to the darkness of the jungle. I figured as long as we didn't make too much noise, we would either go unnoticed or hear someone else if they approached. I was mostly keeping my eyes open for nonhuman predators. Let's hope we can avoid them."

"True," agreed Malone.

Another fifty meters or so forward, they noticed a clearing in the jungle. There was actually festive music playing and lanterns providing light.

With their eyes adjusted to the darkness, it was easy to see with the light provided by the lanterns. The clearing contained at least three similar looking buildings. They were all two to three story buildings approximately the size of a fifty-unit apartment complex. The sides were red panels, and they all had pagoda style roofs of various colors. Wax paper covered openings to allow light and shadows to billow out from the insides. Wooden walkways surrounded the buildings that appeared to be on stilts with stairs leading down from the walkways. These images were only from the second story upward. They couldn't see what was on the ground due to a large privacy fence made entirely of white pickets without any spacing to allow actual fencing in between.

As they approached, screams could be heard, but they coincided with laughing and excited howls of joy. Occasionally, they would hear a whip sound or the cracking of some object against another. They had no idea what these buildings were, but they needed to find out.

"Which way do you want to go?" Malone asked, assuming that they would walk around the wall to find an entrance.

Aaron pointed to his right. Whenever he was presented with a maze, he would always try to take the right, tracing out a path if necessary, unless there was a reason to go another way. He didn't think that this was a maze, but the large wall made it feel similar.

The fence was circular and easy to follow. The jungle had been cleared around it, likely to procure the wood used for the fence. As Aaron spied movement ahead, he put his arm in front of Malone who was moving at his side. Putting his finger in front of his lips, he signaled for Malone to be silent. The two then crept slowly toward the figures ahead.

It was easily noticeable that there were no humans in front of them. At what appeared to be the entrance, due to a large archway and at least four visible guards, stood nothing but what were undoubtedly demons and a couple of demon hounds. As they crouched and watched, several other demons teleported into and out of the compound.

Tapping Malone on the shoulder, the two men quietly backed away. They retraced their steps along the wall. When they reached their starting point, Aaron stopped.

"Aren't we going to walk around it and keep going on the other side?" Malone asked.

"No, there's probably a guarded door on the other side too. We are going forward," said Aaron, pointing at the fence ahead of him. He had no intention of going around the wall. If they did find another entrance, it would surely be guarded or at the very least difficult to pass without being seen. Furthermore, they had no clothes and only the one silver knife.

"You do see the wall in front of us. I don't think we can climb it, and there are demons inside. Whatever is happening doesn't seem pleasant either. Although I do hear laughter and clapping with all of the screaming. Why don't we just skip around it?"

Malone was correct. They probably couldn't climb the wall. Even if one of them stood on the other's shoulders, only one of them would be able to make it over. The wall was at least three meters high and was pointed at the top. Whoever was lifted up would not be able to turn around and lift the other one without being impaled on the spear shaped caps on the fence posts.

Malone was also incorrect. They couldn't go around this compound, even if it wasn't that large. Walking around the perimeter, Aaron had come to a sad realization. He looked at Malone and said, "Za is inside these walls."

"What? Are you sure?" Malone asked.

"As sure as I can be if I'm to trust the feelings we've been following this whole time. We need to try and sneak into this fortress or whatever it is."

"Okay then. Agreed."

Aaron smiled. "I intend for us to charge this wall over and over again until we break the posts enough to get through. With all of the loud noises already coming from inside, I think that any noise we make will go unnoticed. The flimsy walls of the buildings seem to be already shaking, so the shaking of the fence will also appear normal."

"We could run at that for hours before we get through," complained Malone, but before Malone could talk, Aaron continued, "And we have hours, don't we? Because any other plan would take at least that long."

Aaron's smile remained. "Yep," he said.

"More importantly, and I think this will help with any motivation you might need to barrel into a solid wooden wall, I haven't felt Za this close before."

Malone added his smile to Aaron's. The two men then began charging into the wall repeatedly. It was painful. At one point, Malone thought that he broke his arm. He wanted to take a rest, but instead of rushing the wall with his shoulder, he started to kick it in unison with Aaron. After about ten minutes, the wall had been loosened enough to rock the posts back-and-forth enough distance for one of them to slip through. They made sure to rock it slowly to avoid being detected.

Once loose, they pulled the posts outward, and each one picked a side to look into the compound. They were in luck. The demons appeared to only be guarding the entrance. The spaces between the walls and the buildings were empty.

Aaron formulated a plan. "We'll run to the door of the building right in front of us. That's where I'm feeling Za. Once we are in, quickly jump into a room and secure it. Then we can search from there."

"Sounds good," said Malone, knowing that any plan was as good as the other in this situation. "I'm ready when you are."

Quickly, they jumped through the hole in the fence and ran across to the patio and then up the stairwell to the back of the first building. Aaron reacted as a demon came out of the door at the top. As he sliced the demon with the silver-coated knife, the demon turned to ash with his remnants blown in the breeze.

Aaron and Malone successfully snuck into the building. No one was at the back foyer. Everyone was probably in the individual rooms doing God knew what. Rapidly and most silently, Aaron and Malone opened the first sliding panel door that they came across and jumped into the room. Two men were in the room having sex with two women tied to beds. They screamed as they saw Aaron and Malone, but the entire place was filled with screams. No one noticed. As the two men charged at them, Aaron swiftly killed them with his knife. The women in the bed were gagged and crying. They seemed relieved. However, they could not free them without risking getting caught. They sadly had to concentrate only on saving Za and escaping.

No one else was present. They were in.

Once the shock of the moment had passed, Malone bent down and picked up the clothing on the floor left behind by the men. "I know it's gross, but if we put these on and brush blood over our faces, we might be able to pass at a glance."

"Yes, gross, but also a good call," accepted Aaron.

They both apologized to the women as they dressed, sorry that they couldn't save everyone. The clothes left behind were ritualistic red scaly robes. These particular men did not have any weapons either. The robes were slightly large, but once they tore a few centimeters off of the bottom, they fit well enough. The robes also had hoods that allowed Aaron and Malone to hide their faces. If they were to rescue Za, they both knew that they needed stealth to avoid being attacked or reinforcements arriving.

"Are you ready?" Aaron asked.

"No, but I have no choice," replied Malone.

"All I know is that Za is near, I think on this floor, but I can't tell anything else."

"Then we'll have to go room to room." Saying those words sent a chill down Malone's spine. It made sense that they would need to check every room for Za, but it also meant that they would see a new horror in each room, and they would need to proceed quickly and remain inconspicuous. To do so, they would have to do nothing about what they saw. They couldn't afford to pause or to engage in extended conflict.

Aaron secured the knife in his hand with the blade hidden behind his forearm. He slowly slid the door open just enough to peak outside. From the sounds of the commotion, any number of tortures and pleasures were being committed in the rooms of this establishment. No one seemed too concerned about those continuing their business inside the building, and no one was in the hall directly outside their room. The two men decided to try and act natural and just walk through the halls.

Going to the next room, Aaron slid the door just enough to see a man being tortured inside. He knew not how as he kept his gaze into the room at a minimum. Once he knew it was not Za, they moved on.

They split up and each took a door on opposite sides of the hall, slowly sliding the doors open enough to peek inside. Still no Za. Still the people inside were too preoccupied to notice.

Malone slipped as he opened up the door to the next room. He was slightly nauseous from the violation of a man held above the ground by hooks through his skin. Aaron grabbed Malone before he fell. Thankfully, although the assailant briefly looked behind him, nobody was alerted. Seeing the scene was more than either could take.

Once recovered, the two continued checking each room in the same fashion all the way down the hall until it turned to the right at the end. By the end of the hall, they were both sickened by what they had seen. All types of torture bordering on the insane existed in these rooms, but they had to continue. As they turned the corner, they could see that several demons were down the next hallway, presumably guards. As they watched, the demons started to walk toward them.

Immediately, the two jumped into the first door in the new hallway. Thankfully, there was nothing disgusting in that room. Instead, there were two naked young women chained against the back wall with their backs to the men. The girl's backs were surprisingly only mildly scarred from whipping. The wounds did not appear to be fresh but had not healed either. Perhaps being unconscious was slowing recovery or they had been so badly beaten that this was the current state of their healing. The two girls had not moved and appeared to be asleep or passed out. They each had long hair, one red and one black, but both knotted and matted.

A pair of white silk robes, what appeared to be the standard wardrobe of the victims of this demonic brothel, lay on the floor. Malone picked up the one nearest to him and placed it over the dark-haired girl closest to him. As he did so, he uncontrollably let out a shout, "Za!"

Aaron rapidly grabbed Malone's mouth to muffle his sounds. Thankfully, no demons entered the room. The three they had just seen passed by the door, appearing to not care about any screams coming from the rooms. But Aaron was barely able to hold in his own scream when he turned and saw that the remaining naked woman was his own daughter. Aaron reached down, grabbed the remaining white robe, and covered Za's unresponsive body.

Malone, in shock from her visage, stood silently, his hands still clutching the robe he had placed around the other young woman. Tears began to form in his eyes. He held in his vocal cries as the tears increased.

Aaron, holding back his own tears, put his face to Za's. He could feel her breath on his face. "She's alive," he whispered to Malone.

The room in which the girls were confined was only three-by-three meters. Their arms were raised with their hands cuffed to the outer walls. A small whip hung on one wall. Across from the whip was a small cabinet with many small compartments like an oriental apothecary/spice cabinet.

Aaron snapped his fingers in front of Malone's face to try and bring him out of his shocked state enough to speak. "Malone. Look in those drawers. See if you can find a key to these chains."

Malone blinked and came enough to his senses to follow Aaron's orders. He quickly pulled out drawer after draw. Each one had different torture implements from a vial of acid to a box of pins. There were six small drawers across the top of the cabinet, and the sixth one to the far right contained what he hoped he was looking for: two small keys.

Meanwhile, Aaron continued to hold his daughter. His body refused to let her go.

Malone grabbed the keys and ran over to Za. Aaron held her up as Malone tried the keys. The first key slipped into the lock, but it did not turn. For an instant, Malone's brain formulated a secondary plan to find a thin shard of metal in the cabinets to fashion a lock jimmy like he had seen online. Fortunately, the second key slid into the cuffs and turned, releasing Za.

Aaron gently laid her on the ground. He equally gently covered her mouth to prevent her from screaming as she woke, although he realized a woman screaming would draw no attention in a place like this.

Malone knelt on the other side of Za as Aaron softly shook her side to side in an attempt to wake her. He was no expert, but he didn't think that she was drugged because her breathing did not seem abnormal. She also didn't appear to have any broken bones. He shook her again. This time, she thankfully reacted by raising her arm as if to stop whoever was trying to end her slumber.

"Do it again," said Malone, excitedly realizing that Za was waking up.

Aaron smiled at his friend as he gave Za a light tap on her face. "Wake up, sweetie," he spoke gently into her ear.

Za regained consciousness, punching out with both weakened and bruised arms as she struggled to escape the bonds that held her when she fell into her sleep. Aaron held her arms down as her eyes opened. Disoriented, she let out a scream, "Leave me alone!"

Aaron realized that he was still in disguise, uncovered his face, pulling the hood back. "Za, it's me," he said. His face was still blood-covered, but he hoped she would be able to recognize him."

Za continued to struggle as the creature above her uncovered. Then she suddenly recognized the face. "*Dad!*" shouted Za as Aaron covered her mouth to keep the noise down.

She didn't believe her eyes. Was this some new trick the demons were employed to get her to cooperate? The body above her appeared to be her father, but he was wearing demon robes, and his face and hands were covered in blood. "Prove that you're my dad," insisted Za, pulling her father's hand from her face.

"Sweetie, there's no power in hell that could keep me away from you," said her father as he fell on top of his daughter, tears pouring from his eyes.

Her father always called her sweetie, and the sheer force of emotions displayed by the man above had her wanting him to be her father. He also wasn't trying to kill her painfully. But in the last several months, she had seen all types of trickery by the demons to get her to stop killing herself repeatedly to avoid them having any pleasure with her. "Not good enough. What was the last thing my father said to me?"

Aaron could feel Za beginning to pull away. He sat up to give Za room and time to acclimate to her new reality. Holding back his tears enough to compose himself to speak, he said, "The last thing I told you was that I love you and to do well on your biology test."

Za began to cry, not tears of pain or anguish as her body had become accustomed, but tears of joy. It was her father. For the first time, Za turned her head to see the other individual kneeling beside her. The other younger man's face was nearly cleared of blood by the tears flowing down his face. All he could do was smile as Za focused on him. "Aaah!" Za screamed as she jumped up to hug Malone.

Honestly, Aaron was slightly put out. He had to prove who he was, and Malone received the immediate hug. Of course, Malone was her new boyfriend. He would have to get used to that. Still, Aaron realized that the work had been done, and Za accepted who they were.

Not forgetting her father, Za turned around and squeezed him with all of her strength. Modestly, she pulled her robe back closed as it started to open.

Now that the excitement was passed and the tears were drying up, Aaron put one hand on each of Malone and Za's shoulders. "We need to get out of here before the chaos of our entrance disperses."

Za wasn't sure what chaos her father was talking about, but she realized that she needed to do something first. She reached into the drawers of the cabinet and pulled out a small knife. Aaron noticed this move and was surprised not just at how quickly his daughter was adjusting but also that she thought to grab a weapon. He was more surprised when she took the knife and slashed the other woman's neck while she slept.

Malone was speechless. His body biochemistry could not handle any more shock.

Aaron, now only 90 percent sure this was actually his daughter, grabbed the knife out of her fist and handed it to Malone who took the knife more as a reflex than an actual conscious decision. Doing his best not to raise his voice and draw attention to them, Aaron nearly slapped his daughter as he asked her, "What are you doing? Now I'm not sure you're Za either."

Za, quickly realizing the possible confusion but also not happy her knife was taken, responded, "It's not what you think. We had a pact. I'll explain later, but you're right. We need to get out of here quickly. I don't know how long I was out of it, and they never leave us alone for long."

Aaron would make sure that Za explained later. For now, he glared at her and simply said to both her and Malone, "Follow me."

Peeking out the door, Aaron could see that no one was coming. Everyone was still busy torturing or pleasuring. As much as he wished he could save everyone, he realized that it would be futile to try. All he needed to do right now was to escape to semisafety with his daughter.

"Malone, same as before. Sneak along the side, jump in a room if we have to, get out the back door, but this time, run with Za through the opening," Aaron directed.

Quickly, they passed through the door and ran down the hallway to the back door. Without hesitation, Aaron opened the door, and they practically jumped down the stairs. The demonic spa setting was left behind.

As if trying to live out a cliché, Za cried as they crossed through the fence. Her father had rescued her. For the first time since dying, she felt safe.

The three of them continued without thinking into the jungle. They had to keep moving. Surely someone would notice the missing girl.

For as long as they could, the three ran off into the jungle with Aaron and Malone mostly carrying Za in her weakened state. Aaron seemed to have inhuman stamina, but Malone's lungs were burning when they finally came to a stop along a small river running through the area, although unlike the past river, this one actually carried water. Sitting on a fallen log by the water, they came to a temporary rest.

Exhausted, Za laid her head on her father's lap. She wasn't sleepy as you never really had to sleep in the pit, but her body had reached its limit.

Malone sat down beside them. He wanted nothing more than to grab and hold Za but knew she needed time with her father. Instead, he sat, enjoying the simple pleasure of watching his girl-friend breathe. As he caught his breath, he said, "I'm so happy that we found you."

"I'm happy you found me too," replied Za.

Aaron had something else on his mind. "You are the drive that has kept us going, sweetie, but I really need you to answer a question for me."

"What's that, Dad?"

"Why in this crazy messed up world did you kill that girl?" Aaron's voice grew serious as he asked his question. Just as he finished, he realized though that he had done the same thing to several girls in that place too.

"That was kind of messed up, Za. What's going on?" Malone was also confused.

Za sat up between the two men. "It's not what you think."

"Seriously, I don't know what to think," said Malone.

"That was a girl named Sue. We were friends," began Za.

"You sliced your friend's throat right in front of us," uttered Malone, still processing the thought.

"I had to. I couldn't leave her there. You have no idea what they do there."

"I think we saw enough to have a pretty good idea," suggested Aaron.

"I suppose so," admitted Za, "but I couldn't leave Sue alive. It was our agreement."

"I get it. So you were showing her mercy. But what kind of messed up agreement are you talking about?" asked Malone. As he was talking, Malone wondered if they should have killed people too to release them from that place.

"The two of us had been trapped there pretty much since I woke up in this hell. She was the first person I came across after I was captured. We were put in a cage together. She told me about how she had been trapped there for years and had seen all of the horrible things that the demons do to the Christians. The demons would use the Christians for their own pleasure while trying to get them to lose their faith. Before me, there was another girl, I forget her name, that was trapped with Sue. She wasn't sure what happened to her, but they had a pact. Every time that they came together, they would kill each other. They wouldn't kill themselves just in case suicide was irredeemable. But if they killed each other, it was a mercy killing to escape the alternative. Otherwise, the demons would do much worse to them, and when you die, it takes a week or so to respawn. So all you have to do is keep killing yourself if or when you get recaptured to avoid what the demons would do to you. When I was first captured, she told me all of this because the other girl had not respawned near her that time. She needed someone else to help."

"What a horrible alternative," said Malone.

"I'm so sorry that you had to go through that," added Aaron. "I should have been there for you." As Aaron consoled his daughter, he also breathed a sigh of relief internally. As horrible as her experience was, Za had not been violated thanks to her plan. Malone had a similar thought.

"I wasn't planning on going through with her plan until I caught a glimpse of what they do to us. The thought of murdering someone was not high on my list months ago, but in this case, it seemed like the best option. Oh, Daddy, we killed each other several times. It was horrible!" said Za as she embraced her father, finding more tears to shed.

Aaron and Malone also cried once more.

Za turned to Malone. Before speaking, she gave him a hug and kissed his cheek. "You're my hero too, Malone."

Despite all that had happened, Malone was almost the happiest he had been his entire existence. This experience ranked number three behind being rescued from slavery and the first time Za held him. Having been through slavery, it was easy for him to understand what might be going through Za's head. If he knew that he would not die and not be doomed to hell, he would have let someone kill him daily to avoid his life before Aaron and Za.

Za then continued to speak. "I didn't start here. I started on a fire-scorched highway. I walked for days until I thought I saw a group of people up ahead. When I went to ask for help, I saw that they were not the help I sought, but it was too late. These demons captured me and put me in a cage with other girls. That's when I met Sue."

"Then you do spawn near those you were connected with somehow," said Malone, looking at Aaron. The fact that Za appeared on the road and not in the pit also added weight to Aaron being the Angel drawing them there, but he would not press that discussion right now.

"Sue was saying something about that," added Za. "As long as we thought about each other when we died, we would respawn near each other. That way, we could work together to try and stay safe here."

"We should have tried to save her too," thought Aaron out loud.

"From what I've heard, there is nothing we can do until Azriel returns," said Za.

"Where did you hear that?" Aaron asked. It seemed that everyone they met knew information that he needed.

"From the other captives. There are hundreds of thousands of people down here, but it's not supposed to be that way. The evil people or the ones that go against God are supposed to go to hell, but they can't because all of us Christians are stuck here too right now. When I first woke up, I thought my faith was for nothing. I thought that I had been lied to about Christ all of my life. My faith was nearly gone. But then the other imprisoned ladies told me that it wasn't me. It was the afterlife. It was broken right now. Only the absolute true believers were getting into heaven, but countless Christians were stuck in this limbo until angels could lead them to heaven.

"She said something about everyone having to go through trials to test their love for God over themselves and other things. Sometimes, those trials continue after death if their faith wasn't strong. Going through the trials either breaks them or builds their faith stronger. I didn't believe her at first. I was sure that I had strong faith. Somehow, I kept believing. And then you showed up." Za smiled, knowing that she was safe for now. She still wasn't sure why she had not gone to heaven, but if her dad was there, then a reason must exist.

"We showed up on the road first too," explained Malone. "We met this guy, Darda, who explained a lot of things. He thinks, and I believe it too, that the reason we started on the road was your dad."

"Malone, let's not start with that right now," said Aaron with a slight amount of anger. He didn't want to talk about that right now.

"We need to talk about it. Za needs to know everything before we move on," argued Malone.

"What do I need to know?" Za asked.

"It's not important right now," added Aaron. "We can't stay here. We need to move on. Malone, you can talk about what you want, but we can't do it here. We need to keep putting distance between us and that camp."

As much as Malone had to tell Za, not just about her father but about his love for her, he could not argue with Aaron's logic. They did need to keep moving.

They decided to follow the stream. Testing the water first to make sure it wasn't just a flow of acid or something else deadly, they discovered that it appeared to actually be water, and it was comfortably warm. They were careful not to urinate in the water lest some parasite swim up the stream. They were also careful to keep an eye on the water for predatory fish or crocodiles. It was worth the risk. It wasn't as if the jungle was any safer, and Aaron believed that if they walked in the water, the demon dogs would not be able to track them. He was unaware that Zeljabul was still watching them at a distance, but otherwise, he would have been correct. The water was only about two meters deep in the middle and ten meters across, but the rocks along the edge were easy to walk across.

"So what do I need to know?" Za asked Malone again once they were moving down the river.

Aaron smirked but allowed the conversation to continue.

Malone seized the opportunity. He would be able to have a talk with Aaron who had been reluctant to discuss Malone's ideas, but that talk would be hidden within his discussion to Za.

"Don't laugh and hear me out, but all signs point to your dad being an angel, possibly the actual angel of death," started Malone.

"A what?" Za shouted incredulously. "He's my dad! He's not an angel, although he definitely…wait. Tell me what you know." Za was interested. Her father secretly ran a program to help lost children in an organization called Angelic Missions. His whole purpose in life was to help others. She always looked at him like an angel, and now someone was telling her that he might actually be one. The idea was not outside of her realm of possibility, especially considering recent events.

"So we met this guy named Darda. According to him, only an angel could cause people to appear where we appeared," Malone began to present his evidence.

"I'm not sure it was so definitive. It was more like no one had appeared on the road to his knowledge since the angel of death disappeared. That doesn't mean it can't happen," Aaron argued.

"Okay, I'll concede that it isn't a requirement that at least one of us be an angel, but he definitely made it sound likely. But that's only the start. Next, your dad's the only non-demon we've come across who had a demon dog follow him, and what is a demon but a fallen angel?"

"What? You had a demon dog follow you? Did you have to kill it?" Za was surprised.

"No. On the contrary, it died saving us. As scared as I was when I first met him, Lava was a great dog."

"You named it?" asked Za, continuing to be surprised.

"Well, he liked to jump in lava, and I think it actually healed him somewhat," added Malone, trying to defend the fact that they had named a demon dog or even considered it a pet. Although, as Malone thought more about it, Lava was more of a companion than a pet.

Aaron had not actually thought of that. It was true, only demons had demon dogs. Why had Lava been drawn to him?

"The biggest part, though, is that at least twice, I've witnessed your father glow. I'm not sure how bright because any light is bright in this place, but he glowed. Oh, and he had wings. Well, he had long bright ribbons of something come out of his back. They looked like kind of angelic wings. They were angelic looking anyway."

Aaron interjected again, "I'm still on the fence about that. I haven't seen these so-called wings, and they were supposed to come out of me."

"Well, it's like you went into a trance when they came out. You killed at least five demons with a single sword swipe once. It was awesome." As Malone finished, he conceived of another possibility. All of them were strong Christians. They should have gone to heaven in the first place and never gone to the road. Maybe Aaron made them come to the road because he had some connection to it.

Before he could articulate his newest theory, Za spoke, "Dad, is all of this true?" Za looked into her father's eyes. She wanted his thoughts.

"I believe that Malone believes everything he is saying. I know I've killed a lot of demons, and I did have a demon dog, but I'm not sold on the wings yet."

"Well, we'll just have to keep an eye on you then," Za said with a smile.

"I'm not going to argue about it, Aaron, but at some point, you have to accept who you are. God has a purpose for you," said Malone, finishing his argument.

For a short time, everyone was silent. Then Za asked, "Dad, have you seen Mom?"

"Hannah!" gasped Aaron.

Both Aaron and Malone stopped in their tracks. Neither of them had even thought about Hannah. Malone had never met her, but he had often heard Za talk about wishing she had known her mother.

To Aaron, Hannah was the love of his life. She centered him and gave power to the purpose of his life. Before his nightmares, he dreamt of her often. She was the reason that he could never bring himself to date another woman, even though Za pressed sometimes. There was no one else that he could ever spend his life with other than Hannah and, of course, Za.

Even though Aaron would think about Hannah almost every day when he was alive, he had not thought of her once since dying. He was slightly ashamed. How could he forget her for so long? How had he not thought to look for her too? Shame fell over him.

Relief was his next emotion. He had not felt Hannah when he looked for Za. Maybe Hannah was removed enough from his death. She might already be in heaven.

Then he shifted to hope and purpose. They had Za. Now they needed to find Hannah. If she was connected to Aaron the way that Za and Malone were, then maybe she was here. If so, they needed to find her and make sure that she was safe.

Aaron had taken too long to think. "Dad, have you seen Mom?" Za repeated her question, more emphatic this time.

"No," answered Aaron, "but now that we have you, we are going to find her."

As their conversation finished, they appeared to reach the end of the jungle. Instead of a cliff to climb, the pit was taking another downward turn.

As quickly as the humid jungle ended, the temperature shot downward. The stream iced over within twenty meters of the point where the pit took a downturn. Pines, spruce, and other evergreens replaced the jungle terrain. The temperature was definitely near freezing although there was thankfully no wind. They waited on the edge of the jungle for their clothes and bodies to dry before continuing into the cold. It would serve a slow death if they were to succumb to hypothermia.

"We're going to need more than these robes if we continue on," suggested Malone. At least after hours of walking in the small river, they were clean. The filth was washed off their clothes and their bodies. They looked somewhat human. Aaron had even done his best to shave using the sharp edge of his knife.

Aaron decided to sit down for a moment at the border to decide what to do next. As he pondered their situation, Za and Malone had time together.

Without thinking, Za gave Malone a kiss on the lips. Both he and Aaron were shocked. "Sorry," said Za, "I just had to let you know how I felt before anything bad happened."

Malone kissed her back. "Ditto," he said.

"By the way, thank you again," continued Za. "I still can't believe that you rescued me, and I'll never be able to repay it."

"It's been the only thing keeping us going for a while. I dreamed that you were in heaven, but for some reason, Aaron said that he could feel you down here. We followed his feelings or Lava most of the way to you. I'm so sorry that it took so long."

"It's not your fault. I've been moving around a lot, and I keep dying. It's really only been about a week for me that I've been alive."

"But you survived," said Malone.

"You survived too," said Za.

"Thinking of you kept me going," added Malone.

Za smiled and blushed.

"I mean it," added Malone. "I know it might be a bit much, but this place makes you think about all of your life choices. I think that's part of the purpose…of the road part at least. I think I love you."

Malone wasn't sure if it was the fear of death in this place or his actual feelings that made him confess his love, but at the moment, he really did love Za. It was not in the erotic sense either, although he definitely found her amazingly attractive. It was more agape. He would do anything to keep her safe and make her life—or death—better.

Za hugged him saying, "You're the best." Later she would regret not admitting that she loved him too, but in the moment, she didn't want to sound corny or insincere. Instead, she lowered her head to his shoulder and hugged him passionately. She did love him.

Malone grasped Za in return. The two were mentally exhausted and rested in each other's arms.

Za then returned to the discussion about her dad. "I just had a thought. Some say no one has gone to heaven for forty years. Others say that a few make it, but only a very few. Others said this is limbo or purgatory, where we have to stay until we pay off our sins. I found that idea to be the most reasonable."

"It does make sense, but it's broken, and no one is getting a chance at redemption. This breakage is all due to the disappearance of the angel of death. Without him, the other angels that guide the redeemed to heaven have not ventured down here. It's like they're waiting on something."

"And I take it he or she or it has been gone for at least forty years?" asked Za.

"Yes," said Malone. Realizing where Za was going with her argument, he added, "And we know what else is about forty." Malone raised his eyebrow to see if Za would decipher his clue.

"Yes, my father is about forty." Za thought deeply about what she had just said. Maybe Malone was right. Was her father really the angel of death? She could not fathom how any of this could be happening.

Malone had made his point. He could see in Za's eyes that she was beginning to see the sense in his argument. The next time he had to confront Aaron on his true self, she would be on his side.

Aaron looked at them. He could realize that his little daughter had found love. Malone had more than proven himself worthy over the last few months too. Rather than dwell on his heartstrings being pulled, he instead tried to think of a way out of their current situation. A solution was not presenting itself. For some reason, Aaron could only think about Malone's arguments. Was he an angel? Maybe even the angel of death?

It wasn't completely ridiculous. He had fashioned his life helping those that were lost. But he never even once considered killing anyone before he ended in the pit. He might be an angel, but in his mind, he definitely was not the angel of death. No, that he could not accept. But he was finding it nearly impossible to deny that he was probably an angel. He had no knowledge of how to manifest the angel inside of him, though. If that were possible, he felt that he would be able to simply fly them all to safety. Taking people to safety was what he did after all.

Aaron realized that he was exhausted too. His mind would not think straight. He sat down near Malone and Za to relax. Without intending too, he fell slowly into sleep.

# 31

As Aaron slumbered, he immediately began to dream. The rest of the sleep cycle was simply not necessary in the pit, allowing one to instead make other use of dreams.

Across the darkness, Asmodai felt the presence of Aaron's dreaming consciousness. He had become attuned to it over the months that he had been invading Azriel's human dreams. Sitting in his throne room, he felt the perfect chance to confront Azriel again. He dispensed with the theatrics from before and addressed Azriel directly.

In his dream, Aaron found himself in the circular room once more. This time, there were no books or windows, only the chandelier, the table, and two chairs of equal stature. Sitting across from him was the visage of Ash Simpson. Actually curious to talk to Ash, Aaron sat down in the chair on his side of the table.

"Have you seen it yet?" asked Asmodai.

"Seen what?" asked Aaron in return.

"The pitiful, sinful, unworthy humans," answered Asmodai.

"All are unworthy and fall short of His desires," explained Aaron, unwilling to accept Ash's argument that people were unworthy. He didn't care what he had seen in the pit. Definitely, he was constantly surrounded by evil. But there was always the light of love shining, even if slightly under the surface.

"Can't you see yet that the humans are unworthy of saving? They are sin incarnate. They kill each other. They take part in the most despicable sexual acts. They have only ten primary commandments, and yet few survive without breaking them all. Then they try to argue how precious and righteous they are when in His eyes, to even think of harm on another is tantamount to murder."

"Mr. Simpson—Ash—can't you see that it is not about what humans do wrong but about whether they have the desire to seek His grace and mercy. No one, save His Son, can hope to achieve purity on their own. God doesn't so much want them to achieve on their own but to come to the realization that they cannot succeed without Him. All are worthy of love. You and the other fallen have simply lost that ability to love or at least the ability to love others. There seems to be no shortage of self-love here."

"Stop calling me Ash. Such a disgusting human name. My name is Asmodai, and I am a king of hell."

"So you'd rather be a king in hell than a servant in heaven?" retorted Aaron.

"Actually, no, but if I cannot serve Him, then I will serve myself. I knew the love of Him, but He showed me no love when He cast me out. The humans are despicable and deserve death. We cannot be expected to serve such lesser creatures. They should serve us." Asmodai was angry, mostly due to Azriel's lack of understanding.

But Azriel was the only one with true understanding. "You see. Your words give you away. You do not know love, only hate."

"I knew love of God, at least once. I cannot be expected to love those who show Him none in return."

"It's true, some choose not to obey. They choose to hate, to deceive, to live in sin."

"Then you admit it!" Asmodai shouted.

"Absolutely. I won't deny the obvious. But that is part of the meaning of life. We have to decide for ourselves whether we will follow His plan. God wants those who freely choose to follow Him. I'm only now realizing that as a purpose to life. Although what the living call life is really just a slow death. Only here, after death, is there true life for those that seek it. Although with everything so broken, no one is getting that chance. But how we deal with our life experiences helps forge our future choices. Will we or won't we choose to follow God? That's what it boils down to. This place just serves to refine those that still need refining."

"But they do not choose to follow. Surely, you can see that they willfully choose to disobey. They deserve their punishment. We do not. We questioned Him only once, and yet we were cast out. Don't you see that they are unworthy of saving? Didn't your time in the pit show you anything?"

Asmodai was nearly pleading with Azriel now. He deeply desired to convince his old friend. Thousands of years ago, before the fall, Asmodai served under Azriel. He looked up to him. He did not understand how his mentor, the one he once adored, could fail to see what he believed to be the truth.

Aaron responded quickly, "Therein lies the problem. You fail to see that everyone is worth saving."

"Really?" laughed Asmodai. "What about us? We deserve it?"

"No. The moment you think you deserve it, you do not. No one is saved by their own actions, only by those of Jesus. Because you expect it as if you deserve it or can earn it, you never will be redeemed. Any human who thinks that way will suffer the same fate. God does not treat them any differently. The only difference is that they, through an amazing force of faith and will, choose to follow Him independent of any life experiences to the contrary. They realize that only through grace and mercy can they be saved. There is no other way."

Asmodai decided to play his last card. "If you will not condemn the humans directly, then you must surely be able to admit that you are like us, Azriel. You denied God's orders. You refused your purpose. You refused to kill. Why else do you think you fell?"

"Did I fall? Am I even this Azriel?" Aaron asked. "I'm beginning to accept that I have angelic aspects, perhaps as a Nephilim, but I see no evidence that I ever went against God. God has no need for an angel of death that kills. Any angel can kill a human if ordered. From what I'm seeing in this place, God has need of an angel that can lead the dead to new life. If that is the purpose of the angel of death, then I will gladly accept it."

"I honestly thought that you would see it our way this time. Don't you realize how precarious the kingdom is right now? If only one greater angel joined our forces, the balance would shift. We could end this whole façade."

"There is no façade. God did not lie. He told them what was necessary. They needed only believe."

"I honestly thought it would be different. If you will not see reason and join us, then you must die," snarled Asmodai.

"Bring it!" Aaron challenged.

Asmodai grew into his demonic form. From his human neck were added the heads of a bull and ram as his body doubled in size. A caudal serpent's tail protruded three meters from his backside preceded by two great flesh-covered wings. Then flames spit forth from his human mouth as he grabbed a great jeweled lance that appeared at his side.

Aaron was not impressed. The flames encircled him until they burned themselves out, harmless. Aaron grew in size and shone bright as a star. Numerous ribbons of light protruded from his back, enacting pillars of righteous light down upon Asmodai. The light burned his flesh, melting off one of his dragon-like wings.

This was not like earlier dreams. Aaron was in full control and had no need to run or retreat.

Asmodai was injured and surprised. He did not expect Azriel to be so strong so soon. Rather than press, he blinked and disappeared. He did not have to confront Azriel there. Zeljabul would catch him soon in the pit. By opening up his dream, Asmodai now knew exactly where Azriel was and could direct Zeljabul directly to him. It had to be soon. Azriel was gaining power.

With Asmodai, the rest of the room also disappeared. Aaron found himself in darkness, and then he awoke. He smiled as his eyes opened. He was still not sure what he was, but he was at least, in part, an angel, and that gave him power. He didn't want to admit it, but Malone was right. Eventually, Aaron would have to endure an "I told you so" from his young friend.

Aaron reach over and nudged Malone and Za. "It's time to move," he directed.

"It's so cold, Daddy," complained Za.

"I know. We just need to keep moving quickly. If this area is anything like the rest of the pit, we'll find something soon to warm us up." Aaron walked with a new confidence. He could do it now.

As they moved forward, Aaron realized that he had no connection to his long dead wife. He could not tell where she was. Instead, he had to leave it up to the pit to take him where he needed to go. It wasn't much of a plan, but it was all that he had.

Malone and Za walked behind Aaron as fast as they could. Aaron was walking at an abnormally fast pace. More importantly, he seemed to be glowing. From where they were walking, they could even feel the heat coming off of his body. The snow melted at his feet, and the air was tolerable. Malone and Za looked at each other. Neither of them wanted to say anything. They both realized that there was something special about her dad. They also didn't want the warmth to stop.

Aaron was realizing it too. He could feel that the air had warmed, but it was still cold. Their feet were beginning to lose feeling. They needed clothes or shelter soon. Even if they could heal, it would still be painful if they were harmed too much.

At just the right moment, clothes began to appear ahead of them on the ground as if the pit wanted them to survive. Clothes kept appearing of all sizes and types. Jeans, socks, shoes, shirts, even a hat were found. All of them scrambled to find something that fit or that would at least keep them warm. They even found additional swords and a wooden shield. What they did not find were any living humans. The clothes did not appear to be covered in blood. Aaron considered the idea that the individuals had died from some sort of plague. He wasn't sure if the clothes were safe, but if they didn't put them on, they would surely die of hypothermia. Therefore, they searched the increasing supply of clothes for anything in their size.

Their arms filled with apparel, they split up slightly to get dressed with their backs to each other. They wanted to be quick. Whatever was killing the people to make the clothes appear must be close, and they did not want to be unprepared.

Her back turned to the men, Za put on two layers of warm clothes. As she finished, she returned to the men who had already called after her that they were finished. Coming back together, Za was the first to notice that the sky was darkening even more than usual. The darkness was unnerving, and Za pulled closer to Malone, not wanting to be by herself.

Fully clothed and armed but still cold, the group set out to find Hannah. They were not sure where to go, but they knew that they had to keep moving.

Aaron and Malone were also starting to notice the sky getting darker. It was already like nighttime, but now it was like midnight with a storm cloud above.

The cloud was not silent either. Aaron, with his heightened hearing, was the first to notice the buzzing. The sound was alarming, and it was too dark for even him to see any form of shelter. The clothes on the ground may not have been the pit leading them where they needed to be. It may have been a trap to bring them onto the dinner table of some beast.

"Quick, let's get under a tree. Something is coming. Can you hear it?" Aaron said.

"Yes, I'm beginning to hear a buzzing," replied Malone.

"And the darkness is growing. I'm more scared than usual in this place," admitted Za.

The three huddled beneath a spruce. It smelled, and the leaves poked them annoyingly, but they needed to be protected from whatever was approaching.

The buzzing approached closer but oddly did not seem to get much louder. The darkness had grown to a near blackout, though. The three held on to each other. Aaron and Malone were both prepared to jump out at a moment's notice to defend Za.

Jumping out would not have any effect. Finally, the sound and darkness let itself be known. They were suddenly inundated by a swarm of mosquitoes. They couldn't shout lest they risk getting mosquitoes in their mouths. They couldn't run because there were millions of the blood-sucking bugs. They couldn't fight because the targets were too small. All they could do was flail around in the pine needles and pray that they survived. Even with their new clothes on, the insects found ways to bite them everywhere skin was exposed and some places it was not.

Only when they were covered in the guts of the mosquitoes did the swarm seem to die down. Aaron noticed through his swollen eyelids that a light source was approaching. He did not realize that it was him. Azriel's wings were growing and shining, filling the air with their glow. The wings zapped the insects with electricity while simultaneously covering his daughter and friend. Any wings that were not covering their bodies were smashing the swarm or blowing the remaining live insects away. Once they were safe, Azriel returned to his human form completely. Then he passed out.

Only a few minutes passed as Aaron returned to consciousness. He immediately looked around for Za and Malone, but they were no longer to be seen. Instead, only a large grotesque demon remained. Its body was that of a large muscular man, but its face was literally like a pile of feces. Zeljabul stood over him, smiling. A horde of demons surrounded them with torches that fended off the remaining mosquitos after Aaron fainted.

Aaron, in near angelic form, stood up. He was already healed from the bites. Calmly, he looked into Zeljabul's eyes, puffed out his chest, and said with a deep and gruff voice, "Where is my daughter?" It wasn't that he didn't care about Malone also, but Za was the first person to manifest in his mind as the words came out.

"She is safe," said Zeljabul with a smile, "for now." Unimpressed by the posturing of Aaron, Zeljabul was not in fear of the powerful angel knowing that they had someone Aaron wanted.

"If you value your existence, you will hand her over to me now," warned Aaron.

"Oh my, haven't we gotten aggressive? You see the effect that the pit has on us?" Zeljabul referred to Aaron as "us," believing that he would soon be a fallen angel as well.

"I'll show you the pit if you don't give me my daughter. Stop stalling and start talking. Where is she?" Aaron was now glowing and enlarged with at least ten ribbons of light extending from his back.

"You'd settle down if you knew what was good for you and your friends. The light you're giving off is going to attract every demon in the area. Plus, your threats mean nothing if you value their lives."

Aaron settled down, returning to his human form. He knew that he could do nothing until he had Za once again in safety, if that was even possible in the pit. He knew that if she died, she would just respawn, but one could be subjected to many levels of pain without dying. "What do you want?" Aaron asked.

"Asmodai requests the pleasure of your company," directed Zeljabul.

Aaron now knew that Asmodai had been Ash Simpson, the one who sent him to the afterlife in the beginning, which meant that he was also the one responsible for Malone and Za being there. He needed to be careful.

"All right," said Aaron. "I recommend you stay away from me, though." Smiling, Aaron added, "Now that I know where I'm going and that your boss wants to see me, I bet I could just kill you and there would be nothing you could do about it." Aaron knew that if Ash or Asmodai wanted to speak with him again that these demons would not be able to kill him, even if he killed a few of them, not that he was the type of man or angel to do that unless forced.

Zeljabul shuddered slightly at the vindictive streak displayed by Azriel's human form. Maybe the pit was changing Azriel. He also knew that Azriel was correct. He would need to stay back enough to be safe. Zeljabul tried to reason with the angel, "I'll keep my distance, but it will go much faster if we teleport."

"How do I do that?" Aaron asked.

"You'll have to let me get close to you for at least a moment. If you were angelic, you could do it yourself, but you don't know where we are going, and an angel can't teleport directly to one of the primary citadels anyway. Let me take your arm, and we can teleport there together." Zeljabul walked toward Aaron.

"I'd rather walk," growled Aaron. He looked at the demon, practically daring him to come closer, but eventually he gave in. Aaron walked a few steps toward Zeljabul attempting to intimidate him, disgusted by the sight of his face, but then put out his hand, ready to be teleported.

In the blink of an eye, the two were in the fields outside Asmodai's palace.

"Where are we?" Aaron asked.

Although the question had been addressed to Zeljabul, a man sitting on the ground answered, "You are wherever you go."

That was not much of a straight answer, so Aaron tried a different approach. "Hello, I am Aaron. Who might you be?"

"I am god. They all think that they are god, but they are wrong. I am the true god, though I suppose we could all be gods in one sense of another. In a few minutes, I will have to kill them to prove that I am the one true god. Are you a god?"

"No, I'm not a god." Aaron was flabbergasted by the man's comment. While the people in the Bibliotheca thought that they were as good as God, these people apparently thought that they were gods. "Why must you kill all of the others?" Aaron was curious.

"Good that you are not a god," responded the man. "You can be one of my subjects when I am done. I must kill them because they are heretics. They think that they are god. There can be only one god, and that is me."

At that comment, the young man rose up and walked over to a group of dancers. Without remorse or hesitation, he grabbed a woman's throat and ripped out her lower jaw to the pharynx. "Not much of a god, are you?" He laughed at the woman as she bled.

The group instantly became chaotic. Each one with great pomp and eloquence pronounced themselves to be the one true god before lashing out at the others to prove his or her dominance. One woman did nothing but stare at an approaching man, fully expecting that her psionic powers would cause his head to explode. Unfortunately, she had no such powers as she found out when he bashed the top of her head so hard that her medulla oblongata was pushed into her spine.

Aaron did nothing. He did not believe that there was anything he could do to stop these people from killing each other. They were too deeply set in their sin to listen to anyone as they were god in their minds.

Eventually, only one person survived with her left arm and leg severely broken. She lumbered over to the only other individual she could see, ready to kill Aaron.

Reacting to the approaching woman, Aaron yelled, "I am not a god."

The woman slowed. Her breathing was erratic, and the loss of blood was weakening her. Eventually, she fell dead with the others. Although unlike past deaths, these people did not dissolve. Aaron noticed that they were not entirely dead. They were simply unable to move anymore. Saddened by the sight, Aaron began to walk around the carnage. Within moments, Aaron could see that insects and worms were beginning to bore through the bodies. Despite their bodies being slowly eaten away, they were still alive, most likely until the very last moment. Aaron surmised that this whole process would probably start again within hours.

"You wonder why we hate humans," said Zeljabul as he directed Aaron forward toward the imposing fortress ahead.

Asmodai's temple was in the east, and Aaron had finally arrived. Zeljabul wanted to shift Aaron directly to the throne room, but no angel could go directly into one of the bastions without passing through the gates. Upon passing willfully through the gates, they had to give up their aura of protection. They became vulnerable. Aaron did not know this rule. Of course, even a vulnerable angel of the highest order such as Azriel could still take on hundreds of demons in that state before being destroyed and sent back to heaven.

Aaron was simultaneously disgusted and impressed by what he saw. The fortress itself was massive. Passing over the drawbridge that stretched for at least fifty meters over the moats, Aaron was led to a solid black field of sedimentary volcanic rock another fifty meters wide. The entire field was covered with pikes and crosses on which humans had been impaled or crucified, held in stasis so that they could not die or dissolve. Aaron hoped that in this state, the people could not feel pain. Perhaps they were there as a warning to others or simply to put dread in the hearts of men. It did little to put fear into Aaron's heart. The primary effect was that of anger and disgust.

At the first portcullis, Aaron could see that what he hoped was the final gate which was another thirty meters away. Ten snarling demon guards and two demon dogs stood on each side of the doorway as they passed. Another thirty lined each wall of the passage between the outer portcullis and inner gate.

Passing through the inner gate, Zeljabul started walking ahead of Aaron. He was careful to keep what he felt was a safe distance. Zeljabul wanted to be the one to present Azriel at the throne room. The others would have to promote him if he was the one.

As massive as the walls lining the fortress were, the inner citadel was even more so. A field of fifty meters lined with small houses, training areas, animal pens, meal tables, and other typical structures filled the void between the outer wall and inner palace. A huge looming black structure, at least one-hundred meters high, rose in front of him. He followed Zeljabul through the grand entrance of the castle.

Aaron looked into himself. He was an angel. He knew that now. There was no way to continue to deny it. He had power, and he would use it to save his daughter and friend, even if he had to die to do it.

Continuing to follow Zeljabul, Aaron walked straight ahead into the castle. Two bowls of blood sat on top of small pillar-like tables at the entrance. Zeljabul, treating it like holy water, spread some on his forehead.

Continuing down the massive hallway, tapestries of grotesque scenes covered the windowless walls, visible only because of the torches every ten meters. The floor was a black marble, and the ceilings were at least five meters high and arched. There were very few doors, but when they appeared, they were massive metal structures that an elephant could fit through.

The hall stretched to such an extent that as Aaron continued, he eventually could not see the beginning in the low light. At the end was an even more massive double door, twice as large as the ones before. The doors opened, and the throne room was visible ahead.

Aaron slightly recognized the room. It was the not the same, but it was very similar to the circular room in his dream. The throne room included sixteen large black slate pillars leading to a ceiling that was so high and so dark that it was not visible. The pillars rose from marble floors consisting of black and blood red veins. The great circular chamber stretched at least fifty meters across. In the back of the room, Aaron could make out a throne large enough for a huge demon to sit. It was made of the same material as the floor but with gold inlays and a red carpet at the feet. Two burning cauldrons of oil sat on each side of the throne that was raised from the floor by four great steps. The only other furniture, easily recognizable to Aaron, was a table with two gothic chairs with raised wooden backs. The chairs and the table were identical to the ones from his dreams and appeared in the center of the room. He envisioned that if you added bookshelves and draped windows around the sides of the chamber, it would look very familiar.

In the throne room, Asmodai was waiting behind the table with one hundred demon guards. Each guard was clad in thick, heavy armor from neck to toe. Ninety of the demons wore black helmets that covered their faces and had two horns at the top. The others appeared to be higher-ranked and did not wear helmets. Their faces varied from one grotesque anomaly to another. They each had ten of the lesser demons behind them. There were thirty demons to each side of Asmodai and thirty more behind. The other ten guarded the door. Asmodai was not wearing armor. On the contrary, he was wearing an elegant black suit with red pin stripes. He was showing himself in the form of Ash Simpson, even though Aaron knew it was not his true form.

Also in the throne room, waiting to the right of Asmodai, were Malone and Za, both tied in oil-soaked ropes and sitting in two additional chairs like those around the table. Zeljabul had taken a post between them. Aaron, upon seeing his daughter and friend, grew in size. His glow returned. At least twenty ribbons of light emanated from his back. Although dim, a thin sliver of a halo formed over his head. He was finally manifesting as a full angel, but his memory of which angel he was still did not register.

Two other individuals were also similarly tied to chairs to the left of Asmodai. Aaron did not know who these individuals were or why Asmodai had them there.

Seeing Aaron begin to take angelic form, Asmodai said, "Now there he is…the great Azriel. How nice to see you in person again after all of these years."

Aaron was angry. In a booming voice, he bellowed, "Hand them over and live."

"Now that's not a nice way to speak to your host. I know. I know. I did threaten to listen to your screams. But let's not dwell on the past. Water under the bridge and all that you know."

"I won't ask again," warned Aaron.

"Straight to the point then. Can't say I blame you, I guess. Before you go doing something stupid, might I point out that these humans are covered in oil and tied to those chairs? The grate underneath them can release flames at my command. So do calm down. They may not die permanently, but we don't want them to suffer, do we? Let's talk. Look, I brought our favorite chairs." As Asmodai waved his right hand outward, six candles sitting in two large golden three-tiered holders ignited on the table in front of Asmodai. Asmodai took a seat in his human form at the chair on his side of the table. He motioned Aaron to do the same.

Aaron returned to his human form. He was resolved to bide his time while listening to the ramblings of the demon, Asmodai. He would no longer consider him by the name of Ash Simpson. To him, that was the name of a philanthropist. This creature in front of him had never sought to help mankind. His drive had always been to seek out power. Surely, if Aaron could keep him speaking, he could think of a solution to saving Malone and Za while learning more about Asmodai's plan. Aaron walked slowly over to the table and took a seat; however, he maintained his full awareness and avoided becoming too comfortable.

As Aaron sat, Asmodai continued with his discourse. "How nice it is to meet so civilly." Noticing Aaron looking around at the guard, Asmodai concluded that he was seeking a plan to save his friends and escape. "You're looking around at my palace guard. These are some of my favorite warriors. To be honest, I considered posting two hundred, but then, there are two-thousand, five hundred, and fifty from this legion between you and any exit. I think that we can agree that you are my guest for the time being."

Aaron snarled. He would not admit it, but Asmodai was correct. Aaron could not foresee an easy escape that would save his friends some pain. He sat, intent on maintaining a watchful eye over any shenanigans Asmodai might attempt. For now, he would listen.

Asmodai glanced at Aaron but, from his paralanguage, could tell that he had no intention of presently responding. "Let's just agree that I'll keep asking my questions and assume that the answer is yes when you choose not to answer," said Asmodai smiling.

Asmodai continued in his smug cadence, "The last time we spoke, you complained—well, complain may not be the best word. Let's say that you expressed strongly that I and my fellow fallen angels were full of pride. Well, since you chose to walk here, you had the distinct pleasure of witnessing the sin of mankind on full display alongside its many glorifying punishments. You just saw the delusional gods. There are places in Superbia where people prideful of their beauty have the flesh scourged or humans boastful of their intelligence are mindless beasts beaten whenever they try to think or, and this is one of my personal favorites, those prideful of their materials possessions are subjected to their worst fears in a massive dome of doom. It doesn't actually have a name, but you have to admit that dome of doom has a nice ring to it." After a brief giggle having pleased himself immensely, Asmodai looked at Aaron, expecting a response.

Seeing no reaction, Asmodai continued, "Can you see it now, Azriel? We have done nothing beyond the humans. If anything, we served Him through pretime in perfection. Man is not worth it, man's desire to control nature versus just understanding God's work and living in it. We did not fall. Man fell and dragged us with him. It is time that we picked ourselves up and retook our rightful place at God's side. Do you not agree, Azriel? Well?"

Aaron continued to listen but did not respond. He could see Za and Malone along with the other two struggling unsuccessfully to free themselves. He cared more about them than what Asmodai had to say.

"Like I said, I'll assume then, from your silence, that you agree. I'll take it even further, and in this, you must agree. Humans do not just ignore morality. Humans ignore reality. God created a universe that clearly abides by an internal code that humans scoff at. Gender neutrality, moral ambiguity, subjective reality, etcetera—all of these things and more where people put themselves above God and ignore the natural order. They believe that they know everything when they are but a toddler next to true divine knowledge. People fail to find satisfaction in the way things are and instead try to change the world instead of themselves. They are a blight and need to be removed. That is all we want. A return to the natural order where we can once again serve God rather than serve these things."

Asmodai gestured toward Za and Malone to indicate the insignificance of the lowly humans. "And if He cannot recognize the logic and good in that plan, then His will shall not be done."

There it was, two points that made it clear to Aaron that the demon's plan was not as altruistic as they would have one believe. Having listened to Asmodai's rant, Aaron was now willing to speak. "You suffer from the exact same disease that so many humans endure. Demons do not want to accept God's will. They want to change it to their end. You only want to serve a god with the same will as your own rather than to bend your will to that of the one true God. Almost as wrong, and the point that hardened me against any plan that you might have, was that you pointed at my daughter and my friend. Yes, humans are overwhelmingly bad on a global scale. But they also have the overwhelming capacity for goodness when they choose to align their souls properly. Those few who manage to be enlightened, such as Za and Malone, are the few that God seeks to live in His kingdom. Creation was not just about creating a world. It was about creating a system whereby God could allow for others to willfully love Him. In that world, you failed, and that is why you get hell, eternal separation from the light."

Asmodai, surprised that Aaron had spoken, was not pleased at his words. All this time in the pit, all of the failures of the humans, and Azriel was still not accepting his argument. "You're ruining everything," said Asmodai. For a moment, he seemed to be almost pouting. "I get it. For some irrational reason, you have decided to love these humans. My guess is that living amongst them for so long distorted your understanding." Asmodai shuddered at the thought of having to live among humans again. "But you just don't get it. I wasn't showing you the human sin to make you hate them, although you should. I was showing you their sin to show you that God is wrong. Humans are wrong, and we have a plan to fix everything. God knows this plan, but he doesn't want to go through with it. Any god that is too weak to control his subjects does not deserve to be king. But with you, if you would only join us, you could free angels from His control. You could free everyone from His control. You could free yourself."

Asmodai realized that it was time to reveal their primary plan. All else had failed. Surely, Azriel would see the truth in the plan. "If you are beginning to remember, and I sense that you are, then you know that there are seventy-two higher order demons, myself being one. Each of these demons is presided over by a higher order angel. Because of this predication, we are powerless. Each of these angels has absolute authority over the demon beneath them. Each of these angels also knows one of the seventy-two names of God. When God created the universe, he spoke these words in the right sequence. If these names are spoken again in exact reverse, then the world is de-created without humans. It would be as it was before time, before the universe, before we were subjected to their blight. Remember when everything made sense? Remember when all really was good?"

Aaron accepted that some of what Asmodai said was truth. He was beginning to remember. He remembered a time before humans when everything made sense. He remembered how difficult it was with the humans. But he also remembered why he loved them. Despite all of the evil that humans chose to inflict, there was always a glimmer of love and hope. The spirit of a good man could overcome all evil, even if it sped his death. But even that death only led to a rebirth.

Asmodai, sensing a glimmer of understanding from Azriel, continued, "Demons of the covenant would rather not exist than to exist in this world separated from the light. Speaking the names might reset everything. It might also end all existence. We are willing to accept that risk. We cannot accept His decision to give so much power and authority to humans. Even Lucifer agrees. Of course, he would rather be king of hell. He has some fool idea that by abiding in God's plan, he could still be redeemed himself. Ha! He used to understand. With Lucifer, we refused to live by the will of the Creator anymore. But Lucifer will not be redeemed. He will never forgive God because God will not forgive him. So if we cannot return things to the way that they were, then we will end all of existence. Either way, it is better."

The volume of Asmodai's voice lowered. He was ready for his final pitch. "But you are the ace in the hole, Azriel. You do not have a presiding angel. If you join our side, we can actually win. We can take over the heavens if need be. Either we succeed and set things back to the way that they were in the eternal beginning or we end all existence. Likewise, if we fail, we will surely cease to exist. But at least we are taking a stand. I have shown you the horrors of humanity, Azriel, my once friend. You should see the wisdom in our plan. It can work. But only if you join us. And if you will not, then to hell with you and these two behind me." Asmodai pointed at Za and Malone one more time before sitting in silence. He had said what needed to be said. Now it was time for Azriel to either accept reason or to die.

Aaron realized that it was time for him to speak. Afterward, it would be the time for action. "Yes, this pit is filled with the most horrible of sights. I can understand that you have spent so much time here that your view of the grand scope of all that there is has been skewed." As Aaron spoke, his form was transforming halfway between human and angel. "You see only the evil of humankind. But there is so much more. God created them. God is good. His creation is good. When they reach their potential, it is the greatest sight. Someday, I pray that your heart can begin to see that. So, no, I will not join you. You are wrong."

"And what of these two?" asked Asmodai.

"I don't know who they are. Probably some poor souls you brought here to torture," suggested Aaron.

"No." Asmodai smiled. Perhaps this one last surprise would work. He continued, "You see, or perhaps you don't see, demons have no power or authority in the predeath realm. I'll admit, we do manipulate things, often at the forced requests of humans summoning us. But humans have to choose to do evil, and they do it so willingly. These two humans were more than willing to follow the path of evil. In fact, these two are the ones who killed your precious Malone and Za. All for a measly five thousand dollars." Asmodai's smile grew. He could see that he had hit a nerve in Azriel.

Azriel was nearly fully in angelic form before returning to his human form of Aaron. Admittedly, he was surprised by Asmodai's last reveal. He could not deny that he harbored anger over these two. But Asmodai was still wrong.

"Once again, you fail to fully understand the truth, Asmodai," said Aaron. Slowly, he started to grow again. "It is not anger alone that sets one to sin. It would be fully righteous for me to be angry at these two for what they did. But what I do with that anger is what defines me. God will be their judge, not me. That's part of the whole point of the pit."

Asmodai was angered that Azriel was not seeing what he felt was the truth. He quickly and maliciously flipped a switch to the side of his chair. The two murderers dropped through holes that opened up under their chairs. Aaron hated to think where they were headed.

But Aaron was ceasing to be. He loved Za. He loved Malone. He loved humanity. He was beginning to manifest his true self. He remembered.

## 33

Thousands of years had passed since the Trinity was revealed. Azriel had been helping humans ascend since that time. As he hovered over a hollow human form, its corporeal shell slowly dissipated from its seat. Azriel smiled as he watched its reborn soul arise to the heavenly kingdom. He had walked twenty days on the road with that man, showing him the evil and the good in his life, and presenting him with the necessary choices to accept redemption. Thankfully, the man had chosen wisely.

However, with every human he was able to help actualize, nine more fell into the pit en route to their eternal damnation. Azriel could think of nothing in the universe more terrible than to be eternally separated from the light. Of course, there actually was nothing worse in the universe.

As an angel, he was unable to form tears as the humans did, but he knew that in his sadness over the lost souls, he would surely never stop crying. He felt that all he knew was killing and death and suffering. Why else would everyone call him the angel of death?

There was a time when his primary function was to enact God's wrath on the humans. With God's authority, he could rain meteors upon the masses, turn rivers to blood, or release sinners to the afterlife in their sleep. But he wasn't that angel of death now. He was more the angel of deliverance. All these souls would be lost if not for his redemptive work. Yet, no matter how hard he tried, he failed 90 percent of the time.

He remembered God's wrath sending him out to kill countless humans. He did not revel in the blood of the dead. Nor did God.

Every dead evil soul was doomed to suffer, and he knew that God's will was for every human to be saved. Sadly, that never happened.

How could he be such a failure? He failed so many humans. He was unable to turn them from their sin to the will of God. Why did God give them free will? They so often exploited their will and failed. In a world where evil seemed so predisposed to succeed, how did good ever win?

As time had passed, those of Earth seemed more predisposed to accept only their own will. The enlightenment or rational humanism was the start in his view. Once people began to believe that they understood the universe, they sought to control it. Once they could control it, they saw themselves as their own god with no need for an eternal understanding.

Azriel thought that he had achieved eternal understanding. At least, before the time of humanity, before the creation of the physical universe, all that ever existed was the praise of the Supreme. Humans and free will had challenged Azriel's understanding.

Still, he did his best. He had found two primary keys over the course of thousands of years. The first was kindness. Only those willing to care about others above themselves seemed predestined for heaven. The other key was to accept God's will over their own. This one small choice seemed the hardest for most to accept. Humans seemed to have no problem accepting a God of love, a God that they must obey, accepting that by doing so, they would have more abundance than they could ever achieve on their own. That one they had more problems with.

He was told—no, ordered—to love humans and to help them save themselves. Every instance of caring and faith shown by the humans had solidified his love for them, and love them he did. Due to that love, he knew that they had to die. What they called life was only death. Not until death could they hope to achieve life in heaven with the light. Perhaps, in that way, he was the angel of death.

But they failed too often, and their failure was also his failure. He had not led them into a proper life after death. The humans he loved had failed God, and by connection, he was also a failure in his mind. He could not understand the human's predisposition to fail.

Accepting God's will seem so natural. Anything else defied all logic and reasoning that the humans valued so highly anymore.

Unable to understand the failure of the humans and his own failure, Azriel cried out, "Why, my Lord?"

Angels were never to question the authority of God. Not since Lucifer had he been questioned, and that did not turn out well for Lucifer. Those that fell with Lucifer saw the failures of mankind continually. Azriel was the one non-fallen angel destined for the same. God took pity on Azriel because he could see that Azriel had love in his heart but was confused as to his purpose. Once again, Azriel's love of humans had weighed too heavily on his heart.

Immediately after asking the question, Azriel's vision faded. He lost focus on the road. He was surrounded by nothing but divine light. It was instantly apparent to Azriel that he had been called to God's presence. Then he realized his mistake. Without ill intention, without realization, without knowing it was even possible, he had questioned God. Azriel shuddered. Was he to be destroyed? Or worse, sent among the fallen?

No words were needed in the divine tongue. Azriel's mood was shifted from fear to hope. Azriel's work had godly purpose, but even though he lacked free will of his own, God wanted Azriel to carry out his tasks with a clear understanding of its purpose and deep-seated desire to succeed. Only then could he carry out his tasks in delight instead of sadness. It was inevitable. To remain in limbo for so long weighed heavily, even on an angel's heart. It was time for Azriel to learn once more the necessity of his purpose. It was time for him to be given a will to decide for himself the importance of his role.

But only a human could have free will. God could not give Azriel the will to decide as he currently existed. God would have to make him human. The transformation would occur through childbirth into the chosen family. Like childbirth, Azriel would be made clean with no memories of his path that might bias his decision. Azriel would then be presented with a choice. Only through his choice could he continue. He would either choose to live as an angel and do the work designed for him or he could remain a human, forgoing all knowledge of his angelic nature.

If he chose his angelic nature, all would be restored.

If he chose to remain a human, it would shift the universe. Although many angels worked to redeem those on the road, none were as skillful as Azriel. Certainly, more souls would be lost. Also, Azriel would risk being separated from the light. If he chose unwisely as a human, he might end up in hell, and there would be no angel as skillful as he to aid in his redemption on the road.

While Azriel had no way of knowing the outcome, God knew all things. He knew what Azriel would choose, especially since this was the third time that he had enacted this plan. Azriel was just now discovering what that choice would be. Azriel was discovering once again that he had a purpose, and that purpose was good.

## 34

Azriel rose from his chair. "You were right about one thing," he declared to Asmodai. "This place has changed me. Only now because of this experience am I recognizing His true plan." Aaron was no more. Only Azriel remained. He had made his decision.

The energy from his transformation filled the room with the brightest light ever witnessed in that recess of the pit. All but Azriel were blinded.

"You must not value your friends, Azriel," Asmodai screamed through the commotion caused by the light. "I'll give you one more chance to join us or they die!" Asmodai would continue his futile effort to turn Azriel, not realizing that his chances were long past.

The elite demon guards were confused, but they maintained their ranks. Zeljabul cowered and ran for the door.

Azriel knew his purpose. He was destined not to kill but to lead those already dead into life. Malone and Za, as much as he loved them, were dead. They would certainly suffer pain from Asmodai's trap, but they would be redeemed. Azriel's return would light the way for all of the lost that were deserving to ascend. Azriel had returned, and the population of the pit was about to be reduced.

Azriel screamed with a shock wave that shook the thick reinforced walls of the palace. "Do it, and you die!"

As Azriel fully manifested, Asmodai realized that the plan had failed for the third time. Azriel was not coming to reason. He would once again join God, and they would have to find another way. Just like baseball, three strikes, and you were out. They would not pursue this plan any longer. The fact that it failed yet again would temporarily harm Asmodai's demonic standing, but he would recover.

Then again, there were still cards that Asmodai had not played. "I'm a demon at the border of hell. I do what I want!" shouted Asmodai as he flipped a lever hidden by his seat. As everyone's eyes adjusted to the light, flames came from the vent below Za and Malone. Instantly, they were engulfed by an intense fire that incinerated them, their ashes blown upward by the currents created by the heat. Asmodai was slightly angered that the heat was so extreme. He had hoped for more suffering. As his anger consumed him, he shouted out his orders to his demonic soldiers, "Kill him!"

Quickly, ten of Azriel's angelic ribbons shot to the left and ten shot to the right. Ten demons on each side of him were pierced through the neck. Only beheading a demon would ensure that it would dissipate, forced into the dark recesses of hell to reform. Wounding would not suffice today. But as the demons struggled in their last moment before respawning, they held on to Azriel's wings.

Azriel still had his silver-coated hunting knife. As the next twenty demons approached, he fended them off with the silver blade, moving through space faster than the speed of sound, shock waves scattered in all directions, knocking demons over. They realized the nature of the blade and did not want to be poisoned by the silver; however, ten more fell to its edge. In the melee, two of them were able to clip two of Azriel's wings as he withdrew them from their first victims. Such a severe wound caused Azriel to wince in pain and would take several minutes to heal.

Ten of the remaining demons took up guard around Asmodai. As he stood, his full demonic form grew. He kicked the table in front of him, shattering it into shards of wood that exploded in every direction, killing two more demons in the process. Several shards also pierced Aaron, but they were only minor wounds. Azriel was unique among all of the angels. God had gifted him as the only angel able to fully heal in the pandemonium between realms. Without this gift, he probably would not have survived the pit to make it this far.

The door to the chamber swung open. A hundred more battle-ready demons poured into the room. Asmodai shouted out, "Your efforts are futile, Azriel! You cannot win! You may be powerful, but I have legions of demons! Surrender, and maybe I'll reveal my one last surprise!"

"You have no more surprises, Asmodai. You have no power over me. I act as the sword of the Almighty. You will surely pay for your sins today," replied Azriel as his wings took out ten more demons.

The demons were reforming their ranks, shields at the ready. They slowly started to close in on Azriel, on guard against his wings.

Asmodai knew that he had the forces to kill Azriel, but he would only reform and return from heaven. As much as he enjoyed the endless war, he sought more. He clutched onto one last hope that he could convince the angel of death to fall. He had one more secret to reveal, and now was the time. "And what of your wife? Surely, she must matter! You clearly cared so much about those other two to let them die so unceremoniously."

"I did not let them die! You killed them!"

"To-may-to, to-mah-to! You can still save Hannah, though." Asmodai smiled. Asmodai could tell by the look in Azriel's face that he had been caught off guard.

Azriel calmed. He wondered what Asmodai knew of his wife.

Seeing that he had Azriel's attention, Asmodai continued, "You see, I found her soon after you died. She was easy to find since she had eighteen years of history here. Quite a whip that one. Still holds to her faith, even though she had endured much, especially these past few weeks. Oh, but I won't let her die and respawn where you can save her. We wouldn't want to end her suffering. I'll keep her just at that border between death and rebirth. Only when I am done with her will I cut her so that she bleeds the most but lives the longest. One last chance to join us, and if you do, once your fall is complete and irreversible, you can have her."

Azriel was surprised, but he quickly assessed the situation. He was in pain from his severed wings, but they would heal. He could continue to fight, but he would surely lose eventually. It would be satisfying to fell many demons this day, but he could tell that he was not as powerful as he could be. Something about the palace weakened him. He had endured and witnessed so much in the pit. He could not let it end here. Not just him, but many, his wife included, had suffered horrible hardships because he was not there to lead them from the road. His best option was probably to allow himself to be killed. Then he could reform and continue his work.

Azriel loved humanity, but he also loved Hannah. She was special. He knew that the needs of the many outweighed his needs, but he had to save her. But how? If he died now, she may be lost. He would have to continue to fight.

Meanwhile, Azriel's transformation sent shock waves through the ethereal realms. Heaven and hell had felt the change. Asmodai knew that his time was limited. He must turn Azriel now before more angels, or worse, Lucifer appeared. That was the only chance to garner Lucifer's support. No other demon of the covenant would come near at this vital juncture. They would not risk their own demise alongside Asmodai. It was up to him to complete the plan.

Asmodai gave his final signal to his demonic regiment. His private guard of ten demons surrounded him more closely. The hundred demons who had just entered charged at Azriel as another hundred filled the halls outside. Azriel, distracted by his thoughts of Hannah, returned to his senses, but it was too late. There were simply too many demons. No matter his plan to try and fight, it would be for naught.

Another ten demons fell as he fought, some by his wings and some by his blade. But in groups of three, the demons grabbed and restrained Azriel's wings. Ten more demons died as Azriel whipped his wings as best as he could against their rush, but there were simply too many demons, even for him. He tried to take flight, but it was too late. They had already taken hold.

The twenty demons remaining from the original fifty in the room ran at Azriel with hand scythes. In rushed, powerful swings, they cut Azriel's wings back to their base. They then retreated to posts on each side of Asmodai.

"Do not kill him," ordered Asmodai, realizing that he finally had the upper hand. Azriel would not be able to fly off to heal for some time, and if they did not kill him, they could keep him restrained for the time being. But time was limited. Azriel needed to turn now or Asmodai would have to cut his losses, literally.

"One last chance, Azriel. Will you accept the truth and join us? We can bring an end to the war. We will finally regain our rightful place next to Him—no more humans, no more reality, just like it was in the beginning." Asmodai approached Azriel, his guard still surrounding him.

"Your plan is flawed in so many ways," responded Azriel.

"Really? Enlighten me," suggested Asmodai smugly.

"One, even if you ended reality, there are already millions of humans in heaven. I personally guided thousands there myself. Then there are the billions already in hell. If you end creation, the higher realm would still remain. You would not get rid of them."

"Oh, but you are wrong." Asmodai smiled, knowing that in this argument, Azriel could not disagree. "If we end creation, we end all of history. It would be like the humans never even existed." Asmodai looked into Azriel's eyes as he spoke. He could tell that Azriel accepted the truth of what he was saying.

Azriel countered, "Then you still lose. God can just create everything again."

"And we uncreate it again. God would never enter into an endless cycle of death and rebirth, not with the humans He loves so much. The only way He could stop the endless creation/destruction cycle would be to uncreate us, and there are many here who would just as soon have that happen. I, for one, want to continue to exist. If He was going to obliterate us, He would have already done so. We still fit into His plan. Someone has to punish the fallen humans. Might as well be the fallen angels. But maybe we grow tired of tormenting the humans. Yes, we grow tired of it. We want to be loved by Him again. I believe that when He sees our loyalty and love, when things return to the way that they were, then all will be at peace once more."

"You still think in pride that you can exert your will over Him? He will never accept you that way. Even Lucifer knows that even though he led the humans to sin through his hatred of them, he still must do God's will in the end." Azriel felt that he was making satisfactory arguments, but he was not really interested in winning a debate with Asmodai. In truth, he was only stalling. He had heard the wind shift when he rose to his angelic form. Other angels were coming. No one else had noticed yet, but light was coming through the door. The room had grown darker after his wings were severed, but he was no longer the only source of light in the pit.

\*\*\*\*\*

As Azriel and Asmodai had been arguing, heaven reacted to the disturbance in the pit. Angelic legions commissioned to work alongside Azriel to save the lost knew that he had once again made his choice. He was an angel again, ready to do His bidding. Unlike the last times, though, he did not immediately manifest in heaven. Something was different.

The angels could feel the divine authority fill their light. They were to go to Azriel and return his light to its purpose. A legion of six thousand angels descended into the pit, the largest contingent ever. All of them targeted the brightest light seen in the far east. At the speed of thought, they arrived at the outskirts of Asmodai's palace. The war for Azriel had begun.

\*\*\*\*\*

In the throne room, Asmodai continued his war of words. He could sense that another war was waging outside, but he had over one hundred thousand demons at his disposal, even without the other demons of the covenant. Those numbered did not include the million human souls he had organized from hell. The angels that Azriel thought were coming to save him would never make it through his defenses.

"One angel, just one angel. That is all that must fall for everything to return to the way it was. Think about it. Forget about these humans. Does a human cry when an ant dies if that means he can keep his house in order? No, the answer is undeniably no. Our house is out of order. You are the key to bringing everything back. You can help end all of this war between heaven and hell. We can bring peace to the cosmos." By now, Asmodai was within inches of Azriel's face, speaking directly into his eyes.

As an added bonus he had only just then conceived, Asmodai added, "And if you love or have made pets with certain ants, well, we can still design the new creation to include those few. They can be your pets or your friends." Asmodai showed clear disgust at the idea of having a human for a pet and nearly caused himself to regurgitate at the idea of calling one a friend, but he desperately needed Azriel to join him.

The clashing of swords and shields was now audible in the throne room. Shouts and screams filled the halls. The initial descent of the angels had been more to scout for Azriel. Demonic archers and gigantic ballistae littered the sky with ammunition, felling hundreds of angels to be devoured by foot soldiers on the ground.

The angels could not die, but it would take hours for them to respawn in heaven and return to the battlefield. Realizing that they would have to fight their way to Azriel, the angels had formed ranks in the sky, letting loose their own volley of shimmering arrows. Each one exploded when it landed. Thousands of arrows rained down on the outer wall of the citadel. Even with its thick strong design, huge holes opened up on the outer wall.

Demons took to the sky in five thousand groups of three. The angels would be overwhelmed in the sky, but they knew no fear. The Lord was with them in spirit, but they would need to fight this battle themselves in His glory. With a fervor of divine might, swords clashed in the dark skies.

A group of one hundred angels broke off from the main battle and descended upon the inner fortress. Like a bullet of indestructible metal, they formed their wings around them as they plummeted. With the force of a meteor, they blasted into the inner walls, sacrificing themselves to open a way for the others. An entire side of the citadel fell, converted to powder by the blast. The angels knew that none of them would survive this battle as they were severely outnumbered, but through sacrifice, they could set Azriel free.

The last blast sent tremors through the throne room. The floor shook, and pieces of plaster fell from the rafters that were once again invisible in the darkness above. A few demons lost their footing, but they maintained their hold on Azriel.

"Are you sure you have enough demons, Asmodai?" Azriel asked, resolved to wait patiently for his fellow angels to rescue him.

"Don't get your hopes up, Azriel. Hope…what a funny word. It means a belief in something that will not happen just because it is a better option than what is happening. It is a lie one tells one's self to accept the horrid reality they find themselves in. You're better than that, Azriel. Don't lie to yourself. There is no hope. Your angels will not get through my citadel."

Surprisingly, Azriel could sense that Asmodai was not in the least worried. Was it true? Was his rescue hopeless?

Asmodai's forces blackened the sky as they swooped in from all directions at the angels. A rush of power surged through the angelic ranks. They lashed out and fell the first wave of demons. Their small victory was short-lived. Though they fought with valor and honor, every single angel remaining began to fall out of the sky, their wings tattered and torn, their bodies dying. There was no regrouping. There was no retreat to reconsider their actions. The forces were simply too overwhelming. Thousands of corpses fell from the sky, disintegrating like the remnants of a firecracker before they hit the ground. Asmodai's fortress had taken massive damage, but it was still standing. Only two thousand of his forces fell in battle, and they would return from hell faster than the angels could regroup from heaven.

But while the sky had roared at the coming of the angels, the ground now rumbled. Something else was coming. Something that Asmodai feared.

# 35

Several days after being killed by Asmodai, Darda reanimated back on the road. He was none too pleased by the course of events that had befallen him since the arrival of Azriel. *I should have just ascended years ago when I had the chance*, thought Darda.

In the great wisdom bestowed upon him by the Lord, he knew that ascending was the best choice. But his desire for more knowledge of the road and the pit had drawn him to stay, passing up his time of ascension, stranding him in limbo. After centuries on the road, he had seen enough. He had seen the passing of Azriel several times. He had witnessed the rise and fall of many demon kings. He had sorrowed over the souls that refused to be redeemed. Now he would end his purgatory.

Normally, it would have taken months and several respawns to make it where he was heading, but the pit was of divine construction. It knew where Darda needed to go and provided him with a direct path. Within weeks of leaving his once safe house, he arrived. The entrance to hell rose before him. He came prepared, wearing a coat made from the hide of a demon dog and warm clothes long hidden in his house. Interestingly, as if to be a joke on humankind or a final instance of cosmic irony, the gates sat in the middle of a frozen lake, chilling the soul of anyone nearby. In the end, hell would be consumed in a pit of burning sulfur, but for now, it was covered in ice.

The walls surrounding the entrance rose higher than the eye could see. Each door of the gates rose twenty meters high and ten meters wide. In stark contrast to their snowy surrounding, they were each made of a single black opal. The doors were ominously darker than the hell that could barely be seen through their opening. The doors, normally open and welcoming the sinner to enter, were presently closed.

Normally, there would be thralls of weeping humans begging forgiveness, one more chance, or demanding some birthright that did not exist. Today, there were only a few wandering souls lost in the pit and lost in their minds. Darda assumed that they were mostly suicides who otherwise lived a God-fearing life. They could not be redeemed since their final act was a sin, but they could be spared the atrocities of hell because their minds were clouded of all realities.

Like heaven, the gates would normally have been open, but humans could only pass in one direction. It was an entrance, not an exit. Darda dared not enter, even if he were allowed. Minos sat on a great dais in front of the gates. While everyone assumed that Minos was to sort people into hell, he also served the purpose of keeping the good out of hell. With the road not functioning properly in Azriel's absence, it was easiest to keep everyone out. Thus, there were no sinners to sort, and Minos was burdened with inactivity. To a human, the idle hand is the work of the devil. To a demon, an idle hand is near torture.

Since Darda was human, Minos would not allow him entry, and if he were to enter, he would never be able to exit and ascend to heaven. Darda would therefore need a plan. He would play on the insipid boredom shown by Minos' face and posture. If Darda could garner his favor, there was a chance.

"Oh, great and ominous Minos, how fare thee this horrid day?" Darda asked in an effort to break the ice, which seemed fitting in a field covered in it.

Minos rarely spoke. He found it laborious to resort to auditory manifestations of meaning. He preferred physical displays. He lifted his great club with the mass and length of a small bus and let it land directly in front of Darda. Although, if the club had landed on top of Darda, Minos would not have minded.

"Wait, do you think I would travel here just to die? I know your temperament, especially these past decades. You know me as Darda. You know my wisdom." Darda did not consider it his wisdom. He knew that his wisdom was a gift from God, but if he were to say that in front of Minos, the club might just have found its way up and down again. "I came here to offer you respite to your boredom. I know of happenings that will fill the gates of hell."

Minos did not move the club. He did move his head enough to face Darda. That was enough to indicate that he was interested in hearing.

To Darda, the position of Minos meant that he had a chance. "Asmodai leads a covenant intent on changing the status quo. He intends to turn Azriel and lead an army against heaven itself."

Minos let out an echoing laugh that cracked the ice near Darda. Thankfully, there was no water under the ice. The cold came from the ground underneath of it. Unlike on Earth, where a lake was frozen at the top, here it was frozen from the bottom. Nothing lived in this lake, and no amount of cracking would make someone fall through.

"Your response shows your wisdom, mighty Minos. You know that this is not within Lucifer's plan. Wouldn't it just be the most interesting of days if he found out what was happening?" Darda raised his tone to emphasize the question. He would now find out where the loyalties of Minos lay.

Astonishingly, Minos spoke, even if it were only two words. "You wait."

Darda had no intention of disobeying.

In a flash of darkness, Minos dissipated. More time passed than Darda expected. Time was somewhat meaningless in the pit since the sun did not rise and fall, but his past human experiences left him with enough sense of time to know that the sun would have moved far across the sky in the time that Minos was absent.

Finally, Minos did return. In a flash that temporarily sucked the light from the area, Minos landed back at his couch.

As Minos sat, Darda asked, "I feel like you are keeping me in suspense. I feel that I already know the answer. But did you have an audience with Lucifer? What was his reaction?"

Minos smiled one last time. He was not one prone to smiling, but for one moment, he was happy. He did not need to answer Darda. Within moments of the words leaving Darda's mouth, a great swarm of demons flew from the gates of hell. Their gigantic swell created enough wind to nearly knock Darda down. Thousands upon thousands of demonic beings of all shapes and sizes flew into the sky. A quake also shook the ground, this time succeeding in knocking Darda off his feet. Into the fissure that opened, all of the demons flew before it closed behind them. Only one creature, the most massive of demons, remained in the air. Darda knew this creature to be Lucifer. As quickly as the other demons disappeared into the ground, Lucifer darted like a black lightning bolt though the sky.

Now Darda's smile joined that of Minos. "It was a pleasure doing business with you," he quipped. "I feel like my time in the pit is at its end now, Minos. I'm sure no demon will be distraught at my absence. The angels will return soon. It's time for more to ascend." Darda then turned and walked away, heading back to his hidden house on the road to wait for the return of the angels.

Lucifer was even less pleased than usual as he arrived at the eastern castle. From his point above the citadel, he could sense the battle that had just concluded. He could smell the dissolved remnants of both demons and angels. He could also discern the slightest fluctuations in sound and energy to know that another battle was taking place in the main throne room, and humans had been there too in a throne of the pit. How dare Asmodai attempt to undermine his authority. There would literally be hell to pay.

As Lucifer dove down on the main keep, the sky filled with a cloud of darkness. His messengers had ordered every other king and prince of hell to immediately send a legion of demonic minions to his location. All of them complied, especially those in league with Asmodai who now wished to distance themselves as quickly as possible. The sound of the demonic legions' approach was deafening. Sixty thousand demons were in the air, the largest single armada assembled in the history of hell to that point. And these were only the demons called upon as tribute.

Simultaneously, the ground shook, a new fissure opening at the edge of the moat. Despite their massive size and bodies designed for balance, any of Asmodai's demonic forces not already in the sky fell to the ground, losing their balance due to the great quake. Three hundred thousand of Lucifer's own demonic forces then rose from the broken earth.

Like a swarm of locusts, the demonic army confronted Asmodai's legions whose bodies were quickly cleaved, battered, drained, and severed until only shards of flesh and bone remained.

As that war raged, so too did Lucifer's rage. Like a meteor, he crashed through the battered ceiling of the keep. His wrath would be satisfied soon.

For the first time, Azriel was sure where the ceiling was to the throne room. From at least fifty meters above, a great beast had just burst forth, creating a massive orifice and raining debris down on those below. Only a hundred demons remained in the throne room, the rest having joined the lost fight outside. It would be nowhere near enough.

Asmodai looked up in horror. He had failed. Looking once more at Azriel, he implored, "One last chance! We can still do it! You and I could create a perfect universe! If I die, you will never find Hannah!"

"Your time is up. Tell me where she is, and maybe I'll try to help you," replied Azriel. Had he thought about it earlier, he might have imagined himself smiling at that moment. Instead, his true nature shone through. He was saddened at Asmodai. He had once been an angel after all. There was no way to show him the folly of his way or at least no way that he would accept it. Now he would surely suffer, and Azriel hated to see anything suffer, even those that deserved it. If only Asmodai, as all entities, could see the light.

A huge creature, ten meters tall with the eyes of a serpent and twisted cranial structure resembling a python-humanoid hybrid, accelerated as it smashed into the ground. The hooves where his feet would have been each smashed several demons to either side of Asmodai upon impact. The craters created in the marble floor were at least half a meter deep. Everything fell to the ground. With a flaming sword held in his vastly muscular left arm, the creature that was undeniably Lucifer swung inward and severed the head of Asmodai. There was no discussion. There was no mercy. There was only wrath. As the head flew upward, Lucifer lunged forward, catching the head in its mouth and swallowing it in one gulp. Then Lucifer's other arm swung a rather plain spear that plunged into the dark heart within Asmodai while flames from Lucifer swooped downward to engulf the rest of Asmodai's body.

"I considered keeping you in my digestive tract until the chosen time. You would have remained at the border of cessation, burning in the acidic lava of my stomach until we rise for the millennia. But it seemed wiser to end you with my Spear of Destiny." Lucifer looked at Azriel, explaining as he continued, "As above so below. The spear that pierced Jesus has its equivalent in my hand, and Asmodai will never exist again." Satan smiled as he finished his diatribe.

The remaining demons in the room were scurrying to retreat, only to be met by an irresistible force charging into the throne room.

Azriel nearly wept. His search for Za had just ended. He could now go find her and Malone after they respawned in order to lead them to heaven. But now he would need to search for Hannah. Asmodai was right. Wherever she had been hidden, Azriel could not sense her. Za and Malone would surely reform at the road, but not Hannah. And the only one that surely knew where she was no longer existed. Azriel's hope was that since Asmodai commanded thousands of demons, he would be able to question every single one of them after they respawned until he had his answer.

Looking around, Azriel once again found himself surrounded by demons, their leader in front of him. At least now the stubs of his wings were no longer being held down, and they were beginning to heal. He could move freely and would be able to fly within a minute. "Lucifer, I can't believe that you have saved me. But now I must go. Asmodai has hidden something from me that must be found."

Lucifer believed in a much grander plan than Asmodai. The plan set forth by God. By His plan, Lucifer could rule the Earth for a thousand years. Of course, that was nothing compared to the eternity they had already lived. But if Lucifer's plan worked, he would be able to find redemption by following the plan of God. Surely, if God would forgive the humans for their unending sins, Lucifer could be spared his one mistake, maybe two.

But Lucifer had no need for Azriel in his plan, a fact that Azriel was about to discover.

"Oh no, my old friend," said Lucifer, "this is all your fault, and I can't just let you go unpunished." As the final words left his mouth, Lucifer cut off Azriel's head with the flaming sword still coated in a layer of Asmodai's scorched blood. Lucifer knew that he could not kill an angel, but he could at least have him feel some pain. Azriel was so surprised that he did not attempt to block the blow or escape. Lucifer truly was a powerful adversary.

At Azriel's side, Lava appeared. He had respawned and had been taking part in the battle. He thought that he smelled his imprinted master. Looking for the source of the scent, he watched as the head of the being he had sensed fell to the ground. Unfortunately, in his angelic form, Lava did not recognize him. Azriel's form then quickly dissipated, appearing like a thousand fireflies for a moment. Slowly stepping in several circles, Lava could not discern what had happened. He then lay down to wait until his master returned.

## 37

Azriel was not too surprised that Lucifer had taken his head. It was apparent in Lucifer's demeanor that he was full of anger and wanted to punish everything in his sight. The pit was his domain, and others had tried to exert their authority. After months of being tormented by Asmodai's plans, Lucifer had ended his reign. More so, he had literally ended Asmodai. There would soon be a new king to the east of the pit.

Azriel tried to find a way to be angry at Asmodai, but that was simply not in his nature. Asmodai was misguided and mistaken. He had placed his faith in a war with God based on gaining Azriel's allegiance. He was wrong. Azriel would never turn away from the master he loved. Nor would he turn away from the humans he also loved. Azriel may be known as the angel of death, but his heart was full of love. Asmodai had tried to play to his love of God but had not conceived that Azriel would have such a strong love of humans.

Immediately upon his death, Azriel transferred his essence. He was one of the few angels that did not need to reform in heaven. He set his destination as the road, but not just anywhere on the road. His memory was now restored. He was the angel of death after all with full knowledge of this realm.

Knowing who he was for the first time in over forty years, Azriel took flight. As he rose higher and higher above the pit, his full angelic presence formed. He may have fallen from his human form to get to this limbo, but he would rise above it to bring back the heavenly oversight. At least fifty ribbons of light stretched ten meters in every direction from his body. He was as a floating globe of heavenly presence high above the endless road.

Looking down into the pit, he could see the glow of the redeemed, invisible to any but the chosen angels. His light shone now like a sun to those with the heart to look upward to God. Suddenly, the entire pit was engulfed in needles of blue light heading into the sky, emanating from each of those who maintained or grew stronger in their faith while subjected to the pit. Shouts and tears of joy could be heard once more. The entire pit was filled with the joyous screams of the redeemed. Five hundred million people had died while Aaron was in human form. Almost one million were ascended directly to heaven upon death. Of those in the pit, one hundred million of the unfortunate and unintended residents were finally leaving, a greater percentage of saved than ever in human history. "And they were judged, each one of them, according to what they had done," whispered Azriel. The remnants of their physical existence were left behind. Their spiritual rebirth now complete, they rose to their final living place.

Although rejoicing at their salvation, Azriel did not follow. He still had business to attend to. Instead, he lowered himself back to the road. He knew exactly where Malone and Za would reform. Unfortunately, it would take them a few days to do so. In the interim, he would wait.

Fortunately, there was a familiar house to wait in. This position was a junction point on the road. It was why Darda had chosen it after all. The gray house stood in front of Azriel. Slowly and methodically, he shrunk to a human sized form, albeit still angelic and not his once Aaron form, and he entered the house.

Inside the house was a familiar face. Darda was himself waiting. Minos had transported him there, saving him the day of travel back. Darda truly was a wise old man. "I thought you might come here when it was all done. There was a rather high likelihood that Lucifer was going to kill everyone, including your friends. I figured that they would respawn near here too since you started on the road. You know how much of a hobby I liked to make out of tracking angelic movement on the road after all."

"Darda, how nice to see you again. Now I know you so well with my memories returned. You might find it surprising, but Asmodai took Malone's and Za's life, not Lucifer."

"That is surprising. Why would he throw away his strongest bargaining chip?"

"He didn't place enough value in humans."

"That is true," surmised Darda.

"But he also had someone just as important," hinted Azriel.

"Who is more important? No, wait. Your wife. She was in the refugee camp. He must have found her once he realized who you were. Then he would know who she was as well."

"She was in the refugee camp?"

"Yes, for quite some time as I found out. Until Asmodai took her. I did a little searching after you left. Something seemed off about you. You had the hint of angel about you, and I was here the last times you took human form. You were different, but there were definitely similarities to the Azriel I knew. I'm sorry, but I found all of this out after you had left. Of course, then I was taken prisoner and killed by Asmodai."

"And when you respawned, you were the one to warn Lucifer, weren't you?"

"Yes." Darda smiled. "And it wasn't easy, but it was clearly what the pit wanted too. The pit has a calling, you know, and that calling doesn't include all of the Christians walking around."

"Tell me, Darda, do you know where Asmodai was keeping Hannah?"

Darda thought for a moment, but he could think of no positive response. "Sorry, but no. But then, how is it that you don't see her? You're Azriel, for God's literal sake."

"She is hidden deep. She must be surrounded by demons too to cover her scent. Lucifer killed all of Asmodai's forces. There must be a few still loyal, hiding in the depths with Hannah. It will be a while before I can start to round up those that were killed and ask questions. Hopefully, one of them knows something, but there are thousands to check. I can't get her location from Asmodai because he is completely destroyed."

"Lucifer used the Spear?" Darda was momentarily surprised but then reasoned the importance of eliminating Asmodai. "I suppose it was the third strike after all. He couldn't let this situation keep happening or demons would think he was turning soft. By the way, is this the last time?"

"The last time for what?"

"The last time you get tired and have to be taught a lesson. Haven't you figured it out yet? Why does God keep sending you to be with the humans?"

"I'm still sorting it out," responded Azriel.

Darda was displeased at Azriel's inability to understand immediately. "You dunce. Don't you get it? It's not about your or my narrative. It's about God's. You keep wondering if this is all that there is. Are you destined to watch the dying of the humans? Well, yes. But you are also destined to watch and even play a role in the rebirth of the worthy humans. That's the point. Now that I've summed it up for you, maybe you can make use of that purpose."

Azriel thought about Darda's words. All this time, Azriel kept worrying about himself. He may have rationalized his sorrow as due to his love of the humans, but somewhere in his heart, God had given him the ability to think about what he was doing above simply following orders. In the past, thinking angels did not always turn out so well. But Azriel had to be able to see into the hearts of people and reason their eternal love of the Creator. At the same time, Azriel was instilled with a love of the humans that he had to help save. It was the natural order for some to fail because they had free will. By living as a human, Azriel knew that free will now, and he understood the problems it created for those that chose poorly.

But the awesome glory awaiting those that listened to the heart of God was the ultimate prize. God was good. The Bible gave people notice of their fate. In Timothy, "Do your best to present yourself to God as one approved, a worker who has no need to be ashamed, rightly handling the word of truth." A statement that led Azriel to Darda's last request, which Azriel knew was in Darda's heart. Azriel was about to make use of his purpose again.

"You wish to finally ascend, don't you, Darda?" Azriel was being coy. He knew that it was past due for Darda to ascend. In a small way, Azriel wondered if Darda had stayed around so long specifically for this moment as if God had put all of these actions into motion thousands of years ago. He would not be surprised if that were true.

"Yes. Please. I love God, and I only now realize that I have squandered my time on the road when I should have been in His glory. My desire to control my own destiny overwhelmed the gift of wisdom given to me by God. I was not fully submitted."

"It is not I who make you worthy but the Son by his sacrifice and the Father by his gift. Having accepted this truth, you are surely ready to join Him."

"Thank you!" Darda cried tears of joy.

As Darda began to lose his reformed physical self, the entirely spiritual took form. The glow of eternal salvation surrounded him and carried him upward.

As Darda's form disappeared through the ceiling, Azriel had a thought. He should have asked Darda a pressing question on his mind. He could traverse the planes and return to heaven to ask him, but that would draw attention. He also wanted to wait for Za and Malone. Further, he needed to find Hannah. But Darda, with his wisdom, and being the one who watched the angels and demons in the between spaces of heaven, hell, and Earth, was the most likely one to know the answer to his question. He would definitely seek him again in the future.

As he sat thinking, Azriel was alarmed…alarmed that Asmodai was so certain that a single angel could turn the tide between good and evil. His question for Darda that needed to eventually be answered was, "Is the balance really that tenuous?"

Azriel had two days to think of the possible answers to that question and others. The answers did not come. But something else equally as important to him did. He could feel their presence. Their new spiritual forms were taking shape nearby. They were together. He would wait. Malone would recognize this place. It would be a welcome surprise.

## 38

Malone was dizzy. His last memory was of extreme burning pain. Some of that pain still lingered, but he could tell that there was nothing wrong now. His eyes slowly adjusted. He realized the similarity to the feeling he had when he first died. Looking around, he was quickly aware that he was once again on the road. But it was different this time in one very important way.

Za was there too. She had respawned many times in the past months and was getting used to the experience. She was already by Malone's side when he fully regained his faculties.

"Are you all right?" Za asked.

"Yes, sorry. It's only my second time, and it's kind of disorienting, you know?"

"Unfortunately, I do." Za looked into Malone's eyes. What a silly fool. She knew what it was like to respawn. Seeing that he was now fully aware, she put her hands on his face and put her lips to his.

Malone passionately kissed her back. He knew that they were on the road, but in his mind, he was presently in heaven.

They both stood silently for a moment after the kiss, embracing each other.

Malone, returning to his senses, said softly, "Yes, of course you know what it's like. I'm so sorry. But you're here. I'm here. We're both here. Even if we are still in this place, at least we are here together. At least for now, it's over. But—"

His words made up for his initial inability to remember the suffering that Za had gone through. She knew that he loved her, and it filled her with joy, even in this pandemonium. But Za didn't need to hear the rest of his last sentence. She could finish it for him, and it was not related to their spending so much time together. It was obvious and took her joy away. "But what about my dad?"

Malone was almost brought to tears by the look in the eyes of his beloved Za. He immediately thought of something reassuring. "We found you, your dad and me. Now we'll just have to find him. He is the angel of death after all."

"Wow, that's just weird now that I think about it. My dad is Azriel. How is that even possible?" wondered Za.

"I don't know. It's pretty cool when you really think about it. Maybe a bit weird. But more to the point, something about being the angel of death has me believing that whatever happened in the palace, he is still alive."

"You're right," thought Za. "We need a place to think. I know from experience that it isn't safe to remain out in the open. There's a house over there. It's kind of plain, but it looks all right. I didn't see many houses when I was here before, and they were always destroyed."

"Hmm, I wonder," said Malone.

"What do you wonder?"

"I think I've been here before. The road is extremely diverse. You could be on a road that is nearly like heaven or one nearly like hell. Normally, it depends on how you lived, but us, your dad caused us to be sucked into a really bad spot to start, probably directed by the demons that killed him. But after a while, we came upon a single house. The man inside said that the house stood at a junction, sort of where many paths linked. That looks like the same house, although it has been busted up a little since the last time I was here."

"Is it safe to go in? We should probably get out of the open."

"I'm guessing it will be. It might smell, though. I don't think the guy that lives there ever cleans." They both laughed at how preposterous it sounded to try and clean anything in this place.

As they walked quickly toward the house, Aaron had another thought. "Za, you're a Nephilim."

"A what?"

"A Nephilim. It means your half human and half angel. It's supposed to make you super powerful. I know it's not biblical, but you're not supposed to exist."

"We need to get to safety or maybe I won't."

With only about fifty meters left between them and the house, the two started to run. Malone did not even consider being cautious like last time. Darda would let them in.

When they got to the door, Malone grabbed Za. "Wait. The old man that lives here had a shotgun last time. We should probably actually knock, believe it or not."

"If you say so," she agreed.

As Malone knocked on the door, he had one more important item to take care of. "One more thing," he said to Za.

"Yes?"

As the door began to open, Malone stole another kiss from Za. She kissed him passionately back. Despite his delight in the kiss, Malone quickly took a step back when he saw who answered the door.

Za was initially taken aback when Malone ended the kiss. Just as quickly, though, she jumped for joy and into her father's arms. "Dad, you're here!"

Malone waited patiently for his turn to greet Azriel, but Azriel dragged him into the group hug that lasted at least ten seconds. As they entered the house, Malone looked around. "Not that I'm not overwhelmed with joy to see you, but where's Darda?" He looked toward Azriel to see if he knew what had happened to Darda.

"He's gone," replied Azriel.

"Gone where?" asked Malone, concerned that something bad had happened to the man who had helped them.

"Don't worry, my young friend. Darda ascended. He's with God now. It was his time. He'd been on the road for far too long."

"Who's Darda?" Za was confused and had no idea what they were talking about. She wasn't even sure if Darda was a person.

Malone and Azriel looked at one another. "It's a long story," answered Azriel, "but I'm not one to just leave it at that. To put it simply, he was a man who helped us get started on our quest to find you."

"Well, then, I'm glad he got to go to heaven," Za responded, smiling.

Despite all that they had been through for the past several months, the three were happy. They were together, and no one seemed to be trying to kill them. They sat down together in the main room of the house in the three chairs from their last visit.

Azriel told them the story of what had happened after they were killed. In fact, he had to take a step back and tell them how they were killed. Apparently, the death was so drastic and quick that they did not fully remember it. To everyone, that was a blessing.

"So Lucifer saved you and then killed you?" asked Za.

"I've had a few days to think about it. I don't think you could say that he saved me. He was simply angry and perhaps rightly so. Then he killed Asmodai. But that didn't necessarily save me. All I had to do was die, and I would reform at the point of my choosing. No, Lucifer was more cleaning house."

"Interesting way to clean the house," responded Za. "I'd hate to watch him mow the lawn."

After a laugh, Malone interjected. He had waited patiently for the story to finish. Now he had a revelation for Azriel as well. "Now that we know what happened to you after we were killed, I think I should tell you what happened to me after I died again."

"Really, what happened to you?" Azriel wondered.

"Yeah, what do you mean by that?" Za seconded Azriel's question.

"I'm pretty sure the Metatron spoke to me."

"Are you sure?" asked Azriel.

"Yes, I'm pretty sure. He said or it said it was the Metatron anyway."

"What's the Metatron?" Za was getting tired of being the only one out of the loop on everything.

"It's the scribe of God," said Azriel. "If someone thinks that they spoke to God, they probably spoke to the Metatron. If they spoke directly to God, their head would explode. He is one of the highest angels. As the scribe, he is also privy to divine knowledge. Which begs the question, Malone, what did the Metatron say?"

"He was sort of giving me purpose, letting me know that my death had purpose anyway. It's hard to explain because he spoke not with words but with feelings. Basically, I existed to be a messenger, and I had fulfilled my purpose well. I was supposed to tell you that you were Azriel when the time was right. I asked him if my life was not my own then. Did I not have free will? He said yes. I always had a choice, but God knew that the message of your angelic nature was safe with me. I'm still wrapping my head around it, but the main message I got from it was that my suffering and all that I had to go through was all allowed so that I would be prepared to do God's work. And then when he told me that God was pleased, I began to reanimate. I was so happy to see Za that the whole conversation kind of left my mind for a bit. It was like a dream after all."

"Well, the Metatron can come to one like a dream. I'm so glad that you found your purpose, just like I found mine."

"Yes," said Malone. "You are Azriel, the angel of death. I told you so."

To Za, knowing that her father was the angel of death was particularly confusing. "If you're an angel, then what am I?" Za asked, somewhat concerned. "Do I still get to go to heaven? Am I a Nephilim? Do I have a part in God's plan?"

"Those are some difficult questions, sweetie, but the answer is thankfully simple. To the best of my knowledge, I was fully a human when you were my daughter, so you are just as human as every other wonderful member of your highly favored species."

"So that's it? I'm nothing special?" asked Za.

"To me, you are the most special human ever. It's not every day that an angel gets to have a child, you know. We may not know what it is right now, but I feel confident that there is something truly special about you still to be discovered. Maybe you are a Nephilim and maybe not. Time will tell," Azriel explained.

"Thank you for making me feel better. You'll always be my daddy." Za was reassured but still worried. "Now that all of that is out of the way, where do we start to look for Mom?"

"What you mean, sweetie, is where do I start to look for your mother." Azriel took Hannah's right hand and squeezed it gently. "I don't want to let you go, but I have to. You two can't stay here. You need to ascend. You need to find your place in heaven with the light.

As much as it saddens me to lose you, I know that you are going to a much better place. I'm sure that I will be able to visit in time as well."

Za did not want to be separated from her father, but she understood. She could see the sadness growing in his heart and face. "I don't want to leave you, though," she said.

"The time has come when you need to leave the nest, sweetie. I love you, and for that reason, I have to set you free."

Embracing her father again, Za whispered in his ear, "You are loved, and you did your job well. You were the best father ever."

"So that's it then?" asked Malone once the tears had stopped flowing from Za. "We made a good team. Are you sure we can't help you find your wife?" Malone new the answer. Azriel didn't need them. If anything, they would be in the way. Azriel was also right. They did not belong in the pit.

"You two have an amazing adventure still ahead. Heaven is the most wonderful place imaginable. I can't describe it to you because it is different for everyone. You will be filled with love of all, freed from the temptations of the world, free to live for the first time." Azriel tried his best to explain the heavenly realm to the two. He was also trying to distract himself. He knew that it would be some time before he would see them again. The quest for Hannah would not be simple. But they would finally be safe.

"So what happens then?" Malone asked.

"It's already happening," Azriel informed them. With those words, Malone and Za began to shift from their physical manifestation. Their bodily forms dissipated as their reborn spiritual life formed. Then, as they looked down on Azriel, alone in the house, they rose upward into the light.

"You are no longer foreigners and strangers but fellow citizens with God's people and also members of his household," said Azriel as he watched. He needed a moment to process watching his daughter go up to heaven. He had watched millions of humans reach their eternal salvation, but none were ever as close to him.

"Thank you, God, for revealing this new knowledge of rebirth. To see it from a father's perspective helps me to grow."

Once they were gone and no longer within even his sight, he stood up and walked outside of the house before quickly transforming into his full angelic form. In a flash, he teleported to Vorago, the final depth of the pit. A great abyss next to Minos and his gates, Vorago stretched a kilometer deep and a kilometer across before one entered caves that extended countless more kilometers. If one was to fly high enough, Vorago would look like a huge eye staring into the nothing beneath.

Aaron had discovered his purpose. Now he was Azriel. He had directed his most beloved daughter to heaven, but now he set his sights on another mission: his wife.

The last time he stood before the pit, he was questioning his duty. Then God made him a human. This time, he was fully engorged by his duty. The end was the beginning. A cave sat before him. This particular cave extended into the deepest recesses of the pit. The evil behind him potentially paled in comparison to that below. Somewhere in those depths, his wife awaited him. Light from Azriel's eyes blazed a path before him as he stepped downward.

# About the Author

Writer, researcher, educator, and enthusiastic husband and father, Virgil E. Varvel Jr., tries to infuse his hope for the future into all his work. His diverse background includes three postgraduate degrees and awards ranging from education to research. When not writing, he teaches high school science at a private Christian school in the Midwest with a desire to pass his wonder of God's creation on to the next generation.

CPSIA information can be obtained
at www.ICGtesting.com
Printed in the USA
BVHW081548030921
615980BV00007B/188